THE
VISITORS

Simon Sylvester is a writer, teacher and occasional filmmaker. His work has been published in a range of magazines, journals and anthologies, and he has written more than a thousand flash stories on Twitter. He lives in Cumbria with his wife and daughter. *The Visitors* is his first novel.

THE VISITORS

SIMON SYLVESTER

Quercus

First published in Great Britain in 2014 by

Quercus Editions Ltd
55 Baker Street
7th Floor, South Block
London W1U 8EW

A CIP catalogue record for this book is available
from the British Library

HB 978 1 84866 370 1
TPB ISBN 978 1 84866 371 8
EBOOK ISBN 978 1 84866 372 5

10 9 8 7 6 5 4 3 2 1

Typeset by Ellipsis Digital Limited, Glasgow
Printed and bound in Great Britain by Clays Ltd, St Ives plc

For my family

CHAPTER 1

In the bay, a seal bobbed once, dipped and vanished. A light tide sluiced through the ripples and washed the surface clear, leaving no sign. From the headland, the ocean was a lung. Inhale, exhale. Breathe. Focus.

It was the day before Richard left the island, and he was learning how to smoke. The various components were laid out on the grass before him. He broke a pinch of tobacco from the plastic pouch, shaped it into a rough cylinder and tucked it into the fluttering crease of paper. Frowning in concentration, he tried rolling this clumsy package between his fingers, but it kept slipping, and eventually he simply folded it into something like an envelope. He gummed it closed, tongue kitten pink as it slid along the white paper, saliva turning the fibres translucent.

He held it up, proud of his work, crooked and creased, and stuck it in one corner of his lovely, lovely mouth. It was an obvious pose, but it suited him. Hair combed back and ruffled by the breeze, staring out to sea. Sitting down, one knee folded up and close into his body, the other leg sprawled loose in the grass, cigarette in mouth, match in hand. Ready to go. Ready when you are. Ready to light the fuse, blow the keg. Ready for anything. It was the author picture on the jacket of a poetry book. He was practising for the years to come. His own author photos, maybe. The wind puffed out the first match, and it took him a couple of attempts to light the cigarette. He took a deep, dramatic inhalation, then exhaled carefully, a thin white curtain tugged out between his teeth. The smoke was whipped away on the breeze, out to sea, away from here, away from the island, away from me.

'Aye,' said Richard, 'I could get used to this.'

He tried hard to savour the smoke. He held his cigarette like a film star, cupped inside his hand. Looking thoughtful, trying not to cough. Through his cheek, I could see the movement of his tongue inside his mouth, tasting the corners.

He offered me a drag. I shook my head, no, and hugged my knees, slouchy jumper wrapped around my bare shins. He shrugged. He smoked in careful puffs. Exhalation revealed the space inside him, the smoke giving body to the air he breathed. This was the volume of his lungs.

The cigarette was barely halfway smoked when he ground it underfoot. He pocketed the stub, leaving a blackened smudge on the beach grass. My favourite place, charred with ash and tar. I scowled at him. He sat back, wind licking through his hair, and didn't notice.

We sat together on a little headland on the west coast of Bancree, dangling our feet above a narrow inlet and looking out to sea. The cove below the headland was called Still Bay, named after generations of whisky moonshiners. It was a dream landing for smugglers, back when the island creaked with illicit stills and there was money to be made in bootleg whisky. The island was a haven until the customs men started to take it seriously. Faced with jail, the old moonshiners packed it in. They were dead, now, and their grandsons and great-grandsons worked in the fish farm or the big distillery up in Tighna.

Still Bay was sandy but studded with rocks and pebbles. It mapped a long curve of four or five hundred metres, and ended at another headland on the far side. Weeks of receding high tides had left shells and wood and weed in long dark bands, their contours evenly spaced as they spanned the bay. Running parallel to the beach, separated by curtains of dune grass and reeds, a crumbling, potholed single-track road wound along the coast. The road passed through the dozen cottages clustered at the far end of the bay. That was the village of Grogport. A dozen houses and a bus stop. My home.

Beyond the bay, maybe two hundred metres into the water, lay Dog Rock. This tiny islet, barely a hundred metres long, was a curling extension of the southernmost headland, shaped somewhere between a comma and an inkblot. It projected from the sea like an accident, an afterthought in the geography of Bancree. A cottage sat on top of the islet, though I'd never known anyone to live there. It seemed so pointless, its whitewash chipped and faded to nothing, its roof bowed in the middle. Waves licked white against its crooked pontoon. On the far side of Dog Rock lay the full weight of the Atlantic. The coastal currents jumbled blue, reflecting pinpricks of September sun. It was the end of summer, the last weekend before school returned. School, school again. The clouds lay teased in threads like wool on barbed-wire fences.

Richard attempted to light matches on the zip of his jacket. No matter how often he struck the match, it never caught, only chipped the sulphur until the wood was bare. He harrumphed and tried it on his thumb instead, wincing as pieces of the match lodged beneath the nail. He wasted a dozen before I put him out of his misery.

'They're safety matches,' I said. 'You shouldn't play with fire.'

He huffed and tossed them down beside the tobacco. Tomorrow he'd be leaving for university in Bristol, and I wouldn't see him for weeks. Months, maybe. Half-term, perhaps, depending on how it went. But it would be fine. It would be fine, babe. These were his words, not mine. I didn't say much. I ached deep and vague, caught somewhere between melancholy and spite.

'We can always speak on the phone,' he said.

We both thought of the mobile reception on the island. We couldn't always speak on the phone.

'We'll see each other soon, anyway. Of course we will.'

I wasn't sure I'd ever see Richard again. We'd meet, of course. He'd be back for the summer holidays, no doubt, and he'd come home for Christmas. But it wouldn't be him, and I wouldn't be his girlfriend any more. He'd have another girl. She'd be sophisticated and funny and smart and she'd be taller than me and older than me and louder than me and not Scottish. She'd be French, or Spanish, and she'd smoke too. They'd light their cigarettes from the same flame. He'd probably get a Zippo. When he came back to the island, smoking might suit him. With his mini-skirted girlfriend in tow, he'd sneer at everything he used to know and how small it seemed, how quaint. The harbour – the mountains – me.

'We'll be fine, you know,' he said. 'You and me.'

The wind whipped my hair into my face, and I let it. Strands caught in my mouth. Inland, clouds rolled across the ragged top of Ben Sèimh in stupendous white waves. They collided above the little mountain and trailed down the other side, dissolving into blue. The wind farm beat against the breeze. My heart was cumulus, rolling and beaten, tugged into pieces by the turbines.

We'd sat on this little headland hundreds of times in the last few years, looking out onto Still Bay and the sea. We were sitting here when Richard first held my hand. Fingers reaching, creeping across the grass to mine. I'd pretended not to look as he inched nearer, though we both knew what would happen. This was where we came to kiss. And now he needed to shave once or sometimes twice a week, and he was leaving for university, leaving for the mainland.

Leaving the island.

Bancree was small. Barely twenty square miles of long, thin rock, ten or so long and two or so across, stretching out into the ocean. Little mountains bumped along the spine of the island like a pod of orcas, but even Ben Sèimh fell some way short of being a Munro. Our traditional industries were fishing, whisky and peat. Only the whisky had survived. Scores of islanders worked for Clachnabhan Malt, up in Tighna. Without the distillery, Bancree would be deserted. There was nothing on the island that wasn't already dying. Half the houses were for sale. The island population numbered only a few hundred, and that dripped away, year on year. Now Richard was leaving, too. I'd known him all my life, and he was leaving before me.

A slice of me despised him for it.

'Who's that?' he said, squinting in the sun.

I followed his gaze. On the far side of the bay, a grubby white van slowed to a crawl as it passed through Grogport. I could just make out the logo of a mainland hire company. It paused outside each house, looking for something, and passed out the other side, heading up the hill towards the northern end of the island. Then it stopped, lurched backwards, and reversed with a piping sound that floated across the bay. The van turned along the track on the far headland, bumping down towards the decrepit jetty that served only Dog Rock.

'No way,' said Richard. 'No way. Do you think someone's moving in?'

The hire van stopped at the end of the track, lurching with the handbrake. Richard started rolling another cigarette. We were both fascinated. Dog Cottage had been uninhabited as long as I'd been alive. No one ever moved to Bancree, let alone the tiny islet.

On the far side of Still Bay, a man climbed out of the driver's side. He walked around the van and into view. He was middle-aged and dark-haired, wearing dark trousers and a pale T-shirt, but the opposite headland was too far to distinguish any more than that. He arched his back and reached his arms up overhead. Mid-stretch, he saw us. Richard waved enthusiastically, the cigarette hanging crooked from a corner of his mouth. A sour puff of smoke passed across my face. The man gave a curt wave and turned away. On the near side of the van, a girl climbed down and stood beside the driver. She looked a lot younger than him. She looked about my age. All I could see at that distance was that she had dark hair, tied into a bunch behind her head.

'Must be his daughter,' suggested Richard.

'Maybe.'

'Someone for you to talk to.'

When you've gone, I thought.

'I don't even know her,' I said, and tore a blade of grass from the headland.

'Well, yes. But this is Bancree,' said Richard. 'It won't take long, will it?'

She wore shorts and a blue hoodie, hands plunged deep into the pockets. She kicked at the ground. The man walked to the back of the van and opened the doors. He studied the contents, then started to tug and haul on something. He called to her for help, his voice muzzled by the distance between the headlands. The girl joined him, and after a few moments of wrestling, they dragged out an inflatable dinghy, bright yellow against the grass. A foot pump followed, and the man started to inflate the boat with ceaseless, monotonous movement. All the while, he looked across the bay at Dog Rock, sitting squat between Bancree and the sea. I glanced across, too, but the ocean offered only wave upon wave upon wave. The girl carried bags and boxes from the van, wading through the grass and stacking them on the beach.

'I can't quite believe it,' crowed Richard, 'that someone's actually moving into that old place. What kind of idiot would do that?'

As if he'd heard us from across the bay, the man looked up. For a heartbeat, he stared, and then he returned to work. Despite the sun, I felt a cold twist in my neck.

'It's a bit weird,' I murmured.

'Isn't it odd that someone's moving in now, of all times? It's like they know about the disappearances, and they've come to fill the gaps.'

'There aren't any disappearances,' I said.

'Yeah? Tell that to Doug MacLeod and Billy Wright.'

'Wheesht. They can take care of themselves.'

Richard snorted. 'Dougie couldn't care for a cardboard box.'

He played with the matches, trying again to light them on his nail. This time, I let him.

From our perch on the headland, Dog Cottage seemed little better than a wreck. It was still standing, but the walls were compounded as though carrying a great weight, and the door was peeled almost bare. The islet was bounded by a blackened rocky shore, and foxgloves and ferocious weeds sprouted everywhere. Stunted walls of gorse had grown dense since the islet was last inhabited. The scrub was studded yellow with flowers and sculpted the same shape by the Atlantic breezes.

The couple carried the inflatable dinghy down to the shore of Still Bay. He attached an outboard motor, then backed the boat into the surf. The girl began to pass him boxes. When the load was full, she kicked off her shoes and waded in to push out the boat, then hopped up onto the prow. He jerked an arm at the outboard motor, twice, three times, and it coughed into life, farting little blasts of purple smoke, sounding like a wasp against a window. It took them a couple of minutes to reach the pontoon on Dog Rock, their inflatable nodding into shallow waves. The girl stepped out gingerly, hauling herself up on a pole and testing the weight of the boards. As she tethered the dinghy, the man started offloading boxes onto the crooked wood. She took them to solid ground. When they'd finished, they returned to Bancree, immediately packing another round of bags and boxes into the boat.

'It's like everything they own is in that van,' said Richard.

'If they're moving in, it will be.'

'I wonder where they've come from.'

I shrugged. 'Dunno. First people to move in since . . .'

We both paused, thinking. A lot of houses went on sale in Bancree, but there weren't that many bought.

'Do you think they're English? Or foreign? Another holiday cottage,' said Richard, 'just what the island needs. She must be about our age. Your age, anyway. She might go to school. Could be in your year. You'll find out soon enough.'

Like I'd have a choice. The island grapevine would be pounding with the news.

'Well, I guess I'll have to let you know,' I said.

I felt bad about sounding catty, but Richard didn't notice. He rolled another cigarette. This time, it looked like the real thing. I traced pictures in the grass with my fingertip while he smoked. Sometimes he pushed at my shoe or ankle, but I ignored him. The strangers finished their second run in the boat.

'We should go around and help.'

'Your call,' he smirked. 'They're your new neighbours. Not mine.'

Leaning back, he took a deep drag of the cigarette. And then, brow furrowed, Richard tried to blow a smoke ring.

Like a fresh sheet on a bed, realisation settled on me. Watching him flick and fumble with the matches, I suddenly understood that he was trying on a character. A new persona. Right in front of me, testing it on an audience. He hadn't even waited to leave. I wondered how long he'd been planning the new him. Testing new looks in the mirror, testing faces, clothes. Deciding to become a smoker. Learning how to smoke.

I felt nauseous to think of how long I'd missed this truth, even when it stared me in the face. Everything churned and curdled. Everything turned sour.

I was a dress rehearsal.

'It's nice,' said Richard, watching Dog Rock, watching them carry their boxes, 'to be out here with you. To spend this time together. Before I go. Really nice.'

'Is it? Is it really nice?'

He wouldn't meet my eye. He was supposed to be my boyfriend, but I was no longer certain what that meant. We'd known each other all our lives, and had been pretty much a couple for the last two, but he'd become a stranger in the time it took to roll and smoke a cigarette.

Low and fierce, the sun started its retreat into the west. Afternoon shadows crawled out behind us, even as we looked into the sea. Whatever I had with Richard suddenly felt very juvenile. Our relationship sloughed off one skin, and evolved into something new. Once, I'd thought it might be love, but now it felt little better than convenience. We were the only kids on this side of the island, and we'd been bundled together since we were babies. I felt pangs of sluicing sadness. Our parents had declared us childhood sweethearts, and so we were. What choice did we have? There was no one else. It was the easy option.

He was nice. I liked him a lot. He was leaving without me. I couldn't stand to be near him. I stood up and brushed down my legs, sweeping off the crumbs of grass and sand.

'You're going?' he said, surprised.

'Aye. I'm off home.'

'Oh,' he said, turning puppy dog. 'I was going to watch the sunset. It'll be my last one for a while, Flo.'

'Well, don't let me stop you. I'll be watching the sun set every night.'

'You'll come and see me?'

'We've had this conversation a hundred times,' I snapped.

He looked at me, confused.

'OK then,' I told him. 'Sure, of course. Whatever you want.'

He wanted the audience. Standing over him, I'd a sudden urge to slap at him, to lash out. He wasn't sad at all, and it made me boil. He'd brought me out here for a glimpse of his new character. A sneak preview. Not Richard from the island, but Richard who lives in Bristol. Richard who smokes. He was casual, easy, flippant. He was leaving, and I'd be stuck here, trapped on an island that could fit inside a snow globe.

He stood up and came to kiss me. I let him, but didn't kiss back, feeling his hands around my shoulders, his lips pushing against mine. His cigarette breath was acrid on my upper lip. Richard moved his head to one side and pecked my cheek instead.

'Look, it'll be OK. You know that, right?'

'Aye, well. Call me when you're settled. If you like.'

'If I can get through,' he said, wounded.

'If you want to,' I corrected, and turned away, his fingers tugging mine as I let go of his hand. I waded through the deep beach grass and back onto the road. The sun burned hot on one side, the other cool in shadow. I could feel him watching me, but I wouldn't boost his ego by turning for another look. I felt too raw.

'Flo,' he called, 'wait.'

With each step, my left shoe squeaked on the road. Only a few hundred metres to Grogport, and I felt him watching like a weight. A wee stone bridge spanned the creek at the near edge of the village, right beside my house. That bridge meant home and respite. I kept my head down, and forced myself to count the potholes against left shoe squeaks. Locked into myself, and with my gaze fixed on the road, I didn't see the new girl until I'd walked straight into her.

CHAPTER 2

She stood in the centre of the bridge, gazing at the trees beyond the village. She hadn't seen me coming. At the last moment I spotted her feet and jerked my head up, but momentum carried me right into her. She bounced off me, staggering, and I threw out a hand to catch her arm.

'Sorry!' I gasped.

'OK, I'm OK.'

'I'm so sorry,' I said, letting go her arm, 'I wasn't looking.'

'Don't worry about it,' she said, rubbing her side, 'I'm fine.'

'Well,' I hesitated, 'hello, anyway. I'm Flora. I live . . . well. I live right here.'

I pointed at our croft. It stood directly beside us. I felt suddenly ridiculous. The new girl gestured across the bay to Dog Rock.

'That's my new house. I've just moved here with my dad.'

It was weird. She couldn't look me in the face. She was short and skinny and pale. She had dark, wavy hair. Her hands were stuffed into the pockets of her hoodie, and she stood half-on to me. She was quite pretty, but there was something strange about her.

'So . . .' I said, 'where are you from?'

When she frowned, her whole face crumpled.

'All over, really. We only left Islay yesterday.'

'Far enough, I suppose. Welcome to the bustling metropolis of Bancree.'

The half-smile played again, and for an instant, she looked up and right at me. Her face was astonishing. Her cheekbones and jaw were well defined and sinuous. Her mouth was full, but pursed and nervous. She had large, peaty eyes, the iris dark enough to blend into the pupil. The whiteness of her skin made the contrast with her eyes all the more unnerving. Just as quickly, she dropped her gaze back to the road. A horn blast cut through the afternoon. By the jetty, the man stood beside the cabin of the van, waving at the girl.

'Better go. See you later.'

'Aye,' I said, 'see you.'

She turned and jogged to the jetty. Her dad grabbed her roughly by the arm and steered her towards the inflatable dinghy. I watched them pack another load into it before turning back to my house.

The porch was still. Motes of dust hung in sunlight, fostering silence. I kicked off my sneakers and pulled the front door closed. It was that strange summer hour between late afternoon and early evening, and no one was home. I traipsed through the little living room, kicking Jamie's toys under the table, already feeling calmer. In the kitchen, I made a cup of tea and sat at the window, looking out onto Still Bay. We kept binoculars on the sill, and I combed the waves, hoping for otters or dolphins, or perhaps the seal I'd spotted that afternoon. The dune grass was alive with finches, and a heron stalked the shallows, but there was nothing extraordinary. I focused again, looking this time at Dog Rock. Boxes stood in stacks beside the pontoon. I frowned. They were all office storage boxes, the cardboard buckled with use. Some of them spilled paper. There were dozens of them. Who moves house with stationery?

I swung the binos to the headland where I'd sat with Richard, peering along the low line where the land fell into the sea. He'd gone. So much for watching a final sunset.

I simmered in sadness and frustration, furious with Richard for leaving, for changing. I liked him. I did. I'd miss him because he'd always been there. But I didn't need him. It was clear that Richard had pretty much finished with me. Or maybe I'd been the one to do the finishing. Didn't matter. Either way, it was finished.

I felt utterly and suddenly drained.

Across the bay, smoke trailed like handwriting from the Dog Cottage chimney stack. They'd need plenty of fires to dry out that old place. I imagined mushroom carpets, all the floorboards carped and creaking, a thousand cobwebs on the ceiling. Paint and plaster falling from the walls in lumps. I bet they bought the place for a song, hoping to do it up. They hadn't wasted any time. A mound of rubbish had already accumulated outside the door. Through the binoculars, I could make out a roll of lino, dark with dirt. There was a stack of broken tiles, and what looked like old paint tins, and a red-stained electric hob, rusted into disuse. The man appeared at the door, carrying a roll of ratty brown carpet. He dumped it at the door, looked up, then turned back inside. My heart thumped one beat harder. For a moment, I saw him perfectly. Absolutely perfectly. The man. The stranger. Her father.

Even sitting there alone, I blushed red to my roots. I lowered the binoculars, had another sip of tea, thought a moment. He was in his forties or fifties. Medium height, medium build. And he was striking. Handsome, perhaps. No, scratch that. He was pure gorgeous. Really, really good-looking. Almost unnervingly so. Stunning. Weather-beaten. Dark eyes. A full head of dark hair. He had model good looks, his face carved from almost sensual lines. He'd cause quite the stir on the island, if he'd come here alone. There'd be a string of spinsters queuing up to nab him. Andrea Simpson, she'd be there. And that dreadful Janet Campbell. I could just imagine her standing on the shore, waving a tray bake and yoohooing for the dinghy, fishing for an invite in. He'd have every Bancree spinster beating down his door. Poor man wouldn't know what hit him.

There was a flicker of movement on the islet. I jerked the glasses up, hoping to see him again, and banged my eyebrow on the binoculars. By the time I'd settled and focused, all I saw was the strange girl, turning back inside. It was only the briefest of glimpses. I wondered if she'd be in school. Even exuding that odd, skittish atmosphere, she'd probably be popular. With the boys, anyway.

I spied a little longer, but there was no more movement on Dog Rock, and nothing in the sea. No porpoises, no seals. Just gulls and gulls and gulls. It was turning into a glorious evening. I took my tea into my bedroom, and turned on the laptop. There was no internet reception. There was never internet reception. I only checked out of dumb optimism.

The falling sun made half my room glow golden. Books, stereo, a rack of CDs. Clothes bundled in a heap in one corner. There were band posters on the crooked walls, years out of date and suddenly foreign. At that moment, it was someone else's room. I lay back on the bed, stretched out, my arms half-open to grip the edges of the single mattress. The coolness in the sheets washed across me. Sun tumbled through the window on columns of dust, fragments of human skin. I looked at the ceiling and thought numbly of kissing Richard on the bed. This was where we'd lost our virginity. We lit candles. It was all right. It was something to do. It was a secret, something unique between us. And now he was gone, and it wasn't anything at all.

I was furious to find my eyes prickle hot with tears, and bit them back, scrubbing my face with a sleeve. Standing up, I leaned in close to the mirror and studied my reflection. Too serious, no curves, too thin. Dull blonde hair. Romany, Slavic, gypsy, with almond-shaped eyes and broad, high cheeks. I dressed weird. I had no friends. I was a weirdo.

Pathetic, Flora.

I didn't need Richard. Or anyone else. Reaching over, I clicked again on the computer, refreshing the internet. Nothing. I clicked again. Nothing. Page broken. No connection. My phone had no signal and besides, there was no one I could call. I turned on the radio. Static. The hiss and fuzz of static, creeping down the frequencies. Scattered scraps of distant music rang in fragments of pop, hip-hop, classical. The murmur of voices could be talk show radio or walkers on the road outside. It all filtered in the same. It all blended in together. Nothing here worked the way it should.

The island was built of things that had been abandoned and left to waste: houses, boats and people. Especially people. People who would never get away. Stuck here for ever because that was all they knew.

That would never be me.

I didn't know how it would happen, but I was leaving, and soon. My time on the island was drawing to a close. The walls of the snowglobe were pushing in around me, and I was ready to break out, to crack the walls and run. I knew this like I knew the peat blood thrumming in my veins or the salt tracks cracking from the corners of my eyes.

CHAPTER 3

I woke to the sound of fractured voices. The sun had dipped and almost gone, leaving my room a ghostly blue. Voices. I'd left the radio on quiet, and there was a German-sounding talk show fuzzing and crackling at low volume. The words sounded strange, as though the radio was under water. Or maybe it was me. I stretched, cricking my neck, crooked and hazy from the nap. Sleeping during the day always threw me wrong. I'd been asleep for less than an hour, but it had flattened me. I sat on the bed in the gloaming and waited for my brain to catch up. I swung my legs to the floor, and stood up to stretch. Something squelched. I looked down. Beside my bed, small patches of carpet pooled darker. I kneeled to investigate. The floor was sodden.

I prodded at the wet spots, looking around for an explanation. I checked the ceiling for a leak, but it was fine. Beside me, the distorted stereo burbled in the half-dark. Maybe something had burst beneath the floorboards. I'd have to tell Ronny about it. The room was cool. I frowned to see the window open, when I could have sworn I'd left it shut. Outside, Still Bay glowed with dusk, the sky a violet curtain. The breeze blew sharp with the march of autumn. I closed the window, but even as I latched it shut, the radio burbled with a sudden crash of static and I flinched, spooked at the surge in volume.

I turned the stupid thing off. With my room quiet, a muted clatter drifted through the walls. Someone was home. As I moved for the door, my foot caught on something solid, and there was a dull clunk against the leg of the desk. My mug. I'd left my tea beside the bed. I must have knocked it over while dozing, and not realised. It was a weird splash. The damp spots looked like two kidney shapes, quite distinct, shaped the same and evenly spaced. I collected the cup and turned for the door.

In the kitchen, Ronny was making meatballs. Leaning over the worktop, he was wrist-deep in a plastic bowl, shaping mince and onions, parsley and garlic. The mixture escaped between his fingers in a grey paste. He had long hair and seldom shaved, which made him look a bit like a Viking, or a werewolf. Him and Mum had been together five years. I used to fight them both about that, but I grew out of it. They were just trying to get by. They were scared of being alone, just like everyone else. Ronny was a good guy. Plus he was drip-feeding me his 80s and 90s rock records, from AC/DC to ZZ Top. He worked hard at Clachnabhan, he loved his wife and baby, and he cared well enough for me. He had his shirtsleeves rolled high, his hair tied up in a little samurai topknot. His arms wriggled with muscles from raking barley.

'Hey, Ronny,' I said. He started at my voice. He looked tired.

'Hi, Flo. How's it going, poppet?'

I shrugged. 'All right. Richard's away tomorrow.'

'Aye, of course. You OK?'

'I think so,' I said. 'I'll miss him, but maybe it was reaching a finish anyway. We've been sitting out there for ages, not really talking. To be honest, I think he can't wait to get away.'

'Sounds like someone else I know.'

'Right enough.'

He smiled, blankly, shoulders hunched, hands in the bowl of mince. It was rare to see him without a spark of laughter.

'What's the matter, old-timer?'

'Ah, nothing,' he said, feeling for the words. 'Probably nothing. It's just Dougie. I wish he'd turn up.'

'He'll be fine. He'll be on the booze somewhere.'

Ronny shook his head.

'We've called round all the bars, put up posters all over Tanno. It's been more than a week, and no one's seen him. We're worried he might be in a ditch. Or that he fell into the water.'

Ronny sometimes worked with Doug MacLeod at the distillery. He was an odd-job man, equal parts cleaner, labourer and stevedore. He camped out in the woods over summer, and stayed in people's outhouses during winter. He was also a drunkard, but the right sort for all that, soft as butter. Everyone had seen him, mid-afternoon blootered outside the Bull Hotel, or in one of the Tanno harbour bars. He'd sit on a bench outside the pub, a permanent flush to his face, hollering hellos and trying to light cigarettes. He was forty-something, and looked like he was sixty. Most nights he drank until he slid quietly to the floor. Ronny was right. It would be too easy for him to fall into the harbour on his stagger home. A heavy coat and work boots would take care of the rest, and that would be the end of Doug MacLeod.

'He's a daft old lad, but . . . well. We'd miss him.'

Ronny looked into his bowl of meat and onions. I didn't know what to say.

'It'll be fine,' was the best I could manage. 'He'll show up somewhere.'

Ronny paused. 'Billy never did,' he said, and that made me think again.

Bill Wright was another island name. He'd disappeared the previous winter, vanished overnight. Someone had called round his house to give him a lift to work, and he wasn't to be found. The ashes were cold in the grate, the door wide open. The constabulary sent out a dog team and searched the woods and coast around his house, but that was the last anyone had seen of Billy. Even then, it was hard to be especially worried.

'Come on, though. Billy's a wanderer. He likes to walk, he likes to travel. It's just like him to up sticks and vanish for a while.'

'Aye. But he always said goodbye, and he always came home. And now, with Dougie too, it's getting to me.'

'You don't think it's the same thing?'

'Naw,' said Ronny. 'There's lads at the distillery saying as much, but it's only gossip. Sad, that's all.'

We stood and listened to the shoreline, listened to the pan lid clunking on the stove.

'Well. What's next on the CD list? I'm done with the last lot.'

'What did you think of Kyuss?'

I pulled a face. 'Bit monotonous for me. I preferred the Credence Clearwater lot.'

'You're an idiot.'

'Love you too.'

He grinned at me, but his smile was forced and brittle. Dougie MacLeod. Poor old Doug. He looked around the kitchen. He held up gooey hands.

'It's meatballs for tea,' he said.

CHAPTER 4

Mum came home half an hour later, spilling bags of shopping. She was followed through the door by a hulking giant of a man. He carried a kit bag in one hand and a wriggling baby Jamie in the other arm, and all my melancholy vanished in a wink.

'Uncle Anders!' I shouted, and darted to the hallway. I put my arms around him, giving him a delighted hug. He dropped the kit bag, his hand settling on my shoulder like a blanket.

'*Hej*, Flora,' he boomed, crushing me into his stomach, and Jamie giggled as he grabbed for my hair.

'I found this rascal wandering the streets in Tanno,' said Mum, smiling through her tiredness. 'Thought I'd better fetch him in for tea.'

'Are you sure?' I said, suspiciously, and patted his barrel stomach. 'I don't think he needs any more feeding.'

'You cheeky bastard,' growled Anders, then erupted into laughter. He grabbed Ronny's outstretched hand, and hauled him into a bear hug.

Anders Tommasson was an engineer on an oil rig. He had been brought up in Denmark, but he'd been on the island longer than I'd been alive. When he wasn't on the rigs, he lived alone on the north-east coast of Bancree. His was the last house on the island before the abandoned crofts. He and Ronny went back years. They'd worked on the fish farm when they were younger men, before Ronny started with the distillery and Anders found money on the rigs. He was Jamie's godfather. Whenever he was home, the two would meet up for a drink in Tanno or in Tighna, and a grinning, swaying Anders would show up the next morning with Ronny passed out on his shoulder. On one occasion, they turned up three mornings later, having accidentally found themselves in Copenhagen. Ronny was in the doghouse for a month, but Mum had a real soft spot for Anders, and never stayed mad at them for long.

'How you doing, man?' grinned Ronny. 'We weren't expecting you for another couple of weeks.'

'I had to come home early,' said Anders, gravely, and his face fell. 'It is most urgent.'

'Why? What's going on?'

'Perhaps you will understand if I say . . . it is a matter of international importance.'

Ronny's eyes widened.

'You don't mean . . .?'

'I do. I do.'

Laughing, the two men embraced again. Anders thumped Ronny's back, making him cough.

'What on earth is going on?' said Mum.

'It's the football, Cath. He's come back for the game.'

'What game?'

'Scotland–Denmark. Kick-off Friday night.'

'Of course,' grinned Anders, 'I could not allow you to lose all alone. I should be there to make it much worse for you.'

'You wish. This is grand. Dancer. Pure dancer.'

'Never mind your football,' said Mum. 'Dance off to the bathroom and put Jamie through the tub.'

Chuckling, the two of them went to run the baby through his bath and bed routine. Jamie was ridiculously small in the big man's arms, but Anders held him like a bluebird. Mum started setting the table. She looked shattered.

'I'll do that, Mum. You sit down.'

She hesitated, then sunk into a chair. Mum was assistant manager at the Co-op in Tanno. She worked the afternoon shift five days a week. Jamie stayed with my grandparents in Tighna while Mum was at the shop, then she picked him up on the way home. She'd only been back from maternity leave for a couple of months, and the work routine had hit her hard.

'You OK, Mum?'

'I suppose so, love. The delivery was late, as usual, which means I was late, as usual. We were lucky to catch the last ferry.'

I studied her. Mum had me when she was very young, the age I am now. I'd seen the photos of her pregnant, and she was like a girl. She was now in her mid-thirties, and that left seventeen years between me and Jamie. He was pudgy and smiley and thought everything in the world was great. And it probably was, for him. Mum said I was an awful baby. Jamie had proved a nice surprise. I felt more like his babysitter than his sister, most of the time, but it was good to have him in the family. Even with the late nights and early mornings, he'd made things easier in the house. Jamie was something we all had in common, a splash of blood shared amongst us.

Splashing resounded from the bathroom, and Jamie shrieked with delight. I lowered my voice.

'Ronny's really worried about Dougie.'

She softened. 'He's a crooked penny, is Doug. He'll turn up.'

'Aye, I know. I hope so. I'll get tea served up.'

We settled down to eat. Anders plonked a bottle of whisky on the table, and Ronny fetched cold beers from the fridge.

'If I'd known you were coming, I'd have cooked more.'

'I am a growing lad,' said Anders.

'Aye, outwards,' I muttered. He threw a pea at me.

'Come along, children,' warned my mother.

'Sorry, Mum.'

'Sorry, Cath.'

'Hey,' I said. 'Did you know about the people on Dog Rock?'

'No.'

'There's folk moving into the cottage.'

'You're kidding?'

'Really?'

'Aye. We saw them moving in.'

'So what were they like?'

'There's two of them. A father and a daughter. He looks about late-forties, I guess, and she's about my age. They turned up in a van, and shipped all their stuff over in a blow-up dinghy. They had all their stuff in those boxes you get in offices.'

'I thought that place would stay empty until the day it fell over.'

'It's a mess.'

'Would have been a good place for a still,' lamented Anders.

'They've been at it already. Chucking out the old stuff.'

Mum stood up from the kitchen table and crossed to the window. She peered into the evening blues.

'There's a light on,' she confirmed. 'And a fire.'

'Tell you what, though. He's really good-looking,' I said.

'Flora! And with Richard barely gone,' said Ronny, feigning shock.

'That's really funny, Teenwolf. No, I was thinking more about

Andrea Simpson or that Campbell woman hanging round.'

That gave them pause for thought.

'Lord. Imagine having Janet Campbell as a neighbour.'

'Come on. We don't know this new lot at all. They say better the devil you know.'

'Aye, well they never knew Janet Campbell.'

'I knew Janet Campbell,' said Anders, smugly.

'None of that in front of the kids, Tommasson.'

'Sorry, Cath.'

'Dog Cottage. Fancy that.'

'It'll have barely cost them pennies,' said Ronny. 'Still, it'll be nice if the girl's your age, Flo.'

I rolled my eyes. 'We're never back to this again?'

'No attitude, Miss,' said Mum. 'You can share the bus to school.'

'But what if I hate her?'

'Now, whyever would you hate her?'

'I'm just saying. There's no guarantee I'll like her. She might be a terrible person.'

'I suppose so,' said Ronny, then gestured helplessly at the kitchen window. 'But look around, Flo. Who else is there?'

'I've learned something today. I'd sooner be alone than stuck with someone because they're all that's left. No more easy options for me.'

'Only teenagers actually want to be alone. Trust me,' said Mum.

'I'm eighteen next year,' I protested.

'That's exactly what I'm talking about.'

'Come on, Mum. I've always looked after myself.'

'You're very independent, love. And you know your own mind. We just wish you'd spend more time with folk your own age.'

'Like I have a choice,' I said. 'Back to school tomorrow.'

Mum and Ronny exchanged glances.

'Maybe you'll try a little harder with other kids this year,' said Ronny.

'Aye, and maybe they'll try harder with me,' I glowered, and hunkered down into my tea.

I didn't want any friends my own age. With Richard gone, the last thing I needed was something else chaining me to the island.

I didn't speak much for the rest of the meal. My folks and Anders talked a wee while about what might bring people to Bancree, but couldn't find that many reasons. They could only think of reasons to leave.

'Hey,' said Ronny, softly. 'You heard about Dougie?'

'I heard,' said Anders. 'The police called me.'

'What on earth for?' asked Mum.

'Dougie was staying at my house sometimes.'

'When he had nowhere else to go,' chimed in Ronny.

'My place is empty so much. It is not good to be always without a fire in the hearth. It was important to have him there. A house needs a life inside it. And now he is gone. I wanted to see this for myself.'

'That's really why you're back, isn't it?' said Ronny.

'Yes, my friend. They have looked for him, but I must look also.'

'I'll help.'

'Then we will look together. But we must watch the game also. And we must drink to absent friends.'

'Not here you don't,' yelped Mum. 'Last time you two started howling at four in the morning, and the baby's only just gone down.'

'It was a full moon.'

'It was awful. Go on. Bugger off to the Bull, and come in quietly. And you, Ronald McLoughlin, mind you're working tomorrow.'

Ronny and Anders grinned across the table, then headed for the door.

Mum went to read her book, and I did the dishes. The water in the sink ran brown with peat, and my hands disappeared into the murk at the bottom of the basin.

I couldn't stop thinking about Richard and his escape. It was like fumbling at a splinter, but only ever pushing it deeper. I imagined myself on the bus south, the train, my head resting against the window, feeling engines rumble through the glass. New people, new places. Freedom.

The splinter ground in deeper.

It should have been me.

I went to my room.

I felt restless, both wired and exhausted by my afternoon nap. I was uneasy about the new girl, and Richard had left me sad, and angry. Reading didn't help. I was sick of my book, and irritated by everything I knew. The ceiling was too low, the lamplight too invasive. I was sick of my room, sick of my clothes. I wanted something different.

The air felt thick and strange, the evening edgy and unsettled. Part of it was the emptiness of the last night before school, but there was something else, too, something almost tangible. Dusk was growing into night, dark and ribbed with cloud. Scanning through radio channels, I found a rock'n'roll show on Radio 2. The damp spots on the carpet were drying out already. I wandered to the window and tried to relax, losing myself in sunset's shadows.

About now, Richard would be stretched out in an armchair, watching a film or playing cards with his folks. I let my mind wander to his house, his room – his bed – but couldn't place him. There was only laughter in downstairs rooms, and cold sheets on an empty mattress. It was sad to think of how much I might miss him. It was sadder still to think that I might not.

The Atlantic shifted black against a band of pale horizon. A slice of moon shimmered on the crests of scattered waves, turning the sea indigo dark in contrast. There were lights in the windows of Dog Cottage. Being nosy, I trained my binoculars on the islet. Magnified so many times, I caught the tiny windows glowing in the dark. I watched for a while, hating myself for spying, but couldn't see anyone. Bored, I scanned idly to one side, sweeping from Dog Rock out towards the sea, then jerked with shock. I doubled back, training the binoculars again on the islet. There was something in the inky sea. Peering, eyes screwed tight, I scrutinised the waves splashing at Dog Rock. There was definitely something there. A dark shape, black against the blue, bobbing in the surf. Or was it only waves, slopping on the shore? Ducks, feeding late into dusk? The shapes bobbed further from the islet. Not ducks. It was something swimming. It must have been an otter, or a seal, but I'd never seen them out so late. Little wonder when they're so hard to spot, dark on dark on dark.

The clouds drew back, allowing more of the thin moonlight to filter down. I gasped and jammed the binoculars into my sockets. For a fraction of second, the shape in the water was a head. The focus wheel slipped and the image blurred into total blackness. I hastily refocused and looked again, desperate to find the shape in the water. There was nothing but the sea. The shape had gone.

A head. A face. The old man of the sea.

I'd thought it was a head. A human head. I quickly panned across to look at the cottage, but a curtain had been pulled across the window, leaving a dark and muted orange. The strangers were inside, and now the dark sea swelled empty. There was nothing bobbing in the water.

I must have been wrong. It was ridiculous. The moonlight was too dim to see anything for sure, and no one would swim so late at night. It would be stupidly cold and lethally daft. It must have been a seal.

I watched through the window until the last rind of light on the horizon dimmed to black. Waves breathed on the shore. Mad gulls made cat calls in the night, and I looked out onto a magnified nothing.

CHAPTER 5

I didn't sleep well. My dreams were fish, flicking between night and water and Richard and creaking pines and kelp, rivers of kelp, seaweed falling from the sky in endless towers. It drifted down to touch me, and curled around my wrists. It wrapped around my ankles and began to lift me up.

The alarm jolted me awake. I lay in bed for a few welcome moments, looking at the ceiling. I could hear Mum changing the baby in the bathroom, the two of them cooing at each other. It all felt very normal.

The first day back at school. My first day of sixth year, the first day of my last year. Because Richard and I had always commuted together from the island to the mainland, I'd spent most of my time at school hanging out with him and his mates in the year above. They'd been pleasant enough, but now they were all gone. I hadn't any friends of my own. The next year seemed a bleak prospect. But it was only a year. One year, then escape. Freedom. I still wasn't entirely certain what my freedom looked like. I hadn't found any job I wanted to do. All I knew for certain was that involved somewhere away from Bancree.

I showered and dressed.

Sixth year meant I didn't need to wear uniform any more. No

more regulation skirts or stupid blazers. I wore jeans and sneakers, a vest top and a jumper and a jacket. I sat on the edge of my bed to apply mascara, flexing my toes in the trainers. It didn't feel much like going to school. It felt good. A new start. A step up in life.

Anders was passed out in the living room, making a mountain of blankets on the sofa. I hadn't heard them come in, so it couldn't have been a very heavy session.

I wolfed a banana and a cup of tea and stuffed my rucksack with books, notebooks, purse, make-up and phone. Mum came through with Jamie perched on one hip.

'Morning, Mum. Is Ronny still asleep? Can I get a lift with him?'

'He made it to bed at a respectable two o'clock, so no. He's long gone.'

'Two o'clock? Lightweights.'

'I think he's warming up. They want a big night with the football. You'll have to catch the bus.'

Anders appeared in the doorway, blankets gathered around his shoulders.

'Morning, Cath. Morning, Flora.'

'How you doing, trooper?'

'Many things in life become easier as you age. But hangovers, not so much.'

'You look like you've been dug up,' I said. 'Tea?'

'You and your tea. Bring me coffee, child. Coffee.'

I made him some coffee, then yelled my goodbyes and waited for the post bus on the road outside.

The weather had turned overnight. There was no rain yet, but it felt like the end of summer, cooler and blustery, the surf suddenly up and pushing at the shore. Clouds scudded low over the Bancree Sound in blooms of white on grey. On the hills behind

Grogport, rising away from the sea, plantation trees breathed in slow waves, and my dreams returned in the creaking of the pines. It was a great day for driving to Glasgow, Bristol, the world. Good weather for a jailbreak.

There was movement up the road. A man appeared, approaching Grogport from the north. From this far away, I guessed it was some hiker, a tourist out of season. He walked in swift, confident strides, devouring the distance. But as the man moved closer, I found myself shrinking. It was the new neighbour. Despite the coolness in the air, he wore shorts and a T-shirt, a canvas kit bag slung across one shoulder. He faced straight ahead as he crossed the bridge into the village. Even yards away, he radiated a bad mood. I couldn't help but stare, drinking him in. He ignored me completely, not even looking up as he approached my house. He had almost walked past by the time I thought to greet him.

'Hello,' I faltered, then spoke louder. 'Hi!'

He stopped, momentarily, and stared at me, scrutinising. He nodded, once, and continued down the road. Mouth still open, I watched him walk away. He took a piece of my stomach with him. Like his daughter, there was something deeply sensual in his face, but something strange as well, something cold. He had very dark eyes. He was stunning. His hair was wet, soaked into twists and curls.

A thought occurred to me, ringing like a chime. If he was walking home, at this time in the morning – then where had he come from?

I was still lost in contemplation when the minibus arrived. It rolled to a clunking pause outside my house, shunting my daydream to one side. The driver peered out.

'Morning, Flo,' beamed Bev, 'all set for another year?'

'Just about,' I said.

All Bev did every day was drive the post bus, delivering both packets and people. She collected the mail from the first ferry, then drove the minibus round the island four or five times. It took an hour or so to run the perimeter road, delivering parcels and letters and giving lifts to anyone who needed them. This included the school run for the island's dozen children. Bev loved her job. It was my idea of slow death.

We pulled away from my house. I fished in my bag for headphones, but we lurched to a stop almost right away. I looked up. The girl from Dog Rock had hailed the bus. The doors slid open.

'Morning,' said Bev. 'Are you for the school?'

I couldn't hear the response over the noise of the engine.

'Right enough,' she said. 'Hop on. Mind you get yourself a pass from the secretary.'

The girl stepped onto the shaking bus and looked along the aisle. I watched her eyes drift over the school kids and empty seats and wheezing pensioners, resting for a moment on each person. When she looked at me, she offered the same weird half-smile from the day before. With one hand on the rail, she nodded apologetically, walked two steps down the aisle and swung into an empty seat by the window, just across the aisle. The automatic door huffed shut and Bev turned the minibus back onto the single-track road.

From the window, I glimpsed the man in the dinghy. The inflatable raced across Still Bay, leaving a wake of froth on the waves. The girl must have brought it over in time for the bus, and left it for him to get home. The bay heaved grey and fizzing.

Outside the village, the road climbed steeply along the coast. I watched the girl from Dog Rock. I could only see the side of her face. Her skin was stark against such dark hair, tied as before away from her face. Her cheekbone shadowed harsh against the light of the

window, and she sat wrapped up in a thick coat. She put on headphones and didn't look at anything except the window. I wondered
what sort of numpty would move to Dog Rock. If I'd been one of
the island biddies, I'd have crossed the aisle to interrogate her for
information. I'd decided long ago never to be an island biddy, but
that didn't stop me wanting to know. I turned up the volume on
my player instead, and set it to shuffle. Through the window opposite, trees flickered in a kaleidoscope of green and brown and grey.

The road weaved a nauseating zigzag between the hills. The out-
skirts of the town emerged from the crests of hills like ships on a
heaving sea. Isolated crofts gathered steadily towards the larger
settlement. There wasn't much to the island's only town. Tighna
was built around its harbour. A natural breakwater provided shelter
from the Bancree Sound, allowing the harbour to house half a
dozen battered fishing boats and a broad concrete slipway. The
long, whitewashed side of Clachnabhan gleamed above the water.
Situated right beside the slip, the distillery was the first building
anyone noticed when they came to visit. The ferry was the heart of
Tighna, beating half a dozen times a day. There was no other way
to live on the island. Without the ferry, Tighna would be another
coastal ghost town. On the rugged northern coast, ancient crofting
townsteads had fallen in on themselves. Without the ferry, Tighna
would go the same way.

The bus jolted to a halt in the harbour car park, and I knocked
my head on the window. Dog Rock girl was already disembarking.
She was small and neat and I was jealous of her Doc Martens. She
looked around, getting her bearings, then strode towards the slip
and the waiting ferry. The other island schoolkids pushed each
other down the aisle, hooting and joking. I gathered my things
and followed. The girl was well ahead by the time she reached the

ferry. She peered into the passenger lounge, then stepped inside.
I said a quick hello to Jow, the captain. He grunted a vague reply
and waved me on. I climbed straight to the exposed upper deck.

I'd known this ferry all my life. She was called the *Island Queen*,
like a dozen other island ferries. I could just about remember my
first day at secondary school, when Mum rode across with me. It
was thrashing with rain, and we sat in the lounge. Our breath condensed on the windows and we drew pictures in the fog.

The reek of petrol clung heady to the lower deck, but up top, the
sea breeze stripped it clean. The last car inched onto the ferry, and
Jow pushed buttons to raise the loading ramp. With a clank that
shook the boat, it closed. He clambered up the stairs to his cabin. A
moment later, the boat started trembling, sending thin vibrations
into the soles of my feet, and the ferry lurched as he engaged the
engines. Foam churned from the stern.

This was my routine. I knew which corner of the lounge was
the warmest, and which toilet seat tried to tip you off. I knew the
spot where kids from Spain and Greece had chipped their names
into the green gloss. Yannis, Stefanie, Pablo, Esme. They came for
a week's holiday, graffitied their names everywhere, and then they
left.

If I ever went to Spain or Greece, I'd carve my name onto everything I saw.

The Sound was fairly calm, despite the breeze, with only a few
white horses cresting distant waves. In places, the sun was trying to
break through, glowing blinding white behind the banks of cloud.
The mainland crawled closer, its ochre fields and grey-green plan-
tations gaining definition as we approached, divided by long lines
of drystone walling and the whitewashed dots of scattered crofts.
Sprawling back from the sea, like it had washed up on the shore,

lay the harbour town of Tanno, by far the biggest on this stretch of coast. People travelled hours from the smaller islands to come for shopping and cheaper petrol or a big night out, or for appointments with the doctor or the travelling dentist.

A sharp whine cut across the thunder of the ferry's engines. I turned my head to either side, focusing the sound, trying to work out what it was. After a few moments, I knew the noise.

'Lachlan,' I muttered.

Even as I spoke, a motor launch roared in front of us, the noise clarifying as it drew closer to the ferry. Froth rocked a trail of spume behind it. Three or four men hooted and called from the boat, their music thumping loud. Lachlan Crane was steering the launch, his shirt unbuttoned and flapping loose despite the cloud, sunglasses gleaming like a jet pilot.

'Dippit playboy,' I said.

Lachlan was the only child of old Munzie Crane, the distillery owner, and he was next in line to the throne at Clachnabhan. Dozens of islanders worked there, and loads of the Tanno townsfolk, and they all hated Lachlan. He was a bully and a womaniser. He'd tried it on with every girl I knew, including me. Somehow, he'd made it to the age of twenty-five without killing himself through a combination of motorbikes, boats, drugs, drink and fights. He carried a knife. Everybody knew it.

One of Lachie's posse yelled and flung a bottle out behind him, the glass flashing green before it sank into the foam. The others laughed. The motorboat thrashed across the ferry's wake, engines yowling. The noise turned tinny as it raced back into the Sound. The bottle spun madly, bobbed and sank.

I watched the launch out of sight, eyes narrowed, glad to see them go. Lachlan Crane spent half his time abroad, and half at home, where he lived with his father in a vast, empty house on the hill behind Tighna. When he was around, the whole island twitched with trouble. He also had it in for Ronny. I'd have to tell him Lachlan was back in town.

It depressed me beyond words to think of that green bottle, thrown so carelessly, sinking to the bottom of the Sound. It would break and disintegrate, and the pieces would be tugged on the tides, scattered over miles.

The sun had threatened to break through, but now the clouds gathered weight and oozed menace. The air felt too thick. It was intangible and impossible to frame, but I couldn't shake the feeling that something was about to happen.

CHAPTER 6

The feeling underfoot changed as we chugged into the harbour. Jow slowed the ferry to a crawl, and the deck rattled with engine vibration. The shuddering boat churned up water, dredging fragments of weed and wood from the harbour bottom. I leaned over the rail, looking down into the foam. This is me, I thought. Thrashing at nothing. Empty energy, melting back into the sea.

Dark movement flitted through the froth. I frowned and looked again, trying to identify the shape. It crested once more in the agitated water. At first I thought it was a piece of wood, caught in the turbulence, but then I laughed out loud. There was a seal in Tanno harbour.

Seals were common on Bancree, but even then they were shy animals, and it was rare to see them in such a populated place. It was even stranger to see one so close to the ferry. It must have been a very confident animal. I watched for minutes as the speckled seal criss-crossed through the foam. It would have been chasing after crabs, disturbed by the juddering wake. The churning subsided as we approached the harbour wall, and the seal vanished in a wink. I scoured the water in widening circles, but it was gone. Outside the expanding ring of foam, the harbour was still and clear.

The ferry crawled and bobbed up to the slipway, resting against the concrete with the slightest of bumps. Jow left his cabin, and threw down a rope. Onshore, the harbourmaster moored *Island Queen* to a post, then slunk back to his portacabin office. Routine, routine. Jow unshackled the ramp and lowered it to the slipway. The few cars drove off and about their business. Sales, appointments, holidays. They drove south in a convoy on the main road out of town. Some of the island's younger kids disembarked and moved towards the school. Across the road, a gaggle of foreigners laughed and drank coffee from polystyrene cups. They were mostly Poles, and some Lithuanians, tall, broad men working long shifts at the fish farm. Dodging between them, a postie juggled parcels.

I gathered my bag and took the stairs to the lower deck, footsteps ringing on the metal. I nodded goodbye to Jow and drudged up the slipway into Tanno, wondering what it must be like to be a seal, to tumble in the water, to flit and soar and drift, cushioned always by the sea. At the top of the slope, the town opened into a panorama. Pretty houses painted in pinks and pastel yellows lined the harbour on three sides.

Another snowglobe. It felt so small.

I inhaled the rank weedy air, and pulled my hair into a ponytail.

'Excuse me,' said a voice.

I turned. Dog Rock girl stood at the top of the slipway. She looked miserable, her dark, neat features bound in reluctance.

'Oh, hello.'

Only then, facing each other, did it seem suddenly ridiculous not to have spoken sooner. My brand-new neighbour, the only other person my age on Bancree, and we'd travelled the entire way to the mainland without saying a word.

'Sorry,' she said, looking as awkward as I felt, 'but could you show me where the school is? I don't know this place at all.'

'Sure. I'm going too.' I hesitated. 'What's your name?'

She looked briefly at me, then the sky. 'Ailsa,' she said. 'My name is Ailsa Dobie.'

'I'm still Flora. Or Flo. Well, school's just up the road here.'

We left the slipway and walked along the harbourfront. There were some chuckles and jokes when we passed the fish farm work gang. I ignored them, but Ailsa blushed.

'It's only a few minutes,' I said. 'And the kids on the island can only get here by ferry, so there's no big drama if we're late. What year are you in?'

'Sixth.'

'Me too.'

An ugly part of myself lapsed into old biddy mode, craving gossip for handing door-to-door. I choked it down.

'What are you studying?'

'Nothing interesting. Art. Graphic Communication. French.'

'I'm in English,' I said, though it sounded just as bland, 'and Spanish. And History.'

'Right,' she said. She seemed nervous, but I would be too. Her voice was soft and quiet, only tinged with an island accent. 'So what's this place like?'

'Probably about the same as your last spot, I suppose. There's good teachers and bad ones. There's some decent kids and a bunch of neds.'

I thought this would settle her. If anything, her frown creased even deeper.

'Where was your last school? Are you from the islands?'

'Aye. All over, really. Dad moves around for his work. We moved from Islay, like I said. Just outside a wee village called Portnahaven. I went to school in Bowmore.'

'Bit weird for you, moving here just for sixth year.'

'I'm used to moving every year,' she said, glumly. 'But I'm not exactly looking forward to it, no. I don't know anyone. Except you, now.'

'Well, if it helps, I'm hardly Miss Scotland when it comes to popularity. Most of my pals were my boyfriend's pals. They were in the year above. They're all gone now.'

'Was that your boyfriend yesterday? The boy with the cigarettes?'

'Aye, Richard' I said, then reconsidered. 'Well, he was. He's gone to uni. In Bristol. I'm not sure he'll be my boyfriend for much longer.'

'I hate smoking. Do you smoke?'

'No. Never have,' I told her, surprised at the reaction.

'That's good.'

I stopped short as we passed the post office. In grainy black and white, Doug MacLeod grinned from the plastic-fronted notice board. It had been carefully cropped, but I still recognised the Bull Hotel behind him. Even in his own poster, he was pissed. Above his mugshot, the headline said: MISSING. There weren't any more details, just a request to contact the constabulary. I scanned the other cards, then turned away. We fell into step at the bottom of the hill.

'Who was that?' said Ailsa.

'A drunken old fart called Dougie. He's been missing for a week or so. He's pals with a lot of folk round here.'

'What happened?'

'No one knows,' I shrugged. 'He's gone, that's all. He never turned up to work. He used to stay with folk all over the place, in Tighna and Tanno, but now he can't be found, and he's not in any of the pubs. He's vanished.'

We walked a moment in silence.

'Has this happened before?' she asked.

'Not really. Well. This is the second time, I suppose. Another islander vanished a few months ago, a man called Billy Wright. But he often goes travelling by himself. Some folk think they're connected. Personally, I don't think it's a big deal.'

Her frown deepened, lines stark on her white skin.

'Why do you ask?' I said.

'Nothing. It's my dad.'

'Your dad?'

I remembered my glimpse through the binoculars, his face as he'd walked past. I formed the words carefully, but my heart kicked a sudden drum.

'Och, it's nothing. No matter.'

I looked at her, but she wouldn't be drawn. We reached the brow of the hill, where Tanno Academy sat like a long-wrecked hulk. Made of prefab concrete slabs, the school looked more like a prison. The building was mostly three storeys tall, and built on two sides around a central yard. Brightly painted play things sprouted from the middle of the playground. Low football goals, a basketball hoop and swings for children. The school offices sat to one side of the building.

'Here it is. The bunker.'

'Well, cheers,' she said.

Around us, younger kids were running and yelling, playing all the usual games. Fourth- and fifth-year girls stood in gaggles of knee socks, gossiping about boys. Each year they pushed the hems of their skirts and the rules of school uniform as far as they could go. The boys were playing killer basketball, queuing below the playground hoop, taking turns to outdo each other and yell. I recognised other sixth years sloping about in casual clothes, enjoying the step out of uniform and up in status. Teachers crossed the yard in ones or twos.

'That's the office over there,' I said, pointing at the squat extension. 'If Bev needs you to get a bus pass or anything. The bus driver. Did you get your timetable?'

'No,' she said, biting her lower lip. 'Not yet.'

'You'll get that in the office. And anything else you need.'

'Thanks again.'

I checked my phone. It was approaching nine o'clock.

'Look. I've got to go now. I have History.'

'And I'd better check in with the office, I suppose, let them know I'm here.'

'See you round, I guess.'

'OK. Maybe on the ferry home.'

She tried a smile, and started turning away.

'Sorry for not coming over earlier,' I rushed. 'To say hello. On the bus or something.'

'Aye, me too. Bit daft, really.'

'I was in a world of my own.'

'Me too,' said Ailsa, nodding. 'Sometimes, that's the best place to be.'

Like sun from clouds, she flashed a brilliant smile and just as quick, it melted away. She turned. I watched her cross to the office. The glass door closed behind her, and my strange new neighbour was gone.

CHAPTER 7

I walked across the schoolyard. With Richard and his friends moving away, there was no one left who really knew me. I'd never mixed with my own classmates. There was distance between me and the Tanno kids. I was from a different place. A different species, starting my last year as a stranger. Even the other Bancree kids were removed, separate, years younger than me. In a corner near the bins, a flock of sparrows pecked at crumbs. I felt like a cuckoo.

Standing to one side of the playground, leaning against the railings, I could see other sixth years milling around the yard. I knew the students in my year well enough to talk to, but at the same time, I didn't know them at all. Like me, they were dressed in their own clothes. Jeans and T-shirts, skirts and sweaters. It felt weird after spending five years dressed the same as everyone else. Any moment, I expected Mr Baillie to rampage from the staffroom, handing out detentions and yelling about school regulations.

Last year, when I hung out with Richard and his pals, they'd been the ones wearing shorts and hats and trainers. They'd teased me about being the only one in uniform. I'd fumed about it, and willed on the start of sixth year. Now I was wearing my own clothes, just the way I'd wanted, but they were gone and I was still trapped a year behind.

Flotsam.

A year. I could wait that long. A year was nothing. A year, and then my life could begin.

Something banged into my back. Off balance, I stumbled against the railings. Four girls stood in a group behind me. They were all from the fifth year. The shortest of the group stood in the middle. My heart sank. It was Tina Robson.

'All right, Flo?' she sneered. 'Had a pleasant summer?'

'Everything was fine till now,' I said.

At sixteen years old, Tina was an ego in a C-cup. She was queen bee at Tanno Academy. I wanted nothing to do with her, and normally we'd never cross paths. But she hated me for hanging out with older students, and one student in particular: Richard. He and I had come to school a ready-made couple. Tina was used to having any boy she wanted, but she couldn't have Richard, and that meant she wanted him. She was a dog in a manger. She loathed me, but she'd always been on good behaviour while Richard was around. And now he was gone.

Her girls fanned out, hemming me against the railings.

'Things are going to be different for you this year,' she said, 'without your pals to protect you.'

'Will you listen to yourself? Protect me from what? You sound like a gangster.'

'Maybe I am.'

'What's your problem, Tina? What have I done to you?'

'The attitude,' she said. 'The airs and graces. That won't wash any more. You're back down here with the rest of us, and I'm going to make sure you know all about it.'

'Awesome. That sounds peachy. I'll look forward to that, Big Brother.'

'Flat-chested fucking gypsy hipster.'

'Tramp.'

'Better than a prude,' she said, her smile widening into a leer. 'At least I know what boys like. Shame your Richard's not here any more. I'd show him what it's like with a real girl, rather than a stick insect.'

'Well, never mind. You'll have to keep practising with the rest of the rugby team.'

She hissed and lunged at me, and I couldn't help but flinch. She backed off and laughed, her gaggle of pals joining in. They seemed to crowd a little closer. The railings were rigid at my back. I didn't feel scared at that moment, so much as horribly alone.

'Ah, Flora,' said a voice. 'Back with us for another year, I see.'

Tina spun round to see who'd spoken. Her face fell, and relief washed through me.

'Yes, Miss Carlyle,' I said.

The school History teacher shouldered her way into the circle of girls. She was carrying a stack of plastic-jacketed library books in both hands, the volumes piled from waist to her chin. She eyed Tina closely.

'Everything all right here, Tina?'

'Aye, of course, Miss Carlyle,' she sulked.

'Good, good,' replied the teacher. 'Because I'd hate for you and I to start this year in the same fashion we finished the last. Would you like that?'

Tina's eyes shone venom, but she choked out a smile.

'No, Miss. I wouldn't like that at all.'

'Well, that's two of us. Wonderful.'

'Would you like a hand with those books, Miss?' I asked.

She beamed at me. 'That would be delightful, Flo,' she said, leaning towards me. I took the top half of the stack from her, and followed her towards the main block. As I walked away, Tina hissed something vicious, but I didn't catch the words.

Richard had always been my friend, but I'd never seen him as protection. Spending all our time together had felt natural because we lived together, travelled together, schooled together. Richard's friends had become my friends just like Richard had become my boyfriend. Thinking about it now, my life appeared to be a long, bad habit of taking easy options.

With Tina on my case, the year felt a little lonelier and an awful lot longer.

I increased my pace to catch up with the teacher. Still fettered by the books, Miss Carlyle was clawing at the door with her elbow. Weighed down by my own stack, I stuck my foot around the edge, hooking it open.

'Thank you for this, dear,' she said, heading for the stairs inside the door. I followed behind her.

'No bother, Miss. I should be thanking you.'

'Indeed, teacher to the rescue. Was that anything I need to worry about?'

'It was nothing. Did you have a good holiday?'

'That I did, dear. I was on a dig in Turkey.'

'What a completely normal way to spend your holiday, Miss.'

'Enough lip from you, Flora,' she said, smiling. 'And you? What did you get up to?'

I hesitated. We were heading for the top floor.

'It was OK, Miss. You know Richard's gone to Bristol?'

'Ah, yes. Young Mr Macintyre. Your partner in crime, off to university.'

'Aye, well. He's gone.'

She peered at me above her glasses. 'And how does that sit with you?'

'It's fine,' I said, not wanting to make too big a deal of it, 'I'll get by.'

She paused outside her classroom door. 'I'm sure you will, young lady. There are plenty more fish in the sea.'

'Yes, Miss.'

'Or so they tell me, anyway.'

She sighed. I looked at her. She looked at me. I wondered how old she was. 'Another year,' she said. 'Very well. Let battle commence.'

Leaning on the handle, she pushed the door open with her shoulder and went inside. I followed, and placed my stack of books beside hers on the desk at the front.

There were only eight of us studying sixth-year History. As they entered the room, the other students muttered with each other. No one sat beside me.

'Right,' said Miss Carlyle, and the noise fizzled out. 'Let's get started. I'm going to assume you all had a wonderful summer and have arrived back at school feeling refreshed, recharged and full of vigour for the year ahead?'

There was an embarrassed silence.

'No,' she said, pulling up a chair, 'me neither. Well, never mind. You'll be doing more self-guided research this year. We'll start nice and easy, and look at some fairy tales.'

Someone sniggered.

'Yes, Alan. Fairy tales.'

'That's soft, Miss.'

'Soft? Four hundred years ago, if your baby was born deformed, you knew pixies had swapped your infant with a changeling, which made it all the easier to leave it on the hillside. Is that soft?'

'No, Miss.'

'And if a traveller drowned in the river, and their white, bloated corpse was recovered from the shore, covered with toothmarks, you knew a kelpie had been at work. How about that?'

Alan swallowed and shook his head.

'People needed these creatures to explain the events in their lives they couldn't control. I want you to pick a Scottish myth, research its origins, and write a report on how it's evolved over the years. Does everyone understand?'

A mumble of yeses and ayes crept around the desks.

'Good. I've put the full assignment on the board. Now, I suggest you use today's session to research your options and decide upon a topic. You need to manage your own time. By your next lesson, I want a plan of action from each of you, listing potential sources of information. Check those top two shelves for some of my history books, or go and use the computers in the library. Ask me questions, but otherwise,' she beamed, 'I'll see you on Wednesday.'

As one, the other sixth years disembarked for the library, grinning from ear to ear at the newfound liberty. I stayed in class and made some notes on the project. I couldn't work out what to write about. Ghosts, maybe? Or kelpies? I browsed the bookshelves, pulling out occasional titles and flicking through for ideas. Giants? Banshees?

I was no closer to a decision by the end of the lesson. After double History came double Spanish. Unfortunately, the class was combined with the fifth years. I spent two hours in paired conversations, trying to order a three-course meal while Martin MacMillan stared at my chest.

I drifted out of Spanish, still thinking of ideas for my History project, and followed my feet along the corridors. I walked towards the canteen on autopilot, but then came the realisation that I didn't actually have any other lessons that day. Another bonus of sixth year – part-time timetables and a host of study periods. I considered going to the library and doing some work, but the novelty was too much for me. It was a real pleasure to leave school and go home early. One more step to freedom.

Surrounded by her cronies, Tina Robson stood by a near corner of the yard as I walked out through the main gate. She pointed at her own eyes, then at me, just to let me know she'd be watching. I gave her a beaming smile and an upturned middle finger, then passed round the corner out of sight.

CHAPTER 8

Down the hill and back to the postcard harbourfront. The *Island Queen* wouldn't leave for another hour, so I had a quick rummage in the town's two charity shops. I found a bright-blue Sesame Street T-shirt in the first, and a Led Zep CD hiding between boy-band albums in the second. Two good finds. I had a toastie and a cup of tea in Dora's Diner, then decided to pop in and see Mum in the Co-op. As I wandered along the harbourfront, I noticed the parish hall was hosting a jumble sale. With time to kill, I went to have a look.

The hall smelled of badminton and old ladies. Half a dozen biddies guarded half a dozen wallpaper tables, loaded down with books, cakes and battered plastic toys. There was a Teenage Mutant Ninja Turtle annual from before I was born, a shoebox of Nintendo games and a set of lawn bowls. Coffee mugs and walking sticks, ornamental spaniels. Junk, all junk. I did a quick round and was on the way out when something caught my eye. I returned to the stall with the books. One corner of a slim hardback peeked from a box crammed with *Beanos* and *National Geographics*. I teased it free.

It was called *The Truth About The Legend Of The Scottish Selkie*. It was written and illustrated by someone called M.I. Mutch. The cover was a grotesque ink drawing of a fat sleek seal, though there was also something queer about its shape, something at odds with its anatomy. I peered closer. Halfway down its body, emerging at an ungainly, impossible angle, a hand crept out of the skin. The selkie looked so sad, with this obscene hand sprouting from inside it. The hand was beckoning. It gave me the shivers. I flicked through a few pages.

It was most peculiar. Flicking through at random, it seemed Mutch had described the selkies as genuine creatures, rather than fairy tales. They were discussed as though they were native animals, like red deer or rabbits, and the book was a work of zoology, or maybe anthropology, brought to life with lurid illustrations of personal encounters. I flicked to the front of the book, looking for the author's note. There was nothing. It had been published in 1992 by a company called Broch Books. This appeared to be the first edition.

A walking stick waggled in my peripheral vision. I looked up.

'If you want to read that for free, hen,' scowled an old lady, 'piss off and find it in the library.'

I paid my fifty pence, stashed the book in my bag, and left.

Crossing to the Co-op, I strolled the harbour edge, weaving between the mooring posts, looking down into the water. It was tinged turquoise and astoundingly clear. Clusters of weed hung russet in the wash. Tiny fish flickered around a hanging hawser, long-forgotten and now without a purpose, thick with barnacles and slime. For those little fish, that hawser was a universe. I knew how they felt. My shoes scuffed on the old stone blocks that edged the harbour.

Mum was talking on the phone, but smiled and waved me in, gesturing five minutes with her free hand. The shop was empty of customers, the strip lights low on the ceiling and too bright. On a pinboard, classified adverts offered window cleaning or babysitting, drum lessons or chess club, ashtanga or bikram yoga. The magazine racks were pretty much empty, ready for the new editions. I browsed the headlines on the various island papers while Mum chatted with head office, ordering next week's charcoal, wine, flour, sweeties.

The Co-op stocked a host of papers and newsheets from the local islands. Several of them ran small pieces about Doug MacLeod, and a couple of them featured his disappearance as a sidebar on the front page. They didn't have much to say about it. Dougie had last been seen at closing time at the Ship Inn in Tanno on a Friday night, and hadn't showed for work in Clachnabhan on Monday morning. He was a much-loved friend and neighbour. Friends and family were concerned for his safety. Anyone with information was urged to contact DC Duncan of the Northern Constabulary at Tanno police station.

I knew Tom Duncan. He used to live on Bancree. He was seven or eight years older than me, but Ronny knew his parents pretty well. He'd gone to college, joined the police force and come back a detective. He was a nice enough lad. He had an earnest face which was always pink from shaving.

'Such a shame about Dougie,' said Mum. She hung up the phone, walked out from behind the counter and stood beside me.

'Do you think they'll find him?' I said. 'I mean – alive.'

'I don't know, love. Honestly, I don't think it looks good. You don't always know what you're doing when you're drunk, and Dougie was drunk most of the time. He wasn't in great shape.'

'I hope they find him.'

'Hang on,' she said, mildly, 'shouldn't you be in school?'

I grinned. 'Sixth year now, Mum. Study periods. Popped in to see you before the ferry leaves.'

'Studying the charity shops, more like.'

'I bought a Sesame Street T-shirt.'

'Of course you did. How was the first day back?'

'Bits were good. History was good.'

'So what wasn't?'

'Tina Robson.'

'Who's that?' frowned Mum.

'She's a fifth year,' I said. 'Johnny Robson's eldest girl. The hardware guy. She had a crush on Richard, and she's pissed off because he hung out with me instead of her. Now he's gone, she's decided to give me a hard time of it.'

'She might have a point.'

'Mum!'

'Oh, not because of Richard. That's just daft. But you two have done everything together for so long. Ronny and I worry about you. We worry you're not very, well – social. And it's not easy living on the island, I know, but I wish you'd make the effort to get on with a few more people.'

'Well, I met a new person today, if that puts your mind at rest.'

'It does, yes,' she said, surprised. 'Who's that?'

'The girl from Dog Rock. She's called Ailsa.'

'Our next-door neighbour,' said Mum, dripping sarcasm. 'Still, it's a start.'

I tried to remember her surname. 'Ailsa Dobie, I think. They move around all over the islands.'

'Well, good for you. What was she like?'

'She was OK. Seemed quite quiet. And a bit weird. But I would be too. First day at a new school, can't be a lot of fun.'

Mum grinned. 'Quiet and weird sounds like most of the teenagers I know, come to think of it.'

'Very amusing, Mother. I get it all from you.'

'I'd better get back to my orders,' she said, then looked over my shoulder. 'Didn't you say you wanted the afternoon ferry?'

I twirled – sure enough, Jow was cranking the engine, and cars were clattering down the ramp.

'Cheers, Ma. I'm off.'

'You going home to do some work?' called Mum.

'Aye, in a bit,' I said, heading for the door. 'But I'm going to see Izzy first.'

'Izzy? What do you want with that old tinker?'

'I'm pretty sure he can help with my homework,' I said.

Mum looked baffled. I waved goodbye, and raced across the road to catch the claptrap *Island Queen*.

CHAPTER 9

As the lurching ferry crossed the Bancree Sound, I thought about Izzy. He was a beachcomber. He'd moved to Bancree a few years ago, and everyone on the island knew him. When he'd first arrived, bringing nothing but a bulging rucksack, he'd set up beside the last wall of a tumble-down barn, halfway between Tighna and Grogport. Over the next month, he brought more and more timbers to his campsite, sometimes hauling them halfway round the island. He borrowed a shovel. He dug holes and sunk the timbers, making uprights, then lashed perlins and spars all the way around. By the time a tarpaulin had been draped over the top and weighted with stones, he'd built a perfectly respectable shack. He'd dug a pit for a campfire.

Even though it was out of sight, it had rattled a few cages that he'd dared to build there at all. Most islanders were content to leave him alone, but a few sent the council complaints about planning permission. An inspector turned up to examine Izzy's hut, only to find it had disappeared overnight. Someone had tipped him off. The grizzled beachcomber was sitting on an orderly stack of sea-washed timber, quite content, smoking a pipe and warming his hands around a driftwood campfire. He made the inspector a breakfast of sausages in seaweed and stovies with butter, then sent him on his way. By nightfall the shack was up again, and the moaning islanders knew enough not to bother again. And besides, he started coming in useful. He did odd jobs for cheap prices, or sometimes just for food. He mowed lawns and helped people move house. He was there for the lambing, or for picking fruit, or unloading the ferry, and he washed dishes in the Bull when the tourists were in full swing.

Most days, though, Izzy walked the beaches, combing the high-tide line with expert eyes, picking out sea-rinsed glass and the prettiest shells, jetsam logs and useful lengths of net or rope. With the shells and glass, he made wind chimes and necklaces, or simple mosaics glued to planks of wood. He sold them to tourists throughout the summer. He collected mushrooms and berries. He fished the inland burns and kept crab pots in the deepest rock pools. Island rumour said he'd once caught a four-foot lobster. Island rumour also said that he was a practising shaman, that he'd killed a man, and that he used to be a don at Cambridge University. Island rumours weren't worth salt from the sea.

Parents disapproved, but every kid on Bancree loved him, and Izzy loved the kids. He gave away little trinkets he'd found or made. Last summer, he'd given me an old champagne cork he'd carved to look like an Easter Island stone head. He'd become steadily integrated into the community, and now it felt like he'd always been there.

I disembarked the deserted ferry, feeling extremely smug about how early I was back on Bancree. The September sun had finally burned away the cloud and I decided to walk, past Clachnabhan, past the Bull Hotel, past the old building site and the abandoned rows of concrete pipes, across the road and down onto the beach. I took off my shoes and wriggled my feet into the sand, enjoying the cool squeeze of the grains between my toes. The sound of waves relaxed me, hushing always on the shore.

It was a gentle stroll down to Izzy's shack, maybe a couple of miles along, and the afternoon sun soaked soft and woozy. Gulls wheeled in columns, carving and turning on the wind, and tiny birds skipped along the beach ahead of me. On the far side of the Ben, I could just make out the tips of the wind turbines. Two were turning, gently, and one wasn't moving at all. It was a rare day when all three moved at once. Engineers were sent to repair them, but no sooner had they fixed one than the next failed. The dull weight of the mountain grew fainter with haze.

The sand was clean and white and free from tourists. Every now and then, I stopped to examine things caught amongst the seaweed scraps. Izzy would have already been through it, but I enjoyed looking. Dark little spiders rushed beneath the damp, smelly weed, and sand fleas skipped between the bleached and sea-smoothed twigs. Keeping fifty yards ahead of me, a dunlin griped from the flotsam. There were scraps of plastic, old dolls and party poppers, bottles of water or detergent. An old buoy or a ping-pong bat, bald without its rubber skin. A chair leg. A trainer, the sole and laces ripped away. Running through it like a single cord were tangled miles of rope and twine, their faded blues and oranges sewing everything else together. The tide heaved it up in rafts.

Izzy's hut came into view. It wasn't on the beach itself, but well above the high tide line, through a few dozen yards of pitted peat scrub and dune grass. At first sight it looked like a village bonfire, stacked high and ready for a match, but as the distance closed, parts of the building came into focus. Flashes of bright blue tarpaulin showed beneath a corrugated iron roof. Holding the metal up, thicker timbers were planted into the sand, and smaller lengths joined and supported them, making a lattice of old wood. The door was an actual door. He'd found it washed up by the Knorritaven pool. The sea had left it warped and rounded and stripped of paint, but there it stood, hinged to the old railway sleepers that held the whole thing up.

On the higher part of the beach, an array of homemade wind chimes hung on a simple frame. Built of driftwood and stone, glass and bone, they clicked and knocked together, constant, brittle and tuneless. In this breeze, they danced. Whenever I came to visit the old beachcomber, I took a moment to run a hand through them, enjoying their percussion.

Outside the hut was Izzy's campfire. Ringed with smooth grey stones, it was never out for long. A constant supply of wood lay in arm's reach. He spent most of his time beside the fire, making his various trinkets. A number of improvised seats were stationed in a ring around the campfire. People came to see the beachcomber, to swap things and shoot the breeze. It wasn't unusual for Izzy to get drunk with tourists in the beer garden at the Bull, then bring them down the beach to his hut, seat them round the fire and scare them shitless with his ghost stories.

Stories were the reason I'd come to see him.

I knocked on the salt-scrubbed wooden door, tracing my fingers along the whorls.

'Izzy?' I called, 'are you there, old man?'

There was no reply. I hooked my foot around an upturned wine crate, dragged it closer to the fire and took a seat. The fire pit was about a metre or so across and kerbed with hefty stones, spattered with grease from cooking. I'd thought the fire was out, but a low, steady warmth radiated from the ashes. Little zephyrs caught crumbs of ash and sent them soaring in a rush. I reached over, took a handful of driftwood twigs and chucked them into the centre of the fire, scattering more ash on the updraft. They started smoking and smouldering immediately. After a few minutes, flames burst from the wood. I added logs, and the fire caught fast.

While I waited for the beachcomber, I had another flick through the weird selkie book, leafing through in more detail. With the sun at my back and the fire at my shins, I curled up and lost myself in the strangest, saddest book I'd ever read.

CHAPTER 10

I'd always thought of selkies as fairly gentle beasties, but Mutch wrote of seal folk with a wicked rage. According to the book, selkies were wily, malicious, devious, manipulative, contrary, stubborn, twisted, nasty, brutal things, utterly devoid of any good and hell-bent on making people miserable. A bit like Tina Robson, really. The book told tall tales of selkie maidens luring sailors to their deaths by drowning, ambush or assault, stoving their heads in with rocks and oars, tangling them in nets and lines, holding them under. They cast spells, making people fall hopelessly in love with them, then fled, abandoning the stricken men or women to lifetimes of solitude, misery and suicide. In every page, I could feel the frenzy in the author's voice, could trace the spite in every word.

'You're pure crackers, pal,' I muttered.

A strange, strange book.

It was the illustrations that made my mind up. Like the drawing on the cover, each picture was a mess of limbs and stretching skin, showing the selkies in various states of disrobe and transformation. A full-page drawing showed a selkie in seal form, but its entire shape was morphing, disfigured and distorted, the skin loose and jumbled. There were clearly more than two arms and two legs inside the skin, and it bulged with obscenely human shapes. The selkie was sneering, even while its head hung empty as a mask. Low down on the body, in the shadows, the fur drew taut across a screaming face. The fine details were obscured but the expression showed clearly as one of pain and hate, twisted by fury, bulging outwards against the mottled fur.

It repelled me, but my mind was made up. I'd write my school report on selkies. It'd be interesting. I jotted down a few places I could try for information. The library, obviously, for slightly more academic books of myths and legends. And the tiny museum in Tanno might have something. It occurred to me that it would be great to talk to the author, too. I checked the book again for a biography or picture, turning the battered dust jacket inside out, leafing through the pages at the front and back, but there was nothing about him – or her, maybe. Mutch. Odd name. It was almost hidden on the cover.

I studied the pictures closely. They were quite something. Dark and distorted, but beautifully realised, capturing seal and human in single images, both beings combined in a single too-tight skin. Some of them were like that cover image, with body parts emerging from a silken skin. One of the most lurid was of a selkie emerging from its skin in the form of a naked woman. As she stood up from the fur, the skin hung loose from her buttocks, draped loose like a sarong. She was turned away from the artist, but she was looking back over her shoulder, and her face was cruel. Oh, it was cruel. She was icily beautiful but fierce and snide, oozing superiority. Her eyes were inked completely dark. Her breasts jutted a fraction beyond the cover of her arm, catching a curve of light. Fanboy tit-illation. I closed the book with a snap, and reached into my bag for a crumpled A4 pad. Using the hardback Mutch book as a rest, I scribbled some more notes for my project report.

Selkies are evil?! Since when?
Stories – biased? <u>OBVIOUSLY</u>
So, need more information from:
library books (try museum also)
old fishermen from island
internet (ha!)
old songs?
Find Mutch if poss . . . . . . ask publishers direct? <u>Broch Books</u>

I started doodling a selkie of my own. The lines that formed beneath my biro left a crude, crooked-looking thing. It was just a seal, really. I couldn't feel any of Mutch's ferocity towards the creature. Every story I'd ever heard about selkies said they were benign and peaceful, but it wasn't something I knew much about. Then again, everything I'd heard about kelpies said they were evil to the core. That was very one-sided, so maybe that was wrong, too. Maybe kelpies were lovely things. Why was Mutch so blinded by the selkies in particular? I carefully circled his name on my notepad, and added a question mark.

I heard Izzy before I saw him, and returned both book and notepad to my bag. Huffing and gasping, he crested the sand and reached the scrub. He carried a massive piece of wood on one shoulder, bent halfway to double supporting the weight and grunting with each step. I jumped to help him, and took a few quick steps in his direction. With his head bowed, he glanced up, saw me and shook his head, droplets of sweat pinging from his hair. I backed off and let him pass, the pole trailing him by a metre or more. He passed his shack, paused, then hefted the wood from his shoulder to the ground. It dropped on one end, then landed flat with a thud that sent vibrations into the soles of my feet.

'Hey, Izzy. Glad to see you're still here. Worried you'd be next to disappear.'

Still bent double, heaving for air, he waved a hand. After a minute of steady breathing, he inched round and looked up.

'Don't joke about that,' he said, grimacing. 'You fed the fire. Good lass. I was worried it might go out.'

'Just kidding. I don't think there's anything actually happening.'

'Perhaps not, but that's two of my pals gone missing. I'm worried about it, even if you're not.'

'Anders and Ronny are heading out tonight to have a look themselves.'

'Anders is back, is he?'

'Aye. Something to do with a football match. It all seemed very important.'

'Well, good for them.'

Izzy stood up tall and leaned backwards, stretching his arms out and upwards. It was like the timber had squashed him flat, and now he unfolded to full size. He was built like a bear, tall and thickset. He must have been in his fifties, or older, but he worked hard and kept in good health. Framed by a thick straggle of grey hair, his face was angular but friendly.

'This might be a stupid question,' I said, 'but were you carrying a telegraph pole?'

He grinned at me.

'You're right. That is a stupid question. It's only half a telegraph pole.'

'Where's the other half?'

'I'll be back for that tomorrow,' he said, wincing and putting a hand to the small of his back, 'if the body lets me.'

'Where have you come from?'

'MacKendrick's farm. He wanted shot of it.'

I did a quick calculation.

'That's three miles away. You've come all that way?'

'Aye, well. I might have stopped for a wee pint in the Bull.'

'It is important to stay hydrated during exercise,' I said sarcastically, sounding like my mother. I walked along the pole in careful steps, one foot before the other, feeling the warmth of the wood in my bare feet.

'And obviously that was my thinking, doctor. My thanks for your concern.'

'Where's it going?' I asked.

'I thought I'd expand a little. A wee extension. You know me. I'm all about the accumulation of material wealth.'

'I know you need a bath.'

'And I shall have one, in the sea, when you've gone,' he replied with dignity. 'You whippersnapper. When are you going again? In fact, why are you here?'

'I've come to ask you about stories.'

'Stories, is it? Well, I know a few of them.'

'Do you know any about selkies?'

Izzy closed his eyes, thinking, and chewed his lip.

'Selkies? Aye, I've a few of them and all. Every shennachie worth his salt knows a selkie story.'

'What's a shennachie?'

'A storyteller of the oldest sort. He collects stories as he wanders, and tells them from memory. He keeps them stored nice and safe up here,' said Izzy, tapping his temple.

'Well, there you go. And I thought you were a beachcomber.'

'Oh, I'm a lot of things. Take a pew, lass.'

I went back to my upturned crate. Izzy had built himself a chair from driftwood, long ago, and padded it with old cushions taken from the tip in Tanno. He settled himself back into his seat and poked at the fire.

'All right. What do you want to know?' he said, looking up at me. 'What's this all about?'

'It's homework. We're doing a report on Scottish folklore, and I picked selkies. I've got a book already, but I thought I'd see if you knew anything.'

'Books are a waste of time,' he grunted. 'No one remembers what they read in a book. People need to hear it, they need to be involved. That's why we have campfire stories,' he said, nudging the charred logs in their makeshift grate. As he rolled them over, they loosed a new burst of heat.

'Selkies, selkies. All right. Are you ready?'

I drew my feet up onto the crate, hugging my knees.

Izzy started to tell a story.

CHAPTER 11

Once upon a time, there was a poor crofter. He lived alone in his wee cottage on the shores of a windswept island. He kept chickens, and had a pig or two in the byre out back. He grew tatties and turnips. He fished in the river, and set nets in a tidal pool. He kept crab pots by the shore, and collected firewood from the beach. Every few weeks, he'd gather his surplus and take it to sell at market, returning with flour, cloth, salt and whatever else he needed to get by. By night he darned his socks or fixed his nets. The crofter survived, day to day, but his was a lonely, cheerless existence, and there was a sadness inside him that wouldn't leave him be. It nagged at him like a sore tooth.

Now, there came a time when a travelling musician performed at the market. He played the fiddle most beautifully, and the crofter was transfixed. When the fiddle was upbeat, the crofter tapped his foot in time with the music, tasting the warmth of whisky on a hot summer night. And when the fiddle played a lament, the crofter felt the chill of midwinter, all alone in his wee cottage.

The crofter believed with all his heart that this wonderful music would cure the sadness caught inside him. He resolved at once to learn the fiddle for himself. He sold his mother's old loom, some family treasures and two of his piglets, and bought himself a fiddle, the best he could afford. He took his instrument back to his cottage and he started to practice.

O, but how he practised. When he first woke in the morning, he played a little sitting up in bed. He came home for his lunch and played the fiddle while his broth boiled over on the grate. And then, every night, when he returned from the field or from checking on his crab pots, he'd build up his fire, ease off his boots, take up his fiddle and play and play and play. He played until his fingers ached, and his elbows turned stiff, then played until he'd worked them loose again.

After long years of hard practice, that crofter played second to no other. Each night, the sweetest music poured from the windows of his little cottage. He played the fastest dances, conjuring the wildest ceilidh from a few simple notes, and he played the slowest, softest, saddest songs you've ever heard.

The crofter had learned the fiddle as well as any man alive. But no matter how well he played, still that nagging sadness chewed at him, eating at his insides like a rat. He took to sitting on the foreshore every night, playing laments to his own loneliness, and the mournful music slid across the water softer than snowfall. He played until dark. The sadness sounded like night itself.

One night, a selkie swam past the island. She heard the fiddle, and stopped to listen. She was entranced by the music, and coveted the crofter's skill with his instrument. She resolved to take it for her own. Stepping onto the shore, she emerged from her skin and took the form of a beautiful woman. She conjured her skin into the form of a shell, and hid it deep in a rockpool, then ran to the cottage, weeping that she was lost and alone. The crofter was a good man, and of course he gave her shelter. To protect her from the cold, he gave her his jacket and boots. To make her comfortable, he gave up his bed to the selkie woman. He fed her and cared for her.

As time went along, she bewitched him with her beauty, and they became lovers. At last, the crofter felt that heavy sadness lifted from his spirit. As his love for her grew ever stronger, so his music became more wonderful, more entrancing. Invigorated by this new passion, he played his music to the selkie, and she found it more beautiful than ever. She begged him to teach her the fiddle and, of course, crazy with his love for her, he agreed. The selkie woman remembered every note he taught her, and soon she learned to play. She demanded more lessons, and longer lessons. The crofter was so in love that he forgot his duties. His pigs grew sick and died. His chickens stopped laying eggs and shed their feathers, and then the harriers came for them. He forgot to plant new crops. In his abandoned pots, the crabs starved and rotted. All he did, day and night, was teach his woman how to play the fiddle. With each day, he grew thinner and sicker, nourished only by his desire for the beautiful selkie. And all the while, she grew stronger, feeding like a tick on his love and the gift of his music. She gorged herself on all he'd learned, craving more, demanding more. The skill that had taken the crofter years to master was taken from him in a few short months.

He grew ever weaker, and the day came when the crofter was too faint to leave his bed. He called to his woman, his wife, his love, to repay his kindness, and to care for him in turn. Smiling sweetly, the selkie stepped out of bed, as lithe and strong as ever, and took up his fiddle. She began to play, making the instrument sing and dance as though it were alive – as though it were alive and had a voice!

She played fast and she played slow, she played loud and she played soft, she played the music of the heart and the music of the death. The crofter listened and watched from his bed, entranced at the skill of his wonderful bride, his eyes full of tears at how beautifully she played. She played and played for hours, and he felt the sickness overtake him. He called for help, begging her for food and water, but she kept on with the fiddle. He tried to shout above the music, but his voice came out a rasp. Exhausted, he collapsed back on the bed. The selkie lowered her fiddle – for it was her fiddle, now – and laughed at the weakness of the crofter – at the weakness of all men.

She left the cottage, taking the fiddle, and returned to the beach. She retrieved her skin from its hiding place in the rockpool, and slipped back beneath the waves without so much as looking back. From his window, the crofter watched her swim away, only now understanding that she was a selkie, a seal-woman, and his heart broke twice – once for the loss of his beautiful bride, and once for the death of his music. He was a ruined, broken man. The old sadness fell upon him like a boulder, a hundred times harder than before. It pinned misery to the few days left to him, alone in the croft, starving and thirsty and cold.

Outside, his crops rotted in the fields.

The selkie returned to the sea, having stolen the gift of music from the crofter. She played the fiddle for her sisters, and they waltzed beneath the waves. This is why selkies are drawn to the sound of music, and why they shed their skins to dance. This is why drowning men hear the sound of a violin as their lungs begin to flood. This is why they hear a fiddle, the sound muted by the sea, playing laments as soft and sad as snow on water.

CHAPTER 12

I blinked. Izzy watched the fire, his face lit ruddy. He reached down and tossed another branch of bony driftwood onto the embers.

'Wow.' I said.

'Not what you were expecting?'

I thought about it. 'You were different. It's like you took on a character. It was like an act.'

'I told you, I'm a shennachie.'

'I thought selkies were good things.'

Izzy pulled a face. 'They are and they aren't. The stories change as they migrate. See now, up in the Faroe Islands, the selkie is a brutal creature, ambushing lone sailors as they cast their nets, and dragging them under. But off the Isle of Man, a selkie is more like a mermaid from the movies. And there's every kind of selkie in between. That story I've just told you, that's an old one, one from Shetland.'

'I see,' I said, thinking about how that would feed into my report. 'Was there any truth in it?'

'What? The story?'

I nodded. He looked at me like I was crazy.

'It's batshit, lass. Don't be daft. Selkies don't exist. There's no such thing as seals that turn into people.'

'But the way you told it,' I said, frowning.

'It makes for a good story,' he chuckled, 'I grant you that. But that's all it is. Stories. Plenty more of them up here.' He tapped his temples again.

'Any more about selkies?'

'Aye. Three or four more. Maybe half a dozen, once I've had a think. But I'm thinking it's a little late for you and your homework. Will you not be wanted home?'

He was right. It was getting on. The sun was dropping behind Ben Sèimh and the air had grown cool in the mountain's shadow.

'I'll write that story up tonight.'

'Hey there,' growled Izzy. 'No. I'd rather you didn't.'

'But I need to. It's for my project.'

'Write up the bones of it, if you must. Get the basics of it for your homework. But don't write the whole thing like I told it you.'

'Why not?' I said, confused.

He huffed a bit.

'Look,' he said, 'this might sound daft to you, lass. But my stories are about the telling and the hearing, not the writing and the reading. They're all for talking out loud. They're about this, and that, and this,' he said, pointing haplessly at the sky, and the sea, and the crackling fire. 'If you write them down, they'll lose some of the magic.'

'I don't get it.'

'It's like this. If you put a bear in a cage, what do you have?'

'A bear?'

'No. All you have is a cage. It's the same with my story. Do you understand?'

I studied the fire, weighing it up.

'Flora,' he said, 'tell me you understand. They're my words. I don't want them written down for some report.'

'All right, all right. Not if you don't want me to.'

He visibly relaxed.

'Grand. That's fine. And listen. If there's anything else I do to help, come and ask. I'll do whatever I can. Just don't write the stories down for folk.'

'It's a deal. Cheers, Izzy.'

'You'd better go, and I'll off and have my bath. Pop back when you can and I'll sort you out some more.'

'Right you have it, O mighty shennachie,' I said, and began to put my shoes back on.

'That's more like it. Oh, Flora – something else I wanted to ask you.'

'Aye?'

'Happen I've come across some cheap booze.'

'Oh aye? Found it on the beach, I suppose.'

'Something like that,' he grinned. 'Never know what'll wash up next. Anyway, it's almost sort of cherry brandy.'

'"Almost sort of"?'

'I want shot of it. To you, ten quid a bottle.'

'I'm leaving now, Izzy,' I said. 'Stay safe.'

I cut across the fields to reach the road. Having already hiked as far as Izzy's shack, it was just as quick to walk the few miles home, rather than return to Tighna and wait to hitch a ride.

Sheep moved like ghosts in the dusk, startled when I came too close, hooves knocking on the hard turf as they skittered away. The clouds above were glowing orange, but evening was falling hard by the time I vaulted a rundown fence, pushed through the barrier of birch trees and found the road.

As the sky turned ashen, I settled into a rhythm of walking. I thought about Izzy's selkie story, weighing it against what I'd read in the Mutch book. The beachcomber's story had been almost as mean as anything in the book, painting selkies as nasty and cunning. I'd need to write a section about shennachies, explaining the nature of the storyteller. I rankled against Izzy's demand. Traditional stories like that would be brilliant evidence. There was no good reason not to include the story in my homework. The Shetland selkie story was gold dust. I couldn't let it go.

The headlights from an approaching vehicle appeared on the road behind me, throwing my shadow long onto the road in front. I stepped aside and let the post bus roll past. It went too fast to be sure, but I thought I'd seen Ailsa, her face in shadow as she leaned against the window. The tail-lights glowed as they took the corner, then vanished in the gloom.

Mum was right about me. I did cut myself off from people. I was close to a handful of folk – Mum, Ronny, my grandparents. I'd been close to Richard, too, but now he wasn't Richard any more. He was a different person, a thousand miles away. A day away and already I felt completely removed from him. It was as though he'd never even lived on the island. Moss always springs back into shape.

I followed the island bus around the corner, and Still Bay opened up before me. A few lit windows in Grogport blinked between the overhanging lines of birch. The last bats of summer skittered low in the sky above me, weaving their lunatic loops and triangles, almost invisible against the violet gloaming. At this time of year, with autumn settling on the islands, the nights came in quickly, sunset leaching ink drop pinks and blues into the horizon.

Ahead, there was a flicker of light. I pulled off my headphones. A small bright beam reflected in the dark mirror of the sea, then the high whining of an outboard choked into life. The inflatable dinghy. Ailsa was going home. The light traced a bumpy, weaving journey across the bay, then slowed to a stop at the shadow of Dog Rock, the house and islet silhouetted against that indigo sky. The little light was a headlamp. It paused on the mooring, bobbing about. I couldn't see what was happening. The light was laid low on the pontoon. There was a moment of nothing, then a dark shape dived headlong into the sea, held for half a perfect second against the low tan band of sunset in the west.

I stopped, astonished.

Ailsa dived into the Atlantic.

She was swimming.

The thought made me shudder. The water would be far too cold for me. I'd swum in Still Bay plenty of times, growing up. Even with the Gulf Stream washing through the Hebrides, the seas round Bancree were always cold. One summer, Richard and I had swum out to Dog Rock. He'd turned back after a couple of minutes, but I kept swimming, terrified of the riptide tugging at my feet. They'd sent someone to row across and bring me home. Mum had clipped me round the ear for going so far out. My feet had turned blue. Even now, I could remember the prickle as my body thawed, sensation returning to my fingers and toes.

My new neighbour was swimming in the dark, in the cold.

My new neighbour was weird.

I walked the rest of the way home, considering. Evening was drawing into night and Anders was snoozing on the sofa, snoring like an old dog. I stood above him, reassured by his sleeping bulk. His presence gave weight and certainty to everything. I tiptoed to the kitchen. There was some lamb in the fridge, and I decided to make a stew for tea. I rifled through Ronny's albums and popped some Springsteen on the stereo, humming along while I diced onions, crushed garlic and peeled carrots. The stew was simmering nicely by the time Mum and Ronny arrived. Their ruckus woke Anders. He harrumphed for a while, then the three of them played with Jamie by the fire. Ronny came through to help me get tea on the table.

'How was school?'

'It was OK,' I said, 'but I tell you what. I saw Lachlan Crane today.'

'Lachie? Where was he this time?'

'Playing at Top Gun in the Sound, that boat of his packed with cronies.'

'Jesus, really?' said Ronny. 'He's supposed to be in Carlisle, securing a distribution deal.'

Ronny was one of Munzie Crane's favourites at the distillery. He and Lachie did not see eye to eye.

'He's a shirker, that lad. The old man needs to crack his skull, else he'll be the death of Clachnabhan. Mark my words.'

'Be the death of himself, first, if he keeps on driving like that.'

'Chance would be a fine thing,' laughed Ronny, and set bowls on the table. He called the others in from the living room. Mum posted Jamie into his high chair, and tried to feed him mashed carrot. Anders had to stoop to enter the kitchen.

'Hey, Anders, did you go looking for Dougie?' I said, remembering.

'Yes. All day, with my hangover, all day up and down the coast near my house.'

'You were sleeping on the couch when I came home.'

'A man must rest, Flora. A man must recover. And also there is nothing in the fridge at home.'

'Take you it you didn't find anything, then?'

'Alas, no. But tomorrow is another day, and I will be looking some more.'

'I bet you'll be hungover tomorrow, too.'

'Ah! Now, Flora, you begin to understand the world.'

'Because you and Ronny are getting pissed again?'

'Because you know,' he said, sagely, 'what men want.'

'And I took the day off work, too,' said Ronny. 'So we can do this properly. *Skøl.*'

He and Anders chinked their glasses.

'Remind me again, Mum,' I said, 'how this lot wound up running the country?'

'Your problem now, love. I'll stick to running the Co-op.'

It was a good meal.

Anders hogged the conversation, keeping us in stitches with stories of his various mishaps, and updating us on the eternal saga of the distillery he kept hidden on the rig. Oil rigs were supposed to be dry, no booze allowed, but Anders used his spare time to make an infamous moonshine, halfway between a schnapps and a biofuel. All the rig managers knew he kept a still, and searched high and low to find it, but he moved it continually between dozens of secret spots, helped by a network of assistants bought off with free hooch. Once he'd moved the equipment, he'd boobytrap the previous hidey-hole. As I cleared the plates, he told us how one of the managers had finally located the still in an overhead cable locker, and had summoned Anders to witness the big reveal. He opened the compartment with a grand gesture, only to have a bucket of milk drop on him – and then, two perfect seconds later, a bucket of flour.

Ronny was weeping with laughter, and Mum was smiling wide.

'You'll get yourself fired,' she admonished.

'Ah, but, Cath, I can no longer stop myself,' said Anders. 'It has become a game for us all. It keeps me busy. People make many bets on them finding the still.'

'Time to get off the rigs, you numpty.'

'Aye, man, haven't you had enough yet?'

'This is easy for you to say,' he said, pulling faces. 'But what else could I do?'

'I could ask Munzie, see if there's work in the distillery?'

'Anders already has his own distillery.'

'Or the boat yard, then. You have skills. There's work enough round here for someone like you.'

Anders shushed us with his hands.

'It is not so simple for me,' he said. 'I have friends on the rigs.'

'You have friends here,' said Ronny.

'I do, I do. But my friends here have families and small children. My friends on the rigs are men alone, like me, until they go home. In this way, the rigs serve a purpose.'

'You need a woman, Anders,' I announced.

He visibly winced.

'Ah. This is also not so easy on Bancree.'

'You sure as shite won't find one on the rigs,' said Ronny.

'Enough, enough,' said Anders. 'Perhaps I can think about it. But only if you all will shut up.'

'Leave the man in peace,' said Mum, and started stacking dishes.

'This conversation is not over, my friend,' warned Ronny, and topped up Anders' beer.

The pair of them made a half-hearted attempt at washing up before departing for the Bull Hotel and another night on the tiles. Mum lectured them the whole way out the house and halfway down the road, but her heart wasn't really in it. She liked them both too much.

Once they'd gone, I made us both a cup of ginger tea and told her about Izzy the shennachie, rather than Izzy the beachcomber.

This did nothing to improve her opinion of him, but she was as nosy as any other islander, and she was pleased to hear fresh gossip about the old man.

I took my mug to my room. Sitting at my desk, I made a few more notes on my history project. Then, hesitating only briefly, I took my old laptop and started a new document.

As a title, I wrote: 'The Crofter's Lament'.

I'd promised Izzy I wouldn't take his story for my report. I meant to keep that promise. But the story was too good not to write down for myself, and that felt like it was a different matter. I'd include only basics in my homework, like I'd promised, but I'd never heard that selkie story before, and I wanted it kept safe.

I spent the rest of the night writing it out and redrafting it, fitting in as much detail as I could recall. When my memory flagged, I remembered what Izzy had said about the nature of these stories. Concentrating, I drew the smell of wood smoke into my throat and listened to the grinding sea. I wrote down the story of the selkie, word for word. When I'd finished, I went back to the beginning and typed a new line underneath the title:

'A story by Izzy, the Shennachie of Bancree'.

CHAPTER 13

Standing at the bus stop, I ate an apple and watched Ailsa bounce over Still Bay in her inflatable dinghy. The sea was grey and white, the skies low and fat with cloud, but it was warm and blustery. My favourite weather. I walked down through the grass to help her carry the rib up the beach. Several metres out, she cut the engine and let the waves wash the dinghy onto the shore, then jumped barefoot into the shallows. She wore a faded denim skirt and a pale-green T-shirt, with a thick red-and-white plaid shirt as a jacket.

I grabbed a handle on the side of the little boat and helped her drag it over the sand.

'Thanks for this,' she said, panting as we heaved it high above the high-tide mark.

'No bother. Cool shirt.'

'Cheers,' she said, and perched on one side of the inflatable. She took black tights from her bag and peeled them over her feet and ankles.

'So how did you find the school?'

'Spent all morning filling forms and getting the tour,' she said. 'I met all my teachers, I think.'

She hopped up and wriggled, hoiking her tights beneath the waist of her skirt. I looked away.

'Sounds like fun.'

'It was OK,' she said. 'The art teachers seemed sound, anyway. Jackson and um, Creil.'

'Yeah, those two are pretty cool. Creil was in a rock band, way back when.'

'Is that right?'

'He didn't tell you? Lead guitar.'

She nodded sagely. 'That explains the winklepickers.'

I smirked. Ailsa laced her sneakers, then turned the dinghy upside-down, covering the outboard engine.

'All right,' she said, 'I'm good to go.'

We walked up to the bus stop.

'Look, this might sound weird, but did I see you swimming last night? In the sea?'

'Oh,' she said, turning away, 'you saw that?'

'I think so, aye. I mean, yes, I did. I saw you diving in.'

'Exercise,' she shrugged, 'just going for a swim. Yesterday took it out of me. When I got home, I wanted a dip.'

'Were you not freezing?'

'It's cold, I guess, but I don't feel it too badly.'

'You'd better be careful. The currents are pretty tricky outside the bay, especially round Dog Rock. There's a riptide out to sea.'

'I'm strong enough. Don't worry about that,' she said, and flashed me that odd half-smile.

The bus trundled into view. We took seats on opposite sides of the aisle. Almost apologetically, she gestured at me, showing her headphones in one hand. I did the same, smiling, and plugged in. As we rode the bus towards Tighna, I looked out the window. Through the flicker of the birches, I daydreamed about Richard and his new life in Bristol.

I'd tried texting him a few times, during breaktimes at school, but never managed better than bland lines asking how he was, was he OK, was he having fun, what was it like at uni . . . and press to send the text. Strange to watch the little icon flashing on the screen, the phone working out whether or not it could send the message. From Tanno, it usually sent. From Bancree, usually not. He didn't reply, and I pictured all his texts suspended in the airwaves for days at a time, waiting for me to stumble into clear reception. Every day, on the ferry, I waited for the point on the Bancree Sound when the satellites would chatter, our phones would join the dots, and Richard would say hello. He was fine. It was great. But the message never came. Reception, I told myself. There's no reception in a major English city, that's it.

Aye, right.

I had double Spanish in the morning, then English either side of lunch, and study periods in the afternoon. I visited the school library during breaktime. I wanted to research Broch Books and contact them about the Mutch stories, but I checked my email first. I had one new message, and it was from Richard.

Dear Flora, it said.

He'd never called me Flora before. All my life, he'd only ever called me Flo. At that moment I knew exactly what was going to happen.

He went on to say that Bristol was exciting, and sunny, and he was starting to find his way around and that he'd changed his course to Philosophy. He'd met loads of new people already, and made some good friends, and this was hard for him to write but he'd been doing some thinking and look, babe, he was sorry but he simply didn't see how a long-distance relationship could work like this, he really did love me, he really did, but this relationship wasn't fair on either of us, and it was too far, and it was for the best if we moved on from here as friends, you know, blah blah blah, and he couldn't wait to see me at Christmas.

Love, always. Ciao, Rich. Xx

He actually wrote 'blah blah blah'.

Two days away, and he was calling himself Rich.

Love, always.

All the stories I'd ever heard about university magnified in my imagination. I could just see his room in student halls, and a procession of leggy freshers passing through, comparing A-level results, giggling in English accents and taking off their clothes, the room reeling with pot smoke like a caricature. The thought left me blind with sadness. Stuck there in the school library, helpless as a little girl, seeing everything the colour of dark red. For dull, furious moments, my vision darkened. I breathed out, careful in the exhalation, forcing myself not to care. I made a fist and let it go, watching the fingers uncurl as though on a screen. It felt like someone else's hand, rather than my own. A different body.

I steadied myself.

My anger wasn't for Richard. That was only a fleeting thing, a distraction. And it wasn't even anger. It was jealousy.

Going out with him was an escape – my route to freedom, a cord that connected me to the world outside. Richard had cut that cord, and I felt robbed and hollow, the cavern of my stomach writhing with tiny, wormy things. Frustration, envy, sadness. It should have been me who'd escaped into a new life, drinking in bars and meeting new people. It should have been me doing the breaking up. The dumping.

I shouldn't have felt so bad. Everyone knew it was coming. I'd known it before he even left. But still it made me sad.

I turned off the computer without emailing Broch Books. I simmered through my afternoon English class, barely paying attention as Mr McLaggan waxed lyrical about the Dostoevskian scope of *The Silver* bloody *Darlings*. Then he dropped some Shakespeare on us: expectation is the root of all heartache.

I thought a lot about that. I turned it every way, working it out. It didn't make me feel any better. The moment the school bell sounded, I was out the door and gone. I needed to burn. I wanted to explode, just for the sake of something different.

CHAPTER 14

Ailsa sat on a bench by the harbour wall, sketching. I stomped across and sat seething beside her. She glanced up and nodded, but didn't say anything. I took out my headphones. After the music, gulls and cars and people sounded peculiar. A small black cat, greasy with sea salt, detached itself from a crate and wound between my legs.

'Well, Richard's dumped me.'

She didn't look at all surprised. 'Right,' she said. Almost as an afterthought, she added, 'I'm sorry.'

'I'm not,' I said. 'I think.'

Ailsa flipped her pencil and erased a mark, then continued drawing, her pencil scratching lightly on the paper.

'Are you OK?' she said.

In light, confident lines, she was sketching the gaggle of gulls that populated the harbourside, poaching chips and sandwich crusts. Under the mark of her pencil, their heads and backs took shape, all their stupidity and arrogance springing from the page.

'I'm all right. It was going to happen sooner or later.'

She pulled a face. 'Probably. But if something's that inevitable, you should get it over and done with, you know?'

'Aye, maybe.'

'Just accept it, and move on. You never know what's coming next.'

She smiled, sympathetic, and turned back to her pad.

I put my headphones back in and watched Ailsa draw. I felt frustrated whenever I thought about Richard, but her work was mesmerising, and it calmed me down. In her hands, the gulls drew charcoal life from a sky-white page. I found myself hypnotised by the movement of the pencil, the dabs and lines and dots. She was very good. Abruptly, the pencil paused. I looked at Ailsa, then followed her gaze. Behind me, outside the Ship Inn, a gaggle of men yelled and jostled at each other.

'What's going on, Flora?'

'I don't know,' I said, studying the group. Then I worked it out. 'It's Lachlan again.'

'Lachlan?'

'The one in the sunglasses. Look.'

Short and mean and grinning ear to ear, Lachie stood near the centre of the group. Standing behind him, his gang jeered and cursed. In front of him, uncowed and radiating contempt, sat several of the Polish guys from the fish farm. There seemed to be some kind of stand-off over the benches.

'That's the man with the motorboat, right? I saw him from the ferry.'

'That's the one. Lachlan Crane.'

'Who is he?'

'His dad owns Clachnabhan. The distillery. He's next in line for the job. He'll be my stepfather Ronny's boss when the old man dies,' I said, 'and he's a class-A prick.'

'How so?'

'Well, you saw him on the boat. He thrives on trouble. He fancies himself as a bit of a gangster. In fact, he fancies himself full stop.'

'Somebody has to.'

'Aye, well. It's not me. He's tried it on a few times, whenever I've bumped into him.'

'So he likes you?'

'He likes anything in a skirt. There's rumours he's been seeing some of the girls at school, but I don't think any of them would be dumb enough.'

One of the Poles sprang to his feet, knocking his chair back, and the squabble rose an octave, the men bristling as they fronted up to each other. The landlord popped out from behind the bar, trying to placate both groups. Lachlan stood in the centre of the group, beaming as the men buzzed all around him. They looked like little wasps.

'He actually looks happy,' said Ailsa.

'Men,' I muttered. 'Come on. Let's grab the ferry.'

The *Island Queen* was halfway across the Bancree Sound before I noticed that Ailsa was even quieter than usual. Sketchpad stowed in her bag, she sat cross-legged, turned round in her seat, arms folded on the barrier, gazing out to sea.

'Hey,' I asked, finally, 'what about you – are you OK?'

The wind was fairly low, but Ailsa had her hair loose, and it whipped across her eyes. She shrugged.

'I suppose. Today wasn't the best day at school.'

'What happened?'

She picked at the gloss paint on the railing, working loose a blister of the enamel.

'Someone asked me out.'

'On a date? Who?'

'Steven something.'

'Sixth year?'

'Aye. After art class.'

'McLellan,' I said, pulling a face. 'All right, but nothing to write home about.'

'I didn't think so either.'

'You said no, then?'

'I said no. I thought I was pretty nice about it.' Her nail dug beneath the paint and pinged a chip of enamel into the Sound. 'But I guess,' she said, 'that I wasn't nice enough.'

'Was he not too pleased?'

'You could say that. He yelled down the corridor that I,' and here she pronounced her words with a fierce, icy clarity, 'was a frigid dyke. In front of my whole class and half the third year. That was fun.'

'He's a prick. Seriously. What a knob. The closest he's been to a girl is the inside of his right hand.'

'Ouch. Still. Maybe I should have said yes. I could have given him a chance.'

'Did you fancy him?'

She shook her head, digging more paint from the pitted rail. 'Not even a bit.'

'So what's the problem? You can't make yourself fancy someone. You either do or you don't.'

She pursed her lips. 'I don't know. I sometimes wonder if that's true.'

'Of course it's true. You can't force feelings.'

'I think people can convince themselves of anything. Did you always fancy Richard?'

I felt a pang. 'Of course,' I said.

'Really, though? You've known him so long. Before the age you know what it means to fancy someone. I just wondered, that's all.'

I studied my shoes and gave this some thought. Richard was a handsome lad, that much was true. He was growing into pin-up good looks. Loads of girls at school had fancied him, not least Tina Robson. He was considered quite the catch.

'He's good-looking. Everyone said so.'

'That's not the same as you thinking so.'

'Look, I don't know. We were together a long time. He's just Richard.'

'That's not an answer either.'

'Yes, then. Of course I did.'

Ailsa made a vague noise and looked back to sea. In the middle of the Sound, we passed a single swan, glowing white against the cloudy water. I studied my shoes and thought some more about Richard. It was mildly alarming, but already I could only remember his face as it was in photographs. After the cigarettes and smoke rings, everything about him felt so false.

Back on Bancree, the post bus was packed with disgruntled biddies and a day trip of confused Japanese tourists. There weren't enough seats for Ailsa and I to sit together for most of the route, and by the time a space had cleared, we were both engrossed in our music and our daydreams. When the space cleared, I moved across the aisle to the seat in front of hers, perching myself sideways so I could turn easily to talk to her. She smiled, but neither of us said anything. Jimi Hendrix played in my headphones, and I churned all the while at the question she'd asked me, chasing it over and over in my mind.

Had I fancied Richard? Or not?

It should have been a simple enough answer. You either fancied someone or you didn't. I'd said as much myself. But the more

I thought about it, the less certain I became. We were together because we'd always been together.

It had been the easy option.

The answer always came back to this: I don't know.

I didn't know anything.

CHAPTER 15

I helped Ailsa launch the rib, and watched her scooting across Still
Bay. Back in the house, I spied on Dog Rock with the binoculars,
drinking in the cottage, scouring the garden. Small birds flitted in
the gorse. Smoke trickled from the chimney stack. Ailsa's dad was
working on the pontoon. With a hammer and a mouthful of nails,
he was fixing rotten planks. He worked efficiently and without
pause, paying no attention to anything around him. I watched
him for five minutes, trying to focus on his face, but the swaying
pontoon made it impossible.

I sat on the sofa for half an hour, reading the Mutch selkie book.
The man was crackers – I was sure it was a man, it read like a man
– and his madness burned in every word. I could imagine him
frothing and frenzied, carving the words into the page. The illustrations were something else, too. Long after I'd finished the raving
and ranting, I was drawn back to the pictures. Sensuous and cruel,
violent and obscene. The spread and flow of the ink made them
organic. On every page, they crawled.

I closed the book with a whoomp and, for want of anything
better to do, started to run a bath. The sound chundered through
the empty cottage. I used all the hot water, eking every drop from
the boiler, testing the tap till it turned cold. The water ran espe-

cially dark, and the tub filled murky. With the taps off, the house was almost silent – just single drips teardropping on the surface, and the distant heaving of the sea. Our water came from the hillside behind the house. The peat was so dense it obscured the white of the tub beneath, and the bath looked as though it was full of mud. This was what we drank. This was what we washed in. I stripped off and inched myself in, gasping with the heat. I let the heat tease at my muscles, washing away the doubt.

Smothered in the hot, dark water, I let my worries sink beneath the surface. I let go of Richard dumping me, and of Ailsa's challenge. I let go of Tina Robson and her gang of cronies. I let go of my History project, and the weird selkie book, and all my thoughts of escaping Bancree. Hypnotised by hot water and the distant rush of sea, I let myself be lulled.

The dream came to me slowly, as though from a darkness, with someone gradually turning up the light. Richard and I were having sex on my headland. The tide was out, completely out, all the ribs of seabed exposed to air. I was on top of him, my head bowed low and our bodies close together, our faces almost touching but not touching. Above us, the sun spun round so fast that the horizon became a flicker of sunrise and day and sunset and night. The sex was functional, mechanical, without pleasure. His eyes were aligned with mine. Our lips became fused, our faces joined at the mouth. His exhalation was my inhalation. When I breathed out, he breathed my spent air, and his eyes were peatbog blank. Even as I watched, they welled with dark liquid and spilled over. In my dream, I could feel the fluid fill my lungs. Tar. My breathing tightened. I looked again at Richard's face. It was not Richard's face. It was the man from Dog Rock. It was Ailsa's father, and he was staring. He was staring right at me.

A chill clutched at my heart. Even in my dream, he was watching. I felt his presence, watching from inside those dark eyes. The face morphed again, twisting into a grimace, showing a mouthful of nails. In a flash, the face lunged at me – but was caught in a layer of fur, of skin, the weave of it pulled taut. It was the selkie face from the monster book, and it wormed and twisted as though in agony, writhing like a slug in salt.

I jolted awake, startled, slopping water, filmed in sweat, suddenly alert to the sounds of the afternoon. My head was numb. The dark, peaty water had turned tepid. My core felt cool. My hands gripped the sides of the bathtub. Both my hands, each gripping one side of the tub. Beneath the surface of the water, languorous and as gentle as a lover, I felt another hand trace along my inner thigh.

I shrieked and jerked backwards, sending a wave of black water crashing to the bathroom floor. I tumbled from the tub and slammed onto the tiles, taking half the water with me. I scrambled backwards until I banged into the wall, never once taking my eyes from the bathtub. I hauled a towel around myself. Trembling, chest heaving, I found my feet and peered into the bath. The peaty water slopped in a low, quiet wave from side to side. The floor was a sopping puddle.

A pulse hammered madness in my veins. I felt nauseous and exposed, but suddenly uncertain.

I approached the tub in hesitant steps. I leaned low and reached out a hand, moving it slowly over the surface of the water. I took the chain in my hand, tensed and jumped backwards, yanking out the plug.

The water sucked out in a long brown gurgle, leaving a trail of tiny peaty fragments as it drained into the plughole. My adrenaline washed down with it, leaving me hollow, shaken and stupid.

There was nothing in the tub but dirt. I looked around the silent bathroom. The mirror was speckled with scales of condensation, streaks of it running down in thin dark bands.

What an idiot.

I fetched the mop and bucket from the kitchen. Even as I soaked and squeezed the water from the floor, I replayed the moment, over and over again, becoming increasingly less certain of what I'd felt.

It must have been the dream. I'd had a weird dream, that was all. Those twisted drawings from the book. My brain had turned all the dark stuff I'd been studying into something physical. What sort of girl turns that sort of drawing into that sort of fantasy? A rush of shame barrelled through me. And to think I'd seen Ailsa's dad in the dream, too – taking Richard's place, his eyes weeping that dark liquid. His face. It really was a handsome face.

Those eyes. They'd seen so far inside me.

'Don't be ridiculous,' I told myself. 'Don't be daft.'

I took stock and snapped myself out of the fug. I put on my thickest jumper and some leggings, cranked up some music, turned on all the lights and lit a fire, stomping about the house and doing all I could to forget it had ever happened.

CHAPTER 16

Perhaps an hour later, Anders and Ronny clattered into the house, falling over each other and getting stuck in the doorway. Their shambles lifted the weight from my heart. They were company, and they were here.

They were singing something in Danish, extremely badly, at least two seconds out of time with each other. Ronny collapsed onto the living room floor and lay on his back, gasping like a salmon. Anders took to one knee and finished his song as a serenade to me, arms outstretched, holding the last note interminably. Eventually, he stopped braying.

'That was just lovely. What's it about?'

He blinked and swayed, just a little.

'It is a most wonderful fisherman's song,' he said. 'For the fisherman.'

His eyes glistened with tears.

'Home inside twenty-four hours? You two are getting old.'

'We've been. We've been. We've been,' said Ronny, calling from the floor.

I waited.

'We've been . . . for a drink.'

'The fisherman,' whispered Anders.

'Well,' I said, 'I'm going to make you some coffee.'

The coffee helped a little, and the pair were halfway presentable by the time Mum came home. Anders was pretty much his usual self, and Ronny could talk without slurring. Mum gave him the baby, and he skulked off to deal with a dirty nappy, holding Jamie at arm's length like a time-bomb.

I made mackerel and mashed potato for tea, and the food gave them both a second wind. Anders cracked open another bottle of whisky, drinking three times as fast as Ronny. The pair of them kept me laughing, and the laughter kept me from thinking about my bad dream in the bathtub. Simply having Anders in the house helped. He was a one-man army. The more time went on, the more I cursed myself for a daft wee girl.

'How's your day been, sweetheart?' asked Mum.

'Aye, Flo,' croaked Ronny. 'Not your usual chirpy, joy-filled self.'

'Not that great, I suppose. Richard dumped me.'

'The varlet,' growled Anders, 'I'll have his head on a stick.'

'No need for that just yet, thanks.'

'As m'lady commands,' he said, making a theatrical bow.

'I'm sorry, pet,' said my mum.

'It's fine,' I shrugged, spearing a chunk of fish. 'I knew it would happen. We all knew.'

Mum and Ronny glanced at each other guiltily, then me. Aye, they'd known.

'Bristol's a long way away, poppet,' said Ronny, gently.

'Honestly,' I said, putting down my fork, 'I'm fine. I'm a bit sad, but it's hardly come out of the blue.'

'Will you be OK at school?'

'I was getting on before he broke up with me, and I'll get on now. Besides,' I said, gesturing at the hulking Dane, 'I'll always have Anders.'

He put a beefy hand to his chest.

'Be still, my heart!'

'You're a great soft numpty,' said Mum, shushing him. 'You'll let us know, Flora, won't you? If you need help, or – someone to talk to. You could join a club in Tanno. Go to the judo with Ronny. Or something.'

'Or nothing. I'll be fine. I am fine.'

'Of course she's fine,' growled Anders, 'she has me.'

'My prince. That's so sweet.'

'And as for that,' said Mum, rounding on the Dane, 'when are you going to find yourself a woman, Anders?'

'I wouldn't wish that job on anyone,' smirked Ronny. 'Told you that conversation wasn't over.'

'Weasel.'

'Oaf.'

'Wheesht, the pair of you,' said Mum. 'Well? What of it?'

Silence fell. Anders changed. We felt it. In a blink, all his bluster was gone. He shrugged and studied the wooden tabletop, tracing the knots with his big fingers. Finally, he spoke.

'In some ways, I already have a woman.'

'What?' Ronny pricked up his ears. 'You what, now?'

'I've been spoken for since I left Denmark. Since the day I turned fifteen.'

'What the hell?'

'It is true, my friend,' said Anders, and he seemed sadder. He took a slug of whisky and forced a grin.

'Anders! How could you? My heart's broken,' I said, throwing a dramatic hand to my temple.

He spoke low. 'Don't be joking about broken hearts, Flora. This is not a thing to laugh about.'

'I've known you for almost twenty years! How could I not know about this?' exclaimed Ronny. 'What the hell are you talking about? Who is she? Where is she?'

The big Dane was at war with himself, but eventually he decided.

'She is dead.'

We were still, then, and rain surged against the windows.

'I was a boy in Jutland. She lived in the next village. We skipped school to play in the fields. That countryside was ours. We climbed every tree, swam in every stream. We would have been married and so happy.'

'. . . so what happened?'

'One day, I was caught and returned to school. She went without me. The last I saw of her was through my classroom window. She waved and smiled for me to join her. They found her three days later. She was face-down in a pool, drowned like my own true Ophelia.'

'Oh, Anders.'

'But I have learned to live with that. I vowed, then, never to go back. The place and the people are too much for me. Even the language, sometimes. I do not need remembering when already I cannot forget.'

'That's awful.'

'And now you see, how it is not very funny to joke about broken hearts.'

'Perhaps not,' I said, ashamed.

'I can't believe I never knew this,' said Ronny.

'I decided long, long ago I should not talk to anyone about her.'

'But why not, man?'

'Because, my friend, you will try to make me feel better, and you will tell me that the time is now come to move on.'

Ronny shut his mouth.

'So, until today, I do not talk. But lately—' and here Anders sighed, gesturing round the table. 'It's this. It is all of you. Every time I come here, I want this. I wanted a family. I wanted a child. It is hard for me to see this every time.'

'You could still find someone else,' I said. 'You still have time. What about you and Janet? Haven't there been others?'

'As you will learn, Flora, there is love, and there is loneliness, and then, somewhere in between, there is comfort. I will never love anyone the way that I love her. It burns in me like this,' he said, twirling the whisky in its tumbler. Mesmerised, I watched the churn and sparkle. 'And so I am caught, trapped in this amber we call love. I can't go on, and I cannot return. I have the joy of love, and the pain also.'

'This is why you keep working on the rigs,' said Mum, quietly.

Anders nodded.

'On the rigs, there is only the rigs.'

The CD had finished.

'If you are very lucky,' he said, looking only at me, 'then maybe one day you will know what it is to love. And if you are most unlucky, you will know what it is, never to be with that one person you love so much.'

'It's not fair,' I said. I couldn't meet his eye.

'But what is fair? This is the only world we have. Many times, Flora, bad things happen to good people. And the world, still it turns.'

The wind cried into the chimney pots.

'But still,' he said, brightening, 'I have the best next thing. My friends, and my whisky. This is not the same. But I think it comes maybe pretty close.'

He and Ronny chinked their glasses together.

'I should do the dishes,' I said.

We left it at that. The awkward atmosphere didn't dissolve until I'd returned from the washing-up and we started playing cards. Ronny poured me a glass of beer. Anders winked and snuck me foamy top-ups when he thought Mum wasn't looking. But even with the teasing and laughter, I thought of poor Anders and his girl. He soon returned to his usual self, loud and lairy, but Mum and Ronny could see I wasn't right. They would have marked it up to being dumped, and Flo not taking it well, the poor dear . . . She talks tough, but she's soft underneath, the lass, and so on.

Thinking I couldn't cope riled me more than Richard leaving.

Flashes of the bathtub made my skin prickle, but they grew fewer and further between as the evening rolled on. I sought out memories of that presence against my skin, trying to recall what I'd felt, what had happened, but the more we talked – the more beer I drank – the dimmer it became. My heart swelled for the company.

Mum and I drifted to our beds at eleven or so. Anders and Ronny stayed up talking old times over the whisky, with a strict warning not to sing again. Their chuckles and silences kept me awake for hours. When sleep came it was dark and fractured, full of leering ink sketches morphing into people and people turning into seals, flailing about in skins that didn't fit. Kelp and condoms, slack and stretched. Hands appeared from within bodies, searching out seams and thrusting through the skin, fingers clenched in white-tight fists. I woke more than once, heart humming loud, and heard nothing but the low weight of the sea, growling on the shore.

CHAPTER 17

'Right then, folks,' said Miss Carlyle, 'how are we finding the project?'

The class fell into an uncomfortable silence. I'd done loads of work. As well as Izzy's selkie story, I'd ordered two more books on Scottish myths from the library, and already drafted several pages. I felt pretty good about the report, and was genuinely interested in my selkies. But I knew better than to volunteer that sort of information to the class, and I kept my mouth shut.

'I'm struggling to find good sources, Miss.'

'You're doing giants, aren't you, Una? Where have you tried so far?'

'I've used the web, but everything I've found round here says the same thing. The only other source I've got is my grandma, but I didn't think that would count.'

'Why not?'

'Well . . . She's never right, Miss.'

'Ah! What have I taught you? There are no "rights" in history, remember?'

'No, Miss. I mean my grandma's not right. She's mental.'

'Never mind that, Una. She still has important things to say.'

'You've never met my grandma, Miss.'

'Wheesht. She'll have been brought up on songs and folk tales. That's perfect. Use her all you can.'

'Miss Carlyle,' I said, 'what's a shennachie?'

'Ah, now that's an interesting question. Why do you ask, Flora?'

'There's one on Bancree. He has selkie stories.'

'Fascinating. A shennachie – are the rest of you listening? A shennachie is a traditional storyteller. They would be wanderers, performing their stories in exchange for food and lodgings. New stories would be collected on their travels, remembered, told and passed on.'

'He said it was wrong to write his stories down, though.'

'Most shennachies would have been illiterate. The memory was prized above all, because that was all they had. But I'm sure you can get the basics into your report. That will be enough.'

'Yes, Miss,' I said, thinking of my promise to Izzy.

'You're very lucky to have a resource like that, Flora,' she said. 'I suggest you take full advantage of him.'

Halfway through the class, I nipped up to the library. I finally planned to contact Broch Books, the people who'd published Mutch's mental stories. I wanted to know why anyone would print such a peculiar book and, if possible, find out about the mysterious M.I. Mutch. The publishers had to know something about the author, even if no one else did. The book had grown on me day by day. Those demented ink pictures had wormed into my dreams, where they writhed and bunched and bulged. Selkies hid in peaty dishwater, and ducked into the trough of every wave.

Broch Books had no website, but the name returned a couple of positive hits in an Orkney business directory. Intriguingly, Broch claimed to specialise in poetry and island walking guides. Mutch's mad stories seemed a far cry from either of those.

I kept digging, and eventually found an ancient email address. I composed a friendly message, asking for more information about the book – about why it had been commissioned, and about M.I. Mutch – and sent it off.

The library was heavy with the tang of furniture polish. I did some more research online, reading about selkies in the Faroes, and in Iceland. The same stories returned from each culture, give or take minor details.

One, selkie dances on beach.

Two, man steals selkie skin.

Three, selkie lives with man.

Four, selkie steals skin back.

Five, selkie escapes.

Six, man goes wild with grief.

There was a variation on the theme, where the selkie saves the man from drowning, and the two live together happily. But after seven years, the selkie returns to the sea and her own kind. At this point, the story goes back to normal, and the man goes wild with grief. The grief thing was a constant. Whether in blithe myth or Izzy's nasties, the stories always finished with us islanders admonished and humbled, made to pay for chasing fantasies when we should be hard at work.

All selkies have a coat, a sealskin, that allows them to take the form of a seal. Selkies are beautiful and magical creatures, but caught always in the threshold places – between human and seal, between island and ocean.

Selkies were born of the souls of drowned sailors.

That thought made me feel so sad. I imagined sailors looking up, even as they drifted down, limbs loose and suspended in the sea.

After class, I packed my bag and headed down the corridor. I nearly missed the voices talking in the stairwell.

'So who the fuck are you, then?'

The dulcet tones of Tina Robson. I looked around, but she wasn't talking to me. In the darkness beneath the stairs, Tina and her entourage had backed another girl against the wall. They were packed so close I couldn't see who it was. Only her legs showed through the wall of bodies. And if I hadn't recognised the Doc Martens, I might have walked on and left them to it.

'My name's Ailsa Dobie,' she said, quietly.

'What kind of name is that?' laughed Tina.

'My name.'

'Beats the hell out of Robson,' I said, and Tina and her cronies turned to look at me. Ailsa was standing backed against the wall, fists bunched, frame tense.

'You coming?' I said, nodding at the door, trying to be as casual as possible.

Ailsa brushed past Tina and then me, heading for the schoolyard.

'Not making things much better for yourself, Flo,' said Tina, 'are you?'

'After what you told me, I'm done for anyway. With the Tanno gangster queen on my case, I might as well go for broke.'

'Keep it coming, then. You'll get yours.'

'What is it about me that winds you up so much?' I said, suddenly and genuinely curious. 'What do you want from me?'

'I want nothing of yours!' she shrilled. 'Jesus. You think you're so much better than everyone else.'

'No, I don't. But that doesn't mean I'm going to fall in line like your little club of arse-kissers, either.' I waved my arm at her gang. They bristled.

'You might be wanting some friends by the time we're done with you,' said Tina, and her girls pressed closer around her. 'Time goes pretty slowly when everybody hates you.'

She jabbed a finger at me. Her shirt was a size too small and she wore the top two buttons undone, showing glimpses of her chest. She was so transparent, I couldn't help but laugh. This was a mistake. White with rage, Tina reached out and grabbed my arm.

'Shut up!' she hissed. 'Don't laugh at me!'

I jerked my arm away. Tina held fast, even as I pulled, and my jumper bunched and ripped right around the shoulder. Momentum carried Tina backwards. She dropped the torn sleeve. We were both astonished, but I recovered first.

'That was my favourite jumper,' I said, picking up the ripped fabric.

'I warned you,' she replied, uncertain now. 'You'd better show me some respect.'

I gathered my bag.

'Listen to me, Tina. I don't care what you do in the rest of this year, or the rest of your life. It doesn't matter, because you'll still be stuck in this godawful backwater town when I'm long gone. I'm never ever coming back, Tina. Tanno is all yours. And you can fill your boots with it.'

I walked away. Tina's posse chorused nervous giggles, but her fury drilled hot holes into my back.

When I caught her up on the far side of the schoolyard, Ailsa was shaking. At first I thought she was scared, but then I saw her fists balled tight, knuckles glowing white, the bones of her hand straining bright against her skin. I stood beside her, waiting for her to speak.

'One week,' she said, talking to the sky. 'That's all it's taken. First week and already someone's on my case. What is it about me?'

'This has happened before?'

She nodded. She was standing side on to me, but I could see a film of tears in her eyes.

'That's just Tina. She wants to be top dog. She doesn't want anyone new stealing her thunder. That's just the way she is—'

'No,' said Ailsa. 'It's not just her. This always happens. Everywhere I go there are Tinas. In Stornoway, on Lewis, on Harris. Kintyre, Arran, Islay. It doesn't matter where I go. I just want to fit in, but people think I'm different. They always know.'

'Look, I don't know what you're talking about. I guess moving around isn't always easy, but you seem pretty normal to me.'

'Aye?' she said, fiercely, and looked at me. The unshed tears turned her eyes to shifting liquid. 'And remind me what they think of you?'

She summoned a weak smile, and I realised she was making a joke.

'Good point. I'm hardly the most popular girl in school. They think I'm . . .' I searched for the word, 'distant.'

Ailsa rubbed the heel of her hand in her eye, then noticed my ripped sweater. Her face fell.

'Did she do that just now?'

'It's all right.'

'Oh, no,' she said, mortified. 'This is my fault.'

'Don't worry about it. Hopefully Tina will feel that's enough for now and leave me be.'

'But your jumper . . .'

'A small price to pay for a little peace.'

'No. I owe you. It's my fault she ripped it. I've got a couple you could choose from.'

'Honestly, don't worry about it. Every time I run across Tina and her girls, it reminds me that they'll never leave this town. They're lifers.'

'But not you?'

'Christ no. I'm gone as soon as this year's done with.'

'Lucky you.'

'You don't want to leave?'

'I've only just got here. I'm in no hurry to go. We move around a lot. I'd like to stay somewhere longer than six months.'

This needled my curiosity.

'So what's it like on Dog Rock?'

She raised her eyebrows a little, looking down. 'It's an island,' she said, 'and it's ours. I like it.' She turned to look at me again. 'Do you want to come and see it?'

'Wow. Aye, that would be cool.'

'I'll take you after school. You can pinch a jumper.'

'OK, OK,' I laughed. 'I give in.'

'And,' she said, 'you can meet my dad.'

CHAPTER 18

We stepped off the bus and waved goodbye to Bev. Ailsa wound a
path through the waist-high dune grass. I followed, feeling the stems
and blades brushing at my thighs and hips. I really wanted to see
Dog Rock. Part of this was outright island nosiness. Another, smaller
part of me was happy, and even a little shy, to speak to someone who
seemed a bit like me. This was an experience the Tanno kids had all
the time. They knew each other so well. When they were younger,
they played together after school, and then the older kids had parties
and fell out and made friends and drank cider and felt each other up
and bragged about it in the playground. That wasn't something I'd
been able to share. Richard and I had done the drinking, and more,
but on the island we'd always been alone, together.

The inflatable lay metres above the high-tide mark. Ailsa fitted
the engine while I took off my shoes and socks and started rolling
up my jeans. Together, we carried the rib down towards a toothless
surf. Pushing the boat in nose-first, Ailsa hopped over one side and
tinkered with the engine. Standing shin-deep in the icy shallows, I
held the boat by a handle at the stern, waves lapping to my knees.

'Jeez, it's Baltic. How can you swim in this?'

'We'll be over soon enough,' she said, and yanked on the starter
cord.

The engine caught after half-a-dozen attempts, and she dipped the whirring blades into the water. I hopped in, losing my balance, but Ailsa caught my shoulder and I scrambled to the single plank that made a seat in the bows. The bay was fairly calm, despite the bluster, and we scooted over the waves at a decent pace. I reached out and trailed my fingers over the side, gazing into the water. It was a deep, deep blue, and I couldn't see the bottom. Dog Rock grew closer. From nowhere, sunlight bloomed through the clouds.

As we approached the pontoon, Ailsa slowed the engine. Taking the mooring rope in one hand, I hopped up onto the rickety platform and tied the boat to a hitching post. You couldn't hear it from Bancree, but out here the line of floats knocked together constantly, creaking and groaning and clicking where the sea pushed wood against wood. Where her dad had made repairs, new planks glared white against the weathered grey.

'That'll do,' she said, checking my knot.

She skipped onto the floats ahead of me, swaying with the heft of waves. I followed, stumbling to keep my balance.

Dog Rock was bigger than it looked from Bancree. Where the pontoon met the islet, waves frothed gently against the rocky shore. Rimed with weed and muck, a thick cable emerged from the water and into a concrete box marked with a lightning bolt. Electricity. A thought occurred to me as we walked towards the house.

'What would your dad do if the boat was gone, and he needed to get across?'

'He'd swim, if he had to. He's like me. He loves the sea.'

I thought again of that dark shape swimming in the water off Dog Rock, the night they'd first moved in. Could it have been him? Or Ailsa? It felt so long ago.

'He's not really going anywhere at the moment, though. He's

loads to do on the island. We always move to these ancient places that need loads of work. I think he's sorting out a drain, or a generator or something. Come on, come and say hello.'

She set off to one side of the house. I followed, glimpses of his face flashing before me. As we rounded the corner, the rest of Dog Rock opened up. Blocked by the cottage, I'd never seen the inland portion of the islet, and I was amazed to find a perfectly respectable garden hidden behind the house. It was wildly overgrown, and studded with bindweed and thistles, but the old flowerbeds stood quite distinct against the grass and gorse. The sheltered spaces were thick with end-of-season wildflowers. Brambles had exploded along one edge of a fallen-down fence, and blackberries were sleek on the vine.

Passing the house, a red extension lead hung from a ground-floor window and snaked towards a large, dilapidated shed at the far end of the garden. As we approached it, birds erupted from the long grass, and for a moment, the sky danced with chaffinches and waxwings. The door hung from one hinge, and Ailsa pushed it open with a creak. Inside, beneath an electric lantern, her father leaned over a workbench. An engine lay around him, dismantled into component pieces. He looked up briefly at Ailsa, then spotted me, and held my eye as he straightened. Feeling stupid and frightened and shy, I drank him in.

Like his daughter, his hair was very dark and slightly wavy. This close, I could see strands of white and grey. His cheeks were hollow beneath sharp cheekbones, and he wore several days of stubble. He was impossibly striking, and I realised my mouth was open.

'Hi, Dad,' said Ailsa. 'This is Flora, that I told you about. She lives across the way in Grogport.'

'You never said you were bringing someone over.'

'She goes to school with me, Dad.'

He studied me. His dark eyes met mine, and I was rooted to the ground. I'd seen them before. Dark eyes from the bathtub. Standing there, in the shed, I tried to imagine his hand sliding around my leg. Shivers danced across my skin.

'Good to meet you,' he grunted. 'I'm John. Ailsa's mentioned you.'

His name was John.

'I said hello. In the road,' I faltered, hardly trusting myself to speak. For a moment we simply looked at each other. He wasn't so big, but he exuded whipcord strength and I felt absurdly exposed.

'It's a small island,' he said, then turned to Ailsa. 'I should get on.'

'D'you want a cup of tea, Dad?'

'Aye,' he nodded, frowning, 'in a bit.'

Ailsa tugged at my sleeve and drew me away from the shed.

'Don't worry about Dad,' she said, rolling her eyes. 'He's always like that with new folk. He's a pup at heart. Come on, I'll show you the rest of the house.'

She talked as we wandered back towards the house, but I barely heard a word. Before I'd even met him, those dark eyes had been watching in my dream.

The further we moved from the shed, and from John, the more I recovered my senses. Dreams were just dreams, and I was a school-girl feeding a stupid crush. I was cross with myself, and drew in thick lungfuls of air, trying to flush out my stupidity. Another deep breath, and I made myself take stock.

By the front door, a tangle of rotten wood and filthy lino lay stacked where Ailsa and John had cleared the junk. They'd fixed the fallen washing pole with bright-blue nylon, and a few clothes fluttered on the line. Between the shirts and trousers hung a few pairs of underpants – a girl's plain black knickers, and a man's boxer shorts. I blushed, then felt stupid about blushing, and was relieved that she hadn't noticed. She'd moved ahead of me, further up the rough path, and put her shoulder to the front door. Cursing, she banged it open, then waved me inside.

I'd expected it to be dank and dark and miserable, but Dog Cottage was surprisingly cosy. It was small, but not cramped. The door opened straight into a living room, where the Dobies had stripped out the mouldering carpet and laid some rugs across the old stone flags. The bare stone robbed most of the daylight, but a rusty wood-burner stood in the middle of the room, radiating steady heat. A stack of chopped driftwood leaned against one wall. There were a couple of plain wooden chairs and a violently green bean bag. On the far side of the room lay another door. Beside us, steep, crooked stairs led to the top floor.

'Cup of tea?' asked Ailsa, closing the front door with a bang.

'Aye, please,' I said, and followed her across the living room and through the door on the far side. We walked into the kitchen. It was a little lean-to, cobbled onto the side of the house, but it was clean and dry. It was so sparse. A camping gas stove, and some tins and packets on the shelves. The kettle boiled as Ailsa busied herself with mugs and milk and teabags.

There was a frost of sea salt on the window, speckled where the wind had lifted the waves and lashed the house with spindrift. All the village houses had this rime of salt where they faced the sea. It wasn't worth cleaning. The next rainstorm rinsed the house clean. The next windy day left another coat of spray. Beyond the smeary glass, the ocean opened like a bowl. There was nothing between Dog Rock and the horizon but a vast, calm sea, rippled with a thousand little waves, caught upon the sunlight like crumbs of broken glass. The size of it, the emptiness, made my eyes ache.

'Quite something, isn't it?' said Ailsa.

She stood beside me, offering a cup of tea. Still feeling a little unsettled, eyes squinting with sun, I took the mug.

'Incredible view. I mean, you can see Dog Rock from my house,' and I felt suddenly guilty, remembering how I'd spied on them with my binoculars. 'But you can't see the back,' I finished, lamely.

'I'm glad Dad found it. I think I like this place.'

'Not much happens.'

'That's fine with me. I like the quiet.'

We watched the sea for a moment longer.

'Why here in particular,' I said, 'on Dog Rock?'

'Because it was available. And because islands are safe.'

'Bancree is an island.'

'When you're over here,' she grinned, 'Bancree is the mainland. Think about it. Out here, it's small enough that you can see who's coming.'

'What do you mean, "who's coming"? Islands keep you safe from what?'

Her smile dropped away. She looked out the window, and took a long sip of her tea.

'Maybe I shouldn't tell you this,' she said, and paused. Looking out to sea, she weighed a decision, then made her mind up. 'Come and have a look.'

Puzzled, I followed her back into the living room. Upstairs, a tiny landing split the top floor into two bedrooms. Ailsa gestured to one side, and I stuck my head round the door. There was no furniture, and no bed – just a nest of sleeping bags and blankets by one wall. Her father's few clothes lay along one wall in piles of trousers, shirts and jumpers. The rest of the room had been invaded by an avalanche of books, newspapers and notepads. All those office storage boxes were in his room. They lined the walls like bricks, stacked three or four deep. Some were labelled with place names, or people's names, or dates. The small window and the crowding eaves cut a lot of light out of the room, and it was gloomy despite the sunny day.

In the middle of the room, the newspapers formed a clearing, a defined workplace on the floorboards. A very old and very battered laptop was laid to one side.

'This is where he works,' she said. 'Look.'

Pinned almost floor to ceiling was the biggest map of the Western Isles I'd ever seen. When I stepped closer, I realised it was several large-scale maps trimmed and taped together. Scrawled all over it were notes and pins and different-coloured stickers, with looping, dotted lines and arrows and string showing directions, or connecting remote locations. Newspaper cuttings from island chronicles were pinned to the edges of the map, too. They covered a period of many years, but they all said pretty much the same thing:

MISSING

VANISHED

DISAPPEARED

FEARED DEAD

By the dozen, yellowing newspaper clips listed fishermen lost at sea, bartenders who'd never turned up to work, missing babysitters, farm workers vanished on foggy days. I scanned through the clippings, then looked again at the map, focusing on Bancree. Two red dots marked the island, and one yellow. There was a yellow dot in Tanno, too, just across the Sound.

'What is this?' I said, barely breathing.

'It sounds daft, OK? But my dad is sort of a detective.'

'A detective?'

She pulled a face.

'Not a real one. Well, sort of.'

'Like a hobby?'

She grimaced. 'More like a calling. He tries to find missing people when the police stop looking. And there's a lot been going missing round here in the last year, so he's moved over to have a look for himself.'

'You mean Dougie? Doug MacLeod? The man on the poster?'

'Aye, I think he's one of them. Look, there he is.'

She tapped on the map. Sure enough, an arrow drawn from Bancree led to Dougie's newspaper article, and Bill Wright was pinned beside him. Both were marked with red dots.

'There's others, too. Dad doesn't talk much about it. But that's why we move around so much, so he can look for whoever's doing it.'

'You're not saying there's someone here on the island?' I said, incredulous. 'Like a murderer?'

'You tell me,' she shrugged. 'I don't chose where we move to. Dad thinks there's something going on here, so we moved here. If it's anything like usual, we'll be here six months, or maybe a year, then the trail goes cold and we head out somewhere else.'

'Four people missing?' I said, touching the dots around Bancree. 'I thought there were only two?'

Ailsa joined me at the map. 'He has different criteria for each missing person. Red is definitely suspicious. Yellow is a maybe. One of the things he does is join the dots. I mean, some of these people,' and here she gestured at the clippings, 'some of them really have just run away or fallen off boats or got lost walking and that's that. They've got nothing to do with any sort of conspiracy. They were just unlucky. But Dad draws everything together, just in case.'

We studied the map.

'Notice anything?'

'They all point this way,' I said, studying the arrows and lines marked on the map. From the Orkneys to the northern coast on the mainland, then west and south through the Outer Hebrides to Bancree, the lines hopped from island to island. Red dots punctuated each part of the route with reports of another missing person. There was hardly anything further south. The pattern was unmistakable.

The road stopped at Bancree.

CHAPTER 19

'This goes back a long time,' said Ailsa. 'Dad thinks this has been going more than twenty years. Some of these papers are from before I was born. He's been looking for about sixteen, seventeen years.'

I scanned the map.

'There are fourteen – no, fifteen red dots. Fifteen murders. That's not possible. How have the police not worked it out?'

'Time,' she said. 'Effort. I don't know. A lot of the cases are a long way apart. Both in time and distance. Sometimes the cases are years and years apart, then two or three at once. Maybe they haven't made the connection, or maybe they're not bothered. You know what worries me most?'

'What's that?'

'Despite everything, there is no connection. There's nothing but unlucky people, and Dad's got it completely wrong. He'd be devastated. This has become his life's work.'

Headlines blared beside Bancree.

Missing: Doug MacLeod.

Missing: Bill Wright.

The context of the map made it much more real. The pins and arrows made it seem inevitable, a weight of evidence bearing down on the island. I thought about how upset Ronny was. First Billy, then Doug. But I didn't want to believe it.

'What about you?' I said. 'Do you think it's real?'

Ailsa looked out beyond the map, eyes glazed.

'Dad's convinced, but honestly, I don't know. I tell you this much, though. I'd prefer living somewhere long enough to actually know the people who disappear.'

'I've lived here all my life,' I said.

All that moving around sounded great to me.

'It's a lot to take in,' she said. 'Come and see my room.'

A step across the landing led to Ailsa's bedroom. It was smaller than her dad's but far lighter. Again, there was no bed. A sleeping bag and mat lay along one wall, tucked beneath the sloping eaves. A withered wardrobe stood against the wall, and a small suitcase leaned against it. There was a big stack of books piled up in one corner. It was spartan.

'It's not much,' she said, following my gaze around the room, 'but it's home.'

She started fiddling with a little travel radio. I crossed to the window. Her room looked onto some of the sea and some of the main island.

'Hey. I can see my house from here.'

'Aye?'

'That's my bedroom on the right. That wee window.'

'We'll have to get walkie-talkies.'

'Tin-can telephones. You'd get a better signal.'

Ailsa grinned back.

It was surreal to be out there on Dog Rock, looking back at the island. Ailsa was right. From here, Bancree was the mainland.

'If you don't mind me asking,' I said, 'where's your mum?'

Ailsa flushed a little, and wouldn't look up. She teased the embroidered edge of her pillowcase, smoothing it between her fingertips. I wished I hadn't asked.

'Sorry,' I said, 'I didn't mean anything.'

'No, it's not that. It just makes me think about her, that's all.'

She gave up on the lace, and looked me in the eye.

'Mum's the reason we've moved here, I suppose. My mum's one of the missing people.'

It wasn't easy to hear. Ailsa told the story so simply and plainly that it was hard to connect her to it. When she was a baby, only a few months old, her mother had vanished. She was called Annie, and she'd disappeared on a mild midsummer day. Her dad used to run wildlife tours – whale-watching, dolphin-spotting, that sort of thing. He'd been out all day, taking half a dozen tourists on the trail of a rookery of seals. He'd returned to hear his daughter crying hysterically. Puzzled, he'd entered the house, wondering why his wife wasn't seeing to the baby, and moved through the rooms in mounting concern. He'd found the infant Ailsa in her cot, howling and inconsolable. But he couldn't find his wife. Not in the house, not in the garden, and not anywhere. He called the police, but the police couldn't find her either. He trawled the coast, looking for her. He looked for days, then weeks. She was gone. The police gave up the search, but John had never stopped. And the further afield he looked, the more unsolved cases he discovered. To help him track the missing people, he started keeping records. He bought pins. He bought maps.

'And that's that,' said Ailsa.

'Jesus,' I breathed. 'I'm so sorry. I don't know what to say.'

'There's nothing to say. Don't worry about it. I've never known it any different. Dad's been looking for her my entire life. He thinks she was killed.'

'Killed.'

'She might have run away, I guess. But I think they were quite happy.'

She moved to the window. The sun dimmed in the clouds, and the room felt suddenly, incredibly cold. My skin prickled into goosebumps. I ran my fingers along the wooden windowsill, warped with age and damp.

'Those are my only photos of her.'

She gestured at the wall. A single frame hung above her sleeping bag, fixing several photos into a loose collage. All the pictures captured the same woman. Annie looked a lot like her daughter, but she was bigger, brighter, happier. In one image she was hugging John, both of them turned towards the camera. They were grinning. In another picture, a Polaroid with foxed corners, she was sitting with a howling baby on her knee, cupping its seashell hands in her own. I could see Ailsa so clearly in the infant. One of the pictures was newsprint, with Annie hugging her baby close. In the last picture, she stood beside a wall, looking out the window. She didn't know there was a photographer there, and in this image she seemed sadder. They were old photos from film cameras with the edges smoothed off, everything fuzzy, no detail.

The pictures made me feel so sad, and I didn't know what to say. I could sense Ailsa standing close beside me, lost in the photos of her mother. There was nothing I could say to make it better. Her dad's detective work didn't seem so exciting or weird now I knew the truth. He'd lost his wife and maybe a little of his sanity at the same time. He was heartbroken, and it had consumed him. His quest to find his wife, or to track her killer, was – well. Sixteen years. His devotion staggered me.

The last mouthful of my tea had gone cold.

'I don't have a dad,' I volunteered, lamely. 'Ronny's my step-father.'

Ailsa swivelled to look at me. The story was so banal, I almost felt embarrassed to tell her.

'My dad and Mum met young, had me too early, and he wasn't fit for fatherhood. He took himself off when I was a baby, and Mum brought me up without him. She only met Ronny a few years ago.'

'Is he still around?'

'Dunno. Mum might know where he is, but she won't be telling me any time soon.'

'Don't you want to meet him? To know him?'

Her eyes cut into me. I was brutally conscious that knowing her mother was not an option for her, no matter how much she wanted it.

'No one's ever asked me that. In truth, I don't know. I'm like you in that I've never known anything different. I don't know what I'd say to him.'

We stood in silence for a moment.

'Do you want to see the jumpers?' asked Ailsa, abruptly.

'Aye,' I said, grateful to change the subject. 'Are you sure?'

'Go for it. They're all in there somewhere.'

She gestured towards the rickety wardrobe. I wandered over and pulled the doors open. Much like my own clothes rail, several dozen items were crowded on wire hangers. I flicked between jeans and shirts and vest tops, settling on a woollen jumper, green with white crosses near the neck.

'How about this one?'

'Perfect, aye.'

'Certain?'

'Suits you more than me anyway.'

'Well, thanks, then. I love it.'

I bundled the sweater beneath my arm. As I replaced the empty hanger, I spotted a floor-length scarlet dress. It was someone's old prom gown, out of style and just a little tatty. Ailsa saw me looking and grabbed hold if it. She draped it from her shoulders and pulled an exaggerated pose, one hip cocked, pouting for a camera. I laughed.

'Oh, that's you to a T.'

'Should I wear it to school?'

'Oh, every day,' I said, nodding wildly.

'I'll start tomorrow.'

'I'd love to see the look on Tina Robson's face, the day you sweep into school wearing that thing.'

We both sniggered at the thought.

I looked at my watch.

'Look, I'd better go. It's getting on, and I should work on my History report.'

'The selkie thing? How's that going?'

'Good, aye,' I said, standing up. She followed me down the stairs. 'I found some great books in the library, and there's this beach-comber on the island, he's got a load of selkie stories.'

'Has he?' she said, pricking up her ears. 'I'd love to hear them.'

'Go and ask him. He's not shy when it comes to telling tales. Makes the selkies into interesting wee beasties.'

'Could I come with you? Next time you go?'

'Nae bother. Izzy loves an audience.'

We were back in the living room. The little house felt weird.

'Sure you won't stay for dinner with my dad?' asked Ailsa. There was a sudden note of pleading in her voice. With a burst of guilt,

I realised that she must be very lonely. I spent so much of my life seeking out solitude, and here was someone who had no choice about living in isolation. I felt chastened.

'I can't, Ailsa. I'm expected home.'

'Of course,' she said, 'right. Never mind. Maybe another time.'

'Please, aye. I'd like that.'

'Weather's turning anyway. We'd better go.'

I took my schoolbag and we went outside. The sun had weakened, retreating behind a veil of cloud, and Still Bay had turned choppy in the cooling afternoon. We took the dinghy in silence, its engine whining high above the sound of the sloshing waves. A gigantic murder of crows bombed the sky above Grogport. Approaching Bancree, I jumped barefoot onto the beach, dumped my bag and shoes in the sand, and pushed the rib back into the water.

'See you, then. Thanks for the jumper.'

'Thanks for the rescue,' she said.

Still smiling, she turned the yellow inflatable for Dog Rock and didn't look round once. I watched her all the way back to the islet, sitting motionless at the tiller. Just before she reached the pontoon, I turned and walked home through the band of dune grass.

It was clear that she wanted a friend. As weird as she was, I felt drawn to her, to her sadness and loneliness. I'd had a good time with her. I had to remind myself that I was leaving the island inside a year. There wasn't room for anyone else in my life. I was trying to cut my ties to Bancree, not find new ones.

At the edge of Grogport, I felt the first pinpricks of rain on my head and hands. I picked up my pace, even as the rain scattered on the tarmac at my feet. I scampered into the house just before it loosed in volleys, hammering on the porch roof.

There was a fire on, and everyone was in the kitchen. Mum was cooking something with leeks and bacon. Jamie lay on his back, giggling and gurgling and flapping his podgy arms at Ronny, who was busy pulling faces.

'Hey, Flo,' he said, and blew a raspberry.

'Hey, it's the baby. And Jamie, too.'

'Very funny.'

'Hi, Mum. Where's Anders?'

'Dunno,' said Ronny. 'He went home after the pub last night. He was going to get some clean clothes and stop the night, then come back here. But he wasn't in Tighna when we stopped to pick him up just now. I called, but you know the phones.'

'I told you,' said Mum, 'he'll have discovered a bottle of something he'd forgotten about, and he'll be sitting by himself, singing Danish folksongs because I won't let him do it here.'

'Oh, I know, I know. It's a shame though. He's back to the rigs next week, and it's always good to see him.'

'Always good to be out on the lash, more like,' muttered Mum, and poked Ronny in the ribs.

'I'm not sure I could handle another night with Anders. I'm saving myself for the football now.'

'You're getting old. I'll need to find myself a younger model.'

'Steady now, Cath,' he grinned, and went to grab her. Mum squealed and flipped away from him.

'And with that,' I said, 'I'm off to my room.'

I left them laughing in the kitchen, feeling suddenly and sharply unable to share the fun. I understood, then, why I liked having Anders in the house. He made me feel less of a stranger.

Through my bedroom wall, I could hear Jamie shrieking with laughter. There were so many years between me and him. There was a different father between us, and Mum had changed for it, too.

Her and Ronny was not her and my dad, whoever he was. Ronny was a nice guy, and he made me welcome. He treated me like his own daughter. But I was not his own daughter. I was different from them. As time went on, they didn't need me.

The windows of my house cast loose squares of light onto the road. I stood on the fringes, in the shadows. Across the water, Dog Rock showed as lights against the darkness.

Unsure of what to do, I stood in the gloom of my room and listened to the swell of the rain as it stampeded on the road.

CHAPTER 20

A few days later, Ailsa and I skipped school early, because we could. From the top deck of the ferry, she gazed into the shifting Sound. I fought the sea breeze to read the Tanno *Gazetteer*. It was a classified ad rag masquerading as a local news sheet. Three weeks after he'd gone missing, poor Doug MacLeod had dropped down to the middle pages. It was pretty much the same article as the previous edition. Friends and family remained concerned. Report any information to DC Tom Duncan.

'Daft old sod,' I muttered.

'I guess you knew him, then?'

'Everyone knows everyone. He was a janitor at the distillery, some of the time, so he worked a bit with Ronny. Cleaning, odd-jobs, you know. We used to see him out drinking, sitting on the wall.'

I pointed at the harbour, distant but approaching, barely visible as a grey line beneath the Tighna townscape.

'He'd drink his cider, or his brew, or get pints from the hotel when he had the money.'

'Think he fell in?'

'Don't know. It'd happen so quickly.'

'Underwater,' murmured Ailsa, entranced by the sea. Her eyes glowed, sheening blue reflected in the dark pool of each iris.

'Aye. Underwater,' I echoed.

Ailsa would be fine swimming. But we both knew what it meant for Dougie.

'Hey,' I said, 'do you still want to see Izzy?'

'The beachcomber? Aye, sure.'

'I might go now, if you fancy coming.'

'Might be a nice way to kill some time.'

We disembarked and walked down to the beach.

'What's that all about?' asked Ailsa.

She pointed at the building site, a mess of bricks and sand dominated by dozens of gigantic concrete pipes.

'Nothing, in the end. Some kind of tunnel, drainage or gas or something. The project was abandoned, and they left all that stuff. We used to play in the pipes when we were kids.'

'They just left it?'

'This is Bancree. Wasn't worth the cost of shipping back. Come on.'

The tide was at a low point, and we walked barefoot near the shoreline, where the sand was firmest, and the near waves ploshed and sloshed shallow right beside us.

'How exactly does he survive as a beachcomber?' asked Ailsa.

'I don't know if you can. He's an odd-job man, too.'

'Like Dougie?'

'Less organised. Izzy lives off-grid. His shack is his castle. You'll see. But he helps out some of the farmers, and washes dishes for Tony in the hotel sometimes. He makes wind chimes and things for the tourists, too, so I guess you could call him an artist. He does all kinds of things.'

'Strange ways to make a living.'

'It's a calling. His real job is as a shennachie.'

'Ah,' she said, nodding, 'a storyteller.'

'You know the word?' I was a bit disappointed.

'Aye. You don't move about the islands without meeting a shennachie or two. They're always on the go. A few months here and a few years there, and off they go again.'

The sea sighed and fizzed on wet sand. Crows a hundred yards ahead, raking through the weed, and gulls skidding on the waves. Dead crabs, the claws sucked dry, the empty fuselage left to scuttle on the wind.

'I keep thinking that one day I'll decide to come and see him, and he'll be gone. He'll have chucked his shack back into the sea.'

'Not today, though,' she said, squinting up the beach.

A ragged stream of smoke bloomed ahead of us, carried inland on the sea breeze.

'This way,' I said, and picked the path up from the beach.

As I passed the wooden frame, as always, I reached out and let my fingers trail through the bone and wooden wind chimes. Behind me, Ailsa did the same. A heavy figure sat hunched beside the fire. Something bubbled in a large pot, sat directly on the embers, and splashes from the rolling boil sizzled when they hit the fire.

'How do, stranger,' I called out.

The figure jolted and spun, grimacing horribly. I did a double-take. It was Izzy, but one of his eyes was swollen shut, the bruise swelling black. Over his cheek. His knuckles were scraped raw, and there were vicious gashes in his ear and temple. His good eye looked out, clearly startled.

'Izzy?' I gasped, 'What the hell happened to you?'

His battered face broke into a weak smile. He held up a hand.

'Ach, lass,' he said, 'don't worry about it.'

'Don't worry? You're black and blue, man. Who did this to you?'

I walked closer. The beachcomber leaned forward to roll a log onto his fire, and winced with the movement. He noticed Ailsa.

'Who's your pal? Hello, there.'

'Hello,' she mumbled, clearly taken aback.

'This is Ailsa. She wanted to hear your stories. Don't change the subject. Who did this?'

He sighed, and leaned back.

'Look. I'll not be taking this further. So you're not to either, understand?'

I folded my arms. He studied me.

'It was Lachie Crane,' he relented, finally.

'Lachlan? That mad bastard? What's his beef with you?'

'I don't know, lass,' he said, weary as the world. 'I was here as usual the other night, minding my own business, just having a wee smoke and a wee dram, and next thing I know, him and his fancy pals are kicking about the place.'

'What happened?' said Ailsa.

He looked at her warily.

'They had a poke about, and I told them to get away, and they wouldn't, and . . . Well. There was more of them than there was of me.'

Gingerly, he rolled up his sweater. His body was barrel-thick and downed in white hair, but peppered with red and black marks.

'Oh, Izzy. What about your ear?'

The gash was gruesome, the blood crusted black in the curls of skin.

'Lachie had a wee knife with him,' muttered Izzy. 'Think he wanted to make his mark.'

'Jesus Christ.'

'No, I was glad of it. The knife scared his pals. When he got that out, it stopped being funny. They called it a day. Left me to put my things back together.'

'Lachlan Crane is a sewer of a man.'

'He's a wee boy,' corrected Izzy, sadly, 'pulling wings off moths, just to show he can. He'll be no better when his dad gives him Clachnabhan.'

We all brewed on that for a moment. Munzie Crane wasn't getting any younger.

'I don't know,' said Izzy. 'I like it here, but it might be time to move on.'

'You need to tell the police.'

'Aye, right. The Cranes send a dozen crates of whisky to the station every Christmas.'

'Flora's right,' said Ailsa, 'you should report it, at least.'

The beachcomber spat heavily into the fire. It fizzed, boiling to nothing in a flash.

'And how would I prove it, lass? The cops think I'm a bum at the best of times, while Lachie and his pals are perfectly respectable businessmen on a perfectly respectable business trip. Who are they going to believe?'

Ailsa and I looked at each other. He was right.

'And what if I tell, and nothing comes of it. What then? Lachie comes back on his own with that wicked little knife of his, and there'll be no more Izzy, no more shennachie.'

'It's not fair,' I said.

'This is the world,' said the storyteller, opening up his arms, 'and this is how it always goes. You're young, but you'd better get used to it, girl.'

Above us, gulls hacked and swung on updrafts.

'Let me look at your ear, at least.'

Reluctantly, Izzy gave me some strips of rag, halfway to clean, and a bowl of water. He reached beneath his seat and pulled out a bottle of Clachnabhan, sloshed some into the bowl – then took a slug himself. I dabbed the rags in the mix and started to explore the wound. It was thick with blood. The first time, Izzy jerked away from me, and I had to steady him with a hand on his shoulder. His massive body exuded a gravity all of its own. I imagined Lachie's pals buzzing about him like flies.

Gradually, the wet rags dissolved the clotted blood, and rosy water fell from Izzy's ear, dripping down his cheek and into the neck of his thick jumper. Exposed, the wound wasn't as bad as it had first seemed. Poor Izzy flinched each time I daubed it with the whisky, but I cleaned it to a ragged pink slash.

'Have you any plasters?' I said, already knowing the answer.

'Plasters? Do they wash up on the beach, lass?' he replied, indignantly.

'Did the whisky?'

He just winked at me.

'Fine. You need to keep something on it though, at least until it's dry.'

He grumbled, but pressed another of the rags against his ear.

'So why are you two here, anyway? You didn't come to play Mary Seacole to an old fart like me, did you?'

'No. I came in the hope you'd remembered another selkie story. Ailsa wanted to hear them, too.'

'Is that right?' he said, eyeing her up. 'You like a tall tale, do you, Miss?'

She nodded. 'Aye. There was a shennachie on Rum for a while. He stayed a summer. I listened to a few of his stories.'

'So you know the score. Selkies again, is it? I've got others if you prefer.'

'Selkies, please,' I said.

I sat on my usual crate. Ailsa sat cross-legged on the ground beside me, arms folded in front – like a kid at primary school being good for story-time. Sometimes her movements were so childlike.

'Selkies . . .' muttered Izzy, and took another swig of his whisky. 'All right. Here we have it. Listen close, children.'

CHAPTER 21

There was a selkie woman, and she loved a sailor. He was a true lad. Whenever he went to sea, she spied on him from the troughs of waves. She blessed him with fair winds and gifted fish into his nets, though he never knew it. The more she gazed upon him, the more she desired him for a husband. The selkie hatched a plan to seize his heart. She followed him to sea and conjured a terrible storm from the calmest summer day. His smack overturned in the tempest, and the sailor and his mates were cast into the ocean. The selkie approached him in the form of a beautiful woman, and offered to save him. But even in drowning, the sailor refused her. He already had a wife, a lass he loved most dearly, and he could not be swayed, even in the face of death.

The selkie was furious. But a selkie in love is a strange and passionate creature. Angry as she was, she couldn't bear to see him dead. She dragged him to the surface and left him on the beach. The sailor was badly shaken but unharmed, though all his poor shipmates were drowned in the storm.

The story doesn't end there. The selkie resolved to discover more about the sailor and that wife of his. She needed to know what any earthly woman could offer better than a magical, beautiful selkie. She came to land and stowed her sealskin in the dunes. Disguising herself as an old woman, she made her way towards the town. Asking around, she discovered that the sailor and his wife were childhood sweethearts and forever in love, but that they were blighted with great misery. They'd been married three years, and were still without a child. The young bride was beside herself with woe. She'd spoken to the priest and the midwife. She had tried remedies old and new, but nothing worked. She was barren. She could not conceive a child.

On hearing this, the selkie knew in a flash how to steal a portion of the sailor's love. Still disguised as an old crone, she marched right up to their wee croft and hammered on the door. She was answered by the sailor's bride.

The selkie claimed to be a humble midwife, a traveller to the island, who had heard tell of their plight and knew how to help. Despondent but polite, the lass invited her in right away. Inside, the selkie found a sorry house indeed. Both the lassie and her husband sat about, hapless and hopeless, miserable beyond measure. Craving a child, they barely spoke from the fear they would never have what they wanted most.

'Fret not,' said the selkie woman, smiling sweetly. 'For surely I can help you.'

She took the unhappy lass to one side. The problem, she whispered, is not with you, but with your husband. When you go to bed tonight, turn down the light and leave – tell him you've gone to fetch a glass of milk, or to feed the fire. Then light a candle at your door and leave, leave the cottage and run, run as fast as you can. Run to the fairy stones on the hill. Turn thrice about the tallest and run, run back to your husband. If you return before the candle burns out, said the smiling selkie, then you shall right this great injustice.

The young lass studied the ugly old woman. She was doubtful but willing, in her sadness, to try anything for a child. She agreed to the plan. That night, when they turned for bed, the lassie popped out, leaving the room in darkness. She tiptoed to the door. Hands fumbling with a spill, she lit a candle and bolted for the stones, running as though her life depended on it. Back in the cottage, the selkie slipped into the bedroom and changed at once into her proper form, that of a beautiful young woman. Cloaked in night, the sailor believed her to be his bride. In the darkness, the man joined together with the selkie, and they bound themselves in blind, unbridled lust.

Out on the hillside, the young lass reached the stone circle, turned thrice about the tallest stone and sprinted home, reeling with the blood that rushed about her bones. Her craving for a child gave her wings, and soon the cottage came into view, and sure enough! Her candle still burned at the threshold. She seized the lamp and burst into the bedroom, full of joy . . . And, by candlelight, she found the selkie entwined around her own true man. She moaned, sick with horror and betrayal. With a light now in the bedchamber, the sailor realised at once what trickery was afoot. He threw the creature from him, but the damage had been done. The laughing selkie fled back into the sea. As she escaped, she reached out her seal hand and brushed firm and low against the lassie's belly. The candle spilled wax upon the floor.

The sailor and his bride continued in their life together, though their love was cracked in half. The trust between them lay shattered, but what could they do? They spent their nights in sadness and in silence. As the season rolled on, however, things began to change. Three months later, the entire village was amazed when the young lass began to show.

As twisted and polluted as it was, the selkie had kept her word.

A child began to grow within the barren lass. With this, the sailor and his bride rekindled some of their lost love. The selkie had exacted a heavy toll . . . but the couple would pay most anything for a child of their own.

Three months turned to six months, and then to nine. On a dark, rain-spattered morning, the lass began to labour. It was hard. O, it was hard indeed. Nurses were sent for, and the cottage thronged with women. The kettle shrilled on the fire crane, and the shrieks grew louder in the bedroom, louder and more desperate. Then the lass uttered a scream so raw, so dreadful, so awful, that not a soul in earshot ever forgot it. And in that terrible moment, her child was born.

The women gathered close to deliver the baby, but then recoiled in horror.

It was a seal pup.

Cloaked in a caul of blood and matter, it mewled and wriggled in the sheets. Alarmed by the scream, and struck by the sickened silence, the young sailor burst into the room. The seal child squirmed amongst the sodden blankets. Bellowing in anguish, the sailor gathered the pup and dashed down to the shore. Heart pounding, he crashed into the surf. He held the pup beneath the surface of the sea. He didn't blink or flinch as the tiny seal began to buck. After long, awful minutes, it stopped kicking and fell limp in his hands.

At that moment, back in the cottage, the exertions of labour proved too much for the lassie. She expired, giving out her last breath even as the pup fought for air. The sailor slumped home to find the second tragedy – his wife dead. Ripped apart, demolished entirely, betrayed and left bereft, he lost his mind to grief. He took his little boat, and struck out for the New World.

No one heard of him again.

CHAPTER 22

The top of Ben Sèimh dissolved in a haze of green and grey and amber. Gulls swung upon the inland currents.

'Is that it?' said Ailsa quietly.

'That's it,' replied the shennachie, gruffly, turning to face her. He was in profile to me, and I studied his swollen-shut eye.

'How could the sailor not know the difference?'

'What's that?'

'In bed. Even in the dark. He'd have to know the selkie wasn't his wife.'

'It's just a story,' said the shennachie.

Ailsa made as though to speak again, then closed her mouth.

'It was amazing, Izzy,' I said, 'cheers.'

'No bother. Any time. Always good to dust off the older ones, remember how they go.'

'Where was that one from?'

'Raasay, that one,' he said, and stoked the fire with a charred bamboo cane. 'The circle's still there. The stones are fallen in, but still there.'

'I thought there was no truth in any of these tales?'

Izzy made a so-so gesture with his good hand. 'Not like that. There's no selkies, obviously. But some of the stories are pinned to real places, or real people. Creative licence, Flora. It goes a long way.'

'They had to come from somewhere.'

The big man snorted. 'From the bottom of a whisky bottle, maybe.'

'Come on. No smoke without fire.'

He grinned and shook his head.

'Picture the scene, Flo. It's been a long, shitty winter. Your harvest was poor. Your best sow's gone fallow. Your thatch is sodden. There's beasties in your bed, biting your arse every time you try to sleep. Six hours of daylight at best, and everything is piss-wet through.'

'Sounds like fun.'

'Exactly. So you start telling stories to your pals, finding ways to warm the night.'

'You don't just invent a selkie,' I said. 'That needs a spark.'

'Aye, of course. But that's when Fergus falls into the loch and drowns himself, and old Mary sees a seal around the same time, and all of a sudden there's a story to tell.'

'So why are there different sorts of selkie, then?'

'Because it's a good story. Folk remember the good ones, and tell them again. But they tell them different to you, and so the stories change as they go.'

I harrumphed, but didn't argue.

'And that doesn't happen with those books of yours, girl. Stuck on a page, a story has no life. It can't go anywhere. It's fixed down like a butterfly on a pin.'

'Or a bear in a cage,' I murmured.

He beamed at me. 'That's it. Now you understand.'

The fire crackled, and I drew a lungful of wood smoke.

'You seen the stones up on the Ben?' asked the beachcomber.

'Stones? No. What stones?'

'There's pagan spots here, too. From when the Norsemen came, hundreds of years before they converted to Christ.'

'Why don't I know about this?' I said. 'I've lived here all my life. You're only an offcomer.'

'An offcomer that knows more than you, clearly,' he said, tapping his nose, then wincing at the bruise. 'Whenever I move somewhere new, I make it my business to find out all there is about the place and its people.'

'I've been up the Ben dozens of times. There's nothing there.'

'Oh, but there is. You just didn't know where to look.'

'All right, smuggo. Where do we go?'

'Your side, the Atlantic side. When you're right above the wind farm, strike straight up towards the peak. There's a wee corrie up there. In the corrie, there's Viking stones. Covered in moss, but you can still see the carvings.'

'Shouldn't you tell someone? The heritage people, or the tourist board or something?'

'Why should I tell them?' he scoffed. 'All they'll do is bang a roof on top and charge folk to go and see it. No. Everything is designed to fall away, in time.'

'Can we make it today?' said Ailsa.

'Aye. If you go now.'

'So let's go,' she said.

I went to grab my school bag, but Izzy stuck out a paw.

'Flora,' he said, 'stay another second, will you? I've something to tell you.'

I looked at him, puzzled, then Ailsa.

'I don't mind,' she said. 'I'll see you by the fence.'

Standing beside the beachcomber, I watched her go, taking a

thin path that wound between the scrub. When she was out of earshot, I turned to Izzy.

'What's up?'

'Tell me about Ailsa,' he said, still watching after her. 'Who is she?'

'Ach, she's just a friend. She's new to the island. She's moved to Dog Rock. She doesn't know anyone.'

Izzy raised his eyebrows. 'All the way out there? She reminds me of someone. Where's she from?'

'Islay, most recently, I think.'

'Good whisky on Islay,' he said, thoughtfully, as though that was how he judged the quality of a person.

'Is that it? I thought you had some big secret to tell me.'

'No, no. It's just that new people make me nervous, turning up like that.'

'Don't be daft. Don't worry about Ailsa,' I said. 'I'll vouch for her. She's not the police or anything like that. She's like me. One more year of school to go, and then I guess she's leaving. I'd better catch her up. I'm off.'

'All right, lass.'

'You look after yourself, won't you? And watch out for Lachlan coming back.'

'Tell you what. I'll keep my eyes peeled for Lachlan Crane, and you keep your eyes peeled for those stones. They won't come easy. They don't like being found.'

Ailsa waited by the first fence, and I quickly caught her up.

'All good?' I said.

'Hmm? Aye, I'm fine.'

We struck out straight across the field.

'What do you make of Izzy, then?'

'He's quite the character.'

'And the rest. He's a legend.'

'That's pretty bad, what Lachlan did.'

'Lachie's a dick. Izzy wouldn't hurt a fly. If I ever had a problem, he's the first person I'd go to.'

'That's good to know.'

'Did you like the story?'

'Not really,' she said, shaking her head. 'It seemed a bit . . . well, one-sided.'

'How do you mean?'

'Well, it's not like any selkie story I've ever heard. The shennachie on Rum told stories of the seal folk, and they were different. Selkies are supposed to be gentle, aren't they?'

'Aye, that's what I thought, until I started this research. Some stories have them being soft and sad, but this book I found, and Izzy's stories, they're all saying that selkies go out of their way to hurt people and break their hearts.'

'That's not what I've heard. The stories I know are all about heartbreak and loss, that's true. But they're mostly about people and selkies being kept apart. The selkies feel love, too.'

'I'd like some of those stories, too,' I admitted.

'Izzy's story was just mean. It's not like I need a happy ending, but that was plain brutal.'

'That's nothing,' I said. 'You should see this book I found at a jumble sale. Izzy's stories are nothing compared to that.'

Ailsa reached the fence first. Pressing down on the top strand of withered barbed-wire, she vaulted nimbly across.

'It's a shame,' she said, and pinned the wire for me to follow. 'Selkies should be something wonderful and magical, and that sort of story makes them monsters.'

'But selkies aren't real,' I said, 'and history evolves. Over time, people decide what's important.'

I clambered over the fence, and we scrambled through the birches to the road. We fell into easy step on the weathered tarmac. It was only half a mile to the track that led uphill. We huffed a way up the flank of Ben Sèimh, taking a sparse path through the scrubby heather. We walked with trousers tucked into socks, trying to keep the ticks out. Though the mountain was only a few hundred metres high, it was an ordeal to get there. Halfway up, the path forked. Ahead, the main track continued to the summit. Branching right, a fainter route traced a girdle onto the western side of the Ben.

'This way,' I panted. 'He said it was in line with the turbines.'

Ailsa flapped a breathless hand at me, and we plodded on. The walking improved as the gradient levelled, and it became easier to enjoy the view. Panoramas from the Ben were usually spectacular, with the Sound dropping into blue and the Highlands rising in the distance, but the day was cloaked in haze, and the mainland was barely visible, everything washed out to sepia. Crofts and houses whitewashed stark against the heather.

Rounding the Ben, the turbines appeared beneath us. Staring out to sea, they chopped and pounded with the Atlantic gusts. Only one of the three was working, the other two standing impotent, swaying and knocking in the steady breeze. The sounds floated up the hillside in clunks and clanks. We followed the track around the mountain until we were above the wind farm. I kept checking the turbines below me against the peak above.

'It must be about here,' I said, doubtfully. 'Can you see the boulders?'

We both peered up, searching out the stones between the

bracken, and finding only an ocean of green. The ferns shifted together in the sea breeze, swaying like an audience.

'Come on,' said Ailsa. 'Let's get lost.'

She forged off the path, striking out uphill, and in a heartbeat was swallowed by the bracken. For a moment I was alone on the hillside, and then I followed her, plunging myself into a sea of green.

CHAPTER 23

As we entered the belt of bracken, Ailsa raised her arms above the broad fronds and weaved, twisting her body to pass between them with minimal contact. I did the same. It was a bit of a game, trying not to touch them, though the growth was dense throughout, and in places the ferns grew taller than us both.

After twenty hard minutes, the bracken thinned and stopped abruptly, and we emerged into a wide empty bowl, much of the perimeter marked by ancient rockfall. I stepped out after Ailsa and lowered my aching arms.

'Is this it?' she asked, doubtfully.

We were in a corrie, right enough. Long since scoured by glaciation, the broad scoop now provided some shelter from the wind. After the uphill climb and the gusting sea breeze, it felt suddenly, uncomfortably still. The corrie was steep-sided and held the sun at bay. In the shadows, it was cold, and the sweat in the small of my back turned clammy.

'Why does the bracken stop?' I said.

Ailsa frowned and studied the ferns. They ended at the corrie as though at a wall. The scoop should have provided shelter for them to thrive. The ring of large rocks and small boulders lay matted with moss and lichen. No bird song. No wind in the ferns.

No sea. The silence was dense. I looked at Ailsa, spooked by the quiet.

Something small and dark speckled at her throat. It might have been a mole, or a freckle, but it caught my eye, and I leaned close to look.

'Ailsa. Don't freak out, but there's a tick on you. On your neck.'

Her hand flew at once to her throat. She felt the insect, and jerked her hand away.

'Aw, that's disgusting! Will you get it off?'

'Aye,' I said, reluctantly, 'I'll try.'

I leaned closer. The tick was caught fast, denting her skin. The head was buried deep, and its little legs wiggled slowly. It sent shivers straight through me. I brought both hands up and pressed the thumb nails into her neck, bringing one to bear on either side of the tick, and started easing pressure against its burrowed head. Ailsa winced, but kept still. Beneath the pressure of my fingers, her pulse hammered hotly, madly, veins thrumming close to the surface. My nails met around the tick. It wriggled as I pulled it, squeezing gently, careful not to break it off and leave the head embedded. Ailsa's skin tented outwards with the pull of my fingers. The tick popped free after a minute of teasing and pressure, leaving a single, minute bead of blood on her neck. Released, she took a step away, breathing deep and rubbing at her throat.

'I hate those things,' she said. 'Thanks.'

'Nae bother.'

The tiny tick was wriggling madly, trapped between my nails. I pressed both thumbs together, squeezing hard until I felt it pop. When I looked, it was smeared on my nails.

She took her hand away, examining her fingers. There were red wings on her neck from the pressure of my fingers, a red weal at the centre.

'That looks sore. I'm sorry.'

'Better out than in. Don't worry about it. I'm grateful.'

We stood in awkward silence.

'We should get on.'

'Where should we start?'

'You go that way. I'll look this side.'

We worked away from each other, examining the jumbled rocks. The sun finally peeled around the side of the Ben, and I was grateful for the warmth on my back. At first glance, all the stones seemed pretty much the same, but as I moved around the corrie, I approached a couple that looked different from the others, tinged distinctly pink against the flinty greys. They were noticeably longer, too, and thinner.

'Hey, over here,' I called, 'I think I might have found them.'

Ailsa scrambled across the corrie as I kneeled to peel sprigs of heather from the first stone. It was coated in lichen, old man's beard, and I had to snap some of the growth away. Ailsa started on the other. After a minute of work, the stones were clear enough, and we were stilled to see what lay underneath. On the first were animals, creeping in strange, stilted shapes across the eroded surface of the rock. Centuries of moss and rain and wind had dulled their edges, but they were mostly clear enough. Stags, for sure, and something that was either an otter or a dog. There was a border of fish set around the edge, in places so eroded that they were indistinguishable from natural dings in the rock.

On the second stone, men moved in rows, lofting spears and swords. At the foot of the stone, best preserved of all, was a longship. And, there, beneath the boat, was something else. Another animal, carved right at the base of the rock, half-sunk in the ground. I crouched right down and dug the soil away.

'What's that one?' I said.

Ailsa reached in to touch the chiselled shapes, her fingertips brushing across the weals in the stone. She traced an oval around the animal.

'I think it's a seal,' she said after a moment.

'Seals. Cool. I love seals.'

'You do?'

'Who doesn't love seals? Here, stand back. I want to take a rubbing.'

She stepped aside and I kneeled closer. I fished paper and a pencil from my bag, and started shading across the stone. In the end, I had to lie on my belly to get the right angle, stretched out in scrub. I worked gently, wary of tearing the paper on the stone, and slowly men and beasts emerged onto the page, growing into careful layers of graphite. I levered myself up and brushed the curlicues of heather from my jeans.

Ailsa was standing a wee way off from the stones, on a boulder on the edge of the corrie. The clouds were ribbons, bunched up as they fell into distance. For a while, we both looked down onto the sea. This high up, the Atlantic marked a clear curve on the horizon.

'Flo,' she said.

'Aye?'

'What can you actually do for fun on this island?'

'I take it you don't mean like playing solitaire and learning tapestry?'

'No. I was thinking more about getting dressed up and having a drink.'

'Ah. Well, that doesn't happen too often for me. The mainland's not an option. It's not like you can take a taxi back. Richard's dad was good friends with the landlord at the Bull. We used to get a bit pissed there, sometimes, as long as we kept it quiet.'

'Reckon they'd serve you now?'

'I don't know,' I said, weighing the options. 'Richard was closer to eighteen than me. Maybe.'

'Well then. D'you fancy it?'

'Not if Ronny and Anders are there,' I said. 'They turn into boys when they're drinking. They'll take the piss all night.'

'Is that likely?'

'Dunno. Anders might still be staying at his place. He hasn't been at ours for a couple days.'

'How about it, then?'

I thought about it. It would be weird to go there without Richard, and face the stares of island faces who knew precisely how old I was. Maybe it would do me some good, though, to get tarted up and go out for a night. Reclaiming some independence would be a tonic. I thought again of Richard and another girl – any other girl. My imagination always conjured him at the moment of waking, shafts of dusty sun pouring in through floral curtains, the smell of bodies. Waking, stretching, sleepy as cats, they turned to face each other . . .

Ciao, babe. Love always. Xx.

Kisses. Kisses for someone else.

'Well?' said Ailsa.

I made my mind up.

'Hell, yes,' I said.

CHAPTER 24

We settled on Saturday. Ailsa came round late afternoon for tea and to get ready. She wore jeans and a jacket zipped up, and carried a wee rucksack with her. Mum and Ronny managed to rein in most of their nosiness, though they were clearly brimming with questions. I steered her through the introductions and through dinner, then we hurried to my room. With two of us in there, I was conscious that it was even smaller than hers. I put some tunes on the stereo, then pointed out the window.

'Look,' I said, 'd'you see?'

Dog Rock sat in the bay like an actor on an empty stage.

'Tin-can telephones it is, then.'

'Mad to think you're that close, and there's still a wee stretch of Atlantic between us.'

'Islands,' she agreed, non-committal. I waited for more, but she didn't elaborate.

She reached out to touch an old poster. 'I love Idlewild,' she said, the paper buckling under her finger. 'D'you know, I used to have such a crush on Roddy Woomble.'

'Not any more?' I said, pointing her towards the bed. I sat at the desk and poured a can of cider into two glasses.

'Not any more, no. Grew out of that one.'

'Poor Roddy. He'll be gutted. Here you go,' I said, handing one to her.

'Do your folks not mind?' she said, reaching for the glass.

'Mum makes the rules, really. Ronny mostly does what he's told. I'm allowed a wee bit as long as I don't get silly. They're not daft. They knew about me and Richard heading out to the Bull, and they'll have a fair idea that's what we've got planned.'

'That's pretty sound.'

'I suppose,' I said. 'She reckons it'd be a lot worse if I never had alcohol at all, then turned up at a pub when I was eighteen to find out what the fuss was all about.'

'She's probably right. Wish my dad was that sorted.'

'Does he not let you drink?'

'God no. He'd hit the roof.'

'So what have you told him about tonight?'

She looked guilty. 'I told him you and me were watching films, and that I was staying over. I figured, if we took the back door and went out through the woods, he'd never see us leaving.'

'Do you think he'll guess?'

'Maybe. I don't know. But I don't really care, either. I never get to go out. Sláinte.'

'Sláinte,' I replied, chinking glasses. Ailsa took a slug of cider, then placed her glass on the bedside cabinet. She turned her rucksack upside down, and two dozen crumpled tops tumbled out onto the bed.

'Right,' she said. 'Now what are we wearing?'

It took us an hour or so to get there, but in the end we were ready. I wore things I'd never wear, choosing a knee-length skirt and a sleeveless blouse, plus a wee jacket. Ailsa wore skinny jeans and a bomber jacket over one of my vest tops, a flash of stomach on show. Her hair was up. Mine was plaited loosely to the side. Both of us wore heels. It was ridiculously over the top for a Saturday in the Bull, but it was a treat. There wasn't that much skin on show, but we almost had a you're-not-going-out-dressed-like-that moment with my mum. She scanned us up and down, looking for reasons to make us change. When she couldn't find any, I think she realised that we simply looked rather more adult than she'd like. She let us go, lips pursed in disapproval.

'You'll be careful, Flora,' she said, and there was no mistaking the warning in her voice.

'Of course, Mum,' I replied, looking as innocent as I could. 'It's just a few drinks.'

'Aye, well make sure it stays that way. I don't want a call from the landlord. Or the constabulary. Either of you.'

'Course not, Cath,' said Ailsa, wide-eyed.

Mum looked at us, one and then the other, and then she gave up.

'Off you go, then. Behave yourselves. And have a good time.'

'Hang on,' called Ronny, leaning round the door. He had the phone pressed to his ear. 'Before you go, Flo – have you heard from Anders?'

'Not since he was last here. Why?'

'Ach, nothing. I'm still trying to get hold of the galoot. He never showed to watch the football in Tanno yesterday. It's not like him.'

'Who won?'

'Denmark, more's the pity. Two-nil. I could understand him hiding if Scotland had won, but he'd never miss a chance to gloat.'

'He'll be fine. He's Anders.'

'I'm just a bit worried, that's all.'

'Oh no, Teenwolf,' I said. 'You don't think . . . You don't think . . .'

'What?'

'You don't think he's found another man?'

Mum snorted, and Ronny threw a pencil at me. Still laughing, we clattered out the kitchen door, across the stones that passed as a garden path, and through the back gate that opened onto the woods. We must have looked quite the sight, walking through the forest dressed for a night out. The evening was fairly set in, every tree silhouetted black against the deepest violet sky. I carried a headtorch, and the light skittered in twigs and needles. We stumbled and giggled through the trees, emerging onto the road past Grogport and well out of sight of Dog Rock. After walking for ten or fifteen minutes, a muddy estate car scooted by. We shrieked and yelled, and the driver slammed on the brakes. It was McKendrick, the farmer. We bundled into the back seat, giddy from the walk and the cider. We made Tighna in good time, nattering nonsense with McKendrick all the way. He claimed to be seeing a man about a dog. I understood this to mean he'd be tending to his stills. Even now, whisky beat a pulse throughout the island, coursing in the burns and heather. You could squeeze whisky from the stones.

McKendrick dropped us near the Bull, then turned off for the pitted track towards the abandoned northwest coast. Outside the hotel, the gravity of drinking underage weighed a little heavier on me, but Ailsa strode ahead, heels clattering a tattoo on the asphalt. I skipped to catch her up, and caught my breath just as we reached the double doors of the hotel. Painted white, with the sills and drainpipes and woodwork shiny black, the Bull was a focal point for Tighna, and the only pub on Bancree. We paused, looking at each other. As she leaned against the door, a crack of light and noise spilled out. She grinned, and I followed her into the bar.

We moved through the wee hallway, into the public lounge and without breaking stride, crossed the orange carpet to the bar. The locals stared. I knew them all in some small way. We stepped up to the counter, and perched on tall stools. Tony, the landlord, emerged from his hutch at the end of the bar. Ambling down the bar, he sized us up, grinned and shook his head.

'Flora,' he said. 'Lovely to see you. How's school?'

'It's fine thanks, Tony. And, ah, how's business here?'

Pointedly, I looked around the room. It was half-empty, the customers drinking in ones and twos. The only noise came from a couple of Poles from the fish farm, gathered round to swear at the fruit machine.

'Business is extremely slow,' conceded Tony. 'Now, what will you be having?'

'Two pints of Deuchars, please.'

'Here's the deal. You can have two pints of Deuchars shandy. You'll sit in that corner booth, and you'll drink them slowly, and we'll see where we go from there. Fair enough?'

We made our way into the corner.

We drank and nattered. Ailsa told me about the places she'd lived, and everything she'd seen on her travels. As I told stories of island characters like Izzy and Uncle Anders, I realised that each of us had something the other wanted. Ailsa craved community. I needed change. Between us, we had both. Every now and then, I'd glimpse her father in her face – just a little in the nose, in the peatbog eyes – and flush to think of him.

We were onto our third pint of shandy when a small, noisy crowd of men entered the hotel. One stood apart from the others, leading the group to the bar with evident authority.

'Well,' I said, 'there goes the neighbourhood.'

'Who's that?' she said, looking behind her towards the door.

'Lachlan Crane. I always knew he carried a knife.'

'What's he doing in here?'

'To be fair, it's his local. He's in here a couple of times a week. With that boat of his, he considers Tighna part of a Tanno pub crawl. He might be back to pick on Izzy.'

'What about that lot?' she said, studying the group of men. There were four of them, joking and pushing each other, all beer bellies and designer shirts.

'That's his pack. They change every time I see them. Businessmen from all over the world, taking the Clachnabhan tour. Lachie's job is to get them drunk and show them the sights. Some island hospitality before they sign contracts.'

Lachlan scanned the bar. I tried to keep Ailsa between me and him, but he managed to catch my eye. He grinned and sauntered towards us. His gang followed close behind, carrying pints and whiskies.

'And if it isn't Flora Cannan,' he called out as he approached the table. 'How you keeping, honeypie?'

'All the worse for seeing you, Lachie. What are you doing over here? Back to bully the locals?'

'Bully?' smirked Lachie, raising an eyebrow. 'That's not my style, poppet. I was born a charmer. No, me and the boys here, we thought we'd head over to the bright lights of Bancree for a night. Check out the local talent,' he said, pronouncing the last word with a suggestive leer.

'Well, sorry to disappoint you.'

He looked down over me, eyes lingering, then up Ailsa at just as slow a crawl. 'Oh, I'm not disappointed at all.'

'You will be,' I said, then tried a wee lie. 'We both have boyfriends.'

'Really?' he said, gesturing to the empty seats around the booth. 'Still young Richard, is it? Funny, that. I heard he was off to university. Somewhere down south.'

'That's right,' I said. It sounded hollow, even to me.

'Long-distance relationships,' he lamented. 'Abominable success rate. Makes you wonder why some folk even bother.'

Abashed, I looked into my drink. Lachie turned his attention to Ailsa.

'How about you, darlin'? Fancy showing us a good time?'

'Piss off,' she said, mildly.

'Well, now. Listen to the potty mouth. Shame to hear it from such a pretty girl. I should wash your mouth out with soap, lassie.'

'Wash your mind out first.'

'Ah, come off it. Will you come and have a drink with us? You're new around here, aren't you? Come and get to know us.'

'Just passing through. Hardly worth your trouble.'

'We're happy on our own, Lachlan,' I said.

'No man is an island, Flo,' he said, sagely, 'or woman, for that matter. Has Ronald taught you nothing? I'll have words with him.'

'Ronny taught me to stay away from strangers,' I said, then lowered my voice, 'especially strangers with knives. See you later, aye?'

Lachie flinched at the mention of knives, and looked quickly to see if anyone else had heard. He leaned in close. 'Strangers?' he said, coaxing. 'Strangers, is it? Come on, now. We could always do something about that, couldn't we, Flora?'

I leaned in close to match. His aftershave was tinged antiseptic, of lemons, but there was an animal smell on him, too. I thought of him taking a knife to Izzy. The gash on the old man's ear.

'No,' I said. 'We never, ever could.'

His face twitched just a little, flickering, but then he beamed and backed off, laughing out loud.

'Come away, boys. These wee lassies aren't the ones for us. A bleak night for us bold hunters.'

His cronies groaned and laughed along with him, and Lachie led them to a table on the far side of the bar. We watched them leave in silence.

'Think that's the last we'll see of them?'

'Not a chance,' I said. 'There's no one else here. They'll be back in a bit with a few drinks inside them.'

'In that case,' said Ailsa, 'I think I've had enough of this place.'

'Aye, me and all.'

'Should we go home?'

'Let's get some booze from Tony. Come on.'

We finished our drinks, the beer warm and sweet towards the bottom of the glass, then gathered our jackets and bags. Ailsa followed me to the bar.

'My good fellow,' I said, emboldened by the beer, 'might I have a bottle of your finest low-budget wine? To take away, you understand.'

This time, he simply chuckled.

'Not a hope, Flo. But say hi to your mother when you see her.'

'It was worth a shot.'

'No, lass,' he grinned, 'it wasn't.'

We left without the drink, but it was a small relief to close the door on Lachlan and his pack. The autumn night air was fresh and cool and clean. I pulled my jacket closer around me.

'Is that the night over, then?' asked Ailsa, disappointed.

'Not yet. Come on, let's walk back. I've got an idea.'

We passed the abandoned building site, crossed the road, and walked through the playground, swingset squeaking in the breeze. When we reached the beach, I reached down and pulled off my heels. Ailsa did the same and, silently, we stepped barefoot onto the sand.

CHAPTER 25

In the moonlight, the beach was dull silver, and the sea an inky dark. The wind washed waves onto the shore with a hush, and chased through the dune grass in low moans. The stars were pricks of hoar frost.

'This is pretty special,' she said, after we'd walked for maybe half a mile.

Our feet pattered in the cold sand.

'This is how I like the island best,' I said. 'This is when it's perfect. When there's no one else here, and it feels like the island's alive, just me and Bancree.'

'Um, you know I'm here, right?'

'You're my friend. That's different. I mean everyone else.'

'You like your own company, don't you?'

I turned to look at her. 'Don't you?'

'That depends,' she said, 'on what the choices are.'

She grinned and skipped ahead, moving like a dancer with hops and leaps, using her toes to trace shapes on the sand.

As we approached Izzy's shack, woodsmoke resolved into sparks, then tongues of flame that made the smoke glow orange. Ailsa and I walked up the beach and found the path that wound through the scrub. The driftwood chimes clattered in discordant bursts.

For the first time, I wondered if Izzy kept them for the company.

As ever, he sat beside his fire. When the flames licked up, shadows behind him danced black and yellow on the walls of his shack.

'Hey,' I called out, 'hello.'

Despite his bulk, Izzy snapped to his feet, spinning round with fists raised. When he saw it was us, he calmed at once, lowering his hands.

'Hey, now. You OK, Izzy?'

'Flo,' he said, then looked past me, 'and Ailsa.' He did a wee double-take when he took in how we were dressed. 'Big night out, I take it?'

'This?' I said, giving a mock catwalk twirl, 'Why, this is something I just threw on.'

'You won't do my blood pressure any good, dressed like that.'

'My mother was right. You're a dirty old man.'

'And you're a harlot.'

'Pervert.'

'Damn right. What are you doing out here, girls?'

'Actually, I was hoping you could help with something.'

'I didn't think you'd come for company. What do you want?'

'Do you still have any of that cherry stuff?'

A sly grin spread across his face.

'The schnapps? Aye, I do. And I still want shot of it, too.'

'Same price?'

'Ten pounds sterling and it's yours, Flo.'

I handed him the money, and the old beachcomber ducked into his shack. There was knocking and clunking, then the sound of glass on glass. When Izzy emerged again, he held a shockingly pink bottle.

'That's never it,' I said, taken aback.

'No wonder you don't want to be seen out with the stuff,' said Ailsa.

'Look, do you want it, or not?' growled Izzy.

'Go on, then,' I said. The bottle was shaped like a gourd. Tilting it against the firelight, the liquid responded slowly, glopping in the bottle.

'What have we done?' I murmured.

Behind me, Ailsa came closer to the beachcomber.

'Izzy,' she said, 'are you OK?'

'About as much as usual. Why?'

'Only you looked a bit startled to see us.'

'What do you expect, springing at me from the darkness? I thought you were valkyries down from heaven. I thought my time had come. Then I realised it was only you two fishwives.'

'Fuuunny.'

'Ach, I'm kidding. Truth of it is, I'm a bit worried, aye.'

Izzy seemed suddenly crestfallen, all his cheeky swagger deflated. He was getting old.

'What's up?'

'Same old. I keep thinking about Doug MacLeod. First Bill, then Dougie. There's nothing to be done about it. It's daft, but I can't help thinking it'll be me next. If I'm nervous, it's not without reason.'

'That's got nothing to do with you,' I said. 'Don't be daft.'

His sad eyes reflected firelight. 'They were both old men. Both lived alone near the coast. No friends, no family. Sounds pretty much the same to me. Plus there's what happened with Lachie.'

There was nothing I could say to that.

'So, aye, I'm a wee bit anxious about folk sneaking in the dark.'

'Sorry, Izzy,' said Ailsa.

'Don't fret, lass. Beside, it's probably worry over nothing. Wouldn't be surprised if Bill and Dougie showed up hand in hand on a Rio carnival float.'

He grinned, then, but there was no heart in it. Ailsa and I exchanged a glance.

'Hey,' he said. 'I meant to ask you, Ailsa.'

'Me?'

'Who was that shennachie on Rum? Wondering if I know him.'

'Uh, Cormac something. Can't remember. Everyone called him Cormac.'

'Cormac. Rings a bell. How long were you on Rum?'

'A year or so. Not that long.'

'You move about a fair bit, aye? Who's your dad again? I might know him.'

She hesitated.

'John,' she said, her voice brittle. 'Dad's called John Dobie.'

'John Dobie,' he muttered, ransacking his memory. 'No. Maybe not, after all. Shame. Have to meet him soon, eh? Share some of his stories. Might have been to some of the same places.'

'Aye. Maybe.'

'Anyway. Did you lassies want another yarn?'

'Is it about selkies?' I said.

'You not bored of selkies yet?'

'I'm all ears. Bring it on.'

'Then get comfy,' he grinned. 'This is a cracker.'

I grabbed a crate to sit on, hungry for another of the shennachie's stories. Ailsa took the old rubber tyre, and perched alongside me, drawing up her legs and hugging her knees.

On the other side of the circle, Izzy threw half a dozen logs onto his fire, sending sparks cascading into the sky. The wood settled as the heat took hold, blackening and licking green where the fire found salt. He began to speak.

CHAPTER 26

There was once an island woman. She was a fair and bonny lass, and she commanded the attention of all the island men. By the time she'd come of age, she could cook, and sew, and clean. She could manage a household. But more than anything else, she could dance. She loved to dance, and she brought every ceilidh to life with her passion and her grace.

Now, every man on the island wanted her for his own, and many came calling for her hand, from the squires to the swine-herds. But our bonnie lassie knew the choice was hers, and when the time came, she chose a young shepherd. He wasn't the richest man on the island, or the strongest. He wasn't the fairest, or the brightest. But he was the quickest on his feet. Of all the men on the island, he was the only one who could match her in a reel. At the island ceilidhs the bonnie lassie and the shepherd danced every dance there was, and jigged every jig. They reeled till morning, when the band were dead on their feet and everyone else had long since departed. For a courtship, they danced together on the hills, nothing for music but the rhythm of their breath and the drumming of their feet upon the heather. They were very happy together. They decided to be wed.

On the day they were married, there was a ceilidh the likes

of which was never seen again. Every person on the island was invited, from the lowest pauper to the richest laird, and every one of them showed up. Musicians came from miles around, and they lined the walls of the hall two deep. The fiddlers lifted every heart, and the pounding of bodrums fairly raised the roof. The dancing was the loudest, the fastest that had ever been known. The stamping of feet brought dust from the rafters and made the floor shake like a honeymoon bedhead.

But this racket didn't go unnoticed. Down on the shore, a selkie man heard the music. He was intrigued. He wanted some of the celebration for himself. Hiding his sealskin beneath the sand, he stole clothes from a washing line, and dressed himself for the ceilidh. Up at the hall, he found the dancing in full swing, with more than a hundred couples reeling and swinging and carousing. And there, at the centre of it all, was the bride. Glowing with joy, she danced the finest of them all, turning a fair mad jig with her new beau.

When he saw the bonnie lassie, the selkie knew rightaways that he would have her for his own. Nothing would stand in his way. And with that, the selkie started to dance. He matched the islanders step for step, feet flashing as he danced. He joined every reel. Like the lassie and the shepherd, he danced every dance, and he was soon into the thick of it. The selkie man was uncommon fair, and many a fine island girl tried to catch his eye, being unaware of his true nature, but he brushed them aside. He had eyes only for the bonnie bride.

Couple by couple and dance by dance, the islanders fell away exhausted, until only the shepherd, the bride and the selkie were left.

O, but how they danced. The three of them reeled and jigged

like pure mad things, growing flushed with motion, dancing blinder, madder, ever faster. The shepherd and the selkie spun that bonnie bride between them for hours, dancing every dance they knew, then dancing them again, then dancing new reels, ever faster and more frantic. The musicians struggled to keep up and fell away, one by one. But when the last fiddler and the last drummer collapsed and fell quiet, a fiendish music took up the rhythm, pounding out the beat, as though the hall itself had come to life with music. They danced until the sun came up, and only now did the young shepherd grow weary. He didn't know the stranger, but he sensed the danger. Flushed, his heart pounding, he begged his new wife to rest a while. But his new wife was gone and lost to the rhythm. Mad with music, she was in love with her own dancing. As they danced, she grew ever more aware of the handsome stranger who somehow matched her step for step.

Aghast that he might lose his new bride, the shepherd tried again to compete, renewing his pace, but he couldn't match the selkie man. He fought and fought to keep the rhythm, pushing himself harder and faster to match the reel, but the selkie man only grinned and increased his pace again, his feet no more than a blur on the battered floorboards. The bonnie bride now had eyes only for the stranger, and they danced together as though they were a single soul.

The poor young shepherd, well – in the heat of the dance, his heart gave out. Driven by his love for the lassie, he was cheated by the magic of the selkie. Overpowered by the exertion, he collapsed. Even as her poor young love lay dying beside her, the lassie danced on, transfixed by the handsome selkie and his devil's reel. The shepherd's last heartbeats hammered out a rhythm, and this dreadful beat was taken up by the ghostly music. At last, with the shepherd dead, the selkie had her for his own. With the wedding dance become a funeral dervish, the selkie reeled the bride down to the shore. As they danced, he stripped. His stolen clothes turned to rags and flapped and flew away, snagging themselves in trees, hanging from the branches like dead men. Collecting his precious sealskin from the sand, the selkie danced the bonnie lassie straight into the shallows, wrapped her in the fur, and carried her to the bottom of the ocean. Down there, in the darkness, he made good the marriage of the poor dead shepherd. Utterly bewitched, the bride gave birth to a clutch of selkie pups, each with their own little skin.

Given time and madness, the bonnie lassie lost her looks, and so the selkie man lost interest. He sent her back to the shore and there she was found, many a year since that ghastly wedding day. Shivering and senseless, she wandered the rockpools, clawing rags from clootie trees, calling for her long-dead shepherd love. And I tell you this: she never once stopped dancing. Bound over to the rhythm of the selkie's magic, she spent the rest of her miserable days dancing a gruesome jig. Barefoot and bloodied, her legs and feet twitched out of her control, jerking and flitting, tapping to a beat that no one else would ever hear.

CHAPTER 27

I woke to only a moderate headache. I felt a little woolly, certainly, but I'd had worse. It wasn't bad at all. Surprised and pleased with myself, I sat upright, and that was the moment the hangover descended, slopping through my brain like wet concrete. Someone was frying bacon. I stumbled into the bathroom and threw up in the sink. It was tinged pink from the schnapps. Bile ran ragged in my throat. Back in my room, I found some clothes. Any clothes. I dressed like a rag doll, and pulled a brush through my hair.

When I finally dragged myself into the lounge, Ailsa was kneeling on the floor, playing with the baby.

'Morning,' I croaked.

'Morning,' she said, cheerfully. She checked over her shoulder, back towards the kitchen and the smell of bacon. 'How's the hang-over?' she whispered at me.

'Foul. How's yours?'

'Oh, I'm fine. I told you. Nothing like a wee swim to clear the cobwebs.'

'Swimming? You went swimming?'

'Do you not remember?' she grinned at me, wide and clear.

I searched my memory, searched her face for clues. Glimmers emerged, hazy and unsure. Drinking schnapps on the headland.

Cackling like witches. The moon, reflected in the sea, rippled in a shifting jigsaw. Someone jumping into water, over and over again. Ailsa dived into the sea. Ailsa swam in Still Bay.

Startled at the thought, I stared at her. She blew a raspberry at the baby.

'Morning, Flo,' hollered Ronny from the kitchen. 'Want a bacon piece?'

Nausea rose in my throat again.

'Christ, no,' I said. 'I'm turning vegetarian.'

'That bad? You should have drunk some water.'

'Three glasses,' I said, holding up the fingers to match.

He whistled low in understanding. 'I see. Then there's nothing I can do for you but this.'

He stepped out with a glass of orange juice and paracetemol.

I retched over the chalky pills, but the juice was cold and sharp and refreshing. I started making sense of the day.

'OK. What's the plan, Teenwolf?'

'Breakfast first, then off to see Nana and Grandpa for lunch, then we're going on to Anders' place. We're going to drag his Danish arse back here and feed him up before he heads back to the rigs.'

'OK, that's a good plan. I can handle that plan. When are we leaving?'

Ronny took a bite of his sandwich. He checked his watch.

'Five minutes,' he said.

'Two minutes,' called Mum from the hallway.

'Two minutes, Flo,' grinned Ronny, and took another bite. Ketchup burst down his chin. My stomach lurched, and I bolted once more for the bathroom.

We said goodbye to Ailsa and drove off in a rattle of loose gravel. I turned to look out the rear window. As the car turned a corner and Grogport fell out of view, she was walking back along the road towards the rickety jetty.

'How does she get home?' asked Mum.

'I'm not sure,' I said. 'Either her dad comes across to get her, or she'll have left the rib on our side.'

'Fancy that fuss every time you want to pop round and see your neighbours.'

'Can't be easy,' I agreed.

'Still,' said Mum, 'she seems a nice girl. I like her.'

'Yeah, me too.'

'I'm glad you've made a friend.'

In the back seat, I rolled my eyes.

'And it must be hard on her, too. Having no mother. It's not easy for teenage girls.'

'Really? Is that right? Is it hard for teenage girls?'

'Wheesht your cheek, Flora. Remember you've got us.'

'Well, she's got her dad,' I protested.

'I haven't met him yet,' said Ronny.

'No one has,' said Mum. 'He seems to do fine by himself.'

'We should have him over. Ask them both for tea.'

'Aye, I was thinking that too.'

Ronny was a good driver, but the roads were bumpy, rough and bendy, and they did nothing for my hangover. I hunkered down into the car seat. While my folks argued recipes and dates, I spent the rest of the journey trying very hard not to lose my stomach.

My grandparents lived in a bungalow in Tighna, set back from the main road. The decor was about as twee as it comes. Flowery wallpaper, china birds, china dogs. The cup of tea my Nana made me was the best thing that had happened all day. The heat and sugar put some life back in my belly. Ronny talked snooker with Grandpa, and Mum nursed Jamie in the spare room.

'And how about you, Flo?' asked Nana. 'How are you getting on at school?'

'Pretty good,' I said, then wondered if I meant it. 'Well, History is interesting at the moment.'

'What are you working on?'

'We're doing a big project about myths and legends. I'm researching selkies, where they come from, things like that.'

Across the room, there was a startled, harrumphing noise from my grandfather. He struggled to lean forward.

'Selkies,' he said. 'My god, Flora, it's a while since I heard talk of selkies.'

'You know some selkie stories, Grandpa?' I asked, bemused to see the old man so energised.

'Stories that'd curl your toes,' he said, confiding in a conspiratorial whisper.

'Wheesht your noise, Jim,' said my grandmother, 'you daft old fart.'

'But the lassie said,' he protested.

'She doesn't want any of your nonsense,' said Nana, firmly, and that was the end of that.

'Ach, off with you,' he grumbled, settling back into the depths of his chair. I kept watch on him for a minute longer, but he didn't say anything else, his overgrown brows knitted together in concentration, his lips moving with a silent memory.

After a lunch of trout and shrimp and new potatoes, I stacked dishes in the kitchen and started on the washing up. The water ran dark with peat and white with suds, steam filming on my face. The heat stung, tingling my fingers. There was a noise behind me.

'Pst!'

My grandfather grizzled from the gap in the doorway.

'Grandpa?'

'Shhh,' he hissed, 'come on.'

'I'm doing the dishes.'

'Bugger the dishes. You want to know about selkies, I'll tell you about selkies.'

I dropped a mug back into the foam, and rubbed my hands dry on my jeans. I followed him out the back of the house. With exaggerated, nervous secrecy, he opened the door and ushered me into the crisp autumn sun. I followed him, creeping round the bungalow, then down onto the road. He scurried ahead of me, peering round corners, and didn't relax until we were out of sight.

'That was close,' he said.

'What?'

'Never mind that,' he said. 'Now, what was it you wanted to tell me?'

'Grandpa, it was you that brought me out here.'

'I did?'

'Aye. You were going to tell me about selkies.'

'Aye, I know that.'

'Um. OK then.'

'Right, listen, lass. Here's the truth. I knew a selkie.'

I was half-amused. Grandpa's stories were always worth a listen.

'Is that right, Grandpa?'

'It's true. It was right here on the island. Lord help me, but it was the days before I was married to your Nana. She was a fine looking woman, your Nan—' he started.

'Grandpa,' I interrupted, not wanting another rambling story about my grandparents, 'the selkies. You said you knew a selkie.'

His face clouded, then cleared.

'Someone told you about that? They shouldn't of, but I don't mind. The selkie,' he mused. 'Aye, the selkie.'

The conversation was frustrating. I started thinking about steering him back to the bungalow before he got cold. The distraction must have shown on my face, because he caught my arm fast.

'That selkie,' he said, 'saved my life.'

I studied his face. His eyes were more lucid than I'd seen in months, as though a mist had lifted from them.

'I was fishing. I was fourteen, and I was fishing in the Sound.'

Memories passed across his face.

'I was having a terrible day of it, and I stayed out late, setting more lines to try and get a bite. I remember it was uncommon cold. I should have been checking the skies, but I was fourteen and fearless, and stupid, and I was angry. I cursed the sea and the fish and my own bad luck.'

I imagined the boy in his boat, the trailing lines.

'If I'd been watching the skies, I'd have seen the squall. It blew in out of nowhere, coming right across Bancree. By the time I felt the rain, it was too late. I turned and it was on me. The sea blew up something vicious. In a flash, I cut my lines and turned for Tighna, but the seas were rougher than I'd ever seen. I started rowing, but there was no use trying to fight those waves.'

He laid his hand on my arm again. 'I fished the Sound for fifty years,' he said, 'and I've seen worse seas than that. But not often, lass.'

I watched his face as he told the story, talking more to himself, now, than me. I could see him as a boy. I could see the fright in his face.

'I wrestled the boat for God knows how long, turning her to windward, and then it was no good. I was exhausted, and the sea knew it. The boat turned side on and tipped over. I was wearing my boots, my jumper. I was sinking. I could see the boat as a shadow above me, dark against the sky. I was done for, lass. I was done for and I knew it.'

I could barely breathe. 'So what happened?'

'The selkie. I was sinking deep, and she came for me. There was a seal swimming round me, even as I was sinking. It came up close, and it was smiling. Then it was sort of a seal and a woman at the same time. And then it was just a woman. She was in the nip, if you'll forgive me, and she was treading water right beside me. She lifted me up, dragged me to the shore, brought me up on the beach at Rachinch.'

'What was she like?'

'Oh, she was bonny. She was the fairest thing I ever saw. And that includes your Nana. She had dark hair and dark eyes, lovely eyes. She brought me up onto the shore, and she kept me warm the best way she knew how.' He gave me a filthy wink.

'You were fourteen!'

'Damn right. And I'd do it all again, too.'

'Where did she go?'

At this, his face dimmed a little.

'I knew the stories. I knew that I only needed her skin, and she'd be mine for ever. She offered it to me, Flora,' he said, and again he looked directly into my eyes. 'She offered me her skin, held it out to me, like this, in both hands, and asked me to take it. And I thought about it. By God, I thought about it. But there was something there that held me back. I didn't see myself fit to be a selkie's man. She scared me. I could sense the love in her. It was bigger than a sea. It was too much. Damn near broke my heart, but I said no. Besides, there was a lass at home I was fond of . . .'

Grandpa was retreating into himself again.

'. . . so I said no.'

'I hope the lass in Tighna was worth it,' I said, gently.

'Ask her yourself. It was your Nana, even then.'

'Even then?'

'Always,' he said, softly.

'Does she know?'

'About the selkie? Your Nana? Jesus Christ, no. The last thing a fisherman's wife wants to hear is that her man has canoodled with a selkie.'

I leaned against the pebbledashed wall, soaking in the story. The day was bright and cold.

'So did you see her again?'

Grandpa weighed it up. 'In truth, I don't know. I never saw her as a woman, that's for sure. But I've always seen plenty of seals, when I've been out in the boat. More than most. Especially when I've been out alone, just me and the boat. As a seal, well. I think she was there every time I set to sea.'

'That's sad. But sweet, too.'

'What is?' he said.

There was a pained, deliberate mischief in his eyes. The clouds were back. It occurred to me that his eyes had been like that all my life, and I'd simply never noticed.

'Well, the whole story. It's romantic.'

'Story? I could tell you a story or two.'

I studied him. He'd been so lucid when talking about the selkie, and now he was back to himself again. His cloudy eyes met mine. Then he looked up.

'Why are we outside?' he said, baffled. He checked his watch. 'We're missing the snooker.'

'All right then, Grandpa. Let's get you home.'

He waggled a finger in my face. 'Not likely, little miss. Oh no. You'll never get me in a home.'

'Of course not, Grandpa,' I said, and steered him back into the bungalow. Starlings chattered on the roof.

CHAPTER 28

We drove to Anders' house in a stuffed, contented silence. Baby Jamie passed out pretty much as soon as he saw the car, and the lurching island curves never woke him up. I sat in the back, looking out the window, with Mum and Ronny up front.

Grandpa's story stuck with me. His lucid bursts were few, these days, but he still remembered much of his youth, and when it came to the sea, he knew exactly what he was talking about. But he was distant, and easily fuddled. I didn't quite know what to make of his selkie tale. I didn't believe it, of course, but I'd write it up for my report. He would have heard it when he was a boy. Time had transformed the myth into a memory. It was the first story I'd heard in which a selkie had been a kind creature. Even then, Grandpa had spoken of her with sadness and strangeness. She'd been too different, too deep, and that depth had scared him. He'd been frightened by the abyss of her love. She'd asked him to step inside, and he'd been too scared.

Even Izzy's campfire stories were cautionary tales. The selkie was a foreign thing. It wasn't human and it wasn't for humans. It was dangerous. A selkie was too powerful, too strong. Selkies were everything about living on the islands, and dying out at sea. All the stories, good or bad, were about the loneliness or greed of crofters and fisherwives. Selkies tempted them with escape or reward, but punished their greed with heartbreak or death. They offered themselves, offered anything for the warmth of human love. Little wonder that all young men craved a selkie for their own. Once you had a selkie's skin, she was bound for ever to your will. But every time, they turned young men into sad, old, broken men.

The stories were warnings.

Want what you have, I thought. Live humbly. Accept your lot. Because if you can catch a selkie, or if she catches you – if you get what you think you want – you'll regret it. You'll be punished. Selkies taught you to take the safe option, and not to look beyond your horizon.

I simmered in the back seat. Richard had been the safe option. I was done with safe options.

A dark thought crept at me from the corners. I was an islander. I came from the islands, and I wasn't satisfied at all. I wanted to leave the island. They were only stupid old stories, designed to frighten superstitious people, but I was suddenly conscious of how close it struck home.

Why, alone of the entire class, had I chosen selkies for my project?

Looking out the window, trees were skeletons that flickered past the car. The drive north was no distance at all, only a couple of miles, but it seemed so much further than the drive from home.

We pulled up at Anders' place.

It was a monstrous old manse, built squat and square at the top of a field, now surrounded by a dying pine plantation. Patches of dark-grey render had long since fallen from the stone walls, and the north end was carpeted in moss. Virginia Creeper ran rampant from floor to chimney, and the garden was full of weeds the size of triffids. It had stood empty for years before Anders bought it, long since abandoned by the church. He'd moved in at once, and done as little as possible to make it habitable. He lived in a neat annex of rooms on the ground floor, joining the kitchen, bathroom and a makeshift bedroom into a serviceable flat. The rest of the building was given over to wildlife. Swallows, swifts and bats roosted in the attic, but Anders never cared. A hedgehog hibernated in his coal shed. He'd named it Thor.

'There is room for us all,' he said, patting the solid walls. 'Nature is always welcome to my home.'

I smiled to think of him.

The massive front door hung ajar, as usual. Ronny put his shoulder to it, and pushed it open on protesting, squealing hinges. He led the way inside, and I followed.

'Ho, you daft bastard! Where are you?'

Ronny turned from the vast hallway into the front room where Anders kept his bed. I hadn't been to the house in ages, and went to explore the empty side. The drawing room creaked underfoot, cold and mildewed. The light was dark green, shadowed by the creeper that thronged the windows. From inside looking out, I could see the undersides of tiny suckers gripping to the glass.

Ronny called for Anders on the other side of the building, and I moved into one of the back rooms. This room was dusty, with a thin carpet of long-dead leaves crunching underfoot. Through the window, the pines seemed to have grown closer to the house, ready to reach out and touch.

The next door brought me back into the hallway, and I took the sagging stairs, testing each with my weight before stepping up. The landing was gloomy. I couldn't identify a buzz in the dark until my eyes adjusted, and then I saw a wasp, tiny in the huge space. It swayed in woozy lines near the coving, seeking a place to nest for winter. On the ground floor, I could hear Ronny talking indistinctly.

There was a rustle in one of the bedrooms.

I swivelled to look. At one end of the corridor, a shadow passed across the daylight spilling beneath a door. It was one of the rooms above Anders' living quarters. Suddenly cautious, I crept along the hallway, fingers tracing the bumpy wallpaper. The window at the far end was blown out where the creeper had invaded, clinging to the walls and ceiling, tendrils reaching deep into the house. Once again, the shadow fluttered beneath the door, and I slowed to a crawl as I approached. A floorboard moaned underfoot, and I froze. Whoever was behind the door went still, then, and the rustling stopped. The band of daylight was clear, but the corridor felt dark as pitch by contrast. The creeper shifted in draughts I couldn't feel. I gripped the doorknob, tensed, and burst into the room.

A black shape exploded at my face, flailing and beating at my shoulders, and I shrieked, throwing up my arms to shield my head. My hands made contact with something sharp, and then with something feathery, and in a rush I dropped to the floor and cowered. I looked up. The crow flapped and banged into one wall, and banged again, then scrabbled to the window. With my heart hammering, I rocked back to lean against the doorframe. The crow hopped to the window and dropped away from the ledge. I was alone in the room, chest heaving, pulse racing. Creepers gaggled at the empty frame. The crow had scored patterns in the dust, half moons and broken lines.

I didn't know if it was from the beak or talons, but somehow the back of my hand was bleeding.

'Is that Anders?' called Ronny, his voice sharp.

'No, just me. I found a crow. Scared the crap out of me.'

'Have a look, will you? Check the rooms down there.'

'What's up?'

'Don't argue, Flora, just do it. I'll check this side.'

I blinked. I couldn't remember the last time Ronny had ordered me to do anything. I opened each of the doors in the corridor. The bedrooms were empty, paper peeling, floorboards carped. In the unused upstairs bathroom, the tub was full of whatever dark fluids tracked through the ceiling, and a small frog blinked from the oily water.

'Anything over there, Flo?'

'No. Nothing.'

'Shit. Shit.'

Ronny clattered down the stairs again. Suddenly cold with apprehension, I followed. The wasp had left the landing.

On the ground floor, Ronny was dialling a number into Anders' old phone.

Mum stood by the door, her face etched with concern. Jamie was still fast asleep, nestled against her chest.

'Hello? Hello? Is DC Duncan there? No, I'll wait. It's Ronald McLoughlin from Bancree. He knows me. Thanks.'

Ronny was turned away, leaning against the doorframe. I walked past him and looked into Anders' living room. It was in total disarray. Every single thing was smashed. His sofa had been overturned and leaned against the wall. A wooden chair lay in splinters on his futon. Books were tumbled everywhere, and the shelves had been pulled down across the little table. The television lay on its front, the broken screen spreading in crumbs across the floor, and Anders' few pictures hung crooked on the walls. Something that could only be blood spattered on one wall, and a pool of it had crusted brown on the threadbare carpet. I looked up at Mum, but she was looking at Ronny.

A voice garbled on the other end of the line, and he stood up straight.

'Hello there, Tom. No, not great. Not good at all, to be honest. It's Anders,' he said, and held up a hand to pinch the bridge of his nose. 'I think that Anders Tommasson has gone missing.'

There was a pause, then the phone garbled again.

'Since Wednesday, perhaps. He's not answered his phone for a wee while. I'm in his place now, and it's been turned upside-down. It's a shambles. Looks like there's been a massive fight, and he's not anywhere to be seen.'

A porcelain lamp lay in fragments on the floor, though the lightbulb remained stupidly intact.

'I don't know. You'd have to call the rigs. I don't have a number for anyone there. But you need to come across and have a look. There's blood. No, it's definitely blood.'

Ronny twisted to look at Mum.

'Me, and Cath, and the baby, and Flora. Should we wait for you? No, all right. You know to call me if I can help at all. Bye, Tom.'

He looked at the phone for a moment, as though it might ring and tell him this was all a great mistake, then carefully returned it to the plastic cradle. I realised he'd been holding the phone with a dishcloth. Fingerprints.

There was a stupid pause, the three of us stood dumbstruck. Outside, wind shivered in the plantation. A bluebottle hummed madly at the window.

'What's going on, love?' said Mum.

'I don't know. I don't know. That was Tom Duncan from the constabulary. He's in charge of Dougie's case.'

'This can't be a real thing,' I said.

'How real does it need to get, Flo?' said Ronny, gesturing at the devastation in the room.

'We only saw him a few days ago.'

'Aye, but he didn't meet us in Tighna. And then he never showed in Tanno for the football. He's not been round. He's not answered his phone.'

'He'll be drinking,' said Mum, uncertainly. 'Somewhere.'

'Of course he is,' I faltered. 'He has to be. He's Uncle Anders.'

The words hung in the air, empty and pointless.

'This is happening, Cath,' said Ronny. 'It's really happening.'

'Love,' she said, gently, 'we don't know—'

'We know!' he yelled, and slammed his hand into the wall.

Jamie started from his snooze. His face crumpled in slow outrage at being woken, and he waggled his little fists in fury. Mum was looking at the wall.

'I'm sorry to shout, love,' said Ronny, quietly. 'It's just – well. Not Anders, too. It's too much. First Bill, then Dougie, and now Anders. All within half a year. That's not just accidents. Something's going on.'

I'd never seen my stepfather look so lost. Mum crossed the room to stand with Ronny. Jamie was still griping, but she put her free arm around her husband's shoulders. I left them to talk. I walked out to the car and tried not to look up at the manse, because now it felt like all the windows were looking back.

We drove home in numb silence.

There was a full glass of peaty water leftover by my bed. I drank it so fast it slopped over my chin, spilling on my chest, and a lump rose in my throat. It hurt to swallow. I wiped my face with the back of my sleeve. Outside, in the sea, not quite Bancree, and not quite anywhere else, sat the islet of Dog Rock. The wind pounced on wood smoke from the crooked cottage chimney, and tugged it away in wild bursts.

Uncle Anders, the one man army.

MISSING

It wasn't possible. He'd be in a bar somewhere, playing cards, or singing songs and telling tall tales and complaining about the beer . . . Except he'd missed the football. And his house had been smashed up. As though there'd been a fight. Traces of blood. Uncle Anders.

I turned from the window. On the desk, all my selkie research sat beside my laptop in a ruffled stack of books and paper. The Mutch book sat on top. The cover stared at me. I picked it up, balancing the spine, and let the book fall open at random. It turned to the full-page illustration of the evil selkie woman. The sealskin dropped from her hips. Her back was too thin, the spine angled, the ribs askew and waist too narrow. Lip curled, she stared back at me, full of spite and hate.

I did it, she hissed.

It was me, and I'm glad.

Slowly, carefully, I put the book down, cover flat to the desk. I tried to read a detective paperback, but couldn't shake my mood. All I could see was the map of the islands on John Dobie's bedroom wall. A red pin stuck into the northern coast of Bancree. Uncle Anders, our Anders. The sky seemed so much lower. The sea seemed so much deeper, so much darker. I chucked the book onto the floor and tried to sleep. When I dreamed, it was the selkie again. Mad things struggled in her furs. The coat wrapped itself to her, clinging and binding. No matter how I tossed and turned, the shapes were always sliding. Nothing stayed the same. As a backdrop to my dream, vast dark eyes filled the sky.

CHAPTER 29

By the time I was up for school, Mum was ironing her way through a week's-worth of work shirts. Jamie sat between her ankles, baffled by the lurid plastic blocks he held in either hand.

'Where's Ronny?' I said.

'He's gone back to Anders' house,' she replied. 'The police think he might be able to help because he knows the place. He's not good, Flo. He's really upset.'

'Anders will be fine,' I said, and started tying my shoelaces. 'He'll be passed out in a bar, somewhere on the mainland. All that mess will be him fighting his own shadow.'

She frowned, and turned back to her ironing.

'I don't know, pet.'

'Come on, it'll be fine. Remember the time he tried to make a goulash, and he was so drunk he thought mice were heckling him, and he turned his kitchen upside down trying to catch them? That's all that's happened here.'

'I hope so. I'm trying to be strong,' she said. 'I'm trying really hard. He's not officially missing for another day. But Ronny's right. That's three people gone in six months. It doesn't look at all good to me.'

'How about the time they walked naked back from Tighna?' I

said, forcing the grin. 'Or when Ronny called from Inverness after midnight, saying he might be a bit late for tea, and you could hear Anders in the background, singing the Danish national anthem at the top of his voice?'

Mum managed a thin smile. 'Aye. I remember.'

'It'll be something like that. Just wait and see.'

She nodded, and nodded again – too much. She'd ironed the same shirt twice without realising. There was nothing I could say.

Oh, Anders. Where have you gone?

'He'll be back, Mum. He has to be.'

She hung the shirt on the back of the door, and leaned on the ironing board. 'Won't you be late for school?'

'Double History before lunch and double Spanish after, Mum,' I said. 'I'm still working on this selkie project.'

'How's it going?'

'Good. It's good. The selkies are really mysterious, and I enjoy . . . discovering. I like finding out old things and putting them together.'

'In that case, you could excavate the freezer.'

'Not likely. I haven't time to defrost a thousand years of ancient foodstuffs.'

'No,' she said, glumly, 'I suppose not. Never mind.'

'Better go, Mum.'

I kneeled to kiss goodbye to Jamie. He clattered the plastic bricks together. Astonished by the noise they made, he looked up at me for answers.

'Sorry, kid,' I murmured. 'I don't know either.'

I patted him on the head, then grabbed my bag and waited for the bus.

First thing at school, I went up the library and ransacked the net for any mention of Anders. It was a fairly common name in a couple of Scandinavian countries, and I couldn't isolate him. I managed to find him in a roughneck's blog from a few years ago, but that was all about an arm-wrestling tournament. Which Anders had won, I noted with a grin. But that was everything. His disappearance hadn't been announced yet. I sat at my desk for a full half-hour, watching gulls skid past the windows and not crying. The school bell shattered my vigil, and the bustle of changing classes pushed me back to work.

When I finally checked my emails, there were a few bland lines from Richard, talking about his life in Bristol. He'd swapped Philosophy for Art History. It was much more him, babe. He'd started working in a nightclub. Everything was wild. I felt a pang at what my life would look like, if I was in Bristol, then deleted it without a second reading.

The next message was more surprising. A week after I'd sent my query, there was a reply from Broch Books. Or, rather, from the former proprietor of Broch Books, a man called Kenny Lawrence. His email explained that the company had foundered several years ago. And Marcus Mutch, he said, was a reason they'd gone under.

Broch was a tiny press. It made its money in walking guides, and the odd collection of island trivia for the tourists. Marcus had suggested a collection of folk myths, and Kenny had agreed. It seemed just his sort of thing. Over a bottle of whisky, Mutch had talked him into a swingeing advance and a binding contract. He'd promptly disappeared for six months, funded from afar by his increasingly worried publisher. He returned with the selkie manuscript. Horrified, Kenny had tried his best to edit the material into something palatable, but the gruesome pictures limited what he could do. There was no more money, and Mutch refused to change a word, claiming it was all true. Kenny realised he was dealing with a lunatic. In the end, he decided to take a chance on the original manuscript. Seeking at least some small return, he gambled on printing a few dozen copies, and he lost. No one wanted the book, and Mutch was brutalised in both rumour and review. Never much liked, he was now openly ridiculed by his Kirkwall neighbours. Kenny set lawyers on the writer, trying to recover his money, but Mutch fled the island in a fury and Broch Books was bound for bust. The final publication had been a collection of Kenny's own poetry. There were still one or two copies available, said the email, if I ever wanted to read them. All I had to do was send a cheque . . .

I could have perhaps guessed a lot of the story, and it told me nothing about why Mutch hated selkies. But I'd learned two important things. I knew his name, and I knew that he believed in his own ideas.

Marcus Mutch.

I searched for the author online. After refining the search to strip out all the usual junk, I was surprised to discover a few positive hits. *The Truth About the Scottish Selkie* was published in 1992, and Mutch abandoned Kirkwall the following year. In 1996, he was listed as an artist residing in the community in Findhorn, and then his name appeared as part of a writing conference on Lewis in 1998. Two years later, he was listed as part of a green wood workshop in Castlebay, on Barra. All these pages were historic. Mutch was never more than a name on a list. There was no solid information about him, no photographs, and nothing current. The most recent entry came from 2003, when a newsletter announced that he'd joined a crofting co-op outside Tobermory. After that, he disappeared.

Dead ends. All it told me was that he'd moved around the islands.
I sketched the path in my notepad, joining the dots with a biro.

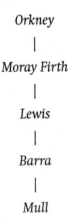

Orkney

|

Moray Firth

|

Lewis

|

Barra

|

Mull

He'd been all over the place.

I tapped my biro on my notepad, but couldn't make any more
sense of it. I spent half an hour tracking down contacts for the different locations, and sent them the same generic message, asking if
they could tell me anything about Marcus Mutch. The green wood
workshop and the writer's conference pinged back immediately
with defunct email addresses. No dice with those two. I kept my
fingers crossed for Findhorn and Tobermory.

The other books I'd ordered had arrived, and I sat with them
for much of the day, making notes on any variations to the selkie
stories, and reading up on Viking shapeshifters. I noticed how
selkie myths only really existed within Viking lands. I was fascinated to think of the codes by which they lived, and those same
stories, filtering through time, diverging and evolving as they travelled. I thought of the pink stones in the corrie. Even as they were
reclaimed by lichen, the stories lived on.

Regardless of how much I discovered about selkies, I kept

returning to Mutch's book. I drowned myself in the dark magic of it. No matter how poisonous his writing, I loved the idea that he truly believed his stories. And even though his work was hateful and unpleasant, I preferred it to the bland, historical accounts of the myths, because it held a cord of magic with both hands and never ever let it go.

I returned the borrowed books to the librarian and drifted out of school. Tanno was dreich. Bursts of rain slanted through the drizzle, and the pavements were slippery with water. I had a toastie and a cup of tea in Dora's Diner. Across the empty café, Jow sat at a formica table. Frowning deep in concentration, he studied the Page 3 girl in his paper. She leaned forward, spilling pink, spilling white, her smile bright and wide and open. She was nothing at all like me.

My phone pipped. It was a text from Ailsa.

Hey Flo. You said you like seals? You should get to Dog Rock soon as.

Out of practice, I thumbed a clumsy reply.

If it's just one or two, don't worry about it. Seen loads.

The reply was swift:

It's not one or two. Trust me. Come home.

Intrigued, I weighed up an afternoon of Spanish irregular verbs. It was no competition.

I'm on my way.

CHAPTER 30

She was waiting on the beach when I arrived into Grogport. I waded through the dune grass, the blades snagging on my clothes. Finches scattered through the thickets. Ailsa smiled and clapped her hands together when she saw me, and hauled the dinghy towards the surf.

'Come on,' she said, 'hurry up!'

'What's the rush?' I asked, fumbling with my laces.

'It's a surprise. Trust me, you'll like it. Come on, hop in.'

I rolled up my jeans and helped her push the boat out. The sand was damp, though the rain had stopped, and the water was shockingly cold. We cast off with me in the prow and Ailsa at the tiller. She fired the little motor into life and, rather than heading for Dog Rock, instead guided the inflatable between the headland and the islet, towards open sea.

'Where are we going?' I yelled. Dog Rock slid by one side of the dinghy, and a net of salt spray misted across us.

She grinned, shook her head, and simply pointed ahead. I turned and looked again, intrigued, seeing nothing before us but the Atlantic. Zipping across the water, we moved out of the bay and into the ocean. Almost at once, the breeze picked up. It was easy to forget how Dog Rock and the twin headlands sheltered Still Bay from the Atlantic. I hunkered deeper into the boat, wishing the dinghy's inflatable walls would dull the wind.

Still smiling, Ailsa looked straight ahead, her hair tugged and thrashed in the breeze. She gave me a thumbs-up. I studied the sea. Like single stars in a vast constellation, orange buoys staked out sporadic lobster pots. The Atlantic rolled for ever. After ten or twelve minutes, Ailsa cut the motor and we glided, carried by momentum. We were about two miles from Bancree. Waves began at once to lift and slop beneath the dinghy. Without the engine, the sounds of the open ocean were devastating. The slosh of water underneath our boat, and the sometime mewling gulls, and the deep, sad, lowing of the sea.

I waited. Ailsa beamed.

'OK, so what is it?' I demanded.

'Shush,' she said, and put a finger to her lips. 'Look.'

I turned and looked again. Ocean. Sky. Ocean and sky. I couldn't work out what I was supposed to be seeing. Ocean and sky and ocean. Then something else, something in the corner of my eye, disappearing. I whirled and looked, but there was nothing there. Then there was something on the other side, again at the fringes of my vision. I turned in time to see something dark sink beneath the surface, a ghost trail of ripples washed away at once. I waited. I watched. Then the seal emerged straight in front of me, almost within arm's reach. Its snub head hung in the water, buoyant on the waves, openly quizzical and looking right into my eyes.

I'd seen seals all my life. Growing up in Grogport, there were always single seals lounging in the bay. I'd seen them basking on the foreshore, playing, and hunting. But I'd never seen one so brazen and close. After half a minute, it simply sunk beneath the surface, straight down. I was close enough to see its nostrils flare and close before it submerged.

'That was incredible,' I breathed, scanning the waves, willing it to come back.

'Isn't it?' said Ailsa. She'd moved a little closer up the boat, the better to see the seal. 'Try the other side.'

I turned round and gasped in astonishment. There were at least a dozen seals watching us. The nearest was within touching distance. They were right there, right there beside the boat. They regarded us with open, sardonic curiosity.

'I've never . . .' I said, and ran out of words.

'I know. It's something else, isn't it?'

Even as we spoke, more seals were appearing, and others sinking down or turning tail, water slicking from their mottled skins. There must have been two dozen overall. They were constantly changing position, swimming towards us or away. As we sat in the boat, bobbing and tossed on the hefting waves, they took turns to study us. The seals came close, and closer, watching us side on, as curious about us as we were them. They came close enough that I saw the bloodshot crazing in their dark, dog-like eyes – the beads of water clinging to their whiskers.

'There are so many. They're amazing,' I said, entranced.

'They are, aye.'

'I've never seen a rookery this size.'

'Or so bold,' grinned Ailsa.

In front of us, a seal yawned wide. As its head tilted up and the lips slipped back, its teeth were exposed, sharp and gnarled, yellowing to white, the roof of the mouth ridged in pink and black. A splosh and it was gone, leaving nothing but ripples lifted on the waves.

'How did you know they were out here?'

'Dad told me. He said they were worth seeing, so I called you.'

'I'm glad you did.'

We'd watched for twenty minutes, or maybe half an hour, when Ailsa looked behind us and tutted. Crouched low in the boat and entranced by the playful seals, neither of us had noticed the clouds gathering darker, or the wind picking up. The weather was turning quickly. I thought of my grandfather's story. The sky to seaward had condensed to deepest grey.

'It's getting a bit rough,' she said, lifting her voice against the wind. 'We should head back, grab a cup of tea.'

'Aye, I suppose so,' I said, reluctantly, drawing back to my seat in the bow of the boat.

As if by a mutual accord, the seals started to slink away, sinking and dropping with gentle splashes, leaving only slight eddies behind them, swirling briefly in the heaving sea. I glimpsed some of them swimming beneath us in those first moments underwater, but their camouflage was good, and their mottled fur hid them from my sight. In a moment, the entire rookery had gone, and there was nothing left but Ailsa and me and wave after wave after wave.

Ailsa fired the engine and turned the boat for home. As before, I sat in the bow, looking over her shoulder, hoping for last glimpses of the seals. Waves licked with shadows, and the sea blended grey into the racing sky. They could have been anywhere out there, and still invisible.

The disguise was perfect.

CHAPTER 31

We left the pontoon and walked to the house. Ailsa led the way, and I followed close behind. As we rounded the corner, her father was working on the far side of the house, loosening the soil with a iron mattock as long as he was tall. With two hands, he lofted it high, then bent his whole body into the downward movement, whipping the spike deep into the hard ground. Then he planted his feet and wrestled the bar, pushing and heaving to lever loose the soil. Once the mattock had broken free, he moved along a half step, raised it and plunged it down again. There was a careful, automaton power in his actions, and he'd already carved a channel from the sea halfway to Dog Cottage. It was clearly hard work. He'd taken his top off, despite the coolness of the day. I let myself study his body. The muscles in his back were tight and defined without being bulky. He was hardened by age, so different to Richard. Again, though, there was that odd quality about him, a base sensuality that didn't make much sense. Curiosity made me want to reach out. I had an urge to touch his back. I wanted to touch him, to lay my palm flat on his back, like a ghost, and for him to never know I'd done it. The thought made me shiver.

He didn't notice until we'd stopped beside him. He was halfway through lifting the iron bar when he turned towards us. Muscles stood out on his body like ropes. Lowering the mattock, he grabbed his shirt and pulled it over his head.

'Hey, Dad,' said Ailsa. 'How's it going?'

He looked back along the channel he'd carved out. 'Aye, all right. Ground's hard, but I'm getting through it.'

'We went to see the rookery.'

John's eyes flashed.

'Did you, now.'

'They were great,' I said, 'amazing. Great.'

I was gabbling, but he ignored me.

'Shouldn't have gone out that far, Ailsa.'

'It was fine, Dad. Don't worry about it.'

'It's a father's job to worry. I didn't even know you were out there. What if you'd capsized?'

'We didn't, though.'

'Or if you'd got lost?'

Ailsa rolled her eyes.

'Flora's just come to hang out for a bit. Is that OK?'

He grunted and turned his gaze to me. I crumbled, but forced myself to meet his stare. His dark eyes studied me, and once again I felt the strangeness, the déjà vu. His gaze exerted its own gravity, drawing me closer.

'Can't do much harm,' he said.

Ailsa led me through the house into the kitchen. Through the window, I watched John at his labour. His motion, lean and muscled . . .

'Just milk, wasn't it, Flo?'

'Please,' I said, clearing my throat.

Ailsa busied herself with the cups and kettle. Again I glanced slyly through the window. The rhythm of his task was hypnotic.

The spike lifted and plunged, lifted and plunged. He was a golem. I remembered the bathtub. The sensation of a hand stroking at my thigh. It had been loving. Not forceful. It didn't fit with John, for all that those eyes watched me.

I jolted to feel Ailsa standing at my shoulder. I turned, too quickly, and snatched the cup from her, slopping hot tea on both our fingers.

'Shit, sorry.'

'Nae bother.'

She crossed the kitchen and knocked on the window. She gestured to John's mug, and laid it on the windowsill. He nodded, let the mattock fall flat with a thump, and moved towards the house. I raced Ailsa out of the kitchen, heading for the safety of her room before he came inside. I stood in her doorway, waiting, already calmer for having a flight of stairs between me and John. What a numpty.

'Oh, by the way,' she said, and pointed to a red skirt hanging on the cupboard door. 'This doesn't fit. Do you want it?'

I held the skirt against my hips. It looked good.

'I dunno,' I said, 'you already gave me that jumper.'

'And you gave me a top last week. Come on, it's no good for me. If you don't want it, I'm giving it to charity. Try it on.'

I hesitated.

'Use my dad's room,' she said. 'It'll be fine.'

John's room was cool and grey. The stacks of paper seemed less well defined than before. They'd collapsed and merged into each other, and in places the floor was thronged deep with reports and newspapers. I stepped out of my jeans and wriggled into the red skirt. I zipped it up and peered down to check the cut. It was a knee-length pencil skirt, and it fit me perfectly. It actually gave some shape to my hips. The colour looked great, too, though I didn't know when I'd ever wear it. As I scanned the room for a mirror, my attention was drawn to John's gigantic map. I studied it anew. It was remarkable how the steadily yellowing papers showed the age of the disappearance. His investigation was marked in time, as well as place, the more the clues deteriorated. The direction was unmistakable. Something caught my eye, and I puzzled at the name. Findhorn. Findhorn wasn't an island, but on the Moray coast, part of the Scottish mainland. Where had I seen it recently?

The answer lurched at me.

Marcus Mutch had lived in Findhorn.

He left Kirkwall in 1993. My head snapped to Orkney on the map. Some of the first disappearances happened near Stromness. Then Findhorn. Then Durness. Gairloch. Lewis. Skye. Barra. Mull. Tiree. Jura. Islay.

John's map had far more locations than I'd found for Mutch, but the two traced the same route through the islands. The pattern was unmistakable.

'Flora? You all right in there?'

I realised I was shaking. Ailsa knocked and stuck her head around the door.

'Hey, that looks great.'

'Stay here,' I said, and grabbed my bag from her room. Wordlessly, I showed her my rough sketch of Mutch's movements. She looked baffled. Then I handed her the selkie book. Her frown deepened as she leafed through, pausing to read tidbits.

'Selkies aren't supposed to be like this.'

'Never mind that. Look,' I said. 'I found traces of the author here, and here, and all the way round. The pattern is identical. And some of the dates are the same, too.'

She puzzled, checking the map against my notes.

'That's crazy,' she said.

'Do you think it's just coincidence?'

'Don't know. I suppose it could be.'

'Should we tell your dad?'

She bit her lip.

'Ailsa?'

'I think . . . no. Not for now.'

'Wouldn't he want to know?'

'He would,' she grimaced. 'It's just . . .'

'What?'

'We've only just got here, Flo. I've half a chance at a normal life for a while. You don't know what that means to me. If Dad gets a sniff at something like this,' she said, tapping the book, 'he'll turn the island upside-down.'

'Isn't that what he wants? It's why he came here.'

She looked at me, then, caught between misery and anger.

'It's not why I've come here,' she said, her voice fierce. 'It's not what I want.'

I softened my voice.

'There's something else, something new. We don't know for certain, but my Uncle Anders might have gone missing, too.'

'What? When?'

'Last week some time. He was supposed to meet Ronny on Friday. We went to his place yesterday. It'd been ransacked, we think, and we can't find him.'

'Do the police know?'

'Ronny called them, aye. He's helping them search. It's not been in the papers yet.'

I tapped the northern coast of Bancree. The road to Anders'

house was clear to see. There was the plantation, too, and the rocky coastline, and the ruined townsteads, and a string of lochans, too small for names of their own. It was a tiny area, really, but with endless places to be lost or hidden.

'I just want this to be over,' said Ailsa. 'I just want him to stop.'

There was a muffled bleeping noise. We looked at each other.

'That your phone?'

'Crap, it is,' I said, and ransacked my bag to find it. After a moment of juggling, I managed to answer.

'Hello?'

'Flo?'

'Mum, is that you? What's going on?'

'I've been trying to call you for an hour, love,' she said. 'It's really annoying, but we're stuck in Tanno. The weather in the Sound has blown right up. Jow won't run the ferry.'

'Oh, no. What will you do?'

'Me and Ronny will grab a B&B. I'm more worried about your brother.'

'Jamie? Is he not still with Nana?'

'Aye, he is, but she's got enough on with Grandpa. You'll have to look after him tonight, Flo.'

'Of course, Mum. But how will I get him from Tighna?'

'I've sorted that out. Nana's bringing him on the bus. That's why I've been trying to call you,' she said. 'They left half an hour ago. They'll be in Grogport any minute. Please tell me you're in the house.'

'I'm not, Mum,' I said, turning to look at Ailsa. 'I'm on Dog Rock.'

'You'll have to get back to Bancree. Your Nana can't be out in this weather with the baby.'

'I'll get back right now.'

'Good girl. Call me if there's any trouble.'

'Call you? Funny one.'

'Scram, go on. Love you.'

'Bye, Mum,' I said, but she'd already hung up.

'Everything all right?' asked Ailsa, concerned. 'Can I help?'

'The ferry's down again. It must be worse up there. I've got to go home. Nana's bringing Jamie down from Tighna.'

'Come on, then,' she said, draining her tea. I wriggled out of the skirt and pulled my jeans back on, then grabbed my rucksack and clattered down the stairs.

Outside, I understood with sudden dismay why the ferry had been cancelled. Still Bay was usually so sheltered, but the sea was up and churning white against the beach. Even as we stood by the open door, a wave ripped along the shore of Dog Rock, and a curtain of spray whipped on the wind, drifting far enough inland to coat us in a mist of salt.

Ailsa pulled a face. 'I can't take the dinghy out in this,' she said. 'It's too strong for me. Hang on, though. Dad will do it.'

CHAPTER 32

'Bye, Flo,' called Ailsa, and tossed the rope into the shaking dinghy.

I waved a hapless goodbye as we drifted from the jetty. John dipped the outboard into the sea. The prop bit fast, and we motored towards Bancree. I could see Ailsa standing at the end of the pontoon, watching us.

For a short while, the sea didn't seem so rough after all, but then I realised the smoothness of the journey was down to how John handled his boat. Under his expert guidance, the rib zipped into the troughs of waves, mostly sheltered from the wind that thrashed above. He slowed the motor according to the rhythm of the sea, or accelerated to match the wave. He didn't control the boat so much as match the movement of the water. Sometimes he was forced to cut across choppy waves, and here the dinghy bottomed out, banging and juddering, leaving my stomach lurching, a reminder of the violence so close to us. Then, halfway across the bay, he had to strike a wave almost head-on, and vibrations rocked the little boat. The force of the hit tumbled loose a bag from the jumble beneath my seat. It was the bulky canvas kit sack he'd carried on the road. I reached down to hold it safe, but when I touched it, John growled. He actually growled. Dark and fierce and low in his throat, the noise cut across the fizzing ocean. He leaned forward, knees bent, ready to spring.

'Leave. That. Alone,' he said.

His dark eyes had no life. His voice was flat and final. Bunched and ferocious, he stared at me, and I stowed the heavy duffel bag back beneath the seat. I was shaken. In the neck of the bag, right on the fringes of vision, almost too dark to make out, I thought I had seen hair. It had looked like human hair. In my paranoia over the disappearances, I could think of just one reason there might be human hair in a heavy bag.

A wave hit us hard. John cursed and with a zip of acceleration, steered us back into the shelter of a trough. As we approached the shore, he slowed the engine right down.

'Get ready,' he yelled, 'and go quick.'

I turned and tensed, crouched and prepared to spring, aching to be off the dinghy. As we closed further, John caught a wave and surfed the rib in towards the beach. We gathered pace as the sea lifted, tilting the little boat. Behind me, he killed the engine and lifted the outboard high. The inflatable slid perfectly, rushing inland on a thick layer of thrashing, foaming surf.

'Now!' he shouted, and I jumped. As my weight pushed it down, the rib touched the sand, giving traction to my leap, and I landed on my feet on the beach. Even as I turned, the backwash was sucking the dinghy back into the deeper water. Not looking back, John dipped the engine and fired it full tilt into the next incoming wave. Climbing steeply up its face, he fired the boat straight over the crest in a burst of froth and spray. He landed on the other side with a resounding slap and raced again into the next wave.

He'd growled at me.

My hands were trembling. I was shaking with fright.

There was a beeping noise behind me. On the other side of the dune grass, parked between two Grogport houses, waited the bus.

I'd seldom been so pleased to see Nana. She waved at me, beckoning one-handed, holding Jamie in the other. Behind her, Bev leaned on the horn again, gesturing up the road and tapping on her watch. I jogged through the grass to collect my baby brother.

There was no time for conversation. Bev was gunning the engine even as I took the baby from Nana. She kissed me on the cheek and climbed back aboard the bus. She gave a thumbs-up as the bus pulled away, rocking in the wind. With the red tail-lights flickering between the trees, the bus disappeared around the corner and I stood in the middle of the road. The gale howled and hissed in the trees, surf pounding on the beach behind me.

In my arms, Jamie lay fast asleep. His soft hair fluttered in the breezes that ducked inside his hood. The brown-black fluff was the same colour as the matter I'd half-seen in John's kit bag. And even then, I'd kid myself it was nothing, just some old piece of cloth or something . . . except that his reaction had been so quick, so vicious. I'd thought he was going to pounce at me, tip me overboard. I turned to sneak a look at Dog Rock. John was still forcing the inflatable through the swell, but he'd almost reached the pontoon. Ailsa flung a rope to him, looping dark against a grey sky. He seized it in a fist and drew in the rib. Together and with evident difficulty, battling both waves and wind, they lashed it to the walkway. The pair left for the cottage, but after a few paces John turned and came back to the dinghy. He reached down to retrieve the kit bag. Casually, he slung it over his shoulder. He followed Ailsa into the house and did not look back.

I didn't know him. I didn't know who he was, or what he was capable of. There must have been some good reason he wouldn't want me to see inside the bag.

Another gust heaved into me, forcing me take a half step to

find my balance. Jamie stirred. The wind chimes hanging from my house clattered in atonal clicks. I started, convinced that someone in Grogport was watching me. The windows of empty houses were blank, reflections showing walls of scudding cloud. The village was deserted. The wind nudged my back. Move. Move. Get indoors. Feeling edgy and exposed, ears ringing with cold and wet, I walked up the road to our cottage.

CHAPTER 33

I mixed up some formula, testing the temperature on my wrist. Sitting in my lap, cradled in the crook of my arm, Jamie guzzled the milk, drinking himself into a contented stupor. I slung him over my shoulder and thumped his back until I'd forced out a burp, then ran him a wee bath and washed him, cleaning him with a sponge. His tiny penis floated in the water, shrimplike and strange. I towelled him dry in Mum and Ronny's room. Fresh and clean and wrapped up in a sleep suit, I sat him on my lap. He cooed and burbled, examining his hands with a baffled frown. I couldn't ever see myself a mother. I felt like I was looking after someone else's kid. Babysitting. Which I was, of course – but he felt like a stranger, not like a brother. Part of that was the age gap. Part of that was having different fathers. And there was something else, too. Mum and Ronny would never say it, but when Jamie came along, I stopped being the kid. Our cottage was small for three, let alone four, and there was only enough space in our lives for one child. Jamie took that spot. He'd need a room of his own, soon, and we all knew that would be my room. It was unspoken, but I'd be leaving home. It made me a little sad, but also fuelled my longing for escape.

I read Jamie a bedtime story about a hungry goat and laid him in his cot. I rocked him for a few moments, then left him to settle.

The rain fell ferociously, hammering the kitchen windows, drumming on the roof. Even the sound of it made me feel cold. I microwaved leftover fish stew for my dinner and sat in a blanket, flicking through the channels. The weather choked the signal, and every station played the same crawling static. Snatches of voices, half-faces. Ghosts. Anders. I turned it off again. The rain was a snare drum.

Idly, I rifled through my History notes, and flicked through the Mutch book. Selkies, selkies wearing skins. They glared at me, challenging, daring, tempting. Come and get me. The selkie woman scowled. I closed the book.

At a loss for what to do, I pinched a slug of whisky from Ronny's cabinet, one of the cheap ones, tipped my head back and relaxed my shoulders as it burned a slow path into my belly. I built a small fire in the lounge, poured another whisky, and sat to watch the fire and think and drink. The whisky flowed better than my thoughts, and I drank more than I meant to, grimacing with each hot sip of spirit, losing myself in the twists and pulses of the embers. Whisky ran warm inside me, glowing from the inside out. At a loss for anything better to do, I went to bed to read.

The wind howled beneath the eaves. Restless and bored and alive to the sounds of the gale, I couldn't concentrate on my book. I turned onto my back and looked at the ceiling. My mind sluiced with thoughts, flitting from Mutch and his twisted pictures to Tina Robson and her gang. Selkies with twisted backs and my Anders, vanished in a wink, gone without goodbyes. Viking stones, and poor Ailsa, so unhappy, craving stillness. I especially thought of John Dobie, of how he'd snapped when I caught the kit bag. It was too much. I couldn't keep it all in perspective. I wanted a moment of distraction, of peace, of nothingness.

I lit a couple of candles and turned off the glaring bedside lamp. This was what Richard and I used to do. Candles and empty houses. Stupid to think so, but the anticipation felt greater alone than I'd ever felt with him. In the flickering gloom, I turned down the volume on the baby monitor, and set it on the bedside cabinet. Jamie hadn't stirred for an hour or more, and I didn't want to be interrupted.

I let my hand slip beneath the covers and drift across my stomach. The candlelight cast ghosts around my room. I pushed my hand beneath my waistband and let my fingertips brush against my inner thigh. I needed something to focus on. I thought of Richard. I pictured his skinny body and mine folded in a jumble on our bed, and remembered how it felt to be with him. I tried recreating the dream I'd had, the two of us on the headland while the sun sped round and round, but it wasn't working. I let my mind drift elsewhere. I tried pop stars and film stars, but nothing clicked.

Another face came to me, unbidden. I tried pushing it away, but it wouldn't go. A sensual, handsome face, even though he scared me. Older than me, with dark, dark eyes. I resisted, but eventually I let my weakness win. I drew John Dobie towards me, and closer still, until he was directly before me, his peaty eyes gazing into mine. Something changed, the closer I drew him in. It was John, and at the same time, it was something else, someone else. But then it didn't matter any more, and the rhythm of my touch carried me a long, long way from Bancree.

Darkness and light washed through me – softer than snow, someone sang a nursery rhyme in Gaelic. Seo mo làimhean: here are my hands.

I surged upwards, back arched – and released, lowering myself slowly back to the mattress. I lay in my cocoon of sheets for long minutes, trembling, soaking in the afterglow of that soft Gaelic croon. The fire receded from my belly, and a soporific looseness washed through me, tinged with prickles of shame. John Dobie was three times my age, and father to my only friend. Looking Ailsa in the eye would take some nerve, next time I saw her. Something else niggled at me, too.

I'd wanted it to happen again.

I wanted that hand on my leg. I wanted to let the fantasy run, to know what happened next. What a stupid thing to wish for.

'Great,' I muttered, out loud, 'just wonderful, Flora. Ridiculous girl.'

With that, I started to heave myself out of bed. But then I stopped.

The nursery rhyme was still playing.

My head snapped towards the baby monitor. The LCD volume bar flickered in time to a quiet soft croon, a gentle voice singing in Gaelic.

'Seo mo làimhean . . .'

The hushed voice crackled through the intercom. In an empty house, someone was singing to Jamie.

In a blur of panic and protection, I hurled myself out of bed and sprinted through the house. I burst into the room, rain still slashing against the windows. Silhouetted against the glow of the night-light, Jamie's cot rocked back and forth, swinging without anyone to swing it. I crossed the carpet, approaching the crib. With no one there to push it, the cot slowed through natural momentum, and then the rocking stopped.

Jamie peered up at me. He gurgled with laughter and waved his arms, wanting to be picked up. The room was empty. He was fine. Numb with relief, I slumped down on the bed. Head in my hands, I shook with the thought of Jamie being hurt or harmed. He was settling, cooing and humming himself back to sleep.

Here are my hands. Here are my hands.

I shivered in the nightlight gloom, trembling with confusion and doubt. The windows were latched. The front door was locked. No one could have found a way inside. That was impossible.

Maybe Jamie had worked out how to rock the cradle by himself.

Maybe I'd daydreamed the nursery rhyme, woozy with sleep, woozy with touch.

Maybe I had an overactive imagination.

And maybe I'd drunk too much whisky.

Jamie had fallen back asleep, snoring with a little whistle, his face lit in the dim yellow of the nightlight. I reached into the cot and gently traced the outline of his tummy. I tried to recall the voice, but the monitor had masked all detail. I only knew it was slow, and sad, and soft.

I checked all the doors and windows, for the first time scared of my own house, painfully aware of how my silhouette would appear to anyone looking in on me. With shivers in my neck, I went back to bed and pulled the covers to my chin. My book gave no respite. Wired awake, I listened to the storm and watched the dancing shadows, afraid to blow the candles out.

CHAPTER 34

The gale relented in the small hours, and the Sound woke calm beneath a crisp, clean sky. I'd already fed and clothed Jamie by the time Mum and Ronny returned on the first morning ferry. We were playing on the lounge floor when they came home. The baby turned upon hearing them enter, and clapped his little hands in glee. Mum swept him up, and Ronny hugged both of them to him. I flushed bittersweet to see them as a complete family, bound together by their blood. I made a pot of coffee while they fussed over each other. The coffee tasted of peat. Everything tasted of peat. I wondered how much of the island had passed through me over the years. How much of the sediment had filtered through my system? Would it fill a shot glass? A tea mug? A pint? A bathtub? The coffee percolated with a gurgle.

Ronny came through to the kitchen. He looked shattered.

'Don't suppose there's been anything from Anders?'

'Sorry, no. Nothing.'

'Didn't think so. I've tried everyone I can think of. Munzie's let me take a couple of days to help out with the search.'

He leaned against the counter, lost in his thoughts.

'I'd better get to school,' I said.

'All right, sweetheart,' said Mum, still cuddling Jamie. He played with curls of her hair. 'See you later. Thanks for having the baby. Was he good?'

The cradle, rocking by itself. The voice on the monitor.

'He was fine,' I said, tying my laces, 'it was a quiet night. Nothing happened at all.'

The ferry took me into Tanno an hour before English, and I idled round the harbour, window-shopping in thrift stores I'd long since exhausted. A hard tap fell upon my shoulder. I turned, surprised, and stumbled.

'Hello, Flora,' said John Dobie.

I gaped at him, and took an involuntary pace away.

'It's John,' he said, stepping closer. 'Ailsa's father.'

'Yes, I know, hi,' I stammered, feeling myself flush red. 'You've actually come to town?'

He gestured at the harbour. 'Clearly.'

Caught between shame and fright, I couldn't meet his eye.

'Don't be scared of me,' he said.

My fantasies, lost in his dark eyes, suddenly repelled me. The tufts in his bag had looked like hair. In the turmoil of my doubt, I stepped away from him again, avoiding his eye. With my gaze lowered, I focused on his hands, his wrists. He was holding a stack of local newspapers, gathered from across the islands. His fingers were gnarled from seawater, engines and nets.

'Listen,' he said. 'I wanted to apologise for yesterday. I don't want you getting the wrong idea. I'm sorry I shouted.'

'No bother,' I said, trying to sound light-hearted.

'Sorry for raising my voice. That's all. I have many things on my mind.'

I shifted on my feet, torn between two Johns: the one I felt magnetised towards, and the one I feared. I couldn't fathom him at all.

'I should push on—' I started, but he cut me off.

'Maybe you're good for Ailsa,' he said, abruptly. 'She's never had many friends. But she can be . . . wayward. I want her keeping safe.'

Nerves or not, this rankled with me.

'She knows her own mind.'

'Aye, that's what worries me. Her own mind might not be best for her.'

'She's old enough to make her own decisions,' I said through gritted teeth. 'We both are.'

He considered carefully before speaking again.

'She's told you about her mother?'

'Aye. And I'm sorry. For you both.'

'That's why she needs looking after. It's not that I mistrust her. It's the rest of the world I don't trust. I won't sit back while trouble finds her. When I'm looking for her mother . . . I can't always be there for Ailsa.'

The sadness turned inside him like a whirlpool.

'In places like pubs,' he said, carefully.

He knew. Somehow, he knew about our night out.

'We weren't in any danger.'

'Are you sure? Ailsa said your dad's friend has vanished, and he's not the only one. Bancree doesn't seem very safe to me.'

'So why did you bring her here?'

His flinched as though he'd been slapped. 'Because I lost my wife,' he said, simply, 'and I need to find her.'

The harbourfront bustle faded to nothing. He was so lost, so alone. I studied his face, seeking out my attraction to him. No matter how I looked, I couldn't place it, couldn't fit it to him. He caught me watching.

'You're too young. You don't know what I'm talking about.'

'I'm an adult,' I replied, calmer than I felt.

'Then understand this. It doesn't heal,' said John, his voice a wound. 'It never gets better. It is always broken.'

Our eyes met fully, and I saw that he was hollow.

'You can't look for her for ever.'

'It might be for the best,' he said, 'if you didn't see Ailsa quite so often.'

My face grew hot.

'We're not kids. And I don't take easy options. I'll do the right thing by my friend, whether you like it or not.'

John considered this. On the far side of the harbour, a car beeped, and a man shouted. Everywhere else, people went about their business. Implacable, he nodded, as though making up his mind.

'Ailsa said you liked selkie stories,' he said, abruptly.

'Excuse me?'

'She said you were collecting them.'

'Oh. Aye. I am.'

'She said you had some where the selkies were wicked.'

'Most of them so far, aye.'

'That's not what I know,' he said. 'So this is a different sort of story.'

The new direction had totally thrown me. I was still working out the selkie angle when John began to talk, and then everything changed.

CHAPTER 35

Selkies danced naked in the surf. Seven of them turned a racing circle, hands linked and heads thrown back, frantic in the salt spray. Their sealskins lay jumbled on the beach as they waltzed and whirled. From the shore, a young crofter watched them dance. He resolved to take a selkie for his wife. He scuttled on his belly like any common crab, sneaking up on the seal girls. He reached out and, with trembling hands, took hold of a precious skin. He retreated, and waited in the rocks.

The selkies danced until they'd tired of dancing. One by one, they retrieved their sealskins from the beach – leaving one poor lass without. Reluctant to leave her but compelled into the sea, her sisters stepped into their skins. Transformed into seals, they vanished beneath the waves. Frantic and weeping, the remaining selkie scrabbled in the sand, but she couldn't find her own coat. Only now did the crofter emerge from his hiding place and approach the selkie. She fell to her knees, pleading for the return of her skin. He refused to give it back, and he took her for his wife. With her sealskin captive, the selkie had no choice but to follow.

For many years, the selkie and the crofter lived together. Entranced by his beautiful bride, the man fell a little more in love each day. He gave his heart and soul to her entirely. For her part, the selkie did her wifely duties without complaint, preparing food and keeping house, though her heart ached always for the sea. Every day, she combed the beach for firewood, so near and so far from her true home. Every day, she lit a fire in the house. In time, she came to welcome the young man's affection, and she became fond of him. The pair muddled on together for seven long years. But throughout that time, she searched low and high for her coat. It simply wasn't there for finding.

There came a day when the crofter went to town. In his absence, the selkie swept the hearth in readiness to build a fire. But as she cleaned, her elbow caught the kettle. The fire crane tumbled over, and split the hearthstone clean in two. The space beneath the hearth rang hollow. At first uncertain, the selkie hauled the stone to one side. Around her, ashes fell like snow. There, beneath the hearth, she discovered an old trunk. With trembling hands, she removed the box, and broke the lock. Inside, she found her skin – her own true skin. Clutching to it like life itself, she turned at once and headed for the sea. She neither faltered nor looked back as she walked down to the ocean.

The young man returned to find the hearthstone split asunder. His trunk lay open and as empty as the sky, and his beautiful bride was nowhere to be found. He bolted for the beach, but he was too late. The selkie stepped into her skin, and was transformed once more into a seal. She dived into the sea and returned to her true home. Her sisters rejoiced to have her back beneath the waves, and she never again returned to land. She never again danced in the surf. Though she was sad to leave the crofter, she remained a seal for the rest of her days.

Back on the beach, the young man lamented, weeping until his eyes turned raw. Love had turned him inside out. He returned to his croft after hours spent waiting in the rain, and he lived on in aching sadness. He grieved for the rest of his days, lost and alone, always in mourning for his missing bride. He lived a long and fruitless life, and only the rain on the flat grey sea knew the measure of his heart.

CHAPTER 36

I stood with my mouth open.

John looked at his watch.

'I'll be on, then,' he said, and took a step back.

'Wait. Wait a second.'

He paused while I gathered my thoughts.

'What does it mean?'

'What any story means, Flora. Whatever you choose to take from it.'

'But if she liked him, why didn't she stay?'

He considered this.

'Because she had a true nature, and she couldn't deny it.'

'No. She had a choice. If she liked him, she could choose to stay.'

John shook his head.

'A comfortable prison is still a prison.'

He turned and walked away. I stood for moments, watching him go, watching the harbour bustle long after he had gone.

The story was gold, but the telling of it had blown me away. His sullen manner had vanished, caught into the swirl of words. And then – like that – it was over, and he was gone.

He was lost so far inside himself. I decided that John was broken. No wonder he kept Ailsa so close. She was all he had left of his wife, his love. If Ailsa went, then Annie went too. All of John was in his boxes of old newspapers. He was haunted by his map, haunted by his red and yellow pins.

I was haunted by his story. I was haunted by his eyes.

What was in that bag?

Distracted, I walked to school.

English was rubbish, as usual. We'd moved on from *The Silver Darlings* to *Middlemarch*. It always seemed to me that I learned more ancient history in English than in History. When I thought no one was looking, I scribbled out John's story. Occasionally I leafed through the Mutch book, soaking up the pictures and slipping into daydreams of selkies. As insane as it was, Mutch felt real. *Middlemarch* felt like a distant joke. I'd ordered a collection of Finnish folk-tales from the library, and I doubled up my books so Mr McLaggan couldn't see. I read a story about a girl who turned into a goose. She flew into the night sky and discovered that the stars were made of frost. Every morning they were melted by the sun, and each night they froze again.

The school bell shook me back to wakefulness. I'd daydreamed through the brief on some new assignment. There were cryptic notes about *Middlemarch* scrawled on the whiteboard, but I had no idea what part of the book they referred to, or what I was supposed to do. I hesitated, almost stopping to ask what we needed to do for the homework, then stepped decisively out the classroom door and didn't look back.

As I walked, I felt little tugs of guilt, telling me to go back, apologise to the teacher, find out what I'd missed. But another voice spoke louder, reasoning that I didn't need or want Higher English.

I didn't need or want any of it.

Someone banged into my shoulder, and I spun into the wall and fell half to the floor. Tina smirked down at me.

'Well, if it isn't the ice queen.'

The corridor was empty but for Tina. I struggled back to my feet, pressing against the wall.

'Shouldn't you be in class with all the other children?' I said, heart racing.

'Just a wee reminder, Flo. I'm still watching. I'm still here.'

'You'll be here for ever,' I muttered.

Tina grinned wider. 'You're not the only one with plans,' she said. 'I've found a handsome prince to take me away from this dump.'

'That's sweet. Who's the victim? Does the poor bastard know yet?'

Mr Baillie rounded the corner, and both of us started with guilt.

'Robson. Cannan. What are you doing out of class?'

'Study period, sir.'

'You always study in school corridors?'

'No, sir.'

'Then be on with you. What about you, Robson?'

'Running a message for Mr Creil, sir,' she said, promptly.

'Really. Why don't we go and ask Mr Creil about that?'

Tina blanched. Baillie grabbed her elbow and steered her towards the stairs. I gave her a cheery wave as they vanished through the door. The corridor hummed with muted classroom noise, and my pulse felt suddenly, stupidly loud.

I steeled myself, steadied my breath.

Tina wasn't going to let me go without a fight. She hadn't yet taken whatever she wanted from me.

I walked out of school. Waiting for the ferry, I made a dutiful attempt to read *Middlemarch*, but Tina's smirk swam through my mind, and I gave up. Fish darted around the harbour, dark slivers of life.

A few more months to go. Only a few more months. I spotted

John Dobie's dinghy moored to the opposite wall. When I replayed our conversation, each time I found myself a little angrier at being told what to do. Once we were underway, Tanno sliding past the ferry, I found my phone and texted Ailsa:

Feeling a bit blue. Fancy another night on the cherry schnapps?

A few minutes later came the reply:

NO! . . . But we could try the pub again? Or that whisky Izzy keeps finding on the beach? Cheer up, kid.

I grinned. Despite everything else, I had a friend.
Things could always be worse.

CHAPTER 37

Tony struck us the same deal as before. Sit at the back, drink shandies and keep quiet. I wore a red halter-top with a mini-skirt and patterned tights. The top made me feel exotic, and I wore far more make-up than usual. Ailsa looked great in a long gypsy skirt, hooped with bands of colour, and a simple black vest. We sat and chatted nonsense about school, clothes and music. She told me more about the places she'd lived in. Beaches, mountains, rivers. She'd been to six schools in the last five years. The more she talked, the more I realised how lonely she'd become. It had only been her and her dad, as long as she'd ever known. No wonder that John needed her so badly. He'd spent half his life chasing ghosts, and now Ailsa was on the cusp of adulthood. Were she to go, ghosts would be all he had left. I imagined him alone on Dog Rock, digging his trench, digging in the dark. Somehow, he'd known we'd been out drinking.

'What would your dad do,' I said, abruptly, 'if he knew we were out like this?'

'He'd be really pissed off. With me, anyway. I don't think he'd mind about you. He hates me being out alone.'

'You're seventeen. He can't keep you locked up for ever.'

'Yeah? Tell him that, would you?'

'Not likely. Then he'd really hate me.'

She shook her head. 'He thinks you're all right.'

'You're kidding? He doesn't even smile when I see him.'

'That's just Dad. He does like you.'

'He told me a great selkie story.'

'I asked him to, if he saw you. For balance.'

'. . . then he walked off with barely a word.'

She winced. 'Ouch. Sorry.'

'Don't worry about it.'

'Look, he wouldn't have told you the story if he didn't think you were all right. You're bringing me out of my shell, apparently.'

I started. 'That's exactly why Mum and Ronny are so keen that I see you. "It's good for me to see girls my own age", you know.'

'What a pair,' she snorted. 'However did we manage beforehand?'

'I don't know,' I said, throwing a dramatic hand to my forehead. 'Save me! Save me from myself!'

Ailsa was giggling, but her face dropped.

'Oh God, no.'

'What is it?'

'It's that awful Lachlan again.'

I turned in my seat. Sure enough, Lachie was approaching us from the far corner of the bar, beaming broadly all the way. He was alone.

'My bonnie lassies,' he leered. 'How lovely to see you again in this wonderful—' he looked around the bar, '—this establishment.'

He leaned low, slopping what looked like half a double whisky onto the table.

'May I join you?' he said, already lowering himself into the booth beside Ailsa.

'No,' I said, pointedly, 'no, you can't.'

His face fell in mock dismay. 'Alas no, Flora. But why not? Surely a dashing young gent such as myself might venture to buy you two ladies a drink?'

'I do not want,' I said sweetly, 'anything from you.'

He turned to Ailsa, shutting me out, and gestured at me with his thumb.

'Barking up the wrong tree with this one. How about you, sweetheart? Care to join me for a tipple?'

'To be honest,' she said, wrinkling her nose, 'I'm already pretty loaded off your aftershave.'

I snorted with laughter. He scowled at her and sat up a little straighter.

'Seriously,' she said, 'have you not got another gear?'

'Aye,' I chimed in, 'change the record, man. Why do you come in here? No one likes you.'

A thin, mean smile slid across his face.

'I'll tell you a secret. I come precisely because no one likes me.'

I glanced at Ailsa, puzzled. Warily, she studied Lachlan.

'I don't understand.'

'No one does,' he sniggered. 'That's the whole point. They hate me because they're scared of me. They're scared because one day soon, the old man will be pushing daisies, and I'll be running Clachnabhan. Half the island will work for me, and the other half will owe me big. They're right to be scared of me.'

'That's so messed up.'

He leaned back, arms behind his head. 'Whatever. Doesn't matter to me. I do what I want. You should be nicer to me, Flora.'

'Or what?'

'Or, when I'm in charge, your daddy loses his job.'

I froze, and he smiled wider. My usual response was to say, 'Ronny's not my dad.' But this time, I didn't. Lachlan wasn't joking.

'You're such a prick.'

'Ah,' he said, holding up an admonishing finger, 'I said play nice. That's not being nice, is it? Is it, Ailsa?'

'My father doesn't work for you. You've nothing on me. Prrrrick.'

He swung his arm to point the finger at her. It looked manicured. The nail gleamed in the bar lights.

'Correction. I've nothing, yet.'

'Keep pointing that at me,' she said, 'and I'll snap it off.'

She beamed at him, but her voiced dripped menace. I believed her, and Lachie must have too, because he dropped his hand back to the table.

'Cool your beans, sweetheart. I'm only messing.'

'We don't want you,' I said. 'We're not interested, either of us. We can't make it plainer. Leave. Us. Alone.'

Lachlan shook his head with amused disbelief.

'Nobody tells me what to do. Nobody. Your father's gonna know about this on Monday,' he said.

'Ronny can take care of himself,' I snapped.

'Just imagine the rumours,' murmured Ailsa, suddenly, 'that all-powerful ladies' man Lachlan Crane fired his best supervisor, and all because a pair of schoolgirls knocked him back.'

Lachie blinked.

'Doesn't sound good, does it?'

'Not at all,' I confirmed. 'People get very sensitive where children are concerned, don't they?'

'And these things spread like wildfire,' she lamented, voice laden with mock concern.

'Quicker, round here.'

'I imagine that sooner or later the police would hear about it, too.'

Lachlan visibly flinched.

'And with something like that, I doubt those Christmas crates of whisky would count for much,' I said.

'Of course,' said Ailsa, sweetly, 'I'm sure there's no need for things to go that far, is there?'

Lachie's face was pulled into a rictus grin.

'No,' he said, 'no.'

His fist was taut against the glass, the tendons straining in his wrist. The tumbler rattled on the table, and the noise took him by surprise. He looked down, saw the trembling glass, and let go his hand with a jolt. We all three watched the glass rumble to a stop. Then Lachie stood up. When he moved, I could scent the wildness on him. He drew out a cigarette and placed it in his mouth.

'I'm going for a breath of fresh air. When you change your mind,' he said, 'I'll be waiting outside.'

He turned around, and walked away from the booth.

I watched him all the way to the door, marching with his head down, feet straight, fists flexing and unclenching at his sides. Relief washed over me. For a moment, the atmosphere brightened throughout the pub. But not for long. As he stormed outside, Lachie barged into a man in the doorway. The man recovered his balance with ease and stepped into the lounge. I froze. It was John Dobie. He stood at the threshold, peering uncertainly into the gloom.

'Oh shit,' I said quietly.

'What's up? Is he coming back for seconds?'

'It's your dad.'

The blood drained from Ailsa's face. She was sitting with her back to the door, and she visibly tensed, as though willing herself smaller, wishing herself invisible. From the doorway, John's dark eyes met mine, and the world stilled a little. The buzz faded as he walked across the room and to the table. Even when he was standing right beside her, Ailsa didn't look up, but stared at the table.

'Come on,' he said, 'let's go home.'

She didn't move.

'Ailsa,' he said, louder, 'we're leaving.'

She chose her words with care.

'I'd prefer to stay, Dad.'

'I'm sure you would. But that is not an option.'

'I want to stay.'

'Get up. Come home. Now.'

What happened next made me spill my drink with fright. Ailsa jumped to her feet and howled in her father's face, screaming at the top of her voice.

'It's not home! It's never home!'

Every conversation died. Every person in the bar was staring. Father and daughter glared at one another, some unspoken communication rattling between them. Then Ailsa reached down, drained her glass to the last drop and replaced it on the table.

'I've nothing to say to you,' she said. 'I'll make my own way back.'

'We'll walk together,' he corrected.

Ailsa grabbed her coat.

'Sorry, Flo,' she muttered. 'I'll see you soon.'

With that, she turned on her heel and walked out, picking her way with care between the tables. The door slammed shut behind her. John stood beside the booth, rocking on his heels.

'I told you,' he said. 'I said she needed keeping safe.'

'And I told you,' I replied, 'that we're old enough to make our own decisions.'

I couldn't keep the tremble from my voice.

John turned without another word and followed his daughter outside. Every person in the room watched the door close behind him, and then, as one, turned to look at me. The hotel bar recovered from silence with a spontaneous burr of conversation. All eyes were on me and my empty table.

Tony wandered over even as I was putting on my cardigan.

'I don't think,' he apologised, gathering the glasses, 'that it's a good idea for you to come here any more.'

'No. Perhaps not.'

'Until you're, well. Old enough, anyway.'

'Don't worry, Tony. We won't darken your tills with our money again.'

I pushed past him and stormed out of the bar, the eyes of every man in there burning in my back. The cool night was an immediate tonic, and the rush began to clear.

I'd been so stupid. I should have known we wouldn't get away with it. I should've known to stay near home. And now I was facing a half-drunk walk back to Grogport. It was going to be a long few miles in bare feet. I kneeled down to undo the straps of my shoes. I could smell lemons. I could smell antiseptic. I looked up.

'I knew you'd change your mind,' said a voice from the dark. Beaming, Lachlan stepped from the shadow of the hotel.

CHAPTER 38

'Oh Jesus. Just piss off, Lachie,' I said, and unhooked my other shoe. I gathered both and stood in bare feet, feeling the chill of tarmac. That would burn off quick enough when I started walking. I looked down the road, but couldn't see either of the Dobies. They'd only had a few minutes' headstart, but they were already lost in the night. I could probably catch them if I ran, but John wouldn't be too pleased to see me. I turned away from the hotel and set off. Lachie caught up with me in a half-jog, and walked beside me.

'Very cold.'

I ignored him.

'Aye, right chillsome. And it's a cold night, too.'

I stopped. He stopped.

'Listen,' I said, 'I don't like you. I don't want anything to do with you. And neither does Ailsa. What'll it take to sink in?'

'So you two have been talking about me?' he grinned. 'That's a good sign. That's a start. You'll warm to me eventually, Flo. They always do. Given enough time, they—'

He was halfway through his spiel when I rolled my eyes and turned back to the road. I'd walked a few steps when he grabbed me. My arm wrenched hot with friction where he gripped it. For a dumb moment, we both looked at his hand on my arm.

Surprised at himself, he released his hand.

'Sorry there, Flora,' he said. 'It's just with that fuss you made in the hotel, and now the cold shoulder, well. A man gets wound up. I don't mean to hassle you. I just want to . . . wind down. You know?'

I stared at him. His eyes speckled white.

'Go away. Leave me alone.'

'Most ladies love my tenacity.'

His smile stretched wider still, and he reached for me again. I slapped his hand down.

'Hey,' said a thick voice, and we both started. It came from the beach side of the road. A man stepped out of the darkness into the slight light cast from the hotel. It was one of the Polish workers from the fish farm. He'd been smoking a cigarette. He dropped the butt at his feet, still half a dozen paces clear of us, and stared at Lachie.

'Lady said you go now. So you go.'

'Why,' smiled Lachie, gesturing with his thumb, 'don't you fuck. Off.'

The Pole looked at him, unblinking. Lachlan bristled.

'D'you not speak English, you prick? I said, jog on.'

'No,' said the Pole, 'you fucks off, motherfucker.'

Lachie detached himself from me and wandered halfway to the Pole. He stood there, waiting. A cloud of his aftershave stayed with me.

What made it worse was that the Pole got in the first blow. It mightn't have been so bad if Lachie had got in a swing or two, made his point, and gone on his way. But the Pole was quick. He pretended to be slow, and threw an inept punch, which Lachie simply stepped away from. He even had enough time to laugh at how clumsy it was. Then the Pole's other hand flew out in a tight blur and connected with Lachie's chin. He fell, more in surprise than anything else, and landed on his backside on the road. He sat there, blinking in astonishment.

Again, it mightn't have been so bad if the Pole had stepped in and hit him again, made sure of things with a follow-up blow. But he didn't. He stepped back, wary, rolling his shoulders, and waited for Lachie to stand up. That was the biggest mistake. He gave Lachie time to stand, to rub his jaw and grimace. He even found that dreadful smile of his, and brushed the dirt from his expensive trousers. He quietly removed his jacket and folded it neatly on the ground. As he stooped, he picked a handful of gravel from the road. That's when I realised how bad this was going to be.

'Lachie—' I said, urgently.

'Be quiet,' he replied, not taking his eyes off the Pole, barely even blinking.

'Run,' I said. 'Run away. Please run.'

The Pole didn't even look at me. The two circled towards each other, closing in. Lachie threw some punches, lashing out, but the Pole was very quick, and simply cuffed his hands away. He managed to catch Lachie with another blow or two, and then Lachie moved up a gear. The two of them circled, coming close, and Lachie paused, feinted and unleashed the handful of gravel. The Pole flinched against the peppering stones and brought a hand to his face. In that flailing second, Lachie kicked out hard, and caught the side of the Pole's leg. He buckled and yelped, falling on his injured knee. Lachlan went to kick him again, and the Pole tried to palm his leg away, but that allowed Lachlan to land a vicious blow directly on his eye. He reeled, and Lachlan made no mistake with a follow-up. He took his time, squared up, and hit the Pole in the same place, right on the side of the eye. The Pole slumped to one side, holding his head in his hands. There was blood between his fingers. I thought of poor Izzy and his ear.

Lachie stood back, breathing hard, and felt at his lip.

'Lachie,' I said, desperate to get him away.

'Shut up,' he hissed, not even looking round, watching the prone man struggle to all fours.

'Lachie, come on. Leave him. You've beaten him.'

He ignored me and reached into his pocket. He pulled out a little knife, and slipped the blade open. He started moving towards the Pole. Desperate, I said the only thing I could to make this stop.

'Wait. This isn't what I want.'

At this, he glanced round.

'What's this?'

'We could be somewhere else. Let's go. The two of us. Just leave him, aye?'

His grin broadened and his entire body visibly loosened up. With great care, he folded the knife and put it back in his pocket.

'You're right, lass. He's not worth the fucking bother.'

I sighed with relief. I'd have to deal with the aftermath, but I'd averted murder. Then Lachlan turned around, still smiling wide and bright, took three steady strides towards the crawling Pole, and kicked him in the face. It happened in a heartbeat, and it happened in for ever. One, two, three, confident, measured steps, his right leg drawn back, his entire body swung into the kick. The noise when his shoe connected with the man's head. Scrunching, wet, raw. The man's head flicked to one side and teeth and blood and snot sprayed out the other side, sprayed into the dark. The Pole dropped like a puppet and slumped face first on the road. Lachie started cleaning his shoe on the man's jacket, rubbing his toe against it, cleaning the blood from his shoe. He walked over to me and took my arm, and this was the point I realised I was moaning. Misery, terror, dismay.

'Come on then, hen,' he said, calm and cool as anything. 'Let's go.'

I tried to shrug him off, but his fist was locked around my arm. He steered me away from the stricken Pole and further down the road.

Meekly, I followed. He stepped a few dozen paces down the road into the darkness of the island road. My shoes clicked in my hand. Lachie pulled me to the right and off the road. Another few paces and we were on the old building site by the hotel. Rooted in the outside world, a single streetlamp glowed in the far corner. Half the site was lit a glaring orange, and half was shrouded black. The abandoned materials cast leering, crouching shadows.

Lachlan steered me into the far corner. There, beneath the streetlamp, lay the stacks of precast concrete pipes. They were easily five or six foot tall, and maybe twenty long. Lachie checked over his shoulder and drew me into the middle pipe. I tried to pull away, but his grip was stone. He led me into the pipe.

Inside, the streetlight slipped, casting a weird slice of orange light. It was cold, colder than outside. The curve of the concrete was disorientating, the perspective twisted, speckles of light at the far end. The arc was vertiginous, and my stomach lurched.

'It's not the Ritz, but it'll do. Any port in a storm, eh honey?'

Lachie was disembodied by the darkness.

'I wanted to take you somewhere nice, Flora.'

His voice floated and rebounded, echoing in the dark.

'Lachie,' I said.

'Treat you right. Spoil you some. I show all my girls a good time.'

'Lachlan.'

'I gave you the chance. Could have taken you to Edinburgh. Edinburgh, eh? That would've been nice. But this will have to do.'

Echoes on the concrete: will have to do . . . have to do . . . have to . . .

And then I said it.

'No,' I whispered.

There was a silence, and a scrape of shoe on concrete. Then a nasty, throaty sound. Laughter. He was laughing. 'No you don't,' he said. 'You wee tramp. No you don't. Nobody gives Lachlan Crane the runaround.'

I found some courage. I tried to be firm.

'Let me go. That man needs help. You can't bully me, like you bullied Izzy.'

He thrust his face in at me, sudden and close. Whisky breath, lemons. Half-lit streetlamp orange, he studied me curiously.

'That old tinker on the beach? What's he got to do with anything?'

'You beat him up,' I faltered, 'you cut him.'

Lachlan grinned broadly. 'Now, where would you hear a thing like that?'

There was a cord of something animal in him, frayed and pulled tight. I'd seen it snap when he fought the Pole, and now, up so close to him, I saw it in his eyes, the cord taut and twisting under strain.

'Listen,' I began, and the word came out a whisper.

'Do not,' he smiled, 'say another fucking word.'

Then he tried to kiss me. His stubble scratched my cheek, his tongue hot against my lips. I felt movement at my waist. Pressed against me, he was touching himself through his trousers. He was rubbing himself, but never took his eyes off mine. He never even blinked. I tried to ease away from him, pushing back into the wall, but he only pressed closer. I turned my head to one side and sucked in a lungful of air. I was halfway through a scream when Lachie clamped his hand across my mouth, pushing into my mouth and nose, stifling my cries. The scream reverberated through the pipe. He reached down with his other arm and hauled up my skirt. I was sobbing, flapping magpie frantic, beating at his arms, but his weight, his proximity, crushed me. With one rough hand at my mouth, the other groped between my legs. I felt his hand push between my teeth, slide into my mouth. As hard as I could, I bit his finger, broke the skin. He jerked his hand away.

'Fuck,' he howled, 'fucking bitch!'

His voice detonated in the pipe. He looked at me. With a steady, measured swipe, he drew back his hand and cuffed me, striking me high on the cheek. My head rang with the slap, clouds and bright stars floating, tingling in my eyes. I tried to raise my arm, but could barely feel my fingers. After that, he made no mistakes. I was vaguely aware of him dismembering my clothes, tugging at the fastenings. Hot breath on my shoulder, hands on my skin. There was a tearing noise, and a rush of cool night air. Buttons skittered in the pipe. I could feel a dim pain in my back where the skin ground into the concrete. Lachlan fumbled at me. I felt the material tauten, bunch and gape as he ripped my tights. Rough fingers groped between my legs, and my knickers rubbed sore where he yanked at them. I twisted and flapped, trying to scream. Lachlan cursed and punched me with a short, hard jab. There was a moment of searing, blinding agony, and then the colour red, pounding in my head, the sound of hurried footsteps, footsteps clattering concrete in the pipe and fading, rebounding ever quieter, dulling through a billion shades of crimson into black.

CHAPTER 39

A dull pulse. Concrete, pressing hard against my skull. The feel of it beneath my fingers, both crinkled and smooth, cool to touch, the slow curve of it lifting my neck into a painful angle. Streetlight fell into the pipe, a shaft of orange cast deep into the darkness. After a while, it occurred to me that Lachlan's breathing had calmed. He slumped over me, his weight pinning me down, his head lolled against my neck.

Something fluid glued his hair to my face. It was getting cold, now. I recalled the echoes of voices I half-recognised. As though it was captured in a shell, I could hear the faintest grinding of the sea. Everything about me felt numb and blunted. I tried to ease myself out from underneath him, but he wouldn't move. I tensed, then shoved and shrieked, expecting violence. But Lachlan didn't move. I pushed him away and he slithered off me, half-lolling on his side. As he rolled, his hairs ripped from where they'd been glued to my cheek. I put a hand to my face and felt a crust of something. He must have broken the skin.

He lay on the ground.

I was puzzled. Something wasn't right. My clothes were in rags. I pulled my ruined top down over my chest and felt in the shadows for my skirt. I was still wearing my knickers. Realisation dawned that I didn't hurt down there. Just about everything else was bruised and sore, but nothing had happened. For some reason, he hadn't gone through with it. Relief flushed through me. I gathered my clothes.

'Lachlan,' I said, then wondered why. My voice rung dully in the pipe.

I looked again at him. In the stark lamplight, he looked asleep. Something glistened in his curly hair. I reached out a hand. It was damp, and came away dark on my fingers. In the streetlight it was black. I raised the finger to my lips, tasted.

Blood.

Lachlan wasn't moving. I stretched a foot and pushed him onto his back. He tumbled over with a low thunk. His arm slithered horribly across his body and crumpled to the ground. His eyes were open. He was looking at me, as though this was my fault. I kneeled in the pipe, dumbly wondering what had happened. He had brought me in here. He'd assaulted me, and tried to do worse. And now . . .

How had this happened?

The concrete radiated cold, and I shivered. There was one button left on my skirt, and I fixed it as best I could. My tights were shredded and useless. I tried to put them on but they were impossible. A sob escaped me and for a few minutes I wept, sitting on my haunches in the pipe, arms wrapped around my knees. Ideas flashed through my brain like slow accidents, like the pulse of a life support machine: I was with him. Who did this? I was with him. It could have been me. Someone did this. Someone knows. Someone knows I was with him.

This last thought stuck on repeat. I'd heard footsteps. Someone knew about me and Lachlan and Lachlan being dead, because someone had killed him, and someone had left me here.

His legs curved sideways up the slope. I had to force myself to recognise he was dead. He was dead. Lachlan Crane was dead. Maybe it was the shock, but I didn't have much of a problem with it. I couldn't feel bad about it, or summon any sorrow. I had bruises and cuts all over my body. He would have done worse if he'd had the chance. Whoever attacked Lachlan had saved me. But I couldn't understand why. If they'd meant to rescue me, why wouldn't they hang around to help? The police would understand. Why would they leave me?

Strangely compelled, I kneeled beside him, the concrete pressing at my knees. I bent low to examine his head. Peering close, I saw his skull stoved in. There was a dent the size of half an orange. It was a stupid image, but it stuck. An orange. His hair was clumped into bloody ringlets, catching slivers of the streetlight.

Lachlan looked back at me, head crocked at a horrible angle, mouth in an obscene half-smile. Someone had struck him, very hard. I couldn't remember. His penis hung from his open trousers, limp and small in a nest of hair. His eyes gleamed.

Thoughts fell into place. Surreal, logical, lucid ideas. What I had to do next. I couldn't be caught here. I couldn't be the one who was found with Lachlan. No one would believe me. If I was caught with his body, I'd be arrested. I tried to imagine my defence. It would be manslaughter at best, and murder at worst. The awful beginnings of a solution swam towards me from the back of my brain.

Lachlan had to disappear. Like all the others, he had to go away.

I stood up, head reeling, and peered outside the pipe. The hotel lights were out, and the only sound came with the calling of the ocean.

The ocean.

I stooped, then, and tried to grab Lachie. I tried to pull him, to push him, to carry him out of the pipe, but his body was rigid and his clothes floopy and his wrists were covered in blood and everything stuck.

I couldn't move his body by myself.

I took another long look at Lachie, committing everything I could to memory. And then I left. There was only one person I could go to about this. I couldn't tell the police, and telling my parents would have the same end result. I wanted to tell Ailsa. She was the only person I completely trusted to keep it to herself, but there wasn't enough time to get back to Grogport, bring her from Dog Rock and deal with Lachie. But more than that, more than anything, I didn't want to disappoint her. What had happened made me toxic. I didn't want her to ever know.

That left me with no choice but to gamble.

Cautiously, checking round me every step of the way, I left the old construction site. The Bull stood quiet and empty. All the windows were dark, and there was no traffic on the road. I didn't know the time – I could have blacked out for minutes or hours. The sky was a deep, dark indigo and the Milky Way a glowing band of light, but I fancied there was a thin line of dawn on the eastern horizon. Maybe not. Either way, I had to hurry. Crossing the island road, I passed through the children's playground, the climbing frame and swingset rusting ghostly through bright paint, then down onto the beach. I took the low tide line. The sand here was firmest and best for walking, but it held the chill of the night and the sea, and my bare feet became very cold very quickly. I wrapped my arms around my chest and pushed on, shivering and scared. Further down the beach burned a low red light. It wavered and guttered the closer I came, until it resolved into the remnants of Izzy's campfire. His shack was quiet. There were no sounds but the rustling embers, the breathing of the sea and the faintest click of the wind chimes.

This was my last chance to find another solution. My clothes were in shreds and I was covered in bruises. I felt gangling and naked, exposed and embarrassed. Maybe I should find the police after all.

No. I had no choice.

I stepped around the fire and knocked quietly on his driftwood door. The noise was barely audible and I rapped again, harder. After a moment, a string of grunts and curses sounded from the guts of the ramshackle hut.

'Izzy?' I hissed.

The curses continued. The door began to open.

'This had better be good,' he growled, and then the door opened fully. A torch shone on my face, blinding me.

'Flora?' he said, astonished. 'What the devil happened to you?'

I'd held it all together until then. I'd thought I was doing OK. But his surprise and concern threw something inside me wide open, and I fell against him, needing the warmth of touch. I sobbed. He put a reluctant arm around me, and for a moment I simply cried. Eventually I gathered my wits and drew away from him, sniffing and wiping my streaming nose.

'Sorry,' I said, 'sorry, sorry.'

'Come in. You'd better tell me what's going on.'

He turned back into his hut. There was a clang and some rustling, then the room was illuminated by a flickering lantern. He turned up the oil and steadied the flame. He started delving into his trunks and boxes.

'Here. Take this. You're freezing.'

He held out a pair of overalls, spattered with streaks of paint. Grateful, I took them and dressed, zipping to the chin. Instantly I felt a little warmer. Izzy threw a blanket on the floor, and I wrapped it around my feet, rubbing them together for warmth. His shack seemed very different by lantern light. The shadows gave depth to the walls, and it seemed bigger. The tarpaulin breathed with the sea breeze. Izzy hefted a crate down across from my seat, plumped himself down and turned to face me.

'Now,' he said, 'it's half-past three in the morning. What the fuck is going on?'

CHAPTER 40

This was my gamble. No turning back. I took a deep breath, and told him about Lachie. I told him everything – when I related how he'd punched me, Izzy leaned in with the lantern and studied my face. I continued, explaining that I'd banged my head, and woken to find Lachlan dead beside me. Tears streamed from my eyes, almost without pause, but I scarcely noticed them. When I'd finished, the beachcomber leaned back. He didn't seem that perturbed. He wriggled a finger in his ear.

'Well,' he said, 'I've had some shit nights out in my life. But this takes some beating.'

I stared at him. Then he grinned, and a burst of hysterical laughter shook from me. It didn't lighten my mood, but it grounded me, gave me focus. Telling Izzy had been the right thing to do.

'All right, Flo. So when are you going to call the good officers of the Northern Constabulary?'

I shook my head. 'I can't, I can't. They'll think I did it. And I don't want them to know what happened.'

Lachlan's hand, fumbling at my legs.

'You have to tell them, lass. A man's been murdered. And Lachlan was a bastard, aye, but he's been murdered nonetheless.'

'They'll blame me.'

'They have . . . forensics and things, these days. There must be a way of working out who did it.'

'I've already thought about this. If it was murder, I mean premeditated, and if it was Lachie they wanted, then whoever did it will have taken care of that. There was no rock there.'

'What?'

'There was no rock, or stone, or whatever it was they used. No weapon.'

'They used a rock?'

He seemed suddenly pained. This was more the reaction I'd expected when I'd first told him.

'His head was cracked in,' I said. 'There was a dent the size of an orange. I could see the bone.'

A sharp white shape.

'Jesus,' said Izzy, clearly shaken. 'You saw that?'

'I can see it right now.'

It sat plainly in my memory, ugly and real, but still divorced of meaning. I couldn't associate that hollow with Lachlan being dead. That part of the night, the moment when Lachie passed from life into death, that part lurked somewhere in the back of my brain. Every time I thought I could see it clearly, it was gone, and I was left to stare at tiny details all over again. The way his hairs tore from my face, glued on with dry blood. The way his ringlets glistened in the orange lamplight. The curved chill of the pipe, creeping higher up above us.

Details. Tiny details.

'Flora,' repeated Izzy. 'Flora, can you hear me?'

I snapped up. 'Aye. I can hear.'

'What do you want me to do, hen?'

'I want you to help me move the body, Izzy.'

Beneath the wan cone cast by the lantern, he smiled and shook his head from side to side.

'I can't do that. No, I can't be doing any of that.'

'You said if I ever needed a hand. If I ever needed help, I had to come and talk to you.'

'Christ, aye, but nothing like this. I meant in finding the Viking stones, help with your homework, something like that.'

'You offered, Izzy. And here I am. I need help.'

'I can't get mixed up in this. I can't. It's madness. I've no beef with Lachlan.'

'He tried to cut your ear off!'

Izzy grimaced and reached for his ear, feeling the wound.

'And one night he would have come down here with his cigarette lighter, and that would've been the end of this,' I said, gesturing at the cluttered shack, 'and you too. I saw him kick a man half to death tonight. He was going to kill him until I got in the way.'

'No, no and no. I don't want to get involved.'

'Listen to me. If the constabulary find him up by the hotel, they won't come looking for me first. They'll ask around for people with grudges against him. And there won't be any shortage, but you'll be near the top. They'll hear about Lachie cutting your ear. That's a pretty good motive.'

Izzy thought about this.

'Where were you between the hours of eleven and three, Izzy?'

'I was right here,' he said, slow and resentful, 'and fast asleep. You know I was here. You woke me up.'

It was hard to lay this on him, but there was no way I could shift Lachlan without him. I needed him.

'Can you prove it? Was anyone here with you? What's your alibi?'

'Don't push me, lass,' he growled. 'Don't you dare. I didn't do a thing.'

'This is what the police will ask.'

Izzy retreated into the shadows, thinking. A gust of wind, and the canvas sucked against the frame of the shack. The lantern scattered shadows into his stacks of junk.

'Jesus,' he muttered. 'All right. He was a bad lad. He was due this sort of end. I just wish it hadn't been you.'

'Thanks, Izzy.'

'So where are you going to put him?'

'I've thought about that, too,' I said. 'We'll put him in the sea.'

He laughed out loud.

'Just like that, we put him in the sea? Bodies float, lass.'

'It's a big ocean. He'll disappear. Just like Dougie. Just like Bill,' I said, sadly. 'Just like Anders. There's been people going missing for years on the islands round here. Loads of them. Sometimes they get pulled out of the sea, and sometimes they're never found at all.'

Izzy stopped laughing. 'I know all about Bill and Doug and Anders,' he said, thickly. 'I didn't know about any others.'

'Not many people do. Not even the police have put it together.'

'So how do you know?'

'It doesn't matter. Lachlan will just be another one. It'll never get out about what he tried to do. None of that.'

'So we put him in the sea,' huffed the beachcomber, shaking his head. 'The mouths of babes and sucklings. All right. I suppose we'd better get on with it.'

He stood and fished inside another box, then threw a pair of battered plimsolls on the floor by my feet.

We trudged back along the beach. The sky was still indigo, but that pale line on the horizon was firing into dawn. The waves lapping on sand sounded like a pulse. It sounded like the beginning of time. I was exhausted. Izzy was a dark figure ahead of me. I scurried to match his bear steps. We walked in silence for the most part. I shouldn't have pushed him so hard to help, but there was no going back now. We let a freak solitary car come down the coast and drive away before crossing the playground and the road. In the hotel, there was the sound of a flush, then a light snapped off in a top window.

Izzy led the way, moving like a shadow, and I followed, praying no one would see. We walked into the construction site and crossed the mud and gravel. My heart beat thicker as we approached the stack of pipes. Gravity seemed to condense, the closer we came. The pipe with Lachlan waited like a black hole, drawing us in.

'Is this the one?' said Izzy, his voice painfully loud in the silence. 'Is this it?'

I nodded, suddenly fearful of going back inside. For stupid seconds I could hear Lachlan's voice, whispering from the darkness. Izzy stooped and stepped inside the pipe. He shuffled in a little way, then paused. He backed out.

'Are you sure this is the right pipe?'

Puzzled, I checked our position. I nodded.

Izzy shone the torch in my face. I scrunched my eyes shut, squinting to see his face. He was furious.

'Are you taking the piss?'

'What? No!'

'Because if it's supposed to be a joke,' he said, and in a single swift motion stepped close, close enough and fast enough to make me gasp, 'it's not even a little bit funny.'

I grabbed the torch from him and ducked around him, darting

to the pipe. I shone the light into the darkness. The darkness shone back at me.

The pipe was empty.

'No. No, he was right here.'

Izzy stood back, scowling, as I raced between the pipes, shining the torch into each one. They were all empty. Slowing down, my pulse racing, I returned to the original one, the one where it had all happened.

'He was here, Izzy,' I said. 'It was here.'

The beachcomber was silent and seething. I climbed inside the pipe and crawled down, down into that pervasive chill. I crawled beyond the cone of orange streetlight, and deeper into the tunnel. The smooth concrete pressed into my palms and bruised knees. It was damp. Under the torchlight, what I'd thought was blood was water, water in a wide arc, running down the sides where it had been sluiced into the pipe. I crawled deeper into the darkness, scuffling along with the torch in my hand, shadows and light jittering along the roof. A few metres in, I felt something beneath my hand that was not smooth concrete. In the torchlight, it was one of the buttons from my miniskirt, pinged into the depths when Lachie tore my clothes. I picked it up, stupidly small to touch. I looked a little further. There was another one. And there, just a little further ahead, lay a narrow, flat, dark object. I crawled deeper into the pipe and took the object in my hand. With some difficulty, feeling all my aches, I turned and shuffled out of the pipe.

I held out my right hand to Izzy. Two buttons.

'You could have easily hidden those,' he said.

I opened my left hand, showing the thin dark object. Izzy picked it up. It was Lachlan's pocket knife. He examined it beneath the streetlight.

'There was nowhere you could have hidden that,' he said, quietly.

'And look at this,' I said.

I drew him over to the pipe. Just inside, where Lachie's body had lain upside down against the curve of the concrete, was the large wet stain.

'When I was here, that was blood,' I said. 'That's where I passed out and he was bleeding. He lay right there.'

Izzy reached into the pipe and ran a finger along the dark stain. It had pooled at the bottom in a puddle, seeping already into the porous concrete. He dipped in his finger, then tasted the liquid.

'Salt. It's sea water.'

'Someone's moved him.'

'Only two people knew he was in here. You, and whoever killed him.'

'But why risk me seeing anything?'

'I don't know,' he said. 'But I tell you this, lass. This puts you in the clear. If the person who did this wanted you in trouble, they'd have left things exactly as they were.'

'You think?'

'Why move it? They must have waited for you to leave before shifting the body. They were watching you.'

'That makes no sense. Why wait?'

He shrugged. 'They're protecting you, Flora. But they don't want you to know.'

I stood lost in thought. The Dobies had been long gone. Besides, anyone who'd been defending me from Lachlan would have called the police.

'You've a guardian angel, lass.'

My brain was scrambled. Behind Izzy, the sky was tanning with dawn, the colour melting into pale blue, then darkening seamlessly through the shades. Night and stars still clung to the west. I felt numb with tension, sharp with lack of sleep. Waves fizzed across the beach, the backwash sighing into sunrise.

'No body, no crime,' said Izzy. 'I think we should leave, right now, and not come back for a long, long time.'

I nodded.

'Should I take the knife, Flo?'

I nodded again. 'Aye. Please.'

'I'll get rid of it. Wouldn't want anybody else getting hold of it.'

'No. OK.'

The beachcomber studied me. 'You're wiped out, lass. Go home. Sleep. We'll see what comes of this in time. You can trust me to stay true.'

We walked out of the construction site in a pale light. It must have been about five o'clock. On the road outside the hotel, we parted ways without a look. Izzy returned to the beach. Still dressed in his overalls, I started the long walk down the coast road home.

CHAPTER 41

Deep. I went very deep, tossed on the thickest sub-sea currents, tumbled over in the flow. A body spiralled from the surface, drifting towards me, creeping closer, the limbs spreadeagled and silhouetted black against the indigo. Each time I tumbled over, Lachlan drifted closer. It took for ever, but he joined me in the current, nose to nose and eye to eye. As I studied his face, his jaw dropped open. Slowly they came forward, pressing tight against each other, emerging from his mouth. Thick, knotted eels. They bobbed on his tongue, blind and grasping, crowded together.

Lachlan blinked.

I gasped for air. Someone hammered on my door.

'Come on, slugabed,' yelled Mum. 'Time to get up.'

I'd slept for three hours. The injuries which had tweaked and niggled on the walk home now cracked and knifed. I eased myself to sitting, using my arms to raise myself up, and my face appeared in the little mirror. In livid red, a bruise marked the place where Lachie struck me.

'Flo,' said Mum, 'come on. Are you up?'

'Aye,' I called, and it came out a croak.

'Well, on with it then.'

Mum didn't hold with lie-ins.

I wore my thickest tights and a long-sleeved sweater with a high rollneck. Even so, nothing was going to hide the marks on my face. I limped out and into the kitchen, pretending that nothing that happened. Mum was draping wet clothes on the drying rack. She did a double-take when she saw me.

'Jesus Christ Almighty. What happened to you?'

I'd practiced this.

'I fell over a wall, Mum,' I said, looking guilty.

'Fell over? It looks more like the wall fell on you.'

'It's not as bad as it looks,' I lied.

'And that's it? That's all you've got to say about it?'

'Aye, well. It was walking back last night. I was. Well, I was maybe a wee bit pissed.'

Her face darkened. I'd known that would do the trick. 'Pissed. Drinking. Flora. We've spoken about this.'

'I know, Mum,' I said, letting the words come out in protest, 'but it's the only thing going on round here, it's the only thing I can do for fun—'

'Enough of that. I gave you the freedom to go out. I'm not daft, Flora. I thought you'd have a drink or two. But I also hoped you'd have the sense to stop. Look at you. Just look. You're a mess.'

'Mum—' I began.

'Be quiet. I'm talking. You could have been killed, by the looks of you.'

'It's not that bad.'

Ronny came into the kitchen.

'Shit the bed,' he said, 'you've been in the wars, Flo.'

'You should see the other guy,' I mumbled, then wished I hadn't.

'Flora. Ronald,' hissed my mother. 'This is not to be taken lightly.'

'No, of course not,' he said. 'Sorry, love.'

'The girl's been drinking. Look at the state of her! She's a mess.'

'So what happened?'

'I fell over. Stacked it on a pothole, fell over a wall. My fault for wearing heels.'

'It was your fault for being drunk!' snapped Mum.

Ronny looked at me strangely.

'Fell over?'

Mum wagged a finger under my nose.

'This is absolutely unacceptable. I expect better of you, Flora Cannan.'

'I'm an adult,' I muttered.

'You're a wee kid. I'm so disappointed in you. I'm just furious.'

I couldn't even look her in the eye. The sodden clothes dripped on the floor.

'Sorry, Mum.'

'I think you should get out of the house right now. Get out of my sight for a bit.'

She spun away from me, arms folded. Numb, bruised, stung by her rage, I turned and walked away. I grabbed my boots and jacket, and went out for a walk. Waves sluiced foam in broad bands onto the beach, and everything was white and grey. Dog Rock looked empty. No smoke, no lights.

I was fifty yards along the road when Ronny caught me up.

'Hey now. You all right?'

'No.'

'I guess not. So you fell over, did you?'

'Like I said, aye.'

'Only it's funny, Flo. Your mum's not seen many fistfights, perhaps. But I have.'

My stomach dropped away. I looked out to Still Bay. Halfway to

Dog Rock, I spotted a seal. The dark head dipped in the foam, bobbing between the waves. Now you see it. Now you don't.

'I know a punch when I see one. So who hit you, Flo?'

I didn't say a thing. I couldn't even meet his eye. On the fringes of my hearing, back in the house, Jamie was screaming.

'I heard there was a fight outside the Bull last night, you know. A man was airlifted to hospital. One of the lads from the fish farm. But there's no way you did something like that. So what happened? Were you there?'

I shook my head.

'All right. You don't have to tell me. I'm disappointed, but it's your call. Listen, Flora. If I see even a hint of anything else, I'll tell your mum, and I'll chase this as far as I have to. Understand?'

I nodded. As if it was copying me, the seal bobbed beneath the waves.

'And give her a couple of hours,' he said, softening. 'She'll calm down.'

'I doubt it.'

'You're her daughter. She's frightened of your freedom. You doing something this stupid tells her you're not ready for it.'

I looked directly at him, then. 'But I need to be ready pretty soon, don't I?'

'Aye,' said Ronny, holding my gaze. 'I think perhaps you do.'

When I looked back to the bay, the seal had gone.

'See you later,' I said.

I walked on along the road then cut off on a footpath heading south, away from Tighna, away from Grogport, away from Izzy. Even away from Dog Rock.

Ailsa. What would she think about last night? She'd been mortified, humiliated, furious. I wanted to speak to her, to piece together

what had happened with her dad. My pace slowed with the realisation that I missed her. I missed my friend. A warning bell sounded
in my head. I couldn't ever tell her about Lachlan. I didn't want
to let her down. She might call the police, though that seemed
unlikely – and besides, without a body, nothing tied me to the
building site. I was more concerned about what she'd think of me,
or that she wouldn't want to be my friend. No, I couldn't tell her.
This was something for me to deal with. Me and Izzy.

There was something very dark and very dangerous on Bancree.

I traipsed along the road, weaving between potholes. The sea
breeze buffeted my coat, barrelling around me. Sea birds skimmed
through the troughs of waves in threes and fours, and the horizon
gathered into murk. I walked for an hour or so, finding my way to
the southwestern tip of the island. A stone monument was dedi-
cated to a sunken troop ship in the Second World War. Scores of
soldiers had drowned. A bunch of dead flowers was wedged against
the plaque, long-since withered to stalks. I sat against the forgotten
concrete, looked out into the grey, and pictured their hundred
hands waving upwards, drifting with the tug of the currents, and
cold streams of sunlight fading to black inside the rusting hull.

For the first time, I considered the reality of Lachie being dead.
Shock hit me like walking alone onto an empty stage.

Him being dead.

His skull broken open like an eggshell.

The things inside that glistened.

The life gone, the blood still. What he'd thought to do to me,
scrabbling between my legs. His penis, pale and limp. My clothes
ripped open. His skull. Orange lamplight. Oranges. The matter
inside.

I clamped my legs tight and tried to hold the halves of my skull together. The first sob rocked me, convulsing my stomach like a punch. I stifled the second sob with my wrist, and lay there, doubled over on the concrete, replaying the night, staring unblinking at the pieces. I cried and cried, howling at the sea, and the clouds and the sea fused into a single band of grey.

I stayed out there for hours. I walked home still numb with it all. My face was sticky with tears. Spots of rain clicked on the road all the way to Grogport. I didn't go in for tea, but splashed my face clean in the sink, then stripped off and fell into bed.

I didn't dream of anything at all.

CHAPTER 42

Over the next days, the world around me became wallpaper. It was there, in the background, but I stopped noticing it. At school, people stared at my bruises, stared at my face, but no one asked how I'd been hurt. Tina Robson growled at me in the corridors, but I ignored her. Whenever I was alone, Lachlan breathed cold air down my neck. I expected to meet him around corners. I felt him watching from the clouds, as though he filled the sky, leering down on all my poor choices. I tried to pay attention, but couldn't focus on anything. When I was challenged by teachers, I told them I was sick, and hid in bathroom stalls for thirty minutes at a time. Lachie was a piece of grit, festering within me, and that made me an oyster, thickening in my shell.

Ailsa didn't go to school for a few days. Dog Rock was quiet and dark. The dinghy disappeared for hours at a time, though I never saw them take it. I didn't see her or John at all, though I thought of them often. I thought about John's broad back, both compelled and repulsed by the thought of reaching out to touch him. I felt magnetised against my will, attracted to the shadows like thread wound to a spool. I wanted Ailsa close, I wanted to tell her what had happened. My tongue thickened in my mouth whenever I thought to put it into words.

The atmosphere in the house remained pinprick anxious for days. We were all bound tightly in our own thoughts, and our conversations were short and irritable. Even baby Jamie soaked up the tension. He was baffled and anxious and quick to cry. The house sweltered in an unbearable bubble, as though the walls themselves, more than a hundred years old, were gently constricting, squeezing us closer together, cramping out the oxygen.

Ronny came home late on Wednesday. We didn't notice him standing darkly in the doorway while me and Mum bathed the baby. Jamie sat up in the tub, fascinated as I steered a wind-up frog across the suddy water, then shrieked with delight to see his daddy.

'Oh, hello, love,' said Mum.

Ronny didn't respond, standing with his brow furrowed. I steeled myself for bad news.

'Hey. What's going on up there?' said Mum.

'Lachie wasn't in the distillery today.'

'So what's new?'

'He wasn't in yesterday, either, or Monday. No one thought a thing of it, but today was a big meeting. He was supposed to be there.'

'Maybe he's giving you the room to shine.'

'If I was on fire,' snorted Ronny, 'Lachlan wouldn't piss to put me out. Old Munzie's fuming.'

'Could he sack his own son?'

'That's not the point, Cath. The point is, where's Lachie? It wouldn't be the first time he'd bunked off work. He always been a skiver. But what with everything else lately . . .'

He and Mum looked at each other. She reached up and squeezed his hand.

'I know the lad has a nasty streak,' said Ronny. 'God alone knows how bad it'll be with him in charge. But all this business with people disappearing. It can't go on like this. There's trouble afoot.'

Nobody spoke. I left Mum and Ronny with the baby.

In my bedroom, I thought of John Dobie's wall map, that miserable, epic chart of disappearing islanders, more than a decade of clues, wrong turns and half-answered questions. With a sudden rush of shame, I realised that Lachie would become a red pin on the map. A red herring.

The island had always seemed such a safe place, such a friendly community. Dull, but safe. Even a month ago, the thought of a murderer living on Bancree would have seemed ridiculous. It no longer felt even slightly far-fetched. Not after all those poor missing people. Not after what had happened with Lachlan. Thinking of him, dead eyes glinting, made me feel ill. And like a nightmare, I had to consider that whoever killed Lachlan also murdered Dougie and Anders. It was an awful possibility, but I couldn't shake it. If John Dobie was right, and there was a killer on the island, then they'd been standing over me with decades of blood on their hands. I'd been helpless, unconscious. There was nothing to stop them.

So why was I still alive?

I sat by the window and watched the sea, lost in the gloaming. Ronny was right. Something was happening. Something was going on. Even as the island emptied and the people disappeared, the animals were returning. Nature was reclaiming old land, good land. I thought of the Norse stones, shrouded in lichen. The moss I'd pulled free would grow back in months, sinking anchors in the rock, eroding and obscuring until the stone was just a stone like every other stone.

What had Izzy told me? All things pass in time, lass. All things fade away. And all things were passing. I was drifting on the edge of something, skirting the surface. I felt as though I could thrust out my arm and break through the crust, reach a hand into another world. It felt so tangible, growing stronger by the hour, yet I somehow never touched it.

I scoured the bay with my binoculars, playing hide-and-seek with the seals. I watched a heron haunt the surf, lashing down at crabs and minnows. Absently, my gaze wandered to Dog Rock, and then to Ailsa's window. I started, then grinned. For the first time in days, she was there, looking back through binoculars of her own and waving enthusiastically. She gestured at me to wait. A moment later, she held a piece of paper to the window. I refocused the glasses.

SO WHAT'S UP?

It was written in fat capitals. I fished about on my desk for an A4 pad and a marker pen.

IN THE DOG HOUSE.

ME TOO. GROUNDED. DAD TAKES THE BOAT
AND I'M STUCK HERE.

THAT'S KIDNAP!

THAT'S MY DAD . . . WHAT HAPPENED TO YOU??

I smiled, but my heart sank. I wanted to tell her about Lachlan. I could never tell her about Lachlan.

DRANK TOO MUCH AFTER YOU'D GONE. MUM FURIOUS.

DAD'S IN A STECKIE, TOO.

NO SCHOOL?

NOT ME. HE'S RAGING. WORKING AT HOME.

I'M SO SICK AND TIRED OF THIS PLACE.

Across the bay, she grinned.

CHEER UP! COULD ALWAYS BE WORSE.

She waved again, and ducked down from her window. Could be
worse, she said. Could be worse. I thought of Anders, missing, and
Lachie, dead, and the ache that billowed in my heart. I reached
down and in slow, careful letters, wrote on the pad:

HOW?

CHAPTER 43

The *Island Queen* churned and trembled as she ploughed home across the Sound, bound for Bancree. I was on the top deck, as always, ignoring spots of rain and thinking about Lachlan and Anders and Ailsa and John and everything else. The day at school had vanished, and the clouds were low. Fog cloaked the distant island, so that all the world was painted in thick bands of blue and grey. I rolled with the waves. Bancree appeared in glimpses through the mist, only to vanish again as clouds drew around the coast like theatre curtains.

We were about halfway across the Sound when Jow cut the engines. The vibration stopped abruptly and for queer seconds we coasted, a ghost ship, turning with the waves. Someone called from the back of the boat, and I turned to follow the commotion. Jow climbed down from his cabin and hurried aft. Compelled to know, I followed, slowly, fingers tracing the guard rail. A small crowd had gathered at the stern of the ferry. With a wall of mist hanging beyond them, they peered down into the water. I joined the fringes of the group. No one spoke. Face down in the water, a body twitched and bobbed with the pull of the tide. Even after days at sea, I recognised the shirt, recognised the trousers, recognised the hair. Sea water sloshed in the dent in the back of his skull. We stood in silence and watched Lachlan float. His shirt had come loose and billowed around him. He wore one sock. His hands and feet were waterlogged and white.

'Jesus,' muttered Jow, 'get back, all of you. Everyone inside. Get below.'

'You want a hand with it, pal?' said one of the passengers.

Jow hesitated, then nodded. He unfastened a boathook from the rail. Everyone else trooped into the little lounge. A few were glued to the windows, wiping condensation clear, watching as the two men tried to fish the body from the water. A teenage girl stood on tiptoes, taking photos with her phone. Low chatter buzzed around the room, but I sat by myself on the far side, chewing my finger and not thinking about crabs in Lachlan's eyes.

It took them twenty minutes to catch him and haul him out. When Jow realised who it was, his voice changed. Even through the glass I could hear the new urgency. He dashed up to the cabin and the radio. The *Island Queen* had drifted on the tide, and he fired the engines back into shuddering life. Slowly, he turned the ferry back to Tanno, and we retreated from the mist into the mist. Jow gunned the engine slower, as though in respect for the dead.

The constabulary were waiting in the harbour. They stood in a grim line, both uniform and detectives. I recognised Tom Duncan right away. He had grown up, but I still saw a schoolboy. A silent crowd had gathered, witness to our arrival. When Jow tossed down the rope, the harbourmaster missed the catch and fumbled the mooring. He looked shaken. Eventually, the ferry was secured and the ramp dropped down. There was an ambulance waiting at the top of the slip. Two paramedics carried a stretcher onto the boat, and reappeared long minutes later with the body beneath a sheet. Tom Duncan and one of the other policeman stooped to look. Even from this distance I could distinguish Lachlan's sharp features, now bloated by exposure to the sea. They replaced the sheet, and Jow conferred with the police. The ambulance trundled away.

By the time we left, the crowd had swelled into dozens. They spoke with their heads on one side, never taking their eyes from the action. As we cast off once more, all I could sense was accusation. I couldn't look back for fear they'd read the truth upon me. I kept to the lounge, near a heater in one wall, and looked into the floor, the ribbing on the carpet, the bolts on the table legs. The other passengers were silent on the return trip. Word had quickly spread that it was Lachlan Crane in the water, Lachlan Crane beneath the sheet. There was a stunned amazement that he was finally dead.

For the first time in years, I felt seasick.

Buoys guided the ferry into Tighna, each crowded with gulls that watched the boat. We arrived into Bancree two hours late. One of Ronny's distillery pals drove past me on the road and gave me a lift most of the way home. I walked the last mile in misty darkness, sea chills crowding at me.

The house was belting heat, but I kept my coat on. Mum and Ronny were watching a film in the living room. He had one arm around her, and she had her legs tucked up on the sofa. The fire blazed, and Ronny's whisky shivered in the glow.

'Look who it is! You're late home, lass,' he said. 'Hot date in Tanno?'

Mum snorted, then saw my face.

'Flora?' she said. Ronny caught her tone, and lowered his glass.

'Everything OK?'

'What's going on, Flo?'

My tongue was too thick for my mouth.

'They've found Lachlan Crane.'

'Is he – Christ, Flora, is he alive?'

'No,' I said. 'They found him in the sea. We saw him from the ferry this afternoon. We had to turn back and go to Tanno. There was an ambulance. And police.'

'You didn't see him yourself?'

'He was floating on his front, but I knew it was him. I knew.'

'Oh, Flo.'

Mum stepped up and embraced me, tightly. After a moment, I thought to hug her back. I noticed for the first time that I was taller than her and from nowhere, I wondered what my father looked like.

'Are you OK, sweetheart?'

'Aye, I think so. I mean, I'm shaken, but aye.'

I could hardly look at Ronny. Dismay carved across his face. He started shaking his head. My head crowded with dark-grey cubes, grinding into splinters. This was what my guilt looked like. I was certain they would hear the sound.

'I'm sorry to tell you,' I said.

'It's not that,' he said. 'I don't give a shite for Lachlan. He was nothing but trouble. It's Anders I'm thinking of, and Bill and Dougie. They were good people. They were my friends. And if Lachie's dead—'

He stopped, caught his breath. Mum shifted uncomfortably, one arm still around me.

'Well,' he said, his face crumpling, 'you know what it means. We all do. It means Anders is done for, too, doesn't it? Oh, Jesus. Jesus.'

I'd never seen Ronny cry before.

'Hush, love. We don't know that yet.'

He pinched the bridge of his nose.

'Come on, Cath. Can't you see it?'

Mum was silent.

'This is no coincidence. It's like we're being hunted.'

'We—' she started, then fell silent. She let go of me and put her arms round Ronny. The teartracks on his face glowed in the firelight. He reached for his whisky, then paused.

'Christ,' he said, sitting upright. 'That's something else.'

'What?'

'Clachnabhan. The distillery. What will Munzie do if Lachie's dead?'

'He'll keep it open, won't he?'

'I don't know.' Ronny was grim. 'He's wanted to retire for years, only Lachlan's been too feckless. I don't know what this means.'

All three of us thought of what would happen if the distillery shut. That would be a farewell to the island. There was nothing else to do.

'I'd better call some of the lads. Better talk to Munzie.'

'All right, love.'

Ronny refilled his whisky and sat down by the phone. He began to dial. Mum stood beside me, chewing her nails, watching her husband.

'What if it's true, Flo? Oh God.'

'There's nothing else it can be,' I said, thickly. 'There were half a dozen policemen at the harbour. This is getting really serious.'

'You be careful, Flora,' she said, urgently, and grabbed my arm. 'Out by yourself all the time, and how you were last week. You promise me you'll stay safe.'

'I promise, Mum.'

It sounded hollow, but she gave me a weak smile. She smoothed the jumper where she'd grabbed my arm.

'I'll head to bed, I think.'

'OK. Yes. Yes. Goodnight, love.'

'Night, Mum.'

I went to my room. The Mutch book lay open on my desk. The voluptuous selkie waited like a centrefold, hand on hip.

This one is all yours, she said.

'It wasn't my fault,' I said, though I didn't believe it. I closed the book with a snap.

Ronny's voice burbled through the wall. The distillery made things even more jumbled. If it closed, we'd have to leave. There was nothing else to do on Bancree.

My reflection fractured darkly in the window condensation. Trickles ran across my face.

Lachlan in the water was worse than Lachlan in the pipe. Until I'd seen him suspended there, lofted in the waves, part of me had clung to the idea that I'd dreamed it all. Now there were witnesses and policemen. There was sodden, swollen white skin, and holes where his eyes should be. Gulls or crabs, scavengers.

No body, no crime, said Izzy.

Now they had a body.

I needed to speak to someone. I needed to see Ailsa.

CHAPTER 44

John Dobie skidded across the bay in the inflatable dinghy. I spied on him, ducking behind my curtains, as he laid it up on the beach. With the rugged kit bag slung over one shoulder, he marched off up the hill, heading south.

While the cat's away, I thought . . .

As I'd seen Ailsa do, I fitted the outboard motor and dragged it across the sand into the shallows. The water was ice cold against my shins as I waded in. The engine started first time, and exhaust passed across my face like cigarette smoke. Travelling slowly, I steered the boat across Still Bay, tiller vibrating in my hand.

I killed the engine on the approach to the islet. I navigated the dinghy towards the pontoon, badly, but managed to lash it to a post and step onto Dog Rock. Wings outspread, a cormorant sat on a rock no more than ten feet from me. It glared, haughty, and didn't move. The cottage seemed empty, but I knocked anyway. The little house was dead. I walked around the islet.

The chaffinches had gone, but a dozen crows waited in the secluded garden. They scrambled into flight as I approached, yelling and screaming down at me. The shed was musty, dark and empty, chinks of daylight showing through the roof. Bits of engine still lay strewn across the bench. I heaved the door closed and walked to the westernmost point. I found Ailsa where the Atlantic breathed against the shore. She sat hunched on a rock, arms wrapped around her knees, and stared into the nearest waves. When she heard me coming, she turned, startled, then broke into the brightest smile and jumped to her feet. She gave me a fierce hug. I found myself hugging her back.

Lachlan, I wanted to say. Lachlan.

'How did you get across?'

'Your dad's going to kill me. I pinched the dinghy.'

'You never did!'

'It's harder than it looks, isn't it? How long's he away for?'

Her smile retreated into melancholy.

'No idea. He's been all over the place this week. He's out every day. He's been going to the library in Tanno, ordering old newspapers. He's searching bits of the coast, too.'

'The police searched when Doug went missing.'

'That's never stopped him before,' she shrugged. 'He's certain the killer is here. But he's said that before, and been wrong. More than once.'

'So . . . how was he after the pub?'

'Furious. I don't think we spoke for three days. Hard to say which of us was madder. I'm so sorry about that.'

'Me too. Mum was raging. I haven't been in that much trouble for ages. She's treating me like a kid.'

'At least you get to be an adult the rest of the time. I get swaddled.'

'He'll have to let you go eventually. For the sake of your schooling, if nothing else.'

'He doesn't care about that. He just wants me locked away and safe. And Dog Rock does that. This is pretty much the edge of the map.'

She flipped a tiny pebble into the sea. It vanished without a splash.

'I don't know,' I said. 'I'm starting to think it's harder out here. It's rougher. There's more space to hide, to do things, and no one sees what's happening.'

She gestured at the bruise on my cheek, concerned, then reached across and almost touched my face.

'What happened to you, Flo?'

It had been a week, and the mark had almost faded, but it was still there, an echo in my skin.

'I fell over on the way home. Daft, I know.'

'You fell?'

'That's right,' I said, studying the sea.

'Oh. Right, OK.'

'You heard about Lachie?' I said, and teased fragments of lichen from the rocks.

'It was on the radio.'

'What do you think?'

'I think he got what was coming to him,' she said.

She sat half-turned away from me. When I looked at her, she followed the gulls. With a start, I realised she was deliberately avoiding my gaze.

Ailsa was hiding something too.

Seaweed sluiced in crannies at our feet.

'Did you and your dad go straight home?'

Still staring into the grey ocean, she nodded, and tucked hair behind her ear. We watched waves slapping on the rocks. The smell of the salt was overwhelming.

'I should get back before your dad comes.'

'Aye, I suppose. Sure you can handle the dinghy?'

'Yeah, it's fine.'

'I'm half-tempted to take you across and bring the boat back here. Make him swim for it.'

'Would he really be OK?'

'He'd be fine with the swimming,' she snorted, 'but not with me leaving Dog Rock. I'm on lockdown.'

'You talk like a prisoner,' I said, half-laughing.

She wiped her nose. 'Sometimes, that's what I am.'

With a jolt, I remembered what John had told me: a comfortable prison is still a prison. I found myself wondering if he'd been thinking of Ailsa. Probably not. In his story, the prisoner escaped.

'Things will get better,' she said. 'Dad will let me out again when this stuff with Lachlan blows over.'

I shook my head. 'You don't know this place like I know it. The Cranes are a big deal round here. I think it's about to get a whole lot heavier.'

'In what way?'

'There's a lad called Tom Duncan who used to go to my school. He's a detective now. I saw him in Tanno when they found Lachlan's body, and I think he's chasing it pretty hard. With someone like Lachlan, they need to show results.'

She chewed her lip. A thought occurred to me.

'Has John ever told the constabulary about his ideas? The map, all his research?'

She shook her head fervently.

'Dad doesn't trust the police at all.'

'Why not?'

'Because they should have found whoever killed my mum.'

The gusts of wind blew colder.

'I'm sorry, Ails,' I said. 'I should have thought.'

'Isn't it funny,' she mused, 'to miss someone you never knew?'

Her voice cracked a little, and she shifted away from me. I took half a step towards her. I reached out and put a hand on her shoulder. Her collarbones were sharp, even through her sweater. She leaned briefly against my hand, then stepped away. She rubbed her eyes with the back of her sleeve.

'Come on,' she said. 'You'd better get yourself home.'

The return trip in the inflatable was easier. A mild breeze blew me straight towards the beach. My inexperience with the dinghy showed on the approach to shore, when slight waves began to lift and drop me onto land. When the rib touched sand, I was bundled headlong into the boat. Lying face up on the floor, just a little shaken, the clouds above me ran like horses. The lift of the waves and the lurch of the backwash spun me in tiny arcs and I lay there for longer than I should have, knowing what it was to be helpless on the sea.

Maybe things would get better. Maybe it would all blow over.

And maybe, I thought, the world will fall down around us.

CHAPTER 45

I wandered into the kitchen in my pyjamas. Jamie grizzled, grinding balled fists into his eyes. He hadn't slept well last night, and that meant neither had Mum. They needed another room for him. Really, they needed my room. There wasn't anywhere else for him to go. He was growing up, and I was being squeezed out. Jamie sat on Mum's lap, grumbling to himself. As I poured a tall glass of orange juice, I became aware that she was staring at me. She looked grim. Something was up, and it was more than just a sleepless night.

'Mum?'

'You tell me, Flora Cannan. Tell me exactly what you've been up to.'

'What do you mean?'

'Is there any good reason why the police might want to see you?' She was shaking. The juice turned sour in my mouth.

'What? What about?'

'You tell me!' she snapped, and Jamie started with fright. A moment later, he started to wail. Mum shushed him, then turned back to me.

'Tom Duncan called this morning, asking for you. Just you, Flora. He requests your presence at the station at Tanno. To assist with an ongoing enquiry. If you can find time, that is,' she seethed, 'in your busy sixth year study schedule.'

'Mum—' I began, but she cut me off.

'Maybe it's nothing,' she said. 'But it didn't sound like nothing. There's so much going on, with Ronny's job, and the baby, and all these terrible disappearances. And the state you came home in the other night!'

'But I didn't do any—'

'Didn't you?'

She glared at me. I thought about Lachlan, and couldn't meet her eye.

'Sorry,' I whispered.

'Not sorry enough to stay out of trouble. Grow up, Flora. Grow up. I've only room in my life for one baby.'

She stood up and stormed away, Jamie perched on her hip and squalling. His cries receded as she crossed the house, getting as far away from me as she could. I stood in the kitchen by myself, feeling guilty, feeling dirty. Sunlight streamed through the windows, but it carried little warmth.

Lachlan was really dead, and the police wanted to see me.

This was happening.

Without really knowing why, I dressed in the red skirt Ailsa had given me. It was totally different to the shapeless clothes I normally wore, and it felt a little like armour, hanging straight and hip to my battered sneakers. I couldn't shake the sense that I was on borrowed time. Something in me decided to go out with a bang. Flushed, I tied my hair back with a handkerchief. It was a style I'd always wanted to wear out, but never had the courage. The skirt made me bold. I wore my large hooped earrings. They called me gypsy, so I'd give them gypsy. There was something defiant in dressing so self-consciously, rather than hiding myself away. I left for school, two fingers upturned to island life.

In the library, I struck out from my usual secluded corner and parked my things in the centre of the room. Curious glances slid over me. I set my jaw, ignored the mutters, kept my head down and worked. If they wanted me to be an outsider, then I'd be an outsider. I started to compile a final draft of my report. Selkies, selkies, selkies.

Born from the spirits of drowned sailors, born into sadness. Caught for ever between the land and the sea, tugged both ways and always torn, hands outstretched and gripping tight to both identities. Pulled both ways by the tide.

Island men coveted selkie maidens for their beauty, their mystique.

Island women craved selkie men for their virility, their authority. Barren girls cried seven tears into the sea to attract a selkie mate.

I realised with a start that selkie men were never captured – only selkie women. Seal men gave their affections gladly to craven, submissive human women. But for the selkie women, their love was held ransom by only the boldest human men. I flicked again through my notes. Regardless of the story, that held true in every case. Selkie girls danced in the surf as though in a shop window.

The selkie myth was a suppression of female sexuality.

I didn't like that at all.

I'd worked for three hours when the lunch bell rang. In minutes, the library filled with younger kids wanting internet access. Ignoring their curious looks, I checked my email once more before leaving. There was a message from the Tobermory crofting commune.

RE: MARCUS MUTCH

In a heartbeat, everything else dropped away. I hovered the cursor over the unread icon for a full minute, wavering, wondering if I really wanted to know. Then I clicked to read it.

It was from a woman called Jacinta. She was fairly new to the commune, she said, but had spoken to some of the older residents. One or two still remembered Marcus Mutch, though not especially fondly. He'd been bolshy and pompous, and hadn't mucked in with the rest of the commune. Rather than working his share, he'd shirked and skived and swapped his tasks. He was remembered as an aspiring writer, working feverishly late into the night, then reading his stories to anyone who cared to listen – and some who didn't care at all. All his work was about selkies and Scottish folklore. He'd passed into commune infamy for insisting that his writing be considered a fair share of the work. Nobody agreed, and he was promptly voted out by the rest of the workers. After barely a year on Mull, he'd stomped off the island in a rage, leaving half his things. He'd claimed he was sick of Scotland, and was going to try his luck elsewhere.

That might have been that, said Jacinta, except that he'd written to the commune a few months later, demanding they forward his remaining possessions to his new address in Brixton. They'd complied, pleased to be completely rid of Marcus Mutch.

No one had heard from him since.

My throat was dry. It hurt to swallow. Brixton, London. Whoever he was, Mutch was in the clear. That was one loose end tied up. I'd have to tell Ailsa before she explained my theory to her dad. Strangely, there was no great sense of relief – only anticlimax.

I sent a quick thanks to Jacinta, packed my things and left, planning to grab a sandwich before my visit to the constabulary. There was a cold bowl in the bottom of my stomach.

Walking down the stairs, not caring about where I put my feet, I heard the muted snuffles of someone crying. At the stairwell, hunched beneath the first flight and hugging her knees, was a schoolgirl. I couldn't see her face. I didn't think I knew her. I approached the shaking figure, cautiously, and bent low to touch her shoulder.

'Hey,' I said, softly, 'are you all right?'

The figure flinched and turned. It took a moment to recognise her through the tear tracks, the smudged mascara. It was Tina Robson. She was equally baffled to see me all dressed up, and for a dumb moment we simply looked at each other. She recovered first.

'P-piss off,' she said, running a sleeve across her eyes, her face. 'Leave me alone.'

'Tina? What's going on?'

'Like you give a shit,' she said, sneering, caught halfway to a sob. I looked at her. This was insane. In five long years, I'd never known her to cry. I'd never known she had heart enough to manage it.

'I'm trying to be nice.'

'Well don't bother.'

She turned away to the wall. Her shoulders shook again.

I stepped back and chewed things over. Something occurred to me, lurching upwards from the dark. There was a reason Tina had a reputation. Older boys, drinking, drugs. The handsome prince who would take her away from it all. I didn't want it to be true, but nothing else could upset her so much. I framed the word, and mouthed it twice before I managed to say it aloud.

'Lachlan. It's Lachie, isn't it?'

She froze. Still facing the wall, she nodded, and then her shoulders shook even harder.

'How long?'

She shifted. When it came, her reply was thick with snot. 'A couple of years.'

I looked up from the stairwell. In decreasing spirals, perspective sent the stairs darkening towards the third storey. Tina sniffled.

'He was. He was my way out of here. He was taking me to Edinburgh. He loved me.'

He didn't love her. Lachie wouldn't have taken her anywhere but Family Planning. But this wasn't the time to tell her that.

'Tina,' I said, 'I'm so sorry—'

Without turning round, she flapped an arm at me, waving me away, and another sob broke loose, high-pitched and ridiculous. I reached out again and touched her shoulder, then withdrew from the stairwell, stepping quietly. The door creaked like a coffin lid, and the sounds of the schoolyard flooded through. It was too bright, with the sun caught low in the clouds. Kids were shrieking too loudly. As the door closed behind me, I caught another of Tina Robson's sobs.

Tina and Lachlan. I hadn't known about that, but I could have guessed. She'd always hung out with older guys. She always partied hard. It boosted her social standing. And as for Lachie – well, it wasn't that big a town. There had always been rumours about him and Tanno schoolgirls. It hadn't mattered much to me, but it mattered to Tina Robson. A shudder passed through me. She'd steer clear of me, for now, after I'd seen her crying. But if she ever discovered that I'd been with Lachlan on the night he died . . .

That thought turned my stomach to ice. She'd either tell the police. Or hunt me down.

It was after lunchtime, but I wasn't hungry any more. The whole thing was such a mess. There was no one adult enough to understand except Ailsa, and I couldn't ever tell her.

I held my breath as I crossed the playground, focusing on my shoes alone. I felt suddenly, oppressively like a fraud, a priss, a fake. The clothes, the hair. It was a costume for an actress, a mask. It was slipping.

I left for the police station and kept my eyes fixed upon the gravel because the entire school, every kid in Tanno, was watching me walk, and all I had to wear was guilt and shame.

CHAPTER 46

The lobby of the police station was like a doctor's waiting room. The floor was laid with carpet tiles, chequered beige and burgundy, the walls a wan green. Placed haphazardly around the room, dog-eared posters advised me to lock up my bike, not to drink and drive. Report Crime.

The room was lit a nervy white-blue by fluorescent lights set into the ceiling. Something somewhere was humming. There were thick veneered doors set into every wall, and a counter cut into one side.

In a dull burst of office noise, the door beside the counter swung open, and DC Duncan emerged carrying several sheets of paper. He scanned the room. I was the only person there. He smiled at me.

'Hi, Flora.'

'Detective Duncan,' I said.

'Please,' he said, wrinkling his nose. 'I'm just Tom. You know that. Nice to see you. How long's it been?'

'Umm, years, I suppose. You went off to Glasgow.'

'Aye, and then I came back. Missed the old hometown, you know.' I grimaced.

He grinned. 'Still at school, then? Mr Baillie still there?'

'Aye, more's the pity. I'm in sixth year.'

'Great years, aren't they? Not long to go.'

'No.'

He stepped back and looked at me.

'It really is good to see you, Flora.'

There was a pause.

'I suppose you're wondering why we wanted to see you.'

'You could say that, aye. My mum's furious.'

'Sorry about that. It's important we speak to you, though. I'm hoping you might be able to help us out. I'm looking for . . . Well, character references, I suppose you might call them. To help me flesh someone out a little.'

'Lachlan.'

'I understand,' said the policeman, 'if it's too difficult for you to speak about.'

I swallowed thickly. 'No,' I said, 'no problem at all. If it helps you work out how he died.'

'Oh, we know how he died.'

'He drowned . . . didn't he?'

The detective was shaking his head. 'He didn't drown.'

'But I thought . . . everyone on the island thinks he drowned.'

'And maybe that's no bad thing for now. But I'm ninety-nine per cent convinced that he was murdered. I think he was killed on Bancree, and his body dumped in the sea. We're still waiting on the autopsy, but I'd bet good money on what it's going to say. And there's more, too.'

Duncan turned around, punched in a code and twisted the latch, holding the door a chink apart so I could look through. Beyond was a little anteroom. Again, my heart leaped, stumbled, and somehow beat on. Hunched in a plastic chair sat the Polish man who'd fought with Lachie. It was more than a week since they'd clashed, and he was in a terrible state. His hands were pitted with scabs. He wore a padded eye patch, and his head was wound about with bandages. Jutting above the collar of his tracksuit, rendering his neck obscenely wide, was a thick brace. His lower lip sagged open. Inside there was a glint of metal and red rawness. A vicious blue bruise crept out from under the eye patch and over his nose to bloom red around his good eye. He stared glumly, fixed, at the floor.

'Jesus,' I breathed.

I was genuinely glad he was still alive, but riddled at once with a dread of being recognised. The Pole was the only person to see me and Lachie alone together. Aside from the killer, he was the only one who could put me in the frame.

'Two fractured vertebrae,' said Duncan, closing the door with a firm clunk. 'The doctors tell me he's lucky to be alive.'

'What happened to him?' I said, trying to hold my desperate nerve.

'I'm pretty sure he had a run-in with Lachlan on the night he died.'

'You think he killed him?'

'No chance,' said Duncan. 'When Polski here was picked up, he was half-dead. He'd nearly drowned on his own blood. The doctors found teeth in his stomach. No, it wasn't him.'

'So how's he connected?' I said, and turned from the closed door to look up at the detective. He gazed directly at me. Inside, I crumbled, but forced myself to hold his gaze.

'Lachlan's body displayed marks consistent with a fist fight. My guess is that they had a set-to, and that Lachlan kicked the shit out of him, minding my language. We suspect that a third party then took advantage of Lachie being distracted by the scrap. In fact,' he said, peering closer, 'you look like you've been in the wars yourself.'

'I fell,' I said shortly, staring him out. 'What third party? Who did it?'

At last, the detective looked away. 'We're not sure,' he said, folding, and for a moment he was a wee boy at Tanno Academy, a few years above me, not even needing to shave. Then he turned back. 'But we'll find out. None of it stacks up. Lachlan isn't the only one, is he? You must have heard the rumours.'

'Of course, aye. Bill. And Doug, and Anders.'

The detective nodded. 'We are pursuing the possibility that all these men are connected. It's hardly a big secret when everyone's talking about it.'

John's map. His newspaper clippings, his mission. He was right after all. I felt a lurch of sadness, a wave of sympathy. Half a lifetime chasing shadows.

'We were hoping,' said Duncan, gesturing with his thumb, 'that the Pole might have seen something.'

'What does he say?' I asked, trying to keep the desperation from my voice.

'Nothing. His jaw's wired shut, and will stay that way for weeks, maybe months. It's broken in three places and he's lost half his teeth. And, somehow, he seems to have forgotten how to write as well.'

'Sorry?'

'He's not talking. He's not saying a word, by mouth or writing. To me or the translator. All I have are the facts that someone beat him half to death, that person was murdered, and that he wants to go home as soon as possible. Omerta. We won't see him again.'

'How do you know he wants to go home?'

'His compatriots from the fish farm assure me that's the only thing on his mind. The mysterious fact that he can make himself understood to them, but not to me, has not escaped my attention.'

'Do you think any of them could have done it?'

Duncan shook his head. 'No. They've good alibis. Some of them were working night shifts. Others were drinking in the Ship. Another was with his girlfriend. She's one of your schoolmates, incidentally,' he said, looking at me with a smirk.

'I haven't any mates at school.'

'Aye, well. They were all in Tanno. I think they're in the clear. Only matey here and a couple of others were drinking in Tighna, and the other two are accounted for until they went to find him. Besides, it doesn't feel right. The bust-up with Lachie was a fluke, as far as I can tell. The murder feels more than that.'

A stern-looking policewoman emerged from the office door, passing behind us, and I looked again into the little anteroom. This time the Pole saw me, and visibly flinched in recognition. He jerked back into his creaking chair, his lip curled, showing more of the metal that wired his jaws together. He emitted a weird, strangled gurgle, whimpering, not blinking, his one good eye staring at me. His reaction made my stomach lurch. He remembered me. He knew exactly who I was. I willed the door closed, closed before someone noticed his reaction. Duncan was still standing beside me, his back squarely to the Pole. Shaking and wincing, the Pole pointed one hand at me. At that moment, the door shut on him.

'You all right there, Flora?'

I nodded too rapidly, feeling a tight hard lump in my throat. My heart thrummed a hollow terror.

'Fine, I'm fine. Just a bit shaken. He's really mashed up, that guy.'

'I'm sorry you had to see it.' He spoke levelly, not sounding sorry at all. He watched me closely. I swallowed hard.

'Why exactly did you ask me here, Tom?'

'We heard that Lachlan had a bit of a thing for you.'

'He had a thing for all women.'

'We heard that he asked you and a pal out for a drink in the Bull Hotel. We heard you turned him down shortly before he left. Don't worry about the drinking,' he said, latching onto my guilt, 'we've bigger fish to fry right now than teenagers on the piss. The point is, you knew him. Tell me about him.'

'There's not much to tell,' I said. 'I only knew Lachie a little, and what I knew, well . . . I hated. I detested him. He tried it on with me and my friend, and we said no. He threatened Ronny's job. We saw him around a few times, but not really to talk to, you know?'

Duncan was nodding. 'What happened when you saw him, not really to talk to, on the night he disappeared?'

'Nothing. He was drunk. He asked us out again. I told him no, again. He went on his way, and I went on mine.'

'Can anyone corroborate this? Was your pal there? Anyone else?'

'My friend had already gone. I was walking back from the pub. Alone. If it helps, Lachie was quite . . .' I looked directly at the DC. 'He was quite insistent, if you understand me, Tom.'

Now it was Duncan's turn to blush.

'I think I understand, aye.'

'So, no,' I concluded. 'I don't know anything else.'

'Where did he go?'

My mouth formed the words before my brain knew what to say. 'To the sea,' I said. 'He walked towards the beach.'

'The beach,' he mused, 'very good. Well, I think that's enough of your time for now, Flora. Thanks for talking to me.'

'No bother.'

'It's been grand to see you. When all this is done, I'd love to see you again, you know? Catch up on old times.'

'Can I go now?'

'Aye,' he said, grin fading. I turned to leave. 'Actually, wait, there is something else. Who was your pal in the Bull? Would I know her?'

'She's new. Her name is Ailsa Dobie,' I said. 'She lives on Dog Rock.'

'Where?'

'You forgotten? The wee islet off Bancree. Opposite Grogport.'

He smiled, remembering, and looked again at the floor. 'Of course, aye. Dog Rock. By herself?'

'With her father. John.'

'John Dobie. OK, grand. If you think of anything else, we're always here. If you need us. I'm always here.'

He smiled, turned and walked back into the depths of the station. The Pole had gone. I waited until the door clicked shut, and then I let my mask slip.

'No,' I whispered, 'you're not.'

CHAPTER 47

I lied to my mother about the police. I told her it was a perfectly routine enquiry, because I'd been in the Bull that night. Everyone was being interviewed. Standard procedure, Mum. She apologised for yelling, and I'd accepted it with all the wounded grace I could muster, Lord help me, chalking up another notch of guilt.

Outside, the day was cool and dry, gusting strongly. There was an edge in the air, too, something draped across the island like a veil. I followed my feet up the coast road, out of Grogport and towards Tighna. Dog Rock watched me go. As I walked further from Still Bay, thinning birch trees obscured the black islet, and soon I could see nothing but the slender silver trunks.

I walked and thought of selkies, of Lachlan, of the sea, of Anders. And of John and Ailsa, too. She still hadn't returned to school. Without her, the ferry felt emptier, the schoolyard louder and more crowded. That dreadful night had put a barrier between us, and there was no getting around it. This made me sadder than I could bear.

I walked about halfway to Tighna. On the right-hand side of the road, the interlocking birches opened onto scrubby pasture. This was where we'd come out from seeing Izzy. Through the slight gap, across the fields, I could see the open space that hung above the

Bancree Sound, the black and white dots of gulls. They made me think of Anders. Where was he now? Underwater with the crabs, or drinking in a bar somewhere?

There was a faint line of smoke from Izzy's campfire, quickly stripped to nothing on the wind. I needed to see the shennachie, too. Walking across the field, the sheep ignored me.

'Hello, lass,' he said, quietly. 'Have you come for another selkie story?'

He was cooking sausages. The buckled frying pan rested on a grill, smoking and spitting fat. I plumped myself down beside the fire pit. Without really knowing why, I ignored my usual crate. Instead, I perched on the same old tyre that Ailsa had used, that night we'd come to see Izzy. I liked the thought that we'd shared the same space, as though my ghost could inhabit hers. Ghosts in high heels. It didn't work. I still felt lonely. I kicked my foot into the ground, scuffing sand. The land underneath was darker.

'Not this time,' I said.

'No,' he agreed, 'maybe not. It doesn't feel quite right, does it?'

I shook my head. He shoogled the pan, turning the sausages. They blazed fat in protest.

'How are you?'

I chose my words with care.

'Part of me,' I said, 'will never be all right. I don't think ever. But it's only been a fortnight, and already I can't remember some of it.'

Izzy nodded.

'That's a healthy reaction. It's how you cope with trauma,' he said.

The dark ground I'd scuffed up was lightening, the exposed moisture evaporating into the afternoon. Soon it would be gone altogether. I dug deeper with the toe of my shoe, turning over new dark soil. Would it get ever darker, the deeper I dug? I imagined the water table welling with Viking blood. Shapeshifters. Selkies.

'It gets better, lass. I promise you. Forgetting is how the brain heals. Plenty of things are better off forgotten.'

I pursed my lips, thinking about his stories. When Izzy died, his stories would die too.

'And some things need remembering,' I said, quietly.

He tended his pan. I don't know if he heard me. Out to sea, the gulls wheeled in dark hooks. Hanging immobile, gliding on the wind, they soared and slid in mean streaks. Clouds curdled on the horizon. The puffs of wind gusted cool, pregnant with rain.

'There's another gale coming. You battened down?'

'As much as ever,' said the beachcomber, without looking up from the fire. 'That's the trade-off for living like this. I always expect collateral damage from a storm.'

'You've seen a few, I guess.'

He grunted. 'What choice do I have, moving to the islands? You learn to live with the weather, and pick up the pieces afterwards.'

'How long have you been a beachcomber?'

He leaned forward and poked the fire, loosing a burst of salty smoke. His lips were moving as he counted. Then he shrugged.

'Pretty much as long as I care to remember. Years and years, anyway.'

'So how old are you now? When's your birthday?'

'I'm not completely sure,' he said, halfway to a grin. 'I stopped counting when people stopped giving me presents.'

'When you started beachcombing?'

'I suppose so, aye. I wanted to see more of the world. Beach-combing and stories became the means to the end.'

'Do you ever regret it?'

'No one's ever asked me that,' he said with surprise. 'I don't know. That's a good question.'

He frowned, and went back to shaping the coals. I thought he'd dropped the subject until he spoke again.

'There are things that I regret, for sure. But those same things brought me to this path. They are not the path itself. If I'd turned off somewhere else, I wouldn't be here now. Does that make sense?'

I turned it over.

'Maybe.'

'What I mean is,' he said, 'I don't regret what I do now. I've found my calling. I know who I am, and what I do. It's all part of the same journey. That's true of every person on the planet.'

I went back to the clouds, the gulls. I imagined the turbines on the Atlantic side of Bancree, stood immobile despite the wind. Sentinels, totem poles. Izzy leaned back in his makeshift throne.

'But you didn't come here to discuss my regrets, did you? And if you're not here for selkie stories, why are you here?'

'I don't know,' I said, miserably.

'I'll tell you, then. You're here because you can't talk to anyone else about Lachlan.'

I kept my eyes on the ground. The scuffmark was gone, faded to nothing without me noticing.

'Have you told your pal? That Ailsa?'

I didn't say anything. The dirt was all the same sandy colour. I couldn't see the scuff at all. It was gone.

'Aye, I thought as much,' said Izzy.

Out to sea, the clouds were growing denser and darker. I held my hand to my eye, and pinched the clouds between my fingertips.

From here, they were tiny. They weren't storm clouds at all. They were cotton pads, stained blue with old mascara.

'Do you ever,' he continued, after a moment, 'wonder who moved Lachlan's body?'

'Every minute of every day.'

'Me too. I wonder, Flora . . .'

'What?'

'Don't you think it's rather suspicious,' he said, 'that islanders have been disappearing since Ailsa and her father moved to Bancree?'

'Bill and Dougie vanished before they arrived.'

'But they were there the night Lachie vanished?'

'They left the pub well before he grabbed me.'

'Could've doubled back,' said the beachcomber.

'They could have,' I admitted, tiredly, 'but I don't think so. John was angry. He took Ailsa straight home. Look, this is daft. He came to look for missing people, not to make more folk vanish.'

Izzy frowned. 'Is that right?'

'Aye, he's been tracing the disappearances for years.'

The beachcomber was baffled. 'Why would he do a thing like that?'

'I'm probably not supposed to tell anyone,' I said, 'but his wife is one of the missing people. Years ago. After she vanished, he started looking for other people who'd gone missing the same way. So it's not John. He's a damaged soul, but that's it.'

Izzy stared to sea, lips moving, then turned back to me. 'What about Ailsa, then?'

'No way. She was a baby when her mother disappeared. This trail goes back decades.'

'Decades?'

'All over the islands.'

Izzy frowned and let out a low whistle, moving the frying pan to a cooler part of the fire. The buttery foam around the sausages subsided. Deep in thought, he ripped a chunk of bread from a loaf. He poured the pan butter onto the bread, and started munching.

'Is this why you thought to put Lachlan in the sea?' he asked through a mouthful of crumbs.

'Aye. I wanted him to disappear, and figured if it was the same as the others, the police wouldn't look as hard. Would have been a different story if they'd found Lachlan in the pipes.'

Izzy's chewing slowed to a stop.

'But that's not public knowledge, lass. Only a few folk know about it. Tell me,' he said, urgently, 'how many people knew enough to make Lachie disappear just like the others?'

The police knew. I knew. Izzy knew, since I'd told him.

John and Ailsa Dobie.

The killer.

No one else.

'There have been rumours,' I said, weakly.

'Come on, lass,' said Izzy. 'There's not that many folk to choose from. And riddle me this. What are the chances of the killer being right there on the night, just in time to save your skin?'

'The Dobies had already left,' I whispered, but my skin goose-bumped.

'It had to be someone in the area. It had to be John.'

'John's looking for the killer himself.'

'What a great cover story. It's the perfect excuse to go wherever you like.'

I thought of the boat ride John had given me. That bag of his, stowed at the stern, and whatever heavy thing he kept hidden in it.

What had looked like hair. His reaction, the fury in his eyes when I'd touched it.

'Bill and Dougie vanished before they came to Bancree,' I protested, fighting against the weight of Izzy's theory.

'So maybe he came here early, scouting round, and did it then. Or maybe they were just accidents, pure and simple.'

My head reeled. It couldn't be. The man had spent almost half his life searching for his missing wife. Or had he? Izzy was right. It would be the perfect cover story. And Ailsa, too. Did she know about this? Or was she part of John's act? She was hiding something. Just like me, she was keeping something secret. In my mind, jigsaw pieces began to fit together.

I just want him to stop, she'd said.

Then I recalled my fantasies in the bathtub, and that hot, stirring passion, the way I'd let myself melt into those dark eyes, the way they'd filled my vision, filled my world. I blushed with shame. Izzy was watching me closely.

'They're my friends,' I said, suddenly bold. 'I don't want to hear this.'

'Ach, it's probably nothing. It's just an idea. There's a chance this is two and two making five. There's not enough to tell the cops.'

'No,' I said, feeling relieved. Even with all the signs pointing towards John, I clung to that fact that there wasn't actually any proof against him, and tried to ignore whatever lived inside his kit bag.

'But I tell you this, Flora.' Izzy leaned closer to me. He smelled strongly of old clothes. 'Be canny. Be very, very careful. I think you should stay away from him. And from Ailsa too.'

'I won't do that,' I said, quiet and fierce. My hands were shaking.

'Because if it is him, and he discovers you know something, there'll be another disappearance.'

Up this close, Izzy's eyes were pale, blinding blue. The corneas tinged a buttery yellow, laced with minute, fragmenting blood vessels. An echo of the black eye, the faintest violet ring was buried in his skin.

'And it'll be you, lass.'

CHAPTER 48

On the ferry, I flicked through my report one last time, rereading words and phrases and thoughts from weeks ago, a lifetime ago. They felt lifeless. Suddenly, I resented what I'd done. I'd stifled the selkies, squeezed all the life from them. I buried the report in my bag and gazed into the Sound, searching for selkies in the choppy sea.

Even in the school corridors, I could smell the ocean.

Miss Carlyle sat at her desk, marking first year jotters. I watched her from the doorway. She was in her late forties, probably, or maybe early fifties. She cycled through the same half-dozen outfits each week. She'd been an inspiring teacher, but seeing her, here, working by herself, made me feel melancholy. Seeing things as they were. Growing up.

Grow up, Flora.

She looked up, though I hadn't knocked, and a smile lit her face.

'Flora!' she said, 'come on in.'

I wandered over to the desk, hefting my report.

'I've finished, Miss.'

'Already? This isn't due until half-term.'

'I know. But . . .'

God, I felt so low.

'But?'

'I don't think I can handle any more, Miss.'

Concerned, she peered at me above her glasses, and started flicking through the report. I leaned back on one of the classroom tables, crossed my legs and looked out the window. Bed and Breakfasts, hotels. Grey vacancies.

Welcome to Tanno. Please Come Again Soon.

'This is clearly very good,' she said, quietly. 'I'll read it properly later, and give you some notes. But . . . tell me, Flora. What's wrong? What can't you handle?'

'I'm not sure, Miss. It's just so . . . dark. It's all so negative.'

'The selkie stories?'

'No. They're just daft. It's history itself, Miss.'

She smiled, blandly, and shook her head.

'I don't follow.'

'There's no more mystery,' I said, blurting it out. 'There's no more magic.'

She traced her fingers over the front sheet.

'I heard the stories,' I said, 'and I was hooked. They were really exciting. I was hooked, Miss. I wanted to know more. And now, I've analysed them, and contrasted them, and explored them, and explained them, and now . . . the magic's gone, Miss.'

Frowning, she thumbed through the report.

'It's hollow,' I said. 'It's all so empty.'

Fragments of words echoed on the whiteboard. Nothing survived entire.

'That's all part of growing up, Flora. You know that, don't you? You must know that? It all goes in the end.'

'I'm not sure,' I managed, thickly, 'that I want that for myself.'

'You may not have a choice. You're a clever girl. The best student I've had in years.'

I shrugged.

'But we're worried about you, Flora. This report is obviously a long way above the standard I expect, but then Mr McLaggan tells me you've been skipping English. What's going on?'

A gull screamed inches from the window, and Izzy's voice echoed in my head.

'If you put a bear in a cage,' I said, 'it stops being a bear.'

She looked exasperated. 'You're too smart to believe in this . . . magic, as you call it.'

'I can try,' I said.

'Then you'll be lying to yourself.'

Somewhere in the school, a bell rang. Moments later a horde of first years streamed into the room.

'Goodbye, Miss.'

'We'll talk some more next week,' she urged. 'I'll see you then.'

I smiled, but couldn't bring myself to say it back.

The playground was deserted. Wind caught crisp packets in eddies, turning them in circles, scooting them into walls and drains. The chatter of classrooms fell away completely as I stepped beyond the gate. Killing time, I turned into Tanno's posh streets and walked the long way to the harbour, old stone buildings all around me.

An ugly tortoiseshell cat hissed at me, then scuttled low beneath a parked van. My sneakers were quiet on the pavement. Turning at random down the avenues, the sharp ring of footfall on stone sparked my attention, sounding out behind me. I turned, casually, but there was no one there. The footsteps had stopped. I watched the empty street. Parked cars and thick sycamore trees lined both pavements, stretching back forty or fifty metres. Plenty of places to hide. At the far end, a car passed across the T-junction, the noise of its engine receding in a purr. Leaves tumbled in the middle of the road.

I turned and continued, newly alert, ears pinned back. Again, I heard the scrape and step of footsteps, echoing my own, the street ringing quietly with the clicks of shoes on stone. They dogged my own. I rounded another corner and accelerated, ducking down a muddy alley between two houses. I splashed through ruts and puddles, emerging into a little courtyard, bounded on all sides by garages. The alley continued through the yard to the other side of the block, but I waited, peering back towards the avenue. I could just see the road. Heart-rate up from the run, I waited to see who'd been following me, who'd been hiding. And I waited. And waited.

I heard the footsteps behind me a moment too late. I spun round even as she shoved me in the back, and I fell, twisting, landing on my hip in the mud. I looked up. She'd doubled back and taken the other alleyway, sneaking round into the courtyard from the other side. She was wearing uniform. She should have been in school. Tina Robson stepped closer.

'What the hell?' I gasped.

Last time I'd seen her, she'd been crying about Lachlan. I'd felt sorry for her. Now she loomed above me, glaring, and she looked vicious.

'I heard something, Flora Cannan.'

'What are you playing at, pushing me?' I spluttered, heaving myself to my knees. I stood up, cold where the mud clung to my clothes, and started brushing myself down.

Her eyes glinted with malice.

'I heard about you and Lachlan,' she said.

I froze. I couldn't blink, or breathe. She leaned in closer, closer, until she whispered directly in my ear.

'I heard you shagged him,' she said, and the heat of her breath was clammy on my skin. 'The night he disappeared. I heard you were with him all night.'

'You heard wrong,' I said, stepping back, barely croaking the words.

'Naw. Naw, I don't think so. Karen's been seeing this Polish guy a few times. His mate was the guy Lachie took to pieces. They've all been talking about it. He told us things he never told the cops. He saw someone who looks a lot like you, Flora, out on Bancree.'

'You've got the wrong idea,' I said, and pushed her away from me. 'I couldn't stand Lachie. I thought he was a prick.'

'Oh, he was a prick, all right. But he was mine.'

'I didn't. Look, I never. I did nothing with him. He tried it on, plenty of times, but I always said no.'

'So why were you with him that night, then?' Her breath smelled of bubblegum.

'It was . . .'

It was an accident, was what I wanted to say. I was supposed to be with my friend. It was Lachie's fault. Someone smashed his head in. Someone put him in the sea, and I don't know who, and every day is limbo.

I closed my mouth.

'. . . or maybe I should just take it to the constabulary,' she hissed, 'and let them ask you themselves?'

I glimpsed an escape route.

'Aye, that's an option. And while you're there, maybe you can explain about you and Lachie being an item, too.'

'Why would that bother them?' she sneered.

'You've been seeing Lachie for a couple of years.'

'So what?'

'So you were fourteen when it started. Or thirteen, even.'

Now it was Tina's turn to freeze.

'And he was . . . how old? Twenty-two? Twenty-four?' I said, as casually as I could, flicking the grit from my shoulder. 'I'm sure they'd like to know all about that, wouldn't they? Bound to be a big fuss. That sort of thing gets around.'

Her face morphed from bafflement to understanding.

'You don't know what you're talking about.'

'Awful young for a trophy girlfriend, Tina.'

'That's nothing compared to murder.'

'Maybe not,' I said, 'but I didn't do it, and you know that, and he's gone. I'm leaving as soon as I can. It's not my reputation the town would be chewing over.'

'It'd blow over in a week,' she faltered.

I shook my head.

'No. You'd be that girl for the rest of your life.'

'Bullshit,' she said, suddenly pale. 'That's bullshit.'

'What was it you told me? Something about time going slower when everybody hates you?'

In the muddy courtyard, we stared at each other.

Tina broke first.

'Fuck you, Cannan. Fuck you. Don't you come near me. Don't speak to me again. Not a word. You or your creepy pal.'

'That suits me fine,' I said. 'Leave us alone, and we'll have nothing to do with you.'

Cats, the pair of us, come together, fighting to be left alone. She turned heel and stormed away, footsteps measured in tight beats. Once she was out of sight around the corner, the courtyard seemed a lot bigger. I looked down at my hands. They were trembling, but I was hot with anger. I'd grazed the heel of one palm when I'd fallen, and blood welled from the skin. A film of sweat chilled on the nape of my neck, but my pulse was hard and high.

Rain fell in isolated drops, spitting and then gone. Single beads struck my head, my face, but the clouds didn't yet have strength enough to burst. Everything was drawing closer. The circle around me was tightening, quickening, still invisible. I could feel it beginning to squeeze.

CHAPTER 49

The clouds streamed low, racing on offshore blasts. The post bus trundled out of Grogport. Hunched low against the sky, a solitary figure sat on my headland. I dumped my bag on the doorstep, and walked towards her through the dune grass. Ailsa sat cross-legged, leaning back, the wind flapping hair into her face. She smiled when I sat down beside her.

'This is my favourite weather.'

'Aye, me too. It feels like anything could happen.'

'So,' she asked, eyeing up my spattered clothes, 'new look?'

'Do you like it? Rockabilly meets muddy puddle. It's all the rage in Paris.'

'Suits you.'

'Cheers,' I grinned. Gulls hurtled a carousel over the bay.

'Want to talk about it, then?'

'I bumped into Tina. She'd heard about . . .'

I bit my tongue. Ailsa still didn't know I'd been alone with Lachlan.

'About . . .?' she prompted.

'She'd heard some daft rumour,' I said, carefully, 'that I'd been seeing Lachlan Crane. Turns out she had a thing for him herself.'

Ailsa frowned. The expression made her seem precocious, a serious six year old despairing at the affairs of grown-ups.

'That's mad. You'd never have anything to do with him.'

I hesitated. At least she hadn't pressed me on it. I wouldn't be able to outright lie to her face. I couldn't. And with that, I realised that I cared desperately what she thought of me. I wanted to be better, and to be a better friend, but my secrets still hung between us. Even as I healed, Lachlan polluted me. I felt dirty to sit beside Ailsa. I couldn't tell her. She'd hate me. I felt sick to have to watch my words.

'The police wanted to see me.'

'What about?' she said, suddenly urgent.

'No big deal,' I said. 'They were trying to find out more about Lachlan, that's all. I explained that he tried to chat us up, then left.'

'That must have been tough.'

'It wasn't too bad. I just told them. You know. What happened.'

Her face relaxed, the frown melting.

If John was a killer, Ailsa had to know about it. She had to. Sitting beside her on the headland, I simply couldn't sense that malice in her. But still I had the sense that she was hiding something. I tried to shake the feeling off. I was becoming paranoid, with every waking minute haunted by doubts and questions.

'That Marcus Mutch is in the clear, by the way,' I ventured. 'I asked around, sent some emails. He took the huff with Scotland years ago. Last seen in London. So that's a dead end.'

She nodded.

'Good,' she said. 'In a way, I'm relieved. Dad would have been impossible if he'd actually had a name to pin it on.'

'Back to square one.'

'Or maybe he's still chasing ghosts.'

The gulls screamed at each other.

'I finished my selkie report. Handed it in this morning.'

'Did you use Izzy's stories?'

'They're all in there somewhere. He may not believe in books and writing, but I do.'

'That's been your life the whole time I've know you,' she said. 'So . . . what will you do now, Flo?'

From the headland, I could reach out and crush Grogport between my fingers. I found myself thinking of the folk tale about the girl who became a goose and simply flew away.

'Flora?'

'Life doesn't get any easier,' I said, quietly.

'Did you really think it would?'

I shook my head.

'The way I see it,' said Ailsa, 'you'll be shot of this whole place inside a year, right?'

'Can't come soon enough.'

'Ach, jog on. With your whole life to come, what does a few more months matter?'

'Not much, I suppose.'

'And look around, look at all this. There are worse places to live, aren't there?'

'Aye. I guess so.'

'Grand. And you can handle Tina?'

'I think me and her have an understanding,' I said, grimly.

'So we've a few more nights on the cherry schnapps to come, right?'

'Oh Jesus, no. Never again. I was puking pink all day.'

'I told you at the time,' she grinned. 'You should've had a swim.'

I smiled and shook my head. Neat terns hung on the breeze.

'I'm glad you came here,' I said.

'Aye. Me too.'

The barrier was still in place, but friendship settled on me like a blanket. I trusted her. I liked her. Whether I'd wanted it or not, we were friends. She tied me to Bancree. And as much as I wanted to flee, I felt good about it.

She offered me one of her headphones. I fitted it into my ear. She grinned and winked, then gazed into the sky. I studied her. The earpiece trailed against her white neck and hid beneath her hair. Her ear was a shell, whorled and sea-washed into smooth twists. We didn't speak, but listened to the music smoulder and build, burning, washing through static into nothing.

'I'd better go,' I said, unplugging the earpiece. She removed her side and stowed the headphones in her bag. It was only when we stood up that I noticed how strong the wind had become. Out of the lee of the headland, the wind buffeted and shoved. I looked at Ailsa. Her hair streamed from her face.

'There's a gale blowing up,' she said.

'Been brewing for days. Something's changing, isn't it?'

'I think so too. But I don't know what.'

I followed her down onto the beach.

Together, we unstaked the dinghy, and flipped it right way up. I sat on the windward side of the inflatable to keep it from blowing away, and Ailsa kicked off her sneakers. Turning half away, she reached beneath her denim skirt and found the hem of her tights, tugging them down, her thighs startlingly white where she stepped out of the dark material. We carried the dinghy down to the sea. The tide was on the ebb, and we walked across metres of cold wet sand, saturated and compact.

Ailsa went in first, wading into the water without breaking

stride, and lowered the bow of the little boat. I laid the stern into the shallows. She stood up to her shins in the bay, wavelets lapping over her bare knees, the wind blowing dark hair in front of her face. She had to raise her voice over the sound of the sea, hissing and shushing on the sand.

'Flora,' she said, 'listen. I want you to know this. I'll always be your friend. Do you hear me?'

'Excuse me?' I replied, lifting my voice into the wind. Salt spray lifted to my face.

'Will you remember?'

'I'll remember, but I don't know why you'd say such a thing.'

'Just in case. If me and Dad have to go away again. Even if you change your mind about me.'

She spoke so lightly, so honestly, it made me uncomfortable. I looked away into the grey green ploughing sea.

'Why would I change my mind?'

'Just remember what I said. Remember that, Flora.'

A wave raced in towards me, sluicing over my feet. I hopped away, uselessly, but my shoes had already filled with frigid water, squelching even as the sea rolled back. I wanted to reach out. I didn't know what she was saying to me, but I sensed there was truth in it, truth and urgency.

A light flared in me. I had to give something back. In case it happened to me. In case she ever found out what I was.

'Ailsa,' I faltered, 'about Lachlan.'

She watched me so closely, her dark features knitted with concern as the water ploshed between her legs. I tried to frame the words, but nothing came. I couldn't say anything, and then the moment was gone. I shut my mouth.

'Lachlan's dead, Flo,' she said. Her voice cut through the busy sea, the blustering wind. 'He's gone. I only met him twice, and I'll never care enough to miss him. It wasn't your fault he died. Was it?'

Her dark eyes, asking, imploring. I was mute.

'Life is tough enough with the people you care about, without wasting time on the ones you don't.'

Spoondrift scattered from the lacing wavecrests, fizzing as it pattered on the water. And then she grinned, wind whipping at her hair. Still beaming, she leaned backwards into the sea. Her skirt dipped two fingers deep as she pulled on the boat, tugging the weight of the dinghy towards her. I let go the handle at the stern and she jumped in, her legs lean white scissors as she swung herself aboard. Already adrift and under momentum, she cranked the outboard once, then twice, the engine caught furiously, and she dipped the whizzing blades beneath the surface. At once the water foamed white. She turned the rib for Dog Rock and didn't once look back.

CHAPTER 50

I stepped out of my wet shoes and knocked them together, shaking loose the crust of sand. I went inside. Ronny sat by himself in the lounge, his hair up in the samurai top knot. He held a tumbler with a mouthful of whisky still sloshing at the bottom. The bottle was uncorked on the floor beside him. The gathering storm let only a little daylight through the window. It was about five in the afternoon. I'd never seen him home so early on a weekday. I'd never seen him drinking during the day, except with Anders.

'Hey, Teenwolf,' I said, cautiously, 'how's it going?'

He'd been lost in thought, and started at my voice, looking up. Amber fluid spun madly in the glass.

'Hey, Flo,' he said, and looked down. He gestured at the tumbler. 'Not great, to be honest.'

'You're back awful early.'

He grinned without humour. 'Not my call. The decision's been made. The distillery's closing, pet. Lachie was the end of it. Old man Munzie's had enough. Clachnabhan is up for sale, and we're on reduced hours while he looks for a buyer. So I came home.'

'Better here than the Bull,' I said, gesturing at the tumbler in his hand.

'Clachnabhan Malt, eighteen years old.'

'That's older than me.'

He raised the glass and peered at me through the whisky.

'There was a time, not long after I'd met your mum. Me and Anders had been out drinking. When the Bull closed, we bought a bottle of whisky, and decided it was a good idea to climb the Ben. The best idea in the world. There was absolutely nothing else we could do instead, you know? So we struggled up it in pitch black, right to the top. And there, at the summit, we drank all the whisky. Man, we were blootered. We had an argument about football, Denmark versus Scotland. It was incredibly important. We decided that the only way to settle the fight was to race each other back to town. And so we go running down the hill, blind drunk, totally out of control. Running into trees, falling over.'

Ronny snorted with laughter, but his eyes glistened.

'So who won?'

'It was an honourable draw. About halfway down, we crashed into each other. Anders cracked his head on a branch, and I twisted my ankle. We limped back to his house, and I remember thinking – things are pretty good. I was with my best mate, the job at Clachnabhan was going grand, and I'd started seeing this amazing woman. That was your mum. Then Jamie came along. Anders has been there, Flora, all the time.'

He brought his sleeve to his eye.

'And now he's not,' finished Ronny, sadly, 'and the distillery's going, too.'

Bear hugs. Big laughs. Holding Jamie like a china doll.

'What will you do?' I asked.

Ronny twisted the tumbler between his fingers, transfixed by the tiny waves in the whisky, watching it slide across the glass. He started shaking his head.

'The question isn't what I'll do, Flo. Here's the question. If the distillery closes,' and here he held up the tumbler, whisky detonating gold in the lamplight, 'then exactly what else is there?'

There was no good answer. With Clachnabhan gone, there was nothing but the fish farm, and Ronny had done his time on that. He grinned wide and wolfish at me, no humour in his smile.

'You know what that means?'

I nodded, mute.

'Sláinte,' he said, and downed the glass in one gulp. He sucked his cheeks, and reached to refill the tumbler.

Ronny would make the only decision he could for the good of his family. If the distillery closed, they'd be leaving Bancree.

Leaving the island.

Leaving the island. It was all I wanted, but even thinking it felt unreal. I tested the weight of the doorframe, pushing against it, pushing until my palm began to burn. I felt cheated. Leaving was supposed to mean something. I felt robbed of the choice. I left Ronny to his whisky, and walked through to my room.

I felt too numb. I imagined Ailsa's face when I told her we were going. For ridiculous moments, I wanted to stay on Bancree more than anything in the world. I wanted to stay on Dog Rock.

I peeled off the muddy clothes and examined myself in the mirror. The ghosts of bruises still marked my ribs, my hips, my thighs. There was a faint red line still clinging to one side of my neck, but it was fading fast. Every day, my body healed a little more, forgot a little more. Soon it would remember nothing. None of my injuries had been bad enough to leave a scar. The memories were fading, as memories always do.

In the mirror, my body was not my own. My breasts were too small. I was too pale, too skinny, too tall, too awkward. There was nothing to my hips, no curves. Nothing feminine, womanly, girly, sexy. The bones stuck out. Flora, virtually fat free. Richard gave me bruises when we had sex. My hair was plain. My cheekbones were too high and broad, gypsy-girl, Romany, Slavic girl. Weirdo. My eyes were cat's eyes, almonds, too pale. I wore weird clothes. I did weird things.

I took off my hoop earrings, dropped them on the floor. Eased off my bangles. They hit the carpet without a sound. I undid the ribbon from my hair. It was cool in the room. The air prickled me, chasing across my skin, raising goosebumps in waves. I reached an arm around my body, spreading my fingers, intertwining ribs and fingers, tracing the channels of my ribcage from the lower floating bones to my sternum. Another ley line, running from my thigh to the sloping underside of my breast. Everything in angles. Where are the curves, skinny bitch? What kind of woman are you? What it's like to fuck a real girl. Real girls, spilling pink and white from tabloid newspapers that men read in their tea breaks. The tiny hairs on my arm stiffened into thin down. I could've had a coat of fur.

I could have been a Viking girl.

I could have been a selkie, rank with salt.

I climbed into bed, despite the early hour, and pulled the covers across my head, and I cried and cried because there was nothing else to do. And when I was done, two voices echoed in my skull.

All things heal in time, said Izzy.

It never gets better, said John.

CHAPTER 51

I was startled awake by a rap at the door. Groggy and disorientated, my eyes gummed with sleep and tears, I gazed at the shadows on the ceiling and tried to make sense of the sounds. Coming round, my attention focused to a point.

'Flora?'

Mum called through the door, and knocked again. I could hear the tension in her voice. 'Flo, it's the constabulary, love. The police. They need to speak to you. Are you decent?'

'Can I call them back?' I yelled.

'It's not the phone, Flo.' Her voice was tight. 'They're here. Now. In the house.'

Something caught high in my throat. I threw on some clothes and stepped warily from the room.

Mum waited in the hallway, sadness and anger and shame all mixed up together.

'You told me it was nothing,' she said, and touched me on the shoulder, pushing me so slightly towards the kitchen.

Tom Duncan sat at the table with Ronny, drinking a cup of tea. In front of him, on the kitchen table, lay a cardboard folder. As I walked into the room, they both turned to look at me. Mum followed close behind. I could feel her at my back. Ronny stood up, clearly pissed from the whisky. He and Mum stood together by the worktop.

'Miss Cannan,' said Duncan, 'good evening.'

Him being on Bancree was bad enough. Calling me Miss Cannan made it worse.

'My name is Flo. You know that. You know me, Tom.'

He looked down at the tablecloth, then cleared his throat.

'This is official business.'

They must know about me and Lachlan. Somehow, they knew. Duncan gestured at the vacant chair. I sat down with a hundred-weight in my stomach.

'What's going on?' I said.

'Soon after talking to you,' he said, 'we received an anonymous phone call.'

Tina Robson. It must have been Tina, calling my bluff. I felt my fist curl. I studied the table, waiting. But what Tom said next surprised me.

'Following that phone call, I made a few enquiries into John Dobie.'

I looked up, baffled.

'John?'

'I now have very good reason to believe he's required to assist in a number of ongoing investigations. I understand you know him and his daughter fairly well.'

They wanted John. The police had finally woken up to Izzy's theory. Two plus two equals five, and torrents of rain burst in rattles on the skylight.

But who would call the cops? Tina didn't know a thing about John Dobie.

'Ailsa's my friend,' I said. 'You already know that. She hasn't done anything.'

'No one's accusing her of anything,' said the detective. 'But her father, well. That's something else. John Dobie may be extremely dangerous.'

'Where's your proof?'

Duncan was silent.

'There's no proof, is there?'

'I have extremely strong suspicions. We'll find evidence on that island. I know it.'

'Leave him alone. He's done nothing wrong. John Dobie's had nothing but bad things happen to him. He lost his wife. He's been looking for her half his life.'

'Yes,' said the detective, queerly, 'he has. It's taken me a while, but I traced him back. I need to inform you, Flora, that his movements match those of several other suspicious disappearances.'

'That's because he's investigating them himself!'

'He's doing what?' asked Duncan, blinking in surprise.

'John believes they're all done by the same person. He thinks it's been going on for years, but your lot haven't made the connection. So he's been looking for the killer himself. And he's tracked them here, to Bancree.'

Duncan leaned back, thinking, and stared at the rain streaking on the window. Then he pinched the bridge of his nose.

'Christ. No, Flora. It's the other way round. He doesn't follow the missing people. They follow him.'

I started shaking my head. Behind him, Mum put her hand to her mouth.

'Do you not see,' said Duncan, 'how this looks?'

'You haven't met him. He couldn't hurt anyone.'

Even as I said it, I faltered. I thought of the sadness in him, but also the menace, the streak of anger.

First Izzy, now the police. The jigsaw pieces rotated, and started making a picture, but it was all wrong. This wasn't how it was supposed to go.

I want him to stop, said Ailsa.

'It's perfect,' said Duncan, softly. 'No wonder they never caught him.'

'But he's heartbroken. His wife was one of the missing people.'

'You've been over there, Flora!' said Mum. 'You've been alone with him.'

'He's looking for his wife, that's all. He's so sad. He's completely broken by it.'

They looked at me.

'I can't explain,' I said. 'It's like he's had his heart ripped out, and now he's walking about without it.'

'That's tripe,' snapped Mum. 'She's talking nonsense, Detective.'

Duncan leaned back in his chair and placed his hands slowly on the edge of the table.

'You could have been killed,' he said. He was trembling.

'And you have no idea what that means to me,' I replied.

'Flora, please. This is a very serious matter. It'll go badly against you if you're seen to be helping them.'

'How will it go for me,' I snapped, 'if they're innocent? What if John has to look for missing people because you can't find them, Detective Constable?'

Rain lashed against the roofs and windows, and ran in streams and spatters down the glass. Duncan looked at Mum, then Ronny, then opened the folder on the table. He slid it over to me. I opened it. Inside a plastic wallet was a *Shetland Times* newspaper report from the 1990s, photocopied in crinkled black and white. The headline shouted in bold capitals:

HUSBAND WANTED
IN SEARCH FOR
MISSING WOMAN

The article went on to say that James Nicol, a fisherman and wildlife guide, was wanted in connection with an ongoing investigation. His wife had gone missing under suspicious circumstances. Soon after, Nicol had vanished, taking his baby daughter with him. Authorities were concerned for the health of the infant. There was a family snap at the bottom of the article, with the names of the husband and wife. The woman was Ailsa's mother. And the baby perched on her knee was Ailsa. It was the same newsprint picture I'd seen at her house. But the man on the right was not James Nicol. Even after seventeen years, he was John Dobie, and my spine had turned to ice.

Everything I'd worried about – everything Izzy had suggested – it yammered at the truth. My pulse pounded with the noise of surf on pebbles.

I didn't want it to be true.

'Well?' said Tom Duncan. 'What now?'

'This doesn't prove anything,' I said, but there was a crack in my voice. 'How could he buy Dog Rock with a false name?'

Tom allowed himself a little smile. It repulsed me.

'He didn't buy Dog Rock. Nobody has. I checked the records this afternoon. It's just an abandoned house that no one else wanted. So he moved in. They're squatting. He didn't even need a key.'

There was a knock on the door. Ronny crossed the lounge to

answer. Four more policemen entered the house. I only knew one – Ivor MacDonald, the senior officer in Tanno. Duncan rose to speak with them. Mum shook her head at me, and went to fill the kettle.

My vision narrowed to the picture on the table. Even through the photocopy, Ailsa's mother's eyes were clear and light. I couldn't see the green irises, the way I had in the colour photos, but I knew they were there. But then there was the infant Ailsa, and John himself, both with such inky-dark eyes, barely a corner of white cornea to frame the peaty iris. Newsprint only emphasised the contrast.

An idea sounded in my mind as a single, clear chime, ringing in the centre of those dark eyes. There was something important. The way the Dobies had captured me so completely, the power they wielded over me. That I let myself be so drawn to them. The idea began to take form, but it was a pale ghost in a peat bath, and I strained to make it out. My name was spoken – the chain was broken.

'Miss Cannan,' said DC Duncan. He'd stepped back into the kitchen. Behind him, the other policemen stood uncomfortably in the little lounge, shedding rainwater onto rugs. He lowered his voice. 'Flora,' he said.

'You played me, Tom Duncan.'

His eyes flickered to the floor, then back at me.

'I'm looking for a murderer, and I believe I've found him. You were a small part of that process.'

'What else do you want from me?' I said, loud enough for the others to hear. 'Still want to catch up some time?'

'Go to your room,' he said, 'and stay there. I think it'd be for the best if you kept out of the way tonight.'

I glared at him.

'I'll keep the heat off you as best I can,' he whispered. 'But there'll be more questions about this. For now, just keep out of the way. We'll talk more in the morning. I know you're angry, but I still hope—'

Wordlessly, I stood and brushed past him.

'Flo,' called Mum, but I couldn't stand to see her. I felt the eyes of the policemen in the lounge, but they stood aside to let me pass. In my room, I closed the door and locked it firmly, forcing the heavy key.

As soon as I was safe, I scrabbled for my old phone. I turned it on, waiting for it to boot up, willing it to work faster. Outside, the wind howled. I could hear it moaning in the chimney pots. Muted in the background, the burn at the bottom of the garden was beginning to roar as the rain swelled into spate.

Why would John Dobie run from the police? Why would he change his name? With all my heart, I believed in his sadness. I believed in Ailsa, weird as she was. Nothing else made sense. The cops were wrong. Izzy was wrong. I believed in my friend because I had to.

'Come on,' I muttered, waving it around the room, praying for a signal. In the corner above the window, a single bar flickered on the little amber screen. I scrolled to Ailsa's number and pressed to call, praying that she had her phone with her. The dial tone rang and rang, measuring in Morse the dots and dashes of my pulse. Looking out the window, I could see a single light somewhere on Dog Rock, faint and shimmering through the sheets of rain. Another torrent burst against my window, rattling the glass in the frame.

The ring tone stopped. There was silence.

'–lo?' said a voice.

My adrenaline surged to hear Ailsa, her speech strangled by static.

'Ailsa,' I hissed, 'listen! You need to get off the island. You need to get away. They're coming for you and John!'

'–lo?' she said again, '–lora? Is tha– you?'

The phone died into a monotonous digital note, killing the signal. The screen registered nothing. She hadn't heard a word I said.

As I watched, peering out the window into the gale, a dark shape obscured some of the distant light on the islet. It must be her. She was standing at the window, looking at me. We were only a few hundred metres apart, but still separated by a scrap of ocean. Almost near enough to shout, but cut off from talking. Too dark for a stupid paper note. I had to tell her, to warn her. At that moment, I'd never in my life wanted to talk to someone so badly. The need to help her blossomed in me, swelling in my heart.

The newspaper story didn't matter. I believed that with everything I had. They were innocent. And now they were being hunted. I had to tell her. Somehow, I had to let her know.

'Get out,' I whispered, willing the words across the thrashing bay, between the lancing rods of rain. 'Get out, get away, get safe. They're coming. They're coming for you.'

As I spoke, my words fogged the glass and faded, leaving only trails of rain. My reflection looked back at me in monochrome, my face reduced to shades of grey on black, a ghost in murky water. In the window reflection, my eyes were sunk as dark as peat.

As dark as John's eyes. As black as Ailsa's.

The other day, I'd seen a seal. A seal that stared back at me. A seal with dark eyes. Eyes as black as peat.

I trembled. It was a ridiculous idea. But now I'd let it out, it wouldn't go away, no matter how daft it seemed. I couldn't shake the thought that the eyes had been the same. Standing at the window, staring out through the rain, the racing rain, I studied the small warm light on Dog Rock and let the idea run.

I turned, compelled, and looked at my desk. The selkie research notes still lay stacked to one side, the spine of the Mutch book peeping out just like that jumble sale, a hundred years ago. I didn't need to open it to think of the madness that boiled inside.

There was absolutely no way it could be true.

In a rush, a string of ideas and memories flooded through my mind. How strange it was for a man and his daughter to move to the middle of nowhere. A man and a daughter without a history. How he knew the ocean like his own blood. How he knew where to spot the seals, how he knew the sea. His wife had died, and it had crippled him. He'd changed his name.

Suppose they could change their names because they were never in the system? Suppose no one knew who they were?

I pictured Ailsa's agility in the water. How cold her skin could be. No matter where she went, people knew she was different. Her strangeness, her sadness, oozing from her like a perfume.

The pieces came together like they'd never been apart.

Her swimming was poetry, simple as breathing . . . and she was her father's daughter. The pair of them, living on my doorstop. I'd even seen her swimming, the night they moved in. A dark shape in black water, not quite real, and I'd mistaken it for ducks or otters.

They were nameless. They moved around because they had to. They lived apart so no one would ever know.

Islands are safe, she said.

And she'd tried to tell me. God, she'd tried to tell me.

Flora, she'd said. I want you to know. Despite everything, she'd said. I'll always be your friend, she'd said.

Even if you change your mind about me.

CHAPTER 52

Outside my bedroom door, police boots tramped through the house. There was no way I'd get out of the cottage through the hallway.

I unlocked the door and peered out. The wind howled around the house, and I made no noise as I crept across the hall. Pressed against the lounge door, I could hear the voices inside.

'It must be him,' urged Duncan, 'it has to be.'

'Not without proof,' said MacDonald.

'We'll find it over there, sir. The girl claims John Dobie has every disappearance mapped out. He's the one to make them disappear.'

'It's far-fetched, Tom.'

'Sir, we could be dealing with the worst serial killer in Scotland's history. He's vanished before. They could be gone tomorrow.'

There was a long pause. Rain rattled the window panes.

'You need to be right about this, Duncan,' said the senior policeman.

'I am, sir. I'm right. It all fits. Dobie moves from island to island, never staying long. He has a boat. He dumps the bodies. If anyone asks, he's grieving for his wife. Everyone feels bad for him, so they leave him alone. No one thinks to ask further, and he's free to kill again. It's too perfect. He's our man.'

There was silence inside, only rain hammering on windows.

Through a gap in the door, I could see Ivor MacDonald deep in thought. Then he made his decision.

'Do it. Arrest him. Get over there now, in case he does a runner.'

'Right,' Duncan said, 'let's go. The dinghy's outside.'

The men headed for the door. I darted into the dark of the coat rack and eased myself between jackets. Four policemen filed out of the living room, along the hall and out through the porch. They passed inches away from me. I held my breath as the last one left. Then I slipped back into my bedroom. I threw the window open, spatters of rain blasting into the room. I swept the books and trinkets off the sill, hoisted myself up, and hopped down into the garden. The rain soaked me in seconds. I crept low along the house, ducking underneath the windows.

I had to warn them. The police were coming, and that was my fault.

I sprinted down the road. The rain battered and stung, thrillingly cold as it lashed down in sheets. I broke right and dived into the beach grass. Fighting my way across the dune, the ground became uneven, and I stumbled, slipping and scrambling back to my feet. I didn't bother looking for paths, but pushed directly through the fronds, blades of grass slicing thinly at my arms and face. I battled my way onto the headland, and here the force of the wind pushed ashore in walls, buffeting me to stand up straight. For a stupid, reeling second, swaying with the gusts, I thought of all the times I'd sat here before. Sunsets and kissing Richard, drinking with Ailsa, watching her take the boat away.

The storm blew rain in rods. On the far side of Still Bay, illuminated by the flickering headlights of their jeep, I could just make out the four policemen wrestling their dinghy from the trailer. It was a powerful semi-rigid craft, and the wind was vicious, tearing it from their grasp as they wrenched the boat down towards the beach.

My face stung with grass cuts and rain. I crouched and hauled off my shoes. Hesitating, I peeled off my sodden jeans, too. They were no use where I was going. My jumper clung to me as I dragged it over my head. I left my clothes in a wringing heap on the grass. In knickers and vest, I turned to face the sea. The surf was up and heavy, churning white against the shore. I stood on the tip of the headland, judging my moment. The waves receded just long enough. I crouched, then sprung. There was a snapshot of time with no noise, no sound at all, everything frozen, hanging head-long and suspended above the water.

I dived into the sea.

For the dumbest second, it was warmer than on land. Then the cold crushed the blood inside my veins. My skin tingled, salt water peppering the hundred tiny grass cuts. And I swam, I swam, arms outstretched, reaching wide and scooping at the water, legs kicking frantic. I came up for air, gasping, breath rushing out and in. Still kicking and swimming, I flipped onto my back and craned for a glimpse of the beach. Behind me, the policemen had wrestled the dinghy into the raging shallows. Ahead, through a gap in the rain, I could just make out the dim light on Dog Rock. It seemed so far away. A wave lifted then dropped me into a trough, giving the shortest of shelters from the wind. The next wave threw me up again. I took a deep breath and dipped my head back below the water.

Beneath the surface, it was calmer. The waves still tugged and twisted at my body as I swam, but down below I could ride with them. The soaked weight of my vest was ballast, helping me sink, keeping me underwater. The world beneath was dark dark blue, inky with

night, and the drumming rain muted to a low, dull roar. I thought
of Ailsa. Things brushed my legs as I swam, seaweed churned in
fragments. I came up for air again. Glancing back, I was already a
frightening distance from the headland, and I took heart from how
far I'd come. But then, looking ahead, Dog Rock seemed impossibly
remote. I was dismayed to realise that the riptide was sucking me
out to sea, away from both the shore and the islet. I felt suddenly
very frightened. This was madness. I dived beneath the surface once
more, suddenly conscious that I was no longer swimming to warn
Ailsa about the police. I was swimming for my life. The ocean pressed
me on all sides, and a rush of terror washed through me. I took an
accidental mouthful of sea water and my heart bucked. Fighting to
the surface, I spluttered, coughing and choking as I trod water. The
policemen were now in the dinghy, but the offshore wind seemed
to blow them away from the islet, and their boat juddered in the
gale. The wind lashed at my face and shoulders, but even as I tried to
hold my position, the riptide tugged me further out to sea. I sobbed
in frustration. Dog Rock was still so far, as though the ocean itself
threw a wall around the Dobies. Weakness soaked through my arms
and legs, and I was doused by a wave. It caught me in a gyre and
spun me round, choking and spluttering for air. I couldn't feel my
toes. Looking over my shoulder, I couldn't even see the headland for
the waves. All I could do was press onwards. I shaped myself against
the tide, and dived down.

A tiny voice in my head told me to stay calm, to stay steady, to
use the currents, to monitor my breathing. Weed licked my ankles
as I kicked. Each time I came to the surface, I gulped in air, took
stock, and dived again. With each surfacing, the islet crept closer.
With each dive, my strength failed a little more. The voice in my
head cooed at me, hummed and crooned, stay calm, stay calm.

My movements were becoming sleepy and weak – I realised with fright that it was not my voice. I'd heard this voice before, humming Gaelic nursery rhymes.

These are my hands.

Even under water, it sounded deliriously clear and real, and this was the moment I knew I was going to die. All burning sensation left my skin. I felt icy sickness, dicing to the marrow. In the dark-blue water, life began to leave my limbs. I no longer owned my arms. When my hand drifted in front of my face, I felt only a detached curiosity. I was not moving. I thought of baby Jamie. I thought of finches in the dune grass.

I started drifting downwards.

I was leaving the island.

These are my hands.

My eyes played tricks. Dreaming and hazy, a ghost flickered in the murk, clarifying as it came closer, gaining depth and focus. It was a face. Ailsa's face swam into focus. In those slow-motion moments, she swam directly to me, and it felt the most natural thing in the world. In lazy movements, she came closer, until her face drew level with my face. She gazed into my eyes and then, at last, lurching madder, I saw the truth of it, round and dark and full of ink.

The eyes, the dark eyes that reeled me in. They weren't John's eyes. They belonged to her. Those inky, peat-black eyes that haunted and watched me. The eyes I couldn't fathom, couldn't understand.

They belonged to Ailsa.

Even dreaming, the last flame in me flared bright with such a crush of understanding. Ailsa moved in close to me. She drew her face to my face – her mouth to my mouth. My lips thawed, slaking off the ice. There was a burst of fire in my throat. Air . . .

Air!

I jolted in the water, awake and aware, alive with oxygen. Ailsa hung suspended in front of me, her face inches from mine, bubbles hung on silver threads around us. She tried to smile at me, cautious and curious, and I stared back, rushing with fear. In the dark water, our hair floated and tangled, tossed and bound together, becoming one, inhaled and exhaled on the currents of the sea. She drew closer, pressing tight against me, and closer still, the contours of her body merging with mine, her fingers stitching fishbone with my fingers.

The last thing I remembered was the feeling of something close and tight being drawn around my head, my throat – of my limbs being gathered and moved, drawn inwards, wrapped up tight with hers. My chest crushed as I dropped deeper in the water. I let myself sink.

Washed on the currents, I let go of everything.

CHAPTER 53

Stars. Sparks. Campfire sparks. The rain had stopped, the storm blown out. The sky was ludicrously clear and clean, the stars cast in shimmering bands. I looked over. I was lying flat beside a fire.

Burning logs collapsed against each other. I pushed myself to sitting, feeling an ache deep inside my chest. Dizziness swam through me in a burst, and then my vision settled. A figure sat across from me, lurching out of focus. Holding myself still, the images resolved into one person, leaning forward to tend the fire.

Izzy. A flood of relief crashed through me. The beachcomber poked at the fire with a thin stick. He looked up when he saw me stir.

'How now, Flora.'

'Izzy,' I said, and my voice sounded not my own. 'What am I doing here? Where's Ailsa? Is she here?'

'She's down on the beach,' he grinned, 'waiting for her father. The police are looking for them, so she couldn't take you home.'

'She told you about the police?'

'I'm no friend to the Northern Constabulary. Don't worry about that.'

He fed the fire with sea-washed logs. It was roaring fiercely now, throwing out a thick, welcome heat. At the edges, the salt-soaked wood coughed with sparks and thin green flame. My throat and lungs felt ragged. Even wrapped in the blankets, I felt cold to my core, but the strength of the fire started to take the chill off my bones. When I moved my head, a rush of nausea washed across me.

'I feel sick.'

'So I should think. She said you nearly drowned. Didn't I warn you to stay away from John Dobie and his girl? I knew you were in danger.'

'But the police wanted them. Ailsa is . . .' I said, pausing to think. What was she? Izzy was watching. 'She's the best friend I've ever had. I had to help her.'

'You had to help her. Aye, of course you had to help her.'

There was something in his voice. His usual, friendly tones sounded strained. He couldn't take his eyes off me. Something stirred in the fringes of my mind.

'You all right there, Flo?'

'I'm fine,' I said, not feeling fine at all. Each breath throbbed in my throat.

Izzy reached into his pocket, and pulled out Lachlan's pocket knife. He spun it gently on his fingers, and it glistened in the firelight.

'I thought you'd got rid of that,' I said, thickly.

'Ach, I know. I should have. But that's the beachcomber in me, Flo. The hoarder. I never throw away anything that might turn out being useful after all.'

'It's evidence.'

He offered me the knife. 'Aye, of course. Here you go. Off and take it to the pigs. Give it to Detective Constable Thomas Duncan. Be sure to tell him where it comes from.'

I didn't move.

'No. I didn't think so.' He slipped the little knife back into his pocket. 'I wish you'd left it alone. I wish you hadn't got involved.'

Izzy stared at me. The vertigo felt worse every time I turned to look at him. I couldn't hold his gaze.

'I know about the selkies,' he said.

For a moment, I was sure I'd misheard him. I forced a recovery.

'We've been talking about them for weeks.'

'Not my selkies. I know about your selkies. The Dobies. Dog Rock.'

'No,' I said, and my voice caught on my teeth. 'Selkies aren't real.'

'That's why you halfway drowned yourself, aye?'

I was silent.

'I won't tell anyone,' he laughed. 'They'd never believe it anyway. They don't listen to me. They never have, no matter where I go, whether it's London or the Isle of Lewis.'

I stared at him.

'London?' I whispered.

'Nasty place,' he said. 'Couldn't even stick a year. I missed the clean air.'

One of the things stacked against John Dobie was his pattern of movement about the islands, following the path of the murders. Suddenly, plainly, I was sharply aware of someone else who'd moved around the islands for years. Someone I didn't know enough about. Someone who told stories about wicked selkies. I looked up at Izzy.

I'd been so stupid.

'You're Mutch,' I said, wearily. 'You're M.I. Mutch. You wrote the book.'

'Clever girl,' he said, grinning, his teeth all crooked. 'The 'I' stands for Isaac. I don't go by that name any more.'

Isaac. The man I knew as Izzy turned his head to gaze into the fire, and the flames reflected in his eyes shone yellow and orange and black, black, black.

'You wrote that terrible book.'

'Someone had to. People had to know the truth about selkies.'

He spoke calmly, with certainty. I felt so tired.

'But you hate books. You can't stand books.'

'My book is the reason I hate books. That book left me a laughing stock. It haunted me for years. Kenny and his vampire lawyers chased me for money. I vowed to keep it all in my head. So I changed my name, and became a shennachie.'

He leaned forward, offering me a mock bow.

'You're insane. Selkies aren't real.'

Izzy closed his eyes.

'You have no idea,' he said, 'of the damage they can do. They don't care about us. They take us. They use us. And then they leave us, empty and alone.'

Baffled, I studied his face, trying to work out what was going on. Another tumbler clicked into place. Something my grandfather had said. I remembered the sadness in his face when he told me the story about his selkie. The thought that she might have followed him to sea, every day of his life, her love burning unrequited. Grandpa had seen the abyss of what it was to love a selkie. With a rush that flooded me from hips to head, I lurched again to think of Ailsa in trouble.

She'd saved my life. The oxygen, so raw in my lungs. She'd kissed me. I didn't know what that meant.

Oh, Ailsa.

'You were in love,' I whispered.

Izzy's eyes squeezed shut.

'I found her by the sea,' he said, 'when I was a young man.'

His eyes opened. He turned to me.

'She was mine, and I kept her. That's how it's supposed to work. That's what all the stories say. And I loved her, truly.'

His face was blank, but his eyes leached tears. In the racing fire-light, they fell in fat and flashing drops. When he spoke, he had to force the words out.

'That's how it works. That's how all the stories go. The selkie loves you back. She gives you children. That's how the story always works.'

'But not for you,' I said, barely breathing.

'No. She was . . . listless. She was useless. She sat slumped against a window, looking out to sea. She didn't speak. She wouldn't tell me her name, so I made one up. She didn't eat, so I had to make her. And she cried, she always cried. She cried herself raw.'

'So why didn't you let her go?'

'Because it wasn't fair!' he exploded, and pounded a fist against his knee. 'I know how it's supposed to work. She should have loved me back, and she wouldn't even touch me. I had to – I had to force her.'

'You forced her,' I repeated dully, and pictured what he meant. The horror of it crept over me. The poor woman, held against her will, aching for escape, trapped by Izzy's delusions.

'But don't you see,' he said to me, suddenly pleading, 'that I had no choice. She was mine. Mine. That's how it always works. I loved her, Flora. I loved her. I only wanted the fairy tale for myself.'

'You let her go, right? You let her go.'

Half his face flickered orange. The other half was black. He had shadows deep inside him.

'Let her go,' he said, and there was something dreadful in his voice, something cracked and always broken. 'Let her go. Yes, I sup-pose I could have let her go.'

I couldn't breathe.

'But I didn't.'

His face crumpled, lips a curling rictus, all his teeth on show. His eyes squeezed with sadness. It was a terrible thing to see.

'I was in my studio. I was painting. I was so used to her crying by the window, I'd forgotten she could do anything else. I heard a smash. She'd thrown herself through the window. By the time I realised, she was outside the house and heading for the shore.'

I imagined the woman, stumbling on bone-thin legs. I could see her eyes, red with years of crying.

'I dropped my brushes,' said Izzy, 'and I chased her.'

Desperate, even as the salt spray touched her skin. I could sense the weakness in her, strength sapping as she hobbled for the surf, daring to hope.

'She was slow, and I caught her. I didn't know myself. I was mad with rage. I picked up a rock.'

I imagined the poor girl, laid flat on the beach, sobbing and coughing, crawling for the sea, reaching out for water, one hand gripped tight to her skin. I imagined Izzy, younger, paint-smeared, flushed with fury, lifting the rock above his head.

'And I smashed her head in. I smashed her pretty selkie skull to pieces.'

Stretched out on the shore, light dimming in her bloodshot eyes. I could see her. The tide coming in to find her, each wave pushing closer than the last, the water reaching out and washing over her outstretched hand, bringing her back home. Blood seeping into sand, flushing pink where it met the sea, and sluicing clear back into the ocean.

We listened to the sea. We listened to the fire, shifting hotter in its cradle.

'She stole my heart,' he said, voice hoarse. 'Even when she was gone, she took my heart with her. And afterwards, I wrote my book. People had to know. I only wanted to help. You understand, Flora. You know what it means.'

It jolted me to see that he was pleading. A vein pulsed in his temple.

'What about the others? All the disappearances? Why would you kill them?'

'Selkies,' he said, and madness boiled inside him. 'They're all selkies. I knew there was one on Bancree. I could smell it. Where there are islands, there are selkies. It was only a matter of time before I caught them.'

'Who? Was it Dougie?'

Izzy snorted.

'Dougie loved nothing but his bottles. He just got in my way. I didn't know the old sot was living with Anders Tommasson.'

'Anders?' I said, incredulous.

'Aye,' said Izzy, and gestured at his sliced ear. 'It was him that did this.'

My stomach bottomed out.

'You said that was Lachlan.'

'I lied. Anders fought like hell. Smashed a lamp upside my head.'

I imagined him sneaking up on Anders' house, spying through the windows. Bursting in, and the two of them brawling, the house trashed by the fight. Izzy was big, but Anders was bigger. Uncle Anders, who told me that bad things happen to good people.

Anders, who was in love.

'You couldn't beat him,' I said, faltering. 'He was too strong.'

'Oh, he fought like a devil. But I winged him before he even knew

I was in the house. He landed some good blows. He gave me that shiner, bruised a couple of ribs.'

That black eye, that ragged ear. I'd washed the blood away, and wept tears for poor old Izzy. Another piece fell into place. When I accused Lachie of attacking the beachcomber, he'd been genuinely puzzled.

'Did you do Lachie, too?'

'Not me,' he said. 'Though I think we know who wants you keeping safe, don't we?'

Ailsa.

'You said she was on the beach.'

Izzy smiled but didn't answer. He stoked his fire, piling more logs onto the furnace. The embers churned red hot, but chills crawled through my stomach. I thought of the void inside John. Always chasing ghosts because no body, no crime. I dreaded the answer, but I needed to know.

'Where are all the bodies, Izzy?'

He gestured at the Sound.

'You had the right idea about the sea, lass, except that bodies float. Amateur mistake. My first few floated. You can't just put them in the water. Bones. Now, bones sink. You need to get rid of the excess first.'

He gestured at the fire.

'Burning does the trick,' he said.

I leaned back in horror, suddenly understanding why he'd stoked it so hot. Oh no. Oh no, no. The raging campfire, spattered with grease. It was a charnel pit. The shape of Izzy's lunacy swelled to fill the world.

It doesn't heal, John said, his voice a wound. It will never get better. It is always broken. When I spoke again, it was in such a small voice. I could barely say her name.

'How do you know about Ailsa?'

'I saw it,' he said, 'when she brought you here. It shines on her. Her love sings.'

'Love,' I repeated, dully.

'Aye, Flora. She loves you. You didn't know?' I could only stare at him. He shrugged.

'That's too bad. When you're dead, that will be gone. She'll live with the heartache for what's rest of her life. She'll understand the pain.'

My tongue had become thick inside my mouth.

'When I'm dead,' I repeated, dully.

Reluctantly, he took out Lachie's pocket knife.

'I like you, Flora. You're a good kid. I'm sorry it has to be this way. You're too young to die for love.'

I thought about Ailsa. In a heartbeat, I replayed the last weeks. I looked into her deep, dark eyes, open now, and saw them for what they were, and perhaps as they had always been: open, guileless, and flooded with love. It was suddenly very simple.

'You will never know,' I said, 'what it means to love.'

For a moment, we stared at each other across the campfire, sparks drifting up between us. Looking sad enough to cry, Izzy unfolded the blade and pointed it at me. It flickered in the firelight.

The fire.

I leaned over, grabbed one end of a blazing log, and swung it up into his face.

CHAPTER 54

Izzy howled and fell backwards, hands clutching to his head, exploded embers falling all around him. I dropped the log and jumped up, ready to flee, and nausea crashed through me. I dropped to my knees and began to crawl away, away, anywhere but Izzy. My stomach churned. I threw up. I was still damp and shivering, sea water sluicing in my brain. I crawled and shuffled on my hands and knees. I was heading for the ocean. Heading for the beach.

Behind me, Izzy clattered round the campfire, kicking crates over as he reached for me.

'Flora!' he screamed. 'I'm going to tear your head off, you wee bitch!'

I had seen his madness close up, lunacy in his inky eyes. The dune grass scratched and cut as I pushed myself towards the beach. Towards Ailsa.

Then, after all the crashing at the shack, there came a sudden, alarming silence. I stopped crawling, frightened of giving myself away.

'Listen to me,' he yelled. 'I was going to make it quick, Flora, because I liked you. But now I'm going to make it hurt. I'll cut your heart out. I'll make her watch!'

Where was she? I turned back to face the sea. Even on all fours, movement was dizzying. I dragged myself towards the ocean. Izzy's curses quietened as I put more space between us. The scrub ended, the gorse fell away behind me, and I dropped down onto the beach. I took fistfuls of cool, silky sand.

Ailsa wasn't there. The beach was bare and silver, stretching in an open curve into the moonlit gloom. Waves shivered where they met the land. Nearby, darkness gathered into angles. It was the rack of windchimes. I crawled past it, growing in strength. There was no sign of Izzy. I'd almost left the chimes behind when something made me stop. Beside me, a shadow slumped at the foot of the rack. I stared into the darkness, and my heart began to pound. Cold sea, cold stars. The shadow whimpered. Low, hurt noises, almost masked by the hollow click of wood on wood.

'No,' I said. 'No, no, no.'

I crawled closer. He'd covered her with some sort of fur or blanket. I peeled it back, and in places it stuck to her. Her wrists were tied above her head, bound to the rack with twine. She was punctured with cuts, each leaking blood and bubbles, and her stomach was slick with red. Even as she breathed, it welled from the holes and spilled down her sides. Her eyes were dull and fixed on me.

'Oh, Ailsa,' I whispered.

She tried to smile.

Somewhere in the night, over near his campfire, Izzy cursed and kicked. I could hear his voice, feral noises in the dark. He was searching for me. It wouldn't take long before he looked this way.

'Flo,' said Ailsa.

'Hush. Don't talk.'

I went to undo the string, but the knots were jammed tight. I picked with my fingernails, desperate for a loose end. Nothing gave. Ailsa lolled against the frame. Panicking, I bent low and began to chew the twine. Fibres frayed between my teeth. Her skin was ice cold, and her hands flopped numb against my face. I finally gnawed through the knot. The string slipped from the frame, and Ailsa's arms dropped down. She let out a tiny yip of pain, loud against the ocean hush, and my head flicked round. Izzy still hadn't reached the beach.

But he would.

The world reeled when I tried to stand, hauling myself upright on the rack, and I sank again to my knees. I brought Ailsa to sitting, and used the twine to bind the blanket around her. In the moonlight, she smiled sickly at me.

'Sorry, Flo. Shouldn't have—'

'Wheesht. Come on. We need to get you out of here.'

She tried to shake her head, but I pulled her forward, and slowly, we began to crawl. She continued to whimper, and we dragged each other along the beach on hands and knees. Ailsa winced with every movement, but forced herself on. I glanced back, dismayed at how little ground we'd covered. Our trail was marked with blood and prints. On the far side of the chimes, Izzy burst onto the beach, and a moan escaped me. He was perhaps fifty metres away, and he held himself awkwardly, head tilted back, as though he was scenting the air, sniffing us out. He turned in a slow circle, peering along the beach. The moonlight showed thick dark lines scored across his face. He'd been half-blinded by the burning log. He held his head back to squint through damaged eyes. He looked directly at us, held my gaze until I thought I would cry out, then continued to turn. He hadn't seen us, but still he stood, head cocked, peering in our direction.

'Come on,' I whispered, 'we have to leave the beach.'

I moved back towards the cover of the scrub, but Ailsa held my arm.

'No,' she said, 'the sea. Always the sea.'

She leaned towards the ocean. I followed down the beach, hand over hand, looking forward and glancing back. Izzy was feeling his way along the beach in careful steps. Even half-blinded, he was a predator, and he was stalking. With his arms outstretched, swiping in the air, he reached the rack of wind chimes. He groped at the space Ailsa had been tied to.

He began to laugh.

'So you found her, did you? That's fine. That means she's still alive. That means she gets to watch.'

Squinting around him, Izzy spotted the blood trail. He prodded at it with his fingers, tracing our marks in the sand. Slowly, he followed the track. We stumbled on. Water sluiced icy at my wrists. We had reached the sea. Ailsa continued to crawl, along the shoreline now, and I realised she was trying to hide our trail in the surf. We were gaining ground when Ailsa slipped in the backwash and fell headlong. The splash carried, and she moaned. Izzy's head snapped towards us.

'Coming, girls, ready or not,' he sang, mocking, and took large steps towards us.

'You go,' whispered Ailsa. She was pale and exhausted. 'It's all right.'

'It's not all right. He wants us both.'

Izzy had halved the distance, sploshing towards us through the surf.

'Listen,' I hissed, 'stay here. I'll come back.'

'Flora,' she said, but I guided her to ground as gently as I could. She grimaced, but let me lay her in the tide line. I squeezed her hand and turned away, heading up the beach, no longer caring about noise.

When I looked back, Izzy had reached the place where the sea met the sand. The trail had been washed clear, and he puzzled, peering about him in the gloom, looking out into the sea. Hardly a dozen paces away, Ailsa was a shadow on the shoreline, invisible against the flotsam and the weed. That was close enough.

I yelled, as though by accident, as though in pain, and watched Izzy spin to find me. Head back, eyes glittering, he stared directly at me.

'Flora,' he whispered. 'I've got you now, petal.'

He took another half-blind step towards me, then another, ploughing through the sand. I crawled along the beach, everything weak and uncoordinated, but Izzy's lurching steps swallowed the distance between us.

'You shouldn't run,' he called out, breathing hard. 'I'm doing you a favour. Given time, you'd thank me for it. You'd beg me for it. Love will strip you to the bone, Flora.'

My hands, my knees, my feet, all sank into the soft, yielding sand. He was almost in touching distance. Even in the dark, his face was seared a vivid pink.

'Compared to a lifetime without love,' he said, 'death is the easy option. Trust me.'

His voice was almost kind. He grabbed my ankle and chuckled, animal noises, and started clawing his way up my leg. I kicked backwards, hard. My free foot smashed directly into Izzy's broken face. He shrieked and fell away from me, landing on his backside in the sand. He groaned, covering his head in both hands. I started crawling again, heading anywhere.

Movement caught my eye. Further down the beach, something crawled from the surf. A seal. It was dark and I was dizzy. It was not a seal. Dripping with water, a man stepped out of the ocean. He was topless, his trousers sodden against his legs. He walked towards me, kneeled down and gently cradled my head in both his hands. He peered at me so sadly.

'Hello, Flora,' said John Dobie.

There was a hiss behind me. Izzy had found his feet. Standing on the beach above us, he seemed a giant. His burned eyes opened a fraction and glittered, glaring at us.

'Selkie,' growled the beachcomber, and drew out Lachlan's knife.

CHAPTER 55

John stepped away from me and waited in the shallows to one side, wavelets lapping at his ankles.

'Step away, old man,' he said. 'Leave the girl alone.'

Izzy held the knife to one side, silhouetted by the fire. He crept down the beach towards John.

'An eye for an eye, selkie. That's how it works. The selkies took from me. So I take from you.'

John hesitated. 'You're insane.'

Izzy lunged blindly with the knife, stabbing forward, and John jumped backwards, tucking in his stomach, the blade whirring without contact. He landed in the surf, spray smashing in an arc.

'You'd deny it, even now?' growled Izzy, and took another step, water washing over his feet. He stabbed again, and again John Dobie threw himself out of reach, further into the ocean. The water now lapped around his knees. Izzy hesitated.

'Oh no,' he said, squinting. 'I'm not stupid. I'll not be coming in there with you. Why don't you come out and fight me fair?'

John said nothing.

'Come out, selkie. Or I'll cut the girl in half.'

Izzy lumbered half towards me, and John crashed through the waves, leaping round to stand before me.

'I thought so,' said the beachcomber. 'Well, I tell you what. I'll be doing that wee traitor anyway.'

'Not while I'm alive,' said John.

'That,' grinned Izzy, 'is absolutely fine with me.'

He lashed again with the knife, swiping in vicious arcs, and time after time John dodged the blade, jumping out of reach. He was too quick for the older man, and Izzy was soon filmed in sweat. John's muscles bunched and looped as he fought back with needle-quick punches. He peppered the beachcomber with jabs, but Izzy soaked up the blows, throwing out half-blind figure-eights with the knife. Frustrated, I saw him tense. He feinted and swung out a meaty hand. John tried to dodge, but Izzy's huge fist clipped him on the temple and he staggered backwards, falling heavily on the sand. Izzy roared with triumph and pounced after him, but John recovered, stumbling out of reach, desperate now as the beachcomber slashed with the knife, batting away his hands, doing everything he could to avoid the flickering blade. Sand kicked in clumps around them, spraying across the beach.

They gradually turned half a circle on the beach. Now John was inland, and Izzy downhill, closer to the sea. With the slope of the dune behind him, John began to gain the advantage, and he pummelled the beachcomber again and again, going for the eyes, for the ribs, forcing Izzy down towards the sea. I scrambled out of their way. The knife swiped hard and sideways, and Izzy overreached. John ducked inside the arc, gathered himself and punched upwards, smashing Izzy on the chin. Now it was the beachcomber's turn to fall, and he tumbled down the slope, down the beach and into the shallows. Chest heaving, John stood back and watched Izzy scrabble in the sand. For a moment, Izzy stayed down. But when he stood again, he held something in his hands.

It was Ailsa.

John yelped and jumped forward, arms outstretched, even as Izzy held the knife above the girl. She dangled loosely in his grip, hanging like a puppet.

'Don't!' cried John. 'She's mine. Don't hurt her.'

Izzy simply shook his head. He ran the knife across Ailsa's arm. She bucked and shrieked, legs kicking. John Dobie moaned.

'Let her go, please, let her go.'

'Tell me what you are,' said Izzy.

John took a lurching step towards the beachcomber, but Izzy pressed the knife against Ailsa's ribs. Again she writhed, and fell still.

'No, no!'

She coughed, and blood skittered on the sand.

'Tell me,' said Izzy, 'what you are.'

Horror flooded through me. We were going to lose. With Ailsa held hostage, Izzy could do anything he liked. And with John gone, who would ever stop him? I came to my knees and crawled up the beach towards them.

'What do I say?' cried John. 'I'll say anything you like.'

Under my hand, fitting in my palm, I felt something round and hard and smooth. It was a perfect sea-washed stone. It was the size of an orange.

'Don't tell me just anything,' said Izzy. Sweat fell in bright beads across his burned face. 'I want the truth.'

I took the stone in my hand. Trembling, I came to one knee, then pushed myself to standing. The world swayed. I took a step and staggered sideways. I took another and somehow tottered forward. I was in touching distance of the beachcomber. I could smell the sweat reek of him.

'Last time,' he growled. 'What are you?'

John shook his head, and sadness cracked in him. He squared up in front of Izzy, but he seemed to be looking directly at me.

'I am alone,' he said.

Izzy shrugged and held the knife out wide.

'Goodbye, selkies,' he said, and began to draw the knife towards Ailsa's throat.

I made no mistake as I smashed the rock down on his head.

The impact jarred along my arm, piercing deep inside. I felt the crunch of bone. For a moment, Izzy simply stood, knife swaying above Ailsa. Then he dropped to his knees and they slumped head-long into the sand. I fell, too, and heaved myself away from the beachcomber. He was down, but not out, and he came to all fours, shaking his head in disbelief. Slowly, he raised a hand to his head. His fingers came away wet. In a quiet, burbling voice, he started talking to himself. He started singing a nursery rhyme.

'Fell down,' he cooed, 'and broke his crown. Fell down.'

John scrambled to grab Ailsa. Sprawling headlong in the sand, he grabbed her and held her close, clutching her to his chest.

'Down will come baby . . .' muttered the beachcomber.

I kicked the knife out of his reach, and it vanished in the darkness.

'. . . cradle and all,' he said. He seemed puzzled.

Moving with studious care, he lay on his side in the sand, drawing his knees to his chest like a child, all the while crooning and muttering. A fat streak of blood flowed from his scalp, dripping through his hair and across his brow. Fringes of the tide crept closer to us.

I heard the ghosts of sirens.

Ailsa was ashen in the moonlight. John peeled back the fur.

When he saw her wounds, he could only put a hand across his mouth.

'Don't worry about it, Dad,' she whispered.

'Oh, my girl. My own girl, my girl.'

'You found him, Dad.'

'Hush, now. Hush.'

'You're free.'

John froze. His lips tried the words.

'Free.'

'No more searching, Dad. You found him.'

John blinked.

'Mum's gone, Dad. No more looking.'

'No more looking.'

His voice was dull.

'You need something else. You need to go on without me.'

'I'll not go anywhere without you,' he said.

She struggled to talk, and I could hardly bear to hear the words.

'You can't decide what's right for me any more,' she said.

'But I love you,' he said, and began to weep.

Ailsa reached out and smudged the tears on his cheeks.

'I love you too. But you have to go, Dad. They're coming.'

'Don't make me go.'

'For once,' she whispered, 'it's my decision. My choice, Dad. I love you, but go.'

'Ailsa . . .'

'Go. I need to speak to Flora. Please.'

Hesitating, he looked at me. Tear tracks streamed a delta on his face. He kissed Ailsa on the forehead, on her cheeks, on her hair. I slumped to my knees beside them and, reluctantly, John eased her body from his care into mine. She weighed nothing. I held her upright with one arm. Her eyes were utterly dark and shining with tears. I had to lean close to hear her talk.

'No more nights in the Bull, then?'

I coughed a laugh, but it caught in my mouth. She smiled. I brushed the hair back from her face. I was vaguely conscious of John splashing in the sea. In the moonlight, Ailsa's face was ever stranger. Her skin was cold.

'What are you?' I whispered.

Still smiling, she studied my face. Her hand found my hand.

'Does it make a difference?'

I remembered how our hands entwined beneath the water, and again locked fingers with her. The way she'd kissed me, hot with oxygen, the way she'd held me close and kept me safe. Ailsa raised her hand and touched my face. She took my chin and tried to bring our mouths together. I rested my forehead on hers, but didn't kiss her. Her fingers brushed against my lips, lingering, and then she drew back.

'I thought you were as lonely as me,' she murmured.

I bit my lip. 'I'm not ready for this.'

She managed another wan smile.

'I've been ready since the day we met . . .'

Dark eyes. My hands. Here I am. Feet by my bed, and a soft voice singing in my head.

'. . . but I don't think it matters any more.'

I forced myself to meet her gaze. In her eyes, I saw an emptiness that only love could fill. Ailsa, always so different and strange, craved love. She needed so much love. She needed me.

I thought again of my grandfather, and how he'd been so scared of the selkie. The abyss of her need, the gulf of what she had to give, and what she needed in return. Sitting with Ailsa, I felt the same gulf open up beneath me. I felt myself teetering on the edge, ready to fall, ready to let it swallow me whole. The weight of her want drew me in like gravity.

It would be so easy to reach back. To kiss.

I couldn't move.

Tears spilled from her eyes, and from mine. They vanished in the sand.

'You saved my life,' I said.

'And you broke my heart.'

She smiled so sadly. Her gaze dropped towards the ocean. I peeked at her cuts. They oozed, still, and her skin was ice cold.

'Help is coming. There'll be an ambulance. You'll be OK.'

'Don't,' she said. 'Don't tell me that now, Flora Cannan.'

'They'll be here soon. They'll be able to do someth—'

'I love you,' she said.

The words twisted deep inside.

'I love you, Flora. With all my heart.'

The words felt insane. They hung between us. She gripped fast around my ribs. Her hair blew against my face, my mouth, and I let it.

I love you.

It would have been so easy to say it back.

I held her closer. She wouldn't let me go. Her life slipped away. It pattered on the beach, and it flowed into the sea. The tide lapped closer and washed against us.

Even as her life flowed into the ocean, her eyes were dark as peat. And then Ailsa was numb weight. I hugged her tighter.

'I'm sorry,' I said. 'I'm so so sorry.'

Here are my hands, Flora.

Her voice echoed in my skull, a thick, close whisper, the brush of lips against my ear.

The sirens whooped and sharpened. Red light, blue light, flickers on the sand. I could hear men shouting, yelling instructions.

Izzy had long since fallen quiet. He lay face down in the surf. The tide washed over his head, and the waves shifted beneath his body, spinning his bulk in quarter circles. I didn't know or care how long he'd been under the water. I clung to Ailsa and let the ocean wash around me.

The men found us in the shallows, half in and half out of the sea.

CHAPTER 56

John stood on the silver beach like a sentinel, pointing at something in the distance. I'd watched him long enough to turn to rust. When I finally looked in the direction he pointed, there she was. There was Ailsa.

On the shoreline, where the sand met the sea, sluiced over by the coming tide, lay a seal. In moonlit greys and blacks, it bellyflopped in the surf, head raised above the flowing tide. It watched me so closely, the wide eyes looking directly at me. Fingertips appeared in the seamless fur, just below the head. Slowly, they peeled back the skin, revealing a hand, and then an arm, and then a skinny girl, soaked with sea. Her white skin glowed in the moonlight, even as the shallows washed around her sealskin. Cautious, Ailsa peered out at me. I could sense the sadness in her, ripe enough to touch. The world turned and the moon waltzed and the tides swelled and sank around us.

I woke slowly in my own bed, knowing there was someone with me. Someone was watching as I slept. Eyes straining in the gloom, I scanned the little room. I felt drained, exhausted. Everything was a dream. A light, uncertain rain tapped irregular rhythms on my window.

I remembered flinging the log into Izzy's face. That part had been real. I played back the memories, shaping events into some kind of sense. I remembered crawling on the sand, sobbing and calling out for help. Finding Ailsa and crawling along the beach, arm in arm. John Dobie, standing on the beach, squaring up to Izzy. I remembered the shennachie's madness, the flickering blade. The stone. And Ailsa. Ailsa was gone.

The policemen had found us on the beach.

It had taken two of them to prise my fingers from her. I'd been brought back to Grogport by concerned, angry people I didn't know. The constabulary were everywhere. Some doctor had given me a sedative and shooed the police away. Ronny carried me to bed, and my mum tucked me in. She waited for the pills to work, her face carved with concern, and blue lights from police cars flickered on the ceiling of my room. The pain melted away, and thick, dark sleep fell upon me in a wave.

I needed to pee. I swung my legs over the side of the bed, discovering all the aches and bruises of the previous night. Still feeling dizzy, I had to hold onto the wall to stand up. Standing by the bedroom door, having walked across the little room, I realised something was wrong. My feet were damp. I snapped on the light. Blinking in the glare, I looked down. On the carpet by my narrow bed were two kidney-shaped wet patches. Bare footprints, clearly marked in water. I bent down and dipped a finger. Salt. Sea water in my room.

As quietly as I could, I hobbled through the house to reach the bathroom. I flushed the toilet, and listened to the pipes quieten. The house shifted in its sleep. Was I dreaming? Back in my room, the footprints were evaporating. There were only toes and heels left on the carpet, as though I'd somehow imagined it. I slipped on a baggy sweater and some jeans, and made to leave the house.

From the hall, I could see a shape in the living room. I looked round the door.

'Hi,' I said. My voice was clogged with rust. I cleared my throat quietly, so as not to wake the baby.

'Hello, sweetheart,' said my mum. She sat in the dark, wee Jamie snuggled into her, as close as he could get, handfuls of her dressing gown clenched in his fists, fast asleep in the pre-morning gloom.

I didn't know what to say to her. I didn't know where to begin, what to tell her of the things I'd seen and done. I didn't know how to describe what had happened. About me, about the island. About Izzy and Lachlan. About John, about Ailsa. I didn't even know how I felt about it myself.

'Mum, listen. There are things I need to say—'

'It's all right, love,' she interrupted.

'Sorry?'

'Just tell me when you're ready.'

I blinked. 'I'm ready now, Mum.'

'There's no rush,' she said, and there was pleading in her voice.

I stared at her. Maybe this wasn't the right time, but there would never be one better. There was a new division between us. I realised, with a sudden rush of sadness, that she was scared of me. She'd seen the bruises on my body, the network of grass cuts on my face. She was scared of what I'd been through, and what I might have done. I'd grown up in a way she would never understand.

She was scared of what I had to tell her.

'OK, Mum,' I said. 'Don't worry about it.'

She gave me a smile, and I knew we'd never speak of it again.

'You going out again? How do you feel?'

'Sore, but I can't sleep. And I think there's someone I need to see.'

She nodded. I reached over and touched her cheek, then reached down and briefly held Jamie's little foot. His breathing altered, snuffling a little, then he nestled deeper into Mum's dressing gown. He was safe and warm and happy. He was my half-brother, but that meant he was half not my brother. He had his mum and dad. If I were to leave now, and never return, he wouldn't remember me. He'd be fine. I turned for the door. I was pulling on my coat when she called out to me.

'Flora?' she called. I stuck my head back around the door.

'Yes, Mum?'

'You know I love you,' she said, hesitant, 'don't you?'

'Yes,' I said. 'Of course I know.'

She leaned back in her chair and looked down on her baby. It was hard to tell in the lightening murk, but she might have been smiling.

CHAPTER 57

The air outside was mild and fresh. A dull pink fringe of sunrise coasted along the horizon. Soon it would be day. A police car was parked outside the house, speckled with beads of rain. In the back seat, Detective Constable Tom Duncan was fast asleep, huddled into one of Mum's blankets. His pink, honest face wrinkled briefly in sleep, then smoothed and settled. He'd blown his big case. He would want answers and evidence, explanations and proof. He'd want to talk to me.

Walking pumped the life into my limbs. I limped down the single-track road, each step loosening and strengthening my stride. I swung my arms as an experiment. It hurt, but in a healthy way. My body would heal.

I couldn't yet fathom the space inside my heart, the ache of absence.

I walked down the road towards my headland, retracing last night's route to the beach. It was a threshold, tides blurring the boundaries of what was land and what was sea. I walked a few hundred metres on the road, then cut across into the grass. Surf fizzed quietly on the beach.

When I emerged from the grass, there was a dark figure sitting hunched on the headland. Stepping from the dip of the dune onto the headland, I increased my pace, feeling suddenly exposed – to the wind, to the sea – to the ebb and flow of my own heart. A few paces away, I pulled up short beside the seated figure. He seemed older and smaller.

'John,' I said. 'Are you OK?'

His eyes were bloodshot.

'No. She's gone.'

'I know.'

'I've been cut in two, Flora.'

Pangs shot through me, even to think of her. But there had been wet feet by my bed. She'd been there in my dream.

'It wasn't for nothing,' I said. 'Ailsa's right. You found Izzy.'

'You found him, not me. I was too slow, like always. She's dead. I brought her here to die. None of the rest of it matters.'

I sat down beside him, and wrapped my arms around my shins.

'He was insane, and she's gone,' he said. 'So what's the point? What do I do now, Flora Cannan?'

'You know, don't you, that you couldn't have watched her forever.'

'I swore to keep her safe. For as long as it took.'

'Like a crofter keeps a selkie?'

His mouth fell open. He looked at me. His eyes were red raw.

'You told me,' I said, 'that a comfortable prison is still prison. In your story, the selkie can't hide her true self.'

He closed his mouth, and turned back to face the sea. For long minutes, we watched the sunrise paint the sky.

'I lost my woman a long time ago, Flora. And now I've lost my daughter. It comes so there's a wee bit less for me on land, each time I come up.'

There are worse places to live, she said.

'Do you understand what I'm telling you?'

My throat was dry. He was saying goodbye.

'I understand.'

He held my gaze a moment longer. His dark eyes had never been the eyes that loved me. I'd been drawn right to the edge of the abyss, thinking it was him.

A gull hawked and called from the shoreline, pecking at the sand. Waves sloshed in the inlet beneath us.

'I'm sorry.'

'Aye. Me too. For all of it.'

John looked out to sea again. Decided, he stood up. He walked down from the headland. He kicked off his shoes. He stripped out of his shirt and his trousers, then his underpants. He left them in a heap, and turned to face the ocean.

'John,' I called, 'wait.'

Impassive, he looked back at me.

'I thought it was you, John. All that time, I thought you were watching me. I thought I was falling in love with you.'

'It was never me, lass.'

'So why didn't I know?'

Sunrise spilled rosy light across his face.

'You once told me something about never taking easy options. You remember?'

I nodded.

'Who was the easier option? Me, or Ailsa?'

I'd missed the truth, even when it stared me in the face.

The new sun was upon us, fire cresting at the horizon. But even as it lightened, the pale sky cast peculiar shadows and I saw Ailsa, for the briefest of moments, hiding in the shadows of her father's face.

Behind me in Grogport, a car horn beeped, blasting through the millpond silence. A second police car had parked beside my house. Bodies queued at the door. I squinted, trying to make out faces. When I turned around again, John was already gone.

Still Bay was flat calm and the ripples spread in widening circles, reaching further and wider into the oil-dark water. When he popped up again, he was more than a quarter of the way into the bay, gliding with eerie silence. He continued to dip and swim beneath the water. He vanished behind Dog Rock. I thought I saw the curved head appear once more, when it was well past the islet and into the Atlantic Ocean, but out there waves lapped around the distant headland, crests tipping at the flat morning sun, and it might have been a shadow. It was strange, from a distance, how closely he resembled a seal.

I gathered his clothes and shoes. Halfway home, I stashed them in a thicket of the dune grass and left them to moulder. Even if the police found John's clothes, they'd never find him. By the jetty, grim-looking frogmen tinkered with the police launch and stared at me. Inside the crofthouse, the baby was crying.

I carried with me things that could never happen. Everything had changed. Bancree used to be my prison. Now it was only one small part of a wide, blank map. I'd grown up.

I opened the door to what was once my home. I walked inside to face the questions and lie to the police about everything.

CHAPTER 58

The autopsy on Izzy's body noted a badly fractured skull and unexplained burns to the face and head, but the examiner concluded that the final cause of death was drowning. I stuck to my story. I'd woken on the beach with Ailsa and Izzy dead, and couldn't tell them any more than that.

When the police searched his shack, they discovered a stash of objects belonging to the missing island men. Doug MacLeod's cigarette lighter, and a Saint Christopher that belonged to Billy Wright. They found Anders' hip flask. They found Lachlan's pocket knife on the beach, gummed with someone's blood.

It was impossible that Izzy could have found all those things from beachcombing. Without friends or family to vouch for his innocence, his movements throughout the islands were traced and gradually matched to a host of suspicious disappearances. John Dobie was never found, but his map, abandoned in Dog Cottage, proved invaluable in closing the case. Back in the beachcomber's shack, the constabulary also found a series of scrawled and often illegible notes, ranting and raving about sea monsters, about old wives' tales and ancient myths. From these, it was discovered that Izzy had written a book on the subject, long ago, under the name of Mutch. This added a dash of celebrity and intrigue to the story, and for a few weeks it was all the island papers had to talk about. Eventually interest waned, and the beachcomber's life concluded with a string of lewd obituaries:

Marcus Isaac Mutch, little-known writer and artist, had turned beachcomber and lost his mind to isolation. Alone and haunted by his own lunatic convictions, he'd attacked and murdered a number of innocent people throughout the Scottish isles, believing them to be selkies.

Selkies, of all things.

Most of the papers printed extracts from his book. His writing was generally taken as evidence for his insanity. Some papers printed his illustrations – the lurid ink sketches, dripping venom, a slender human hand sliding from the folds of sealskin.

After a few months, with no sign of John, I was permitted to claim Ailsa's body. She was cremated, and I scattered her ashes on the low-tide beach. I sat alone in winter sun and waited for the tide to take them home. A film of white ash clung to my fingertips.

Mum and Ronny moved away. The decision wasn't so difficult, in the end. When Munzie Crane sold Clachnabhan, the new owners cut half the staff and brought their own managers, so Ronny looked elsewhere. He found a supervisor's job with Dalwhinnie, up in the Highlands, and Mum put the croft up for sale. They were lucky. A nice couple from Hampshire bought it for a song, hoping to do it up. They planned to use it as a holiday cottage. Grogport became a ghost town, empty but for mice and tourists. Mum and Ronny moved out within weeks, taking all their things in a battered hire van. My grandparents planned to follow, if they could sell the bungalow. They wanted to be near their family.

I stayed long enough to finish school. I missed them all, but things would never be the same. A new family didn't need old baggage. Ronny made it clear there would always be room for me in their new house. But it would never be my home. For all the months of hugs and promises that came after, Mum and I had said our goodbyes on that half-light morning.

One family at a time, people drained from Bancree. Up on the Ben, the wind farm died, abandoned by the cost of maintenance. The electricity company stopped sending repairmen, and so the island ran on diesel. The huge blades flapped and knocked on gusty days, but didn't turn. One day, they might dismantle the turbines and recycle the steel. Or the turbines might stand for centuries like Easter Island moai, staring out to sea, waiting for another culture to come and gaze in wonder.

We only stay for a short while, and then we go. Sometimes we leave traces of ourselves behind, and sometimes we are remembered. Every one of us is a visitor.

The only question in this life is who we choose to travel with.

EPILOGUE

I walked down the village street towards the end of the harbour. A cleft had been gouged into the cliff, creating a steep, narrow inlet. The rocks on either side were dense with weed, and the shingle dropped sharply through gorse into sand and sea. The harbour was surrounded by horseshoes of pastel houses.

South and west of the Rinns, about a hundred yards from shore, the tide rose and fell dramatically on either side of Orsay and Eilean Mhic Coinnich. The two small islands created mad currents that raced and boomed and towered as they smashed into each other. Tucked behind them, the harbour at Portnahaven was remarkably sheltered from the chaos, and seals congregated on the rocks by the dozen.

I watched them from the harbour wall. Their blunt heads dived and dipped in the evening murk. I found steps in the sea-washed concrete and stepped down for a closer look. Here the weed lay piled in low tide heaps, and crabs haunted the slivers between rocks. I stood on the edge of the land, and my reflection heaved and gently slid upon the waves.

I slowed my breathing to match the rhythm of the tide.

Inhale, exhale. Breathe. Focus.

Cautiously, one of the seals swam closer. It bobbed in the water, almost within arm's reach, gazing up at me with frank curiosity. It was speckled grey and black and glossy with water. Droplets clung to its whiskers, and its eyes were round black pools, deep enough to drown in. For heartbeats, we looked at one another. Moving slowly, I kneeled on the rocks, and reached out my hand. I was near enough to touch when it flinched away and began to sink, nostrils closing tight as it dropped beneath the surface. There was a flicker of a pale ghost in the water, and then only ripples, floating on the ocean, moving apart, washing away.

Islay wasn't even a hundred miles from Bancree, but at the same time, it was another world.

Smiling, I clambered back across the rocks and onto the harbour road. A wall of cloud hung on the horizon, but it was moving out to westward. I watched the sea and sky dance together. Spring was late, this year, and when the cold nipped at me, I ducked into the tiny pub on the corner. Inside was fiercely hot, peat popping like firecrackers in the stove. After a cold, brisk day walking on Islay's rocky western beaches, the racing heat was welcome, and soon I took my jacket off. I sat in the corner, reading my book and making occasional notes. After a while, Fraser brought me a pint and a toastie. His hand lingered on mine as I took the glass.

The room began to fill as evening deepened into night. After a month in Portnahaven, and more than one late night in the pub, I knew many of the faces, and most people nodded hello or stopped to chat. After an hour or so, the tiny room was full, and the villagers gathered shoulder to shoulder. Fraser cast me another of his looks. He was a handsome lad, all corkscrew curls and blue eyes and sleeves rolled up. I smiled back, remembering last night's lock-in, me and Keira and Fraser and two Kiwi backpackers dancing and singing till dawn.

It was pitch dark by eight, and the pub was in full swing. Sitting quietly by myself, I rested in the shadows and studied every face. I memorised their laughter, watching how they moved, how they talked to each other. I was learning to see patterns in people.

It was busier than previous nights. Word had spread, and folk had come through from Port Charlotte. One couple had driven round Loch Indaal from Bowmore. The tiny pub was close and loud and dark. There was movement by the door, and the crowd shifted to let Keira in. She slipped through to the bar and ordered a cider. She grinned and raised her glass.

When I felt ready, I waved at Fraser, and he ducked behind the bar. A moment later, the lights dimmed low.

I stood up, then. The villagers nearest to me fell quiet, and their silence spread around the pub. Fraser killed the jukebox. The distant booming of the Orsay and Coinnich currents sounded through the room. In the stove, the fire slumped upon itself, sending sparks against the glass.

Stories are written in woodsmoke and salt.

Every face was turned to mine.

'I'm going to tell you a story,' I said, 'because stories explain the things we can't control.'

I spoke calmly, but my voice carried in the bar. Ruddy in the firelight and hidden by the dancing shadows, the villagers looked at me. Standing behind the counter, one hand on the beer pumps, Fraser watched me wide-eyed. He looked like a wee boy when I told my stories.

'It's about a lot of things . . .'

Keira joined the fringes of the circle.

'. . . but it's mostly about love. It's about finding love in peculiar places. It's about finding love, even when it's hidden in plain sight.'

She held my gaze.

'And it goes like this.'

I lowered my voice, and pindrop silence needled through the bar. I enjoyed it, making them wait. The night was full of promise. And then I opened up my heart, and I let them in.